TWILIGHT ZONE

TWILIGHT ZONE

19 ORIGINAL STORIES ON THE 50TH ANNIVERSARY

EDITED BY Carol Serling

TOR®

A TOM DOHERTY ASSOCIATES BOOK • New York

TWILIGHT ZONE: 19 ORIGINAL STORIES ON THE 50TH ANNIVERSARY

Copyright © 2009 by Carol Serling and Tekno Books

A Tor Book
Published by Tom Doherty Associates, LLC
175 Fifth Avenue
New York, NY 10010

www.tor-forge.com

Tor® is a registered trademark of Tom Doherty Associates, LLC.

Library of Congress Cataloging-in-Publication Data

Twilight zone anthology / edited by Carol Serling.—1st ed.
　　　p. cm.
　　"A Tom Doherty Associates book."
　　ISBN 978-0-7653-2434-4 — ISBN 978-0-7653-2433-7 (trade pbk.) 1. Fantasy fiction, American.　2. Psychological fiction, American.　3. Twilight zone (Television program : 1959–1964)—Influence.　4. Short stories.　I. Serling, Carol.
II. Serling, Rod, 1924–1975.
　　PS648.F3T78 2009
　　813'.07660806—dc22

2009018661

First Edition: September 2009

Printed in the United States of America

0　9　8　7　6　5　4　3　2　1

COPYRIGHT ACKNOWLEDGMENTS

CONTENTS

INTRODUCTION

The highway leads to the shadowy tip of reality; you're on a through route to the land of the different, the bizarre, the unexplainable. . . . Go as far as you like on this road. Its limits are only those of the mind itself. You're entering the wondrous dimensions of the imagination. Next stop . . . the Twilight Zone.

—ROD SERLING

It was fifty years ago that CBS announced that *The Twilight Zone*, an unusual new series of dramas dealing with tales stranger than fiction scripted by Rod Serling, would make its debut on CBS, Friday, October 2, at 10 P.M. "Where Is Everybody" was aired that night and proved to be the beginning of a groundbreaking television series.

Actually, the series had its origins in a teleplay that Rod had written in 1957 called "The Time Element." It was a fascinating story of time travel, in which our modern man travels back to Pearl Harbor (December 7, 1941) right before the Japanese attack. Rod had planned it as a pilot for a TV series, but CBS shelved the script and it remained unproduced until Bert Granet found it in the archives and filmed it for the Westinghouse *Desilu Playhouse*. "Element" was first shown on November 24, 1958, and received overwhelming viewer acclaim, with thousands of letters pouring into Granet's office. Encouraged by this success, CBS entered into serious talks with Rod about producing *The Twilight Zone* as a series, and, as we all know, the rest is history.

Although Rod had firmly established himself in the television world of the 1950s, he was frustrated by the strict limitations placed on the TV medium by the networks and sponsors. So ... speaking in the phraseology of fantasy and within the perimeters of his own show, Rod found that he could comment allegorically on universal themes ... the social evils and issues of the day ... prejudice, politics, nuclear fears, bigotry, the holocaust, conformity, war, racism ... and the TV censors left him alone because either they didn't understand what he was saying or they truly believed he was in outer space.

Rod cast far and wide for stories, writing many himself (92 out of 156), but he also bought scripts or adapted classic stories by authors such as Charles Beaumont, Richard Matheson, Earl Hamner, George Clayton Johnson, Ray Bradbury, Jerome Bixby, Damon Knight, and many others. The series also featured incredible actors from the forties and fifties, a Who's Who of actors both well known and soon to become well known, including Ida Lupino, Robert Cummings, Robert Duvall, Robert Redford, Jack Klugman, Burgess Meredith, Cliff Robertson, Lee Marvin, William Shatner, Peter Falk, Leonard Nimoy, Carol Burnett, Dennis Hopper, Charles Bronson, Mickey Rooney, and many more.

Today, the show has inspired two television revivals as well as a feature film, many *TZ* books including graphic novels, a published series of the TV scripts, a magazine, and even a pinball game, a slot machine, and a theme-park ride. Just as important, it sparked the imaginations of countless writers, filmmakers, and fans around the world, and is considered a seminal show for broadening the horizons of both television and fiction.

It is this last intersection from which this anthology sprang. In conjunction with the celebration of the fiftieth anniversary of the first broadcast episode of *The Twilight Zone* in 2009, this original collection of stories celebrating the unique vision and power of Rod's landmark series was commissioned, and the range and diversity of the resulting stories surprised even me. Within these pages are brand-new stories by authors that span the last half century, from original series writer Earl Hamner's twisted tale of a bonsai enthusiast who wreaks his subtle revenge on a careless groundskeeper, to William F. Wu's story of two chance acquaintances on the road again decades later, each heading toward a meeting with destiny—or not. There are also new stories by acclaimed bestselling authors such as Carole Nelson Douglas, whose spinster retiree takes a Southwestern road trip into terror, and the master of suspense Whitley Strieber, whose tale of suburban neighbors versus the monsters moving in next door rivals anything that *The Twilight Zone* would have produced.

I was hoping for stories that would celebrate the best of what *The Twilight Zone* offered its viewers every week, and I'm pleased to say that this anthology has succeeded in bringing together an incredible roster of talented authors, each with his or her unique take on Rod's legendary creation. I hope you will enjoy these stories as much as I have.

CAROL SERLING

TWILIGHT ZONE

GENESIS

David Hagberg

This is The Corporal, age twenty-one, a paratrooper, who is secure in his own mortality, held together only by the thin thread of his memories. But in a few moments a Japanese sniper's bullet will hit him in the wrist and knee, bringing him into a reality that he's been trying to escape from since leaving Cayuga Lake. He'll be brought back to face an enemy he's never met, nor ever wanted to. His small-town upbringing and loving family will work against him. He can recall in detail a simpler, easier existence, which his wounds will erase from his life as if it never existed. The Corporal, demolitions expert, who in the next seconds will move into the Twilight Zone—in a desperate search for survival.

It was fast approaching night when the oppressive heat of the day would be replaced by the oppressive humidity. The only good thing about the darkness was that the tracer rounds could be seen walking toward their positions. And the Japanese were proving to be an even tougher, more accurate, and certainly more tenacious foe than MacArthur had warned they would be.

This was Leyte Island, in the Philippines, a place that The Corporal and the others in the 11th Airborne Division's 511th Parachute Regiment had come to hate and fear after only the first few days of the fierce battle that would never end—except for the ones who bought it, and there were a lot of those. Too many of them.

A heavy mortar round struck about twenty feet from where The Corporal and a half-dozen other paratroopers were hunkered down behind a jumble of boulders that looked as if they'd been dropped into the middle of the jungle. After the initial concussion, a rain of black dirt, chewed-up vegetation, and something else that smelled strongly of copper and something sweet and horribly sour at the same time fell down on them, peppering their helmets.

A young man, even younger than The Corporal, and slighter and shorter than The Corporal's slender five-four, suddenly leaped up and tried to run. His helmet, face, and shoulders were covered in blood, and a long, twisted rope of intestine that had fallen from the sky was plastered down one arm from his shoulder to his elbow. He was screaming, his words not recognizable in the almost constant din of battle because the noises coming from his throat were not human. Only the desperate sounds of a frantically frightened man.

"Down!" The Corporal shouted. "Get down!"

But the private didn't or couldn't hear; it was as if he had turned to run for home and nothing in the world could make him look back, nothing would stop him, until a Japanese Type 92 7.7-mm machine-gun round slammed into the back of his head, exiting out the front of his helmet, and he was thrown forward onto his face, dead before he hit the ground.

The Corporal, his mouth slightly open, knew that he shouldn't be affected by this—just the latest death in the dozens, probably hundreds, that he had personally witnessed since New Guinea in June—but he had a vivid imagination.

Ernie Pyle or someone like that, he thought, had written something to the effect that a moron died only once but a bright guy died a thousand deaths because he could think out ahead and figure the odds, figure his chances. Probably had something to do with cowardice versus heroism, but right at this moment The Corporal wanted to be anywhere but here, because he'd been figuring the odds for a long time.

He hunkered down a little lower into the jungle mud and gore, into his own sweat and the foul body odors of the other grunts packed around him like untidy sardines in a can, and allowed his mind to drift into a fantasy world.

Like the war and Leyte, the errant thought intruded in The Corporal's head, the intense noises of the heavy machine-gun fire and mortar rounds they were taking from the Japanese who were steadily sending in reinforcements from Luzon, inescapable.

He could see a man aboard a train hurtling down a track somewhere back in the States. He was an ordinary man, maybe in some business that he'd grown tired of; a job and very likely a place from which he wanted to escape.

The man was looking up at the conductor who'd come around to collect tickets, and it was clear from the expression on his face that he wasn't happy. That he might have wanted to take off into a dream world. That he would be hurtling down some other track, for someplace else, for a place where he could be happy, could be at peace with himself.

Maybe it would happen in his dreams.

The Corporal opened his eyes, and he could see pretty much the entire scene. The man was wishing for a better life, not in terms of money but in terms of no stress, and he would fall asleep during his daily commute and dream of such a place. Small-town USA.

Only on this day, he gets up in the middle of his dream and sleepwalks to the end of the passenger car, opens the door to the connecting platform, and then without hesitation, with a smile on his face, opens the outer door and, still sleepwalking, steps off the speeding train to his death.

. . .

Maybe it's wishful thinking nestled in the hidden part of a man's mind, or maybe it's the last stop in the vast design of things, or perhaps for this man it's a place around the bend where he could jump off.

. . .

Someone was calling his name, but for a moment it didn't register. When his time came, he wouldn't jump up and try to run away, nor would he sleepwalk off a speeding train. It would be different for him. He knew it, could feel it in his gut. There was more for him, more life, more dreams, more everything.

"Corporal, for Christ's sake, get your head out!"

The Corporal looked to the left, into the eyes of Tom Hafner, his squad sergeant, not two feet away. "What?" he said. But then he had to shout to be heard over the din. "What?"

"That Jap pillbox is chewing us up. I'll try to find some defilade around the mound at two eighty, come in from his blind side. I need covering fire."

The Corporal looked out and saw the low mound of a hillock to the left. If the Sarge could reach that far, he'd be blocked from view by the Japanese gunners from their heavily fortified position.

The others had looked up and were listening to the sergeant, and nodding uncertainly. Fear was on their faces, but determination, too. The only way this war was ever going to end was for them to take orders and to fight as hard as humanly possible. But the fog seemed to be everywhere. Surrounding a man. Making any future less than certain, even improbable.

Their platoon of two squads, eight guys and one sergeant in each, plus Lieutenant Henderson from Minnesota, was down to one undermanned squad, one sergeant, and no officer, with no re-placements expected anytime soon.

"Let's do it." The Sarge motioned toward the hillock about twenty-five yards out. He hesitated a moment, then shouted: "Now!"

The Corporal popped up and began firing his M3 Grease Gun on full automatic, short bursts as they'd been taught. The other four grunts did the same, laying down a heavy screen of fire out ahead, walking the line up toward the machine-gun slits in the Japanese position of palm logs and sandbags.

The Sarge, a heavyset man ten years older than everyone else in the combined squad, had a potbelly, a fact everyone marveled at because all they'd been eating for the past two weeks were C-rats, and looking at him no one would ever guess he could get to his feet from behind a boulder, let alone do a broken field run, in full kit, faster than any of the kids.

But then incoming rounds, which had the right-of-way, were definite motivators.

The Sarge, hunched behind the end of the mound of boulders, suddenly leaped forward, making a diagonal path toward the hill. He moved very fast, bent over at the waist, zigzagging through the sometimes thick jungle growth.

Almost immediately the Japs spotted him and moved their fire to the left, trying to cut him off. They knew what he was trying to do.

The Corporal increased his rate of fire, almost immediately running dry, but it took him only a couple of seconds to reload with a fresh thirty-round box magazine of .45 ammo, slam the bolt back, then pop up again to fire.

It was the same thing that everyone else was doing.

Larry Pechstein pulled out a grenade, yanked the pin, and tossed it overhand to hit the ground within ten or fifteen yards of the pill-box, and it went off with an impressive bang. It hadn't caused any damage, yet the pop must have impressed the Japs, because their fire diminished, just as the Sarge flopped down behind the hummock, putting it between him and the pillbox.

He gave the squad a thumbs-up, and The Corporal and the others hunkered back down behind the boulders, and the Japan-ese machine guns opened up again on their position.

From somewhere off to the right were a mortar launcher and crew, and they began to lob round after round over the trees again, bracketing the squad's position.

The Corporal looked over at Pechstein, who was from some-where near Jacksonville, he thought, and at the others, Yablonski from Hackensack, Lamb from Waterloo, and Horvak from Cleve-land, who'd claimed at one time or another to have owned just about every model Detroit had ever made before the war, and him-self, of course from Syracuse.

· · ·

Five young men, soldiers all. Florida, New Jersey, Iowa, Ohio, and New York, with the usual backgrounds, all stuck in a situation beyond their making or understanding. There is no logic here, just a seem-ingly endless nightmare from which the only escape might be death. In the next second we'll begin to see the situation for what it really is—the past, the present, and, more important to them, the future.

· · ·

A mortar round struck ten yards to the left and slightly behind their position. Someone from the other side of the tall palm tree began returning fire, momentarily breaking The Corporal out of his reveries.

He cautiously raised up so that he could just see over the top of the boulders, but the Sarge was gone from behind the hill. Nowhere in sight, but then the machine-gun fire from the pillbox concentrated on their position again, and he ducked back down.

In his head he could see the five of them desperately trying to get away, but none of them knew to where or what they might find if they got there. At first they made a human pyramid, climbing on one another's shoulders, but they couldn't reach the top.

Of the boulders?

He didn't know. He couldn't see that far.

Another mortar round landed nearby, and The Corporal rose up again to look for the Sarge, but machine-gun fire from the pillbox forced him back.

To his imagination.

The five of them took off their web belts, linked them together, and attached a bayonet to one end. Like a grappling hook. One of the soldiers, The Corporal couldn't see who—but maybe it was himself because his need to escape was even stronger than the others'—tossed the bayonet up over the top.

Three times before it finally caught on something and he climbed over the top of the boulder and tumbled down to the other side. Where he . . . ?

The Corporal opened his eyes again, confused in the first instant. He had escaped, in his mind, but he had no idea to where. He thought he might have seen snow; maybe he was lying facedown. And when he looked up he'd been seeing something, perhaps a person, but not a Japanese soldier, and not the Sarge.

Pechstein was looking at him, an odd expression on his red, freckled face smudged with grease and mud.

"What?" The Corporal asked.

"You fall asleep or something? You okay?"

It struck The Corporal that the mortar shells had stopped coming, and the machine gun in the pillbox had gone silent.

"What's going on? What's happening?"

"Beats the shit outta me," Pechstein said. "Maybe the Sarge got lucky."

The Corporal rose up and took a quick look at the low hill and to the right, at the pillbox, but there was no movement, no sound. It was as if the five of them had been dropped off the face of the earth, or at least out of the battlefield.

Then a mortar round dropped so close in front of them that one of the larger boulders was dislodged and came tumbling down, missing Horvak by less than one foot.

Then he had it, the place to which he had escaped by climbing up the boulders, and the figure. He was a doll, or something; the figure above him was that of a little girl, who picked him up and threw him back over the boulders. Into a barrel with other dolls being collected for Christmas.

. . .

Just a barrel where are kept make-believe figures made in the shape of human beings. Of soldiers unloved and in mortal danger for the moment. But somewhere just on the other side is a place of peace and home and love. If only they can get there, out of this dream world and into another.

. . .

But the machine-gun fire hadn't resumed and The Corporal chanced another look over the top. Nothing had changed. No sounds of gunfire anywhere, and now the mortar rounds stopped.

He glanced down at Pechstein and the others, who were watching him.

"What do you see?" Pechstein asked.

"Nothing."

"What about the Sarge? Can you see him?" Horvak asked. "Has he made it to the pillbox?"

"I told you, nothing's moving out there," The Corporal said sharply. He was getting spooked. He'd been through lulls on the battlefield before, but never like this one, which seemed to have dropped over them like a thick blanket.

He eased down and sat, his back against the boulders, his Grease Gun cradled between his knees.

"What're we supposed to do?" Yablonski asked. Like the others, he looked up to The Corporal.

"Wait for the Sarge," The Corporal replied absently. He was thinking of something, his focus on the here and now going soft.

"But what if he doesn't come back? Fer Christ's sake, we can't sit here forever, waiting for somebody to show up."

Here and now.

. . .

The place is here on the battlefield, the time is now, mid-November 1944, and the journey is just about to start.

. . .

But it isn't the jungle battlefield he's seeing with his mind's eye. It's a small town somewhere, maybe in the Midwest, and he can't remember his name, or how he got there, except that the place seems to be deserted. Nothing moves, no sounds, not the rustling of the leaves in a breeze, not a child's laugh or a dog's bark.

But people were here just a second ago. He walks into a diner on Main Street and a burger is frying on the grill; a lit cigarette is perched on the edge of an ashtray. Across the street, he looks through the window of the barbershop and sees water dribbling from a faucet into the sink.

He turns around and races up the street. "No one's here!" he shouts. "Everyone's gone!"

Pechstein was there beside him, a wild look in his eyes. "What the hell's the matter with you?"

"What do mean?"

"You were shouting something crazy."

The Corporal shook his head. He couldn't see the rest of it. The town, where the people had gone. The ending. But he desperately wanted to see, wanted to understand, because he felt that his life, his future, might depend on it.

Something nagging at the back of his head, something from the future-wonder stories he'd read as a boy, something just beyond his ken, wanting to take him away from this place, wanting to pull his concentration away from the struggle here to the mystery out there.

. . .

Up there is an enemy known as isolation. It sits in the stars, waiting, waiting with the patience of aeons.

. . .

But he didn't know what that meant. The thoughts were merely random snippets, popping off in his head like a photographer's flashbulbs, clear for just an instant before nothing was left except the afterimage of a dark spot in the retina.

Pechstein and the others were watching him. They were worried. With the Sarge gone, The Corporal was all they had to lead them. He had a bachelor's degree from Antioch, which meant he knew things none of them knew, he could figure out stuff. They were depending on him.

"Well, at least they've stopped shooting at us," The Corporal said.

"Do you think it's because of the Sarge?" Horvak asked. "Maybe he took out the pillbox."

"We would have heard something," Lamb said. He was the shy one of the squad and usually the butt of the jokes. But what he'd just said made sense, and no one ribbed him. They would have heard the Sarge's Grease Gun, or maybe a grenade.

But nothing, and now this ominous silence.

The Corporal peered over the top of the boulders again, but still there was no sign of the Sarge.

"Anything?" Pechstein asked.

The Corporal dropped back and shook his head. "We'll give him a couple more minutes."

"Then what?"

"We'll see," The Corporal said, and suddenly he remembered something in the face of the young private who'd tried to run away and had gotten himself killed.

It had been a momentary flash of light, the sun streaming through the palm fronds ruffling in the breeze, and he'd had the strangest sensation that he knew the kid was going to buy it.

· · ·

U.S. Army paratroopers, Philippine Islands, gathered behind a pile of boulders in the middle of the jungle. Their sweating faces are covered in mud and grime and blood, their eyes wide with a curious mix of fear and resignation. Some of them will die, and all of them know it, though no one is sure who'll be next. Except perhaps for one man who can see the light.

· · ·

He could see the story in his head, visualize the men—Pechstein and Lamb and the others—he could even hear himself telling the Sarge, and later an officer in the rear, that he could see death. It was the light on their faces.

They didn't believe him, and the more he tried to convince them that he had this terrible gift, the more they pushed him away, sending him back to the front.

"Why don't you look in the mirror," someone suggested.

And he remembered a line he'd read at Antioch from Shakespeare's

Richard the Third: *"He has come to open the purple testament of bleeding war."*

In his imagination they were calling him a nutcase, and here and now he was beginning to wonder if it was true. He was seeing things, hearing things, trying to step off the speeding train. The private wanted to go home, the businessman just wanted peace, and The Corporal wanted the same things.

He looked up into the sky, the sun low now off to the right, and thought for a moment that he'd heard the engines of an airplane. The Navy was flying air cover, but just not here today. Anyway the plane sounded too big to operate off an aircraft carrier, and they were too far from Australia for land-based planes.

It didn't make any sense to The Corporal.

He looked over the boulders toward the hillock and then the pillbox. The Sarge was gone and it was up to him to make the decision.

"Check your ammo," he told them. "We're going in the same way the Sarge did."

"Jesus," Yablonski said, but they hurriedly did as they'd been instructed.

"I'm down to two magazines," Lamb said.

"I only have two grenades," Pechstein told him.

The Corporal had five grenades and five magazines of ammo plus the half-empty one in his weapon, which he swapped out for a full one.

"Lamb, strip the bodies," he ordered. "Horvak, you and the rest of your guys help him. We're going in with as much firepower as we can carry."

They nodded, their eyes wide, and hurried off to do as they'd been ordered, their fear no less than before, but with a sense of relief that they were going to be doing something. They had an objective.

The Corporal thought he heard the airplane again, maybe above the clouds. Circling. Searching for something, maybe for a way down.

. . .

Unknown to the pilot and his crew, this airplane is heading into an uncharted region well off the beaten path, perhaps on an odyssey. Perhaps reported overdue and missing by now, the object of a frantic search on land and especially in the sea. An Army Air Corps plane trying to get home. But we know where she is, and maybe we should shoot up a flare or something.

. . .

"Who goes first," Pechstein was saying, and The Corporal looked at him and the others blankly for just an instant.

The battlefield continued to be silent, and eerie, and The Corporal got the strong impression that he and his four squad mates were the last people on the planet. Even the plane circling overhead was gone.

"I'll go first," he said. "But spread out, left and right; keep low and keep firing."

"Grenades?" Horvak asked.

"Save them until later," The Corporal said. "Look, it's only twenty-five yards and we'll have a defilade."

"Unless the Sarge is dead and we run into a trap," Pechstein suggested. "Could be that's just what they want us to do. They stop shooting and like a bunch of saps we run right out there into an ambush."

The Corporal ignored him, looking up over the top of the boulders one last time. Still no movement.

"Let's go," he said. Without looking over his shoulder to make sure the four others were with him, he started running, half bent over at the waist, his legs pumping, and he began firing short bursts toward the pillbox.

Almost immediately Pechstein and the others opened fire.

The Corporal had another crazy thought: What if he could invent a time machine, to go back to just before the Japs manning the pillbox had been inducted into the service, and kill them? They wouldn't be here now.

The Sarge's body lay sprawled on the west side of the hillock, most of the front of his head blown away. He couldn't be seen from behind the boulders.

The Corporal started to turn when the sniper's bullet hit his wrist, fragmented, and the pieces slammed into his knee, knocking him to the ground.

Pechstein and the others were firing, and one of the guys started lobbing grenades over the hill, all of it in stop-action in The Corporal's head.

He heard the airplane again, only this time there were two of them, small, fighters from off the aircraft carriers, come to the rescue.

Someone—Horvak or perhaps Lamb or perhaps both of them—dragged him to the safety of the hillock, and as he phased in an out of consciousness, he realized that if he didn't die here in this place, today, in the island jungle twilight, he would be going home.

Pechstein loomed above, a big grin on his face. "Serling, can you hear me?" he said. "Listen, Rod, you're going to be okay. You just got your million-dollar wound."

Horvak was there too, smiling like a kid at a birthday. "Yeah, you're going home." He shook his head. "I'm gonna miss your stories."

Lying wounded in the Leyte jungle, Corporal Rod Serling has his strangest thought of the day. There is a fifth dimension, beyond that which is known to man. It is a dimension as vast as space and as timeless as infinity. It is the middle ground between light and shadow, and it lies between the pit of man's fears and the summit of his knowledge. This is the dimension of imagination. It is an area that might be called . . . the Twilight Zone.

A HAUNTED HOUSE OF HER OWN

Kelley Armstrong

Consider one Tanya Evans, a woman who believes she can mold any situation to her own desires. What Tanya desires most is a haunted house, or a country inn that she can advertise as haunted, since she is far too rational to believe in ghosts. But houses, haunted or not, contain their own unrealized desires, as Tanya is about to find out when she signs on the dotted line, opens her inn's front door, and enters . . . the Twilight Zone.

T anya couldn't understand why realtors failed to recognize the commercial potential of haunted houses. This one, it seemed, was no different.

"Now, these railings need work," the woman said as she led Tanya and Nathan out onto one of the balconies. "But the floor is structurally sound, and that's the main thing. I'm sure these would be an attractive selling point to your bed-and-breakfast guests."

Not as attractive as ghosts . . .

"You're sure the house doesn't have a history?" Tanya prodded again. "I thought I heard something in town. . . ."

She'd hadn't, but the way the realtor stiffened told Tanya that she was onto something. After pointed reminders about disclosing the house's full history, the woman admitted there was, indeed, something. Apparently a kid had murdered his family here, back in the seventies.

"A tragedy, but it's long past," the realtor assured her. "Never a spot of trouble since."

"Damn," Tanya murmured under her breath, and followed the realtor back inside.

Nathan wanted to check out the coach house, to see if there was any chance of converting it into a separate "honeymoon hideaway."

Tanya was thrilled to see him taking an interest. Opening the inn had been her idea. An unexpected windfall from a great-aunt had come right after she'd lost her teaching job and Nathan's office-manager position teetered under end-of-year budget cuts. It seemed like the perfect time to try something new.

"You two go on ahead," she said. "I'll poke around in here, maybe check out the gardens."

"Did I see a greenhouse out back?" Nathan asked the realtor.

She beamed. "You most certainly did."

"Why don't you go take a look, hon? You were talking about growing organic vegetables."

"Oh, what a wonderful idea," the realtor said. "That is *so* popular right now. Organic local produce is all the rage. There's a shop in town that supplies all the . . ."

As the woman gushed, Tanya backed away slowly, then escaped.

The house was perfect—a six-bedroom, rambling Victorian perched on a hill three miles from a suitably quaint village. What more could she want in a bed-and-breakfast? Well, ghosts. Not that Tanya believed in such things, but haunted inns in Vermont were all the rage, and she was determined to own one.

When she saw the octagonal Victorian greenhouse, though, she decided that if it turned out there'd never been so much as a ghostly candle spotted on the property, she'd light one herself. She had to have this place.

She stepped inside and pictured it with lounge chairs, a book-shelf, maybe a little woodstove for winter. Not a greenhouse, but a sunroom. First, though, they'd need to do some serious weeding. The greenhouse—*conservatory*, she amended—sat in a nest of thorny vines dotted with red. Raspberries? She cleaned a peephole in the grime and peered out.

A head popped up from the thicket. Tanya fell back with a yelp. Sunken brown eyes widened, and wizened lips parted in a matching shriek of surprise.

Tanya hurried out as the old woman made her way from the thicket, a basket of red berries in one hand.

"I'm sorry, dear," she said. "We gave each other quite a fright."

Tanya motioned at the basket. "Late for raspberries, isn't it?"

The old woman smiled. "They're double-blooming. At least there's one good thing to come out of this place." She looked over at the house. "You aren't . . . looking to buy, are you?"

"I might be."

The woman's free hand gripped Tanya's arm. "No, dear. You don't want to do that."

"I hear there's some history."

"History?" The old woman shivered. "Horrors. Blasphemies. Murders. Foul murders. No, dear, you don't want this house, not at all."

Foul murders? Tanya tried not to laugh. If they ever did a promotional video, she was hiring this woman.

"Whatever happened was a tragedy," Tanya said. "But it's long past, and it's time—"

"Long past? Never. At night, I still hear the moans. The screams. The chanting. The chanting is the worst, as if they're trying to call up the devil himself."

"I see." Tanya squinted out at the late-day sun, dropping beneath the horizon. "Do you live around here, then?"

"Just over there."

The woman pointed, then shuffled around the conservatory, still pointing. When she didn't come back, Tanya followed, wanting to make note of her name. But the yard was empty.

Tanya poked around a bit after that, but the sun dropped fast over the mountain ridge. As she picked her way through the brambles, she looked up at the house looming in the twilight—a hulking shadow against the night, the lights inside seeming to flicker like candles behind the old glass.

The wind sighed past and she swore she heard voices in it, sibilant whispers snaking around her. A shadow moved across an upper window. She'd blame a drape caught in a draft . . . only she couldn't see any window coverings.

She smiled as she shivered. For someone who didn't believe in ghosts, she was quite caught up in the fantasy. Imagine how guests who *did* believe would react.

She found Nathan still in the coach house, measuring tape extended. When she walked up, he grinned, his boyish face lighting up.

"It's perfect," he said. "Ten grand and we'd have ourselves a honeymoon suite."

Tanya turned to the realtor. "How soon can we close?"

The owners were as anxious to sell as Tanya was to buy, and three weeks later, they were in the house, with the hired contractors hard at work. Tanya and Nathan were working, too, researching the house's background, both history and legend.

The first part was giving them trouble. The only online mention Nathan found was a secondary reference. But it proved that a family *had* died in their house, so that morning he'd gone to the library in nearby Beamsville, hoping a search there would produce details.

Meanwhile, Tanya would try to dig up the less-tangible ghosts of the past.

She started in the gardening shop, and made the mistake of mentioning the house's history. The girl at the counter shut right down, murmuring, "We don't talk about that," then bustled off to help the next customer. That was fine. If the town didn't like to talk about the tragedy, she was free to tweak the facts and her guests would never hear anything different.

Next, she headed for the general store, complete with rocking chairs on the front porch and a tub of salty pickles beside the counter. She bought supplies, then struck up a conversation with the owner. She mentioned that she'd bought the Sullivan place, and worked the conversation around to, "Someone over in Beamsville told me the house is supposed to be haunted."

"Can't say I ever heard that," he said, filling her bag. "This is a nice, quiet town."

"Oh, that's too bad." She laughed. "Not the quiet part but . . ." She lowered her voice. "You wouldn't believe the advertising value of ghosts."

His wife poked her head in from the back room. "She's right, Tom. Folks pay extra to stay in those places. I saw it on TV."

"A full house for me means more customers for you," Tanya said.

"Well, now that you mention it, when my boys were young, they said they saw lights. . . ."

And so it went. People might not want to talk about the true horrors of what had happened at the Sullivan place, but with a little prodding they spun tales of imagined ones. Most were secondhand accounts, but Tanya didn't even care if they were true. Someone in town said it, and that was all that mattered. By the time she headed home, her notebook was filled with stories.

She was at the bottom of the road when she saw the postwoman putting along in her little car, driving from the passenger seat so she could stuff the mailboxes. Tanya got out to introduce herself. As they chatted, Tanya mentioned the raspberry-picking neighbor, hoping to get a name.

"No old ladies around here," the postwoman said. "You've got Mr. McNally to the north. The Lee gang to the south. And to the back, it's a couple of new women. Don't recall the names—it isn't my route—but they're young."

"Maybe a little farther? She didn't exactly say she was a neighbor. Just pointed over there."

The woman followed her finger. "That's the Lee place."

"Past that, then."

"Past that?" The woman eyed her. "Only thing past that is the cemetery."

Tanya made mental notes as she pulled into the darkening drive. She'd have to send Nathan to the clerk's office, see if he could find a dead resident that resembled a description of the woman she'd seen.

Not that she thought she'd seen a ghost, of course. The woman probably lived farther down the hill. But if she found a similar deceased neighbor, she could add her own spooky tale to the collection.

She stepped out of the car. When a whisper snaked around her, she jumped. Then she stood there, holding the car door, peering into the night and listening. It definitely sounded like whispering. She could even pick up a word or two, like *come* and *join*. Well, at least the ghosts weren't telling her to get lost, she thought, her laugh strained and harsh against the quiet night.

The whispers stopped. She glanced up at the trees. The dead leaves were still. No wind. Which explained why the sound had stopped. As she headed for the house, she glanced over her shoulder, checking for Nathan's SUV. It was there, but the house was pitch black.

She opened the door. It creaked. Naturally. No oil for that baby, she thought with a smile. No fixing the loose boards on the steps, either. Someone was bound to hear another guest sneaking down for a midnight snack and blame ghosts. More stories to add to the guest book.

She tossed her keys onto the table. They hit with a jangle, the sound echoing through the silent hall. When she turned on the light switch, the hall stayed dark. She tried not to shiver as she peered around. *That's quite enough ghost stories for you,* she told herself as she marched into the next room, heading for the lamp. She tripped over a throw rug and stopped.

"Nathan?"

No answer. She hoped he wasn't poking around in the basement. He'd been curious about some boxes down there, but she didn't want to get into that. There was too much else to be done.

She eased forward, feeling the way with her foot until she reached the lamp. When she hit the switch, light flooded the room. Not a power outage, then. Good; though it reminded her they had to pick up a generator. Blackouts would be a little more atmosphere than guests would appreciate.

"Nathan?"

She heard something in the back rooms. She walked through, hitting lights as she went—for safety, she told herself.

"Umm-hmm." Nathan's voice echoed down the hall. "Umm-hmm."

On the phone, she thought, too caught up in the call to realize how dark it had gotten and turn on a light. She hoped it wasn't the licensing board. The inspector had been out to assess the ongoing work yesterday. He'd seemed happy with it, but you never knew.

She let her shoes click a little harder as she walked over the hardwood floor, so she wouldn't startle Nathan. She followed his voice to the office. From the doorway, she could see his back in the desk chair.

"Umm-hmm."

Her gaze went to the phone on the desk. Still in the cradle. Nathan's hands were at his sides. He was sitting in the dark, looking straight ahead, at the wall.

Tanya rubbed down the hairs on her neck. He was using his cell phone earpiece, that was all. Guys and their gadgets. She stepped into the room and looked at his ear. No headset.

"Nathan?"

He jumped, wheeling so fast that the chair skidded across the floor. He caught it and gave a laugh, shaking his head sharply as he reached for the desk lamp.

"Must have dozed off. Not used to staring at a computer screen all day anymore."

He rubbed his eyes, and blinked up at her.

"Everything okay, hon?" he asked.

She said it was and gave him a rundown of what she'd found, and they had a good laugh at that, all the shopkeepers rushing in with their stories once they realized the tourism potential.

"Did *you* find anything?"

"I did indeed." He flourished a file folder stuffed with printouts. "The Rowe family. Nineteen seventy-eight. Parents, two children, and the housekeeper, all killed by the seventeen-year-old son."

"Under the influence of Satan?"

"Rock music. Close enough." Nathan grinned. "It was the seventies. Kid had long hair, played in a garage band, partial to Iron Maiden and Black Sabbath. Clearly a Satanist."

"Works for me."

Tanya took the folder just as the phone started to ring. The caller ID showed the inspector's name. She set the pages aside and answered as Nathan whispered that he'd start dinner.

There was a problem with the inspection—the guy had forgotten to check a few things, and he had to come back on the weekend, when they were supposed to be away scouring estate auctions and flea markets to furnish the house. The workmen would be there, but apparently that wasn't good enough. And on Monday, the inspector would leave for two weeks in California with the wife and kids.

Not surprisingly, Nathan offered to stay. Jumped at the chance, actually. His enthusiasm for the project didn't extend to bargain hunting for Victorian beds. He joked that he'd have enough work to do when she wanted her treasures refinished. So he'd stay home and supervise the workers, which was probably wise anyway.

It was an exhausting but fruitful weekend. Tanya crossed off all the necessities and even a few wish-list items, like a couple of old-fashioned washbasins.

When she called Nathan an hour before arriving home, he sounded exhausted and strained, and she hoped the workers hadn't given him too much trouble. Sometimes they were like her grade-five pupils, needing a watchful eye and firm, clear commands. Nathan wasn't good at either. When she pulled into the drive and found him waiting on the porch, she knew there was trouble.

She wasn't even out of the car before the workmen filed out, toolboxes in hand.

"We quit," the foreman said.

"What's wrong?" she asked.

"The house. Everything about it is wrong."

"Haunted," an older man behind him muttered.

The younger two shifted behind their elders, clearly uncomfortable with this old-man talk, but not denying it, either.

"All right," she said slowly. "What happened?"

They rhymed off a litany of haunted-house tropes—knocking inside the walls, footsteps in the attic, whispering voices, flickering lights, strains of music.

"Music?"

"Seventies rock music," Nathan said, rolling his eyes behind their backs. "Andy found those papers in my office, about the Rowe family."

"You should have warned us," the foreman said, scowling. "Working where som ething like that happened? It isn't right. The place should be burned to the ground."

"It's evil," the older man said. "Evil soaked right into the walls. You can feel it."

The only thing Tanya felt was the recurring sensation of being trapped in a B movie. Did people actually talk like this? First the old woman. Then the townspeople. Now the contractors.

They argued, of course, but the workmen were leaving. When Tanya started to threaten, Nathan pulled her aside. The work was almost done, he said. They could finish up themselves, save some money, and guilt these guys into cutting their bill even more.

Tanya hated to back down, but he had a point. She negotiated 20 percent off for the unfinished work and another 15 for the inconvenience—unless they wanted her spreading the word that grown men were afraid of ghosts. They grumbled, but agreed.

The human mind can be as impressionable as a child. Tanya might not believe in ghosts, but the more stories she heard, the more her mind began to believe, with or without her permission. Drafts became cold spots. Thumping pipes became the knocks of unseen hands. The hisses and sighs of the old furnace became the whispers and moans of those who could not rest. She knew better: that was the worst of it. She'd hear a pipe thump and she'd jump, heart pounding, even as she knew there was a logical explanation.

Nathan wasn't helping. Every time she jumped, he'd laugh. He'd goof off and play ghost, sneaking into the bathroom while she was in the shower and writing dirty messages in the condensation on the mirror. She was spooked; he thought it was adorable.

The joking and teasing she could take. It was the other times, the ones when she'd walk into a room and he'd be standing or sitting, staring into nothing, confused, when he'd start out of his reverie, laughing about daydreaming, but nervously, like he didn't exactly know what he'd been doing.

They were three weeks from opening when she returned from picking up the brochures and, once again, found the house in darkness. This time, the hall light worked—it'd been nothing more sinister than a burned-out bulb before. And this time she didn't call Nathan's name, but crept through the halls looking for him, feeling silly, and yet . . .

When she approached the kitchen, she heard a strange rasping sound. She followed it and found Nathan standing in the twilight, staring out the window, hands moving, a *skritch-skritch* filling the silence.

The fading light caught something in his hands—a flash of silver that became a knife, a huge butcher's knife moving back and forth across a whetting stone.

"N-nathan?"

He jumped, nearly dropping the knife, then stared down at it, frowning. A sharp shake of his head and he laid the knife and stone on the counter, then flipped on the kitchen light.

"Really not something I should be doing in the dark, huh?" He laughed and moved a carrot from the counter to the cutting board, picked up the knife, then stopped. "Little big for the job, isn't it?"

She moved closer. "Where did it come from?"

"Hmm?" He followed her gaze to the unfamiliar knife. "Ours, isn't it? Part of the set your sister gave us for our anniversary? It was in the drawer." He grabbed a smaller knife from the wooden block. "So, how did the brochures turn out?"

Two nights later, Tanya was startled awake and bolted up, blinking hard, hearing music. She rubbed her ears, telling herself it was a dream, but she could definitely hear something. She turned to Nathan's side of the bed. Empty.

Okay, he couldn't sleep, so he'd gone downstairs. She could barely hear the music, so he was being considerate, keeping it low, probably doing paperwork in the office.

Even as she told herself this, though, she kept envisioning the knife. The big butcher's knife that seemed to have come from nowhere.

Nonsense. Her sister *had* given them a new set, and Nathan did most of the cooking, so it wasn't surprising that she hadn't recognized it. But as hard as she tried to convince herself, she just kept seeing Nathan standing in the twilight, sharpening that knife, the *skritch-skritch* getting louder, the blade getting sharper. . . .

Damn her sister. And not for the knives, either. Last time they'd been up, her sister and boyfriend had insisted on picking the night's video. *The Shining.* New caretaker at inn is possessed by a murderous ghost and hacks up his wife. There was a reason Tanya didn't watch horror movies, and now she remembered why.

She turned on the bedside lamp, then pushed out of bed and flicked on the overhead light. The hall one went on, too. So did the one leading downstairs. Just being careful, of course. You never knew where a stray hammer or board could be lying around.

As she descended the stairs, the music got louder, the thump of the bass and the wail of the singer. Seventies' heavy-metal music. Hadn't the Rowe kid—? She squeezed her eyes shut and forced the thought out. Like she'd know seventies heavy metal from modern stuff anyway. And hadn't Nathan picked up that new AC/DC disk last month? *Before* they came to live here. He was probably listening to that, not realizing how loud it was.

When she got downstairs, though, she could feel the bass vibrating through the floorboards. Great. He couldn't sleep, so he was poking through those boxes in the basement.

Boxes belonging to the Rowe family. To the Rowe kid.

Oh, please. The Rowes had been gone for almost thirty years. Anything in the basement would belong to the Sullivans, a lovely old couple now living in Florida.

On the way to the basement, Tanya passed the kitchen. She stopped. She looked at the drawer where Nathan kept the knife, then walked over and opened it. Just taking a look, seeing if she remembered her sister giving it to them, not making sure it was still there. It was. And it still didn't look familiar.

She started to leave, then went back, took out the knife, wrapped it in a dish towel, and stuck it under the sink. And, yes, she felt like an idiot. But she felt relief even more.

She slipped down to the basement, praying she wouldn't find Nathan sitting on the floor, staring into nothing, nodding to voices she couldn't hear. Again, she felt foolish for thinking it, and again she felt relief when she heard him digging through boxes, and more relief yet when she walked in and he looked up, grinning sheepishly like a kid caught sneaking into his Christmas presents.

"Caught me," he said. "Was it the music? I thought I had it low enough."

She followed his gaze and a chill ran through her. Across the room was a record player, an album spinning on the turntable, more stacked on the floor.

"Wh-where—?" she began.

"Found it down here with the albums. Been a while since you've seen one of those, I bet."

"Was it . . . his? The Rowe boy?"

Nathan frowned, as if it hadn't occurred to him. "Could be, I guess. I didn't think of that."

He walked over and shut the player off. Tanya picked up an album. Initials had been scrawled in black marker in the corner. T.R. What was the Rowe boy's name? She didn't know and couldn't bring herself to ask Nathan, would rather believe he didn't know, either.

She glanced at him. "Are you okay?"

"Sure. I think I napped this afternoon, while you were out. Couldn't get to sleep."

"And otherwise . . . ?"

He looked at her, trying to figure out what she meant, but what could she say? *Have you had the feeling of being not yourself lately? Hearing voices telling you to murder your family?*

She had to laugh at that. Yes, it was a ragged laugh, a little unsure of itself, but a laugh nonetheless. No more horror movies for her, however much her sister pleaded.

"Are *you* okay?" Nathan asked.

She nodded. "Just tired."

"I don't doubt it, the way you've been going. Come on. Let's get up to bed." He grinned. "See if I can't help us both get to sleep."

The next day, she was in the office, adding her first bookings to the ledger when she saw the folder pushed off to the side, the one Nathan had compiled on the Rowe murders. She'd set it down that day and never picked it up again. She could tell herself she'd simply forgotten, but she was never that careless. She hadn't read it because her newly traitorous imagination didn't need any more grist for its mill.

But now she thought of that album cover in the basement. Those initials. If it didn't belong to the Rowe boy, then this was an easy way to confirm that and set her mind at ease.

The first report was right there on top, the names listed, the family first, then the housekeeper, Madelyn Levy, and finally, the supposed killer, seventeen-year-old Timothy Rowe.

Tanya sucked in a deep breath, then chastised herself. What did that prove? She'd known he listened to that kind of music, and that's all Nathan had been doing—listening to it, not sharpening a knife, laughing maniacally.

Was it so surprising that the Rowes' things were still down there? Who else would claim them? The Sullivans had been over fifty when they moved in—maybe they'd never ventured down into the basement. There had certainly been enough room to store things upstairs.

And speaking of the Sullivans, they'd lived in this house for twenty-five years. If it was haunted, would they have stayed so long?

If it was *haunted*? Was she really considering the possibility? She squeezed her eyes shut. She was not that kind of person. She would not become that kind of person. She was rational and logical, and until she saw something that couldn't be explained by simple common sense, she was sending her imagination to the corner for a time-out.

The image made her smile a little, enough to settle back and read the article, determined now to prove her fancies wrong. She found her proof in the next paragraph, where it said that Timothy Rowe shot his father. *Shot*. No big, scary butcher—

Her gaze stuttered on the rest of the line. She went back to the beginning, rereading. Timothy Rowe had apparently started his rampage by shooting his father, then continued on to brutally murder the rest of his family with a ten-inch kitchen carving knife.

And what did that prove? Did she think Nathan had dug up the murder weapon with those old LPs? Of course not. A few lines down, it said that both the gun and knife had been recovered.

What if Nathan bought a matching one? Compelled to reenact—

She pressed her fists against her eyes. Nathan possessed by a killer teen, plotting to kill her? Was she losing her mind? It was Nathan—the same good-natured, carefree guy she'd lived with for ten years. Other than a few bouts of confusion, he was his usual self, and those bouts were cause for a doctor's appointment, not paranoia.

She skimmed through the rest of the articles. Nothing new there, just the tale retold again and again, until—the suspect dead—the story died a natural death, relegated to being a skeleton in the town's closet.

The last page was a memorial published on the first anniversary of the killings, with all the photos of the victims. Tanya glanced at the family photo and was about to close the folder when her gaze lit on the picture of the housekeeper: Madelyn Levy.

When Nathan came in a few minutes later, she was still staring at the picture.

"Hey, hon. What's wrong?"

"I—" She pointed at the housekeeper's photo. "I've seen this woman. She—she was outside, when we were looking at the house. She was picking raspberries."

The corners of Nathan's mouth twitched, as if he was expecting—hoping—that she was making a bad joke. When her gaze met his, the smile vanished and he took the folder from her hands, then sat on the edge of the desk.

"I think we should consider selling," he said.

"Wh-what? No. I—"

"This place is getting to you. Maybe—I don't know. Maybe

there is something. Those workers certainly thought so. Some people could be more susceptible—"

She jerked up straight. "I am not susceptible—"

"You lost a job you loved. You left your home, your family, gave up everything to start over, and now it's not going the way you dreamed. You're under a lot of stress and it's only going to get worse when we open."

He took her hands and tugged her up, his arms going around her. "The guy who owns the Beamsville bed-and-breakfast has been asking about this place. He'd been eyeing it before, but with all the work it needed, it was too much for him. Now he's seen what we've done and, well, he's interested. Very interested. You wouldn't be giving up; you'd be renovating an old place and flipping it for a profit. Nothing wrong with that."

She stood. "No. I'm being silly, and I'm not giving in. We have two weeks until opening, and there's a lot of work to be done."

She turned back to her paperwork. He sighed and left the room.

It got worse after that, as if in refusing to leave, she'd issued a challenge to whatever lived there. She'd now stopped laughing when she caught herself referring to the spirits as if they were real. They were. She'd come to accept that. Seeing the housekeeper's picture had exploded the last obstacle. She'd wanted a haunted house and she'd gotten it.

For the last two nights, she'd woken to find herself alone in bed. Both times, Nathan had been downstairs listening to that damned music. The first time, he'd been digging through the boxes, wide awake, blaming insomnia. But last night . . .

Last night, she'd gone down to find him talking to someone. She'd tried to listen, but he was doing more listening than talking himself, and she caught only a few *um-hmms* and *okays* before he'd apparently woken up, startled and confused. They'd made an appointment to see the doctor after that. An appointment that was still a week away, which didn't do Tanya any good now, sitting awake in bed alone on the third night, listening to the strains of distant music.

She forced herself to lie back down. Just ignore it. Call the doctor in the morning, tell him Nathan would take any cancellation.

But lying down didn't mean falling asleep. As she lay there, staring at the ceiling, she made a decision. Nathan was right. There was no shame in flipping the house for a profit. Tell their friends and family they'd decided small-town life wasn't for them. Smile coyly when asked how much they'd made on the deal.

No shame in that. None at all. No one ever needed to know what had driven her from this house.

She closed her eyes and was actually on the verge of drifting off when she heard Nathan's footsteps climbing the basement stairs. Coming to bed? She hoped so, but she could still hear the boom and wail of the music.

Nathan's steps creaked across the first level. A door opened. Then the squeak of a cupboard door. A *kitchen* cupboard door.

Grabbing something to eat before going back downstairs.

Only he didn't go downstairs. His footsteps headed upstairs.

He's coming up to bed—just forgot to turn off the music.

All very logical, but logical explanations didn't work for Tanya anymore. She got out of bed and went into the dark hall. She reached for the light switch, but stopped. She didn't dare announce herself like that.

Clinging to the shadows, she crept along the wall until she could make out the top of Nathan's blond head as he slowly climbed the stairs. Her gaze dropped, waiting for his hands to come into view.

A flash of silver winked in the pale glow of a nightlight. Her breath caught. She forced herself to stay still just a moment longer, to be sure, and then she saw it, the knife gripped in his hand, the angry set of his expression, the emptiness in his eyes, and she turned and fled.

A room. Any room. Just get into one, lock the door, and climb over the balcony.

The first one she tried was locked. She wrenched on the door-knob, certain she was wrong.

"Mom?" Nathan said, his voice gruff, unrecognizable. "Are you up here, Mom?"

Tanya turned. She looked down the row of doors. All closed. Only theirs was open, at the end. She ran for it as Nathan's footsteps thumped behind her.

She dashed into the room, slammed the door, and locked it. As she raced for the balcony, she heard the knob turn behind her. Then the creak of the door opening. But that couldn't be. She'd locked—

Tanya glanced over her shoulder and saw Nathan, his face twisted with rage.

"Hello, Mom. I have something for you."

Tanya grabbed the balcony door. It was already cracked open, since Nathan always insisted on fresh air. She ran out onto the balcony and looked down to the concrete patio twenty feet below. No way she could jump that, not without breaking both legs, and then she'd be trapped. Maybe if she could hang from it, then drop—

Nathan stepped onto the balcony. Tanya backed up. She called his name, begged him to snap out of it, but he just kept coming, kept smiling, knife raised. She backed up, leaning against the railing.

"Nathan. Plea—"

There was a tremendous crack, and the railing gave way. She

felt herself falling, dropping backward so fast that she didn't have time to twist, to scream, and then—

Nothing.

Nathan escorted the innkeeper from Beamsville to the door.

"You folks did an incredible job," the man said. "But I really do hate to take advantage of a tragedy. . . ."

Nathan managed a wan smile. "You'd be doing me a favor. The sooner I can get away, the happier I'll be. Every time I drive in, I see that balcony, and I—" His voice hitched. "I keep asking myself why she went out there. I know she loved the view; she must have woken up and seen the moon and wanted a better look." He shook his head. "I meant to fix that balcony. We did the others, but she said ours could wait, and now . . ."

The man laid a hand on Nathan's shoulder. "Let me talk to my real estate agent and I'll get an offer drawn up, see if I can't take this place off your hands."

"Thank you."

Nathan closed the door and took a deep breath. He was making good use of those community-theater skills, but he really hoped he didn't have to keep this up much longer.

He headed into the office, giving it yet another once-over, making sure he'd gotten rid of all the evidence. He'd already checked, twice, but he couldn't be too careful.

There wasn't much to hide. The old woman had been an actor friend of one of his theater buddies, and even if she came forward, what of it? Tanya had wanted a haunted house and he'd hired her to indulge his wife's fancy.

Adding the woman's photo to the article had been simple Photoshop work, the files—paper and electronic—long gone now. The workmen really had been scared off by the haunting, which he'd orchestrated. The only person who knew about his "bouts" was Tanya. And he'd been very careful with the balcony, loosening the nails just enough that her weight would rip them from the rotting wood.

Killing Tanya hadn't been his original intention. But when she'd refused to leave, he'd been almost relieved. As if he didn't mind having to fall back on the more permanent solution, get the insurance money as well as the inheritance, go back home, hook up with Denise again—if she'd still have him—and open the kind of business he wanted. There'd been no chance of that while Tanya was alive. Her money. Her rules. Always.

He opened the basement door, stepped down, and almost went flying, his foot sending a hammer clunking down a few stairs. He retrieved it, wondering how it got there, then shoved it into his back pocket and—

The ring of the phone stopped his descent. He headed back up to answer it.

"Restrictions?" Nathan bellowed into the phone. "What do you mean *restrictions*? How long—?"

He paused.

"A year? I have to *live* here a year?"

Pause.

"Look, can't there be an exception under the circumstances? My wife died in this house. I need to get out of here."

Tanya stepped up behind Nathan and watched the hair on his neck rise. He rubbed it down and absently looked over his shoulder, then returned to his conversation. She stepped back, caught a glimpse of the hammer in his pocket, and sighed. So much for that idea. But she had plenty more, and it didn't sound like Nathan was leaving anytime soon.

She slid up behind him, arms going around his waist, smiling as he jumped and looked around.

Her house might not have been haunted when she'd bought it. But it was now.

It seems that husbands have their unrealized desires, too. Leaving Tanya Evans, the woman who couldn't get what she desired in life, all the time in the world to fulfill her desires in death. Perhaps she will, too, with a little help from . . . the Twilight Zone.

ON THE ROAD

William F. Wu

Two young people, alone and searching for meaning in their lives, meet by chance. They share their hopes and doubts, then go their separate ways. Seeing each other again on some far-off day would normally involve impossible odds. Coincidence, however, does not exist . . . when you hitchhike into the Twilight Zone.

An abrupt surge of anger overwhelmed Tod Kwan, anger at the painting on his easel, at his routine, at the repetition. In fury, he flung the palette and brush as if they were diseased, to clatter on the polished red-cedar floor. His heart pounding, he grabbed his canvas off the easel and smashed it over the back of a wooden chair as if he were destroying giant vermin. The wood ripped through the canvas and the torn fabric slapped his left forearm with wet paint.

Sweaty and breathless, Tod stared at the split canvas and the destruction of his artistic effort. He had never done anything like that before. Then he glanced up like a child caught misbehaving.

Amber Leon, his assistant, stood in the interior doorway with the mail. A student at the Colorado School of Mines in Golden, she looked from him to the palette lying in smeared paint.

Tod felt foolish, his rage spent. "I, uh. . . ."

"I'll get it." She knelt to pick up the palette.

Embarrassed and confused, Tod turned away and gazed up

through the glass wall of his home studio at the beautiful Rocky Mountain slopes he had known for so many years.

Just moments ago, he had been catching the morning sunlight on his palette of mixed oils like a makeup artist angling a mirror. Fifty-eight years old with a lifetime of painting behind him, he knew his work. He had dipped his 000 brush into the forest green he had just mixed. With fine strokes, he had used the tiny point to delineate curving edges on individual leaves, creating the illusion of depth where no depth existed.

Then he had smashed it.

Mystified by his actions, Tod massaged the ache of arthritis in his finger joints. The effort to paint had been familiar and the strokes had come easily, without thought. With growing unease, he glanced across the studio at his wall calendar.

Tod painted photo-realistic landscapes. He specialized in the peaks and slopes of the Rockies that had fascinated him since his first visit to Boulder, when he was in his twenties. His work was his life. Yet, in this moment, it seemed like no life at all.

Divorced, without children, he lived simply. With financial success, he had built this ranch-style home outside Boulder, away from the zigzagged, interlaced highways, off a two-lane blacktop, down a graded gravel road, at the end of a long, uneven, rocky driveway where the way finally stopped.

The mountains he loved looked like walls. His house was a trap at the end of the road. He felt lost, abandoned, left behind.

As Amber wiped the mess off the shiny floor, Tod stared at the grid of black lines forming the squares on his wall calendar.

"Do you want me to get a new canvas out?" Amber asked.

"No." Tod eyed the empty white calendar squares, defined by the lines and corners of black ink. Down in the flatlands, where no mountains blocked the way, these straight lines and right angles could almost be county-line roads seen from an airliner. "I want to take a trip." He worked his arthritic fingers harder.

"Okay. I'm already on the Internet. What should I look for?"

"Get me the first major flight from Denver I can catch."

"But where are you going?"

"I don't know—don't care. Get me the first flight, any airline, any direction."

"But why?"

"No reason! I have to shower and dress."

In Springfield, Missouri, Connie Watts Dreyer sat in the breakfast nook of her modest, two-story house, staring into her cereal bowl as though the puddle of nonfat milk in the bottom held the secrets to her life that she could not seem to find.

Her son, Barry, was thirty-four years old and lived in St. Louis with his family. He had been moody and belligerent ever since Connie and his father had agreed to a separation. His sister, Ann, two years younger, had a job in the Kansas City area. She thought it was crazy for her mother, fifty-seven years old, even to consider a separation and divorce. Ann had not returned her mother's calls this week.

Connie sighed, glancing at the calendar on the angled latticework separating the breakfast nook from the kitchen. She supposed that Ann, always Daddy's girl, was trying to persuade Don to move back home. He had been gone for three weeks. Connie still felt they could work out their marriage somehow.

Feeling guilty about the kids' unhappiness, she studied the calendar, where it hung among supermarket coupons she had stuck in the latticework like some sort of discount mosaic.

She stared at the intersecting shapes formed by the morning sunlight shining through the lattice onto the counter. Idly, she ran her forefinger along a narrow, diagonal shadow, following the angle and turning at the corner to follow another. She traced the angled, crisscrossed shadows in fascinated despair, gazing at the lines and corners of the pattern, each edge leading to another, every corner a chance to go somewhere else or just back where she started, around in circles—no, around in little parallelograms, she thought wistfully, remembering her high-school geometry.

Suddenly she grabbed the cereal bowl, walked to the sink, and tossed it in with a clatter. She hated the thought of being a depressed empty-nest mother and an abandoned wife, after a lifetime as a career woman. She just didn't feel old. Her blond hair was streaked with gray, but was artfully blended, and still nearly shoulder-length. She looked much younger than the grandmothers she recalled during her own childhood, who had been stout and matronly in shapeless flower-print dresses. Anxious to leave the silent house, she hurried to the garage, her high heels tapping on the floor tiles like an engine desperately low on oil.

In August 1970, Tod Kwan stood on the shoulder of Interstate 270, somewhere north of St. Louis. A sheen of sweat covered him in the muggy evening as the sun blazed over the prairie country ahead of him. Crickets chirped loudly, mourning late summer.

He had tied a dark blue work shirt around his waist by the sleeves, over the wide belt holding up his low-slung brown jeans. His feet were hot inside weather-beaten, square-toed boots with scratched decorative buckles. When traffic came by, he held out his right arm, thumb up; his shoulder-length freak flag tossed away from his face in the wind of each passing vehicle.

An old VW bus rattled toward him, painted in swirls of blue and chartreuse dotted with white peace symbols. Its driver would be more likely to give him a ride than the Missouri farmers glaring at him from passing pickups. However, it pulled over about thirty feet up.

The passenger door opened and a slender young woman jumped out. She whirled, swinging long, blond hair, and shouted angrily, though traffic roar drowned out her words. A full, khaki backpack with the Boy Scout insignia hit the pavement. The minibus rumbled away, another chance lost.

Tod admired the blonde as she bent over for her pack.

She slung it over one shoulder with the ease of experience. Then she saw him. She paused, appraising him like he was a bag of seeds in a health food store, and walked toward him.

Watching her, he lifted his thumb again. She had straight blond hair parted in the middle, a slender frame, and a willowy walk, even while burdened by the backpack. A faded blue denim microskirt left her legs bare; sandals adorned her feet. She wore a loose, white peasant blouse with red embroidery at the neck.

"Hi." She stopped about fifteen feet from him, like a cat judging whether or not to run.

"Have some trouble back there?"

"Oh, that jackass. I mean, not the driver, but this guy I was hitching with. The driver has this mattress in the back, you know, and he had some wine in this little refrigerator?"

"Right. I think I get the point."

"I'm not a prude or anything, but I have to like the guy." She watched him anxiously, still feline in her readiness to flee.

"Yeah, right." He didn't know what to say.

"So, um, where you headed?" Her blue eyes searched his face.

"Berkeley."

"Oh, wow. Really?" Her eyes widened. "Are you from there?"

Tod stifled a laugh; he knew she asked in part because of his Asian descent. "No, I live in Ann Arbor. But I've been on the road most of the summer. I'm going to see some friends."

"Ann Arbor." She drew a stray strand of hair out of her mouth. "Michigan, right? That's supposed to be really cool, too."

He grinned. "Seven student strikes this past school year."

"Oh, wow. Um, I go to K.U. in Lawrence."

"University of Kansas."

"Right. This friend and I were going to spend the summer in this commune in Yellow Springs, Ohio, but I didn't like it. So I've been kind of going home, but a girl shouldn't hitch alone if she can avoid it. I do if I have to. But I've found lots of beautiful people with crash pads, so . . ." She shrugged again.

"Lawrence is on the way to Berkeley." Tod could hardly believe what she wanted. "You want to hitch together? Uh, okay."

"Cool. I mean, really great." Relief washed over her face. She glanced at the shirt tied around his waist. "Is that it?"

"Uh, yeah."

"That's cool. I mean, you can really live off the land, huh?"

"I had some money, but that's gone now. There's a real community out on the road nowadays. Lots of college campuses have soup kitchens where you can eat and crash in exchange for work."

"Communes, too. That one in Ohio helped people passing through."

"Right, right. I've been to a few."

"Doesn't this highway meet I-70? That goes right to Lawrence. Don't you think we'll get someone going straight west?"

"Yeah."

In early afternoon, dressed in his jeans and his white Western shirt, Tod took a flight to Wichita Falls, Texas. Denver was an airline hub; Amber had located planes headed for New York, Chicago, and Los Angeles. She had also found flights to Jackson Hole, Gunnison, and Wichita Falls. He had picked one on impulse and had chided himself after takeoff, looking out the window at rural roads that looked nothing like the grid on his calendar.

Tod put on his headset and surfed channels. Chad and Jeremy sang about how that was yesterday and yesterday's gone. This channel played all folk music. He whisper-sang about a man named Charlie on a tragic and fateful day and this train that don't carry no gamblers.

The songs spoke of adventure and penniless wandering. They stung. His years of spontaneous risk were as lost as Charlie. Long ago, he had mastered every angle in his paintings, the slopes and peaks, each tree and rock, the snow or leaves. His work remained good and it remained the same.

He cranked up the volume to drown out his thoughts.

Just before the plane began its descent, another song told Tod you can't hop a jet plane like you can a freight train, but he had come close. At the terminal, as passengers dispersed, Tod gazed out at the flat Texas plains. A highway led from the airport below a deep blue sky. The pavement beckoned as the grid on his wall calendar had drawn him—only this road was real.

By now he knew that his anger today was more than just a fit of temper. He had been a man of constant sorrow for a long time; how many leaves can one man paint before they make him cry? Amused at his absurd, bitter humor, he adjusted the strap of his carry-on bag and stepped out into the air of northeast Texas, humming a tune about how it was green, green on the far side of the hill.

Connie revved the engine of her rusted green sedan like a teenager. She pulled into the flow of traffic and snapped on the radio. Then she called her supervisor at the civil rights commission. As the phone rang, Connie sang in a whisper along with the stereo about a man walking down roads and a white dove sleeping in the sand.

"This is Brenda."

"It's Connie. I'm not coming in today."

"Are you okay? Wait, is it something about Don?"

"No, nothing like that. I just ... need some time."

"You have lots of vacation time. Just let me know, okay?"

"Thanks, Brenda." Connie hung up, aware that her exhilaration had vanished. Her abrupt freedom left her shocked.

Singing softly about how many times a man must look up to see the sky, she reflected that she was a blank slate now: free from work, hardly a wife, the kids long grown. She could do anything she wanted.

Of course, if freedom was just another word for nothing left to lose, her life today was empty after all.

Ahead of young Tod and his new companion, the sun blazed red, low on the horizon. Mosquitoes buzzed around them. The evening rush from St. Louis had passed them by like a stampeding herd.

Finally a big, rusting, dirty, white Chevy Impala slowed down and pulled onto the shoulder to an abrupt stop. A young woman was driving. Another woman leaned out the open passenger window, looking at his blond friend and pointedly not at him.

"Where're you headed?" The woman on the passenger side had short, curly, dark brown hair and gold-wire-rimmed glasses.

"Lawrence, Kansas," said the blonde. "Where are you going?"

"Taos, New Mexico." The woman in the car giggled.

The driver leaned toward the passenger side, swaying a wild triangle of curly brown hair. "We're driving down across Missouri. We'll pass through Tulsa on our way to Texas."

The blonde glanced back at him.

"Let's do it. You can go north from Tulsa up to Lawrence. The rides might be better there."

"Okay." She turned back to the car. "Sure, that'll be great."

"Outta sight. Get in."

The blonde slid into the back and wedged her backpack behind the driver. Tod followed her and slammed the door. The car rumbled up the road, its power undaunted by age or rust. Both front windows were down, blasting summer wind into the back.

"I'm Deb," the driver called over her shoulder.

"Sarah," said her friend, opening the glove compartment.

"I'm Tod." He was looking at his companion.

"Connie." She smiled shyly as her long, blond hair fluttered.

The driver turned up the radio, loud. ". . . Tonight on this Million Dollar Weekend. Now here's Tommy Roe with—"

A cassette tape snapped into place, shutting up the deejay.

"Yuck," Deb said loudly, laughing. "Hey, you like acid rock?"

"Sure," Tod yelled over the rush of air, but the fast, driving guitar of Cream's "Crossroads," starting in midsong, drowned him out. He turned to Connie, and they laughed together.

Sarah toked on a small, handheld brass water pipe, then handed it to Deb. The wind from the open windows swirled the smoke out of the car. Deb passed the pipe over her shoulder to Connie in a motion of casual trust.

Tod rocked in his seat to the song, observing that Connie knew how to use the pipe. He took a turn and passed it back to Sarah. Connie met his gaze, smiling tightly, and also bounced in her seat to the beat with him.

Finally, Connie let out a breath. "So, like, you must have been born here, right? I mean, you don't have an accent or anything."

"Right." Tod heard that all the time, especially on the road.

Another Cream song followed on the stereo.

"Did you ever read anything by Alan Watts? He writes about yin and yang and balance and stuff. Or do you already know all that?"

Tod laughed, not sure how to answer. "I read a book of his for a class." In fact, he had been raised with some of the values and principles she meant, but that didn't make him an expert.

"I have one. And R. D. Laing. And *On the Road*, by Jack Kerouac."

"Yeah, I've read something by all of them."

"Cool." She accepted the pipe from Deb again and drew on it.

Tod took his turn, then passed the pipe back to Sarah.

Idly massaging his arthritic finger joints, Tod walked along the sidewalk outside the airport, exulting in his unaccustomed freedom. Since he was doing nothing, he could neither succeed nor fail. He found a bus going into downtown Wichita Falls and got on. As the bus rumbled away, he felt an anticipation he did not understand. After all, he had never been there and had never wanted to go there.

He had no direction, like a rolling stone.

Connie drove cheerfully, with no thoughts beyond the traffic in front of her. She turned on the stereo and pressed the scanner. When she heard "Oh, Pretty Woman," she stopped it to sing with Roy Orbison.

She smiled with lighthearted amusement as the song ended with the guy picking up a woman on the street. Today she could pick up a guy. She was long past worrying about pregnancy, and her husband had moved out. Her kids would never know.

Connie sobered, thinking about her job again. It was steady, being a civil service position. She had been idealistic when she had started. Now it was just work.

When Connie saw the entrance ramp to I-44 west, she took it.

A young guy in faded blue jeans and a sweaty, orange tank top stood on the shoulder with this thumb out. His long, straight brown hair was pulled back into a ponytail. Of course, nowadays she was much too cautious to offer a lift to a strange man.

That made her sad.

As the Impala rumbled across Missouri, cornfields with green stalks and ripening silk tassels blurred past them, ghostly and mysterious in the deepening twilight.

"What are you majoring in?" Connie asked.

"I thought about trying fine arts, but . . . I don't know."

"Oh, wow, you play music or write poetry or something?"

"I used to paint." He folded his arms. "I'm not very good. I ought to find something I'm good at." He shrugged.

"Like you'd be a doctor or an engineer or something instead?"

Suddenly Tod grinned, amused that she had picked professions often associated with someone of Asian descent. "I don't know."

"I get it. You don't want to sell out." Her blue eyes looked large and guileless. "But painting's great. It's your own thing."

"Nobody would want the stuff I paint. What about you?"

"I'm a sociology major." She wrinkled her nose. "But I don't know if I'll stay with it. So, is Alan Watts cool?"

"Yeah." Tod laughed; her question seemed absurd, but she'd meant it. "He writes for average Americans. Maybe kind of simplified."

She nodded, studying his face intently. "Sometimes I just feel so, you know, being a white girl . . . you know?"

"Huh?" Tod wasn't sure if his confusion was her fault or his.

"I mean, I'm not black, so the civil rights thing, I mean, I'm in favor of it, but I'm not in the middle of it. And I can't be drafted, so I kind of feel guilty about all that. I want to contribute something. I don't know what."

"Oh." Tod was lost. He accepted the pipe from Connie again. It wouldn't help him sort it out, but right now he didn't care.

"So, like, you do get prejudiced against?"

He laughed at her garbled phrasing.

"No, really, I mean it."

He shrugged again, aware that she wanted to hear dramatic stories of being mistreated. The truth was more subtle. Many incidents were well intended—effusive appreciation of sweet-and-sour pork or Connie assuming he might become an engineer.

The demanding, incessant roar of "Sunshine of Your Love" came on as he took another turn with the pipe and passed it.

"That's *The Very Best of Cream*," Tod said suddenly.

"I guess you really don't want to talk about it, huh?"

Tod sighed. "Look, most white liberals haven't taken up my people as a cause. That's fine—but when I answer a question like yours, I get arguments—that we don't really have any problems."

"I'd believe you," she said softly.

He heard the sincerity in her voice. "Okay. You have any idea how racial the war is? The way most GIs talk about the Vietnamese? Or how they treat guys like me who go over? If I went, I figure if the enemy didn't kill me, the guys in my own platoon would."

Her blue eyes searched his face as though trying to see inside him.

Uncounted years later, Tod got off the cool bus in the heart of Wichita Falls, back into the blazing heat and stifling humidity. Feeling like a drifter, he looked for a place to eat, squinting up and down city blocks laid out on a grid like the days on a calendar.

Tod found a coffee shop, where he ordered a meatloaf special. Edgy and restless, he ate quickly. He mused that everything he had ever done in his life had brought him here for this meatloaf.

When he finished, the city grid no longer beckoned. Instead, he felt like a rat in a laboratory maze of city streets, local roads, and major highways that would take him on an inevitable route no matter which way he turned. Outside, he strode up the sidewalk, afraid to question a growing sense of purpose. He hurried even faster, going anywhere and going nowhere, but always going where he had been headed since he had smashed his painting.

Connie relaxed behind the wheel. She still didn't have a destination in mind. Among green cornfields and tall trees, she watched signs go by: Mt. Vernon, Sarcoxie, Joplin.

Her route clipped a corner of Kansas and entered Oklahoma. She drove through prairies of varied greenery under a bright blue sky, with subtle hues mixed as though on a palette. The signs continued: Miami, Afton, Vinita.

She stopped in Claremore for chicken-fried steak, an unhealthy midwestern indulgence from her childhood that she had shunned for years. Then she filled the gas tank and drove on through Tulsa, where she found an oldies station playing "Me and You and a Dog Named Boo." She sang along, about lazily wandering the country in the early seventies. Long ago, she had ridden through Tulsa one night. Beyond Oklahoma City, the signs picked up new names: Chickasha, Lawton, Wichita Falls.

Connie read the last name again. Once, she had almost reached Wichita Falls. Now she knew where she had been going all day.

By the time the Cream tape started "Crossroads" again, Connie had snuggled close to Tod. The headlights cut into the darkness ahead. They had stopped for gas and restrooms and returned to the road.

"I overdid the grass," said Deb. "I got to switch to Dex." She ejected the eight-track tape.

Mungo Jerry came on the radio with "In the Summertime."

"I like this song," said Connie. "What do you like?"

"I like it, too. And Peter, Paul and Mary. Folk, acid rock."

"Me too. And Dylan. Ooh, I haven't been this ripped since I saw *2001: A Space Odyssey* on campus. It's cooler being high."

"So's *Alice in Wonderland*." Tod gave her bony shoulder a squeeze. The car felt like a self-contained world, moving through a vacuum with only stars and space around them.

"So are you into Zen or anything? That's real big now."

Tod laughed. "No." He felt light-headed but not totally ripped. "I learned in a class that Zen started in China. Existentialists have a lot in common with Zen."

"I read Sartre and Camus last year. *No Exit*, *The Stranger*, stuff like that." She paused. "What do you mean?"

"They both emphasize the moment—living in the present. But also, Buddhists believe in karma—what you do, good or bad, brings the same kind of vibes back to you someday."

"I heard once, everything you've ever done led to where you are at that exact moment." Her blue eyes were big with wonder.

"So it's cause and effect, but we don't control it."

"That's the existential part." She nodded solemn recognition.

The Grass Roots had come onto the Million Dollar Weekend with their clear, stinging guitar in minor key, followed breathlessly by their insistent refrain to live for today.

"Oh, wow, do you believe this? Listen."

"*Doo, doo*, doo doo, *doo doo*, doo doo." Tod sang a different, wordless melody.

"No, really, listen. This is so . . . Zen." She gazed at him.

As Tod looked at her mouth, she eyed his, expectantly.

His mind whirled: Was this cause and effect? Did a coincidence between their talk and a song on the radio turn her on? Was their discussion turning on "The Great Mandela" as the deejay spun a platter, so no coincidence could possibly exist?

More likely, it was just the grass.

Maybe this was her way of feeling less white.

Maybe she didn't like him, the individual. Maybe she saw him only as a guy of his race. Maybe he should see that as an insult.

Hell with that; he could feel insulted later. Into the moment, Tod kissed her. She drew him down on top of her; he felt a slender hand brush through his shoulder-length hair.

They lay awkwardly across the seat. She slid one of his hands under her peasant blouse.

Creedence's current hit of psychedelic absurdities, "Lookin' Out My Back Door," came on. It was a perfect backdrop to kissing Connie while almost falling off the backseat.

Connie raised a knee and pulled his hand up her denim skirt.

They were On the Road, had met at the Crossroads. He hoped Deb would find No Exit anytime soon, and he laughed way too hard.

Then Connie tugged at the big metal buckle on his wide belt.

Live for Today.

Mystified by his own actions, Tod leaned forward in the backseat of the cab, pretending he was not a rat in a maze.

"That's I-44 comin' up," drawled the driver, a young, skinny guy who truly sounded like a cowboy in an old Western movie.

Tod looked in both directions. His heart pounded. He recognized nothing, but he pointed anyway, to his right. "That way."

"Are ya sure ya know where you're goin', sir?"

"I know." Tod squinted blindly into the sunlight ahead.

Connie raced down the highway, amazed at herself. She was a good mother who really enjoyed her family and her job. Yet she was miles from home, driving, as trees threw long shadows angling over her like the latticework shapes on her breakfast counter.

She hadn't been so spontaneous in years. All day, she had driven in an excited rush of freedom and solitude, playfully ignoring what she was doing. Now, for the first time, she snapped off the radio and drove in silence except for the rush of air outside the car and the quiet, lonely hum of the engine.

The car rumbled on through the night. Deb and Sarah had rolled up the windows. "Hitchin' a Ride," the light, bouncy song from earlier that summer, came from another Million Dollar Weekend out of another city. Sleepy yet wide awake, Tod knew that a lot of time had passed. He and Connie huddled together.

"You want to come to Berkeley with me?" Tod asked quietly.

"I'd like that. But I have to get back to Lawrence."

"It won't be for long. I'll go back to Ann Arbor soon."

She squeezed him. "Thanks for asking. But I want to go home."

"You don't mind hitching alone again?"

"You could come to Lawrence."

"I guess." He was pleased, but it felt wrong.

"Living the moment," she said. "We should go our separate ways."

In that moment, he wanted the night, and the ride, to go on forever like some hell-bound train. "I'll never see you again."

"We could run into each other again," she said. "Somehow."

He grinned. "We could agree to meet after the Revolution."

"You really think there's going to be a revolution?"

"No." He laughed.

She laughed, too. "Me neither. Okay, after the Revolution. But when? And where?"

"No planning. It should just happen."

"Right, right. It should be, you know, in the moment." She nodded, intense and somber again. "When the moment's right for both of us. Wherever it has to be."

"And karma, too." He meant to say it lightly, but it came out serious. It was all a big joke, and yet he felt it, deep inside: the moment, the karma.

She held one of his hands. "You have long fingers. I bet you can paint. Would you paint something for me?"

"You'd never see it, anyway. No point."

"Paint something for me. If you say yes, I'll know."

"I can't paint. I don't want to face that again."

"And not just any painting. Something that's really you."

"I don't paint," he said quietly. "Not anymore."

"What were you going to paint? Tell me about one of them."

"Oh . . . like a Chinese dragon in the Sierra Nevada. I read about Chinese immigrants building the railroad there."

"Ooh, cool. Do that one for me." Her tone turned playful. "When we meet after the Revolution, you can bring it to me."

He smiled weakly and shrugged.

"Promise me," she whispered solemnly.

He stared into her deep blue eyes, amazed. The moment grew inside him. Her intense gaze seemed to lift him, to make him more than he had been just moments ago. "All right," he whispered, and in that moment, he meant it.

She squeezed him, as though trying to cling to that moment.

They cuddled silently. The sky was growing light. Ahead, the lights of a town lay scattered in the fading darkness like stars from a space odyssey lying across the Texas plains.

Deb bounced energetically behind the wheel.

"What's that town ahead?" Tod asked.

"Wichita Falls, Texas," Deb called over her shoulder.

"Texas?" Connie sat up in surprise.

"Whoa! We were going to get out in Tulsa."

"Sorry! I forgot!" Deb giggled. "Took you long enough! Tulsa was three hours back, before Okie City. What do you want to do?"

"I have to go northwest," said Tod. "Connie has to go back to Oklahoma City. Then she can take I-35 north to Lawrence." He grinned at her. "I guess we were, uh, busy through Oklahoma."

Hiding a shy little smile, Connie snuggled close again.

"A highway's coming up for Amarillo," said Deb. "I'll pull up at that diner." She nodded toward the nearest exit.

Tod saw a small diner just off the exit. An Open sign stood in one window. Some pickup trucks were already parked outside.

In the parking lot, he got out and adjusted his clothes. Connie climbed out with her backpack. Sarah followed Deb into the restaurant.

"I have to use the restroom, too," said Connie. "Time to split, huh?"

"Uh, yeah. Be careful, okay?" His farewell sounded shallow, but he did not know how to express his fondness for her. She had given him a gift, one that swelled inside him but had no name.

"Sure. Take care." Connie kissed him lightly and gave him a sad, wistful smile, peering into his eyes again. "Don't forget."

As she walked away in the pale dawn light, Tod watched her little blue skirt twitch, and her long, blond hair sway.

In the parking lot, as the taxi drove away, Tod stared at the diner, a very vague memory made real. From here, through Amarillo, he had reached I-70 at Denver. He had seen Boulder for the first time during a random side trip on his way to Berkeley.

He found the place empty of customers. A waitress in a timeless white uniform refilled the sugar canisters on each table. He sat down at the counter and ordered iced tea.

Tod gazed straight ahead. He could hide here and never paint those tiny leaves or familiar peaks again. No one in his life knew where he was. Today he had nothing left to lose.

A petite blonde entered the diner. She hesitated, looking at him. Then she sat at the far end of the counter, adjusting her skirt.

"Coffee?" The waitress reached for the coffeepot.

"Yes, please."

The woman glanced at Tod again.

Behind the counter, Tod saw the red lights of a digital clock showing today's date and time. It was a calendar with no grid.

"I had a funny day." The blonde sat in a bright shaft of angled afternoon sunlight from a big window, with no shadows crossing her. "This morning I skipped out on my job. Like I knew what I was doing, but I didn't. I just left Springfield and drove." She paused. "Sorry for the chatter; I guess I'm wired."

Tod nodded politely. He saw that she was pretty, her pale complexion finely lined and her blond hair blended with gray. Then he looked away and sipped his iced tea.

"I didn't even call my husband—not that he'd care. We're separated." She stopped. "Would you rather I left you alone?" She stirred her coffee in a nervous, clackety rhythm.

"I don't mind. I had a weird day, myself."

"Do you live in Wichita Falls?" She watched her coffee spin.

"No. I live near Boulder."

"Boulder, Colorado? It's an artistic community, isn't it?"

"That's right."

"Are you an artist?" Her blue eyes searched his face.

He wondered if he should speak in past tense. "I paint."

Her eyes widened. "I've always admired creative people."

He didn't want to talk about his art. "What do you do?"

"I work in the women's rights division of a civil rights commission."

"You don't sound very enthusiastic."

"I wanted to change the world. But I'm not that special."

"Are you a lawyer?"

"No, I just push paper in management now. Got my degree in sociology." She sipped her coffee and looked into it as she spoke. "I admit I was surprised to see an Asian American in a Wichita Falls highway stop like this. Have you been here before?"

"Not really."

"I'm sorry." She closed her eyes.

"What?" He looked at her, uncomprehending.

"For categorizing you that way. Occupational hazard. Everyone's in a category at a civil rights commission. Race, gender, disabled, all the others. I'm really sorry."

"Don't worry about it." Amused, he gave her a little smile.

She smiled back. "I listened to oldies radio stations all day. They made me feel old, but I knew the songs. I forgot my iPod today—but I have one. My daughter gave it to me."

He knew she wanted to change the subject. "I listened to folk songs today. They remind me of protests, the draft, hippies. . . ."

"Free love." She smiled slightly, down at her cup.

"Yeah." Ted grinned at the phrase from his youth.

"You know, my job didn't even exist back then. If I look at it that way, I suppose I make a contribution."

Tod nodded. The frantic wheel of his career had stopped spinning, leaving him floating free. He just wanted to listen to her talk, here in this place at the crossroads.

"Sometimes I work with young people who say that period made no difference—there was no revolution, that nothing really changed. But women have many more options than we used to."

"I know what you mean. Asian Americans developed their own movement from that time."

"When I was young, I didn't think I could be an activist. I met a guy once who expressed something different about race and the war. I always remembered that. There was a revolution."

"Damn right there was. Life's very different now."

"A lifetime later." She smiled to herself. "I found my niche through . . . an indirect cause and effect. Like art, I suppose."

"Not what I've been doing. It's nothing."

"I think art must be a very personal expression."

"It should be," he said softly. "I just followed the market."

"What would you have done that was different?"

"Oh . . . once I thought I might paint Chinese mythic motifs in American settings." He glanced at her. "But I never did."

Curious blue eyes studied him silently.

Tod's heart pounded crazily and he looked away from her gaze. "I told a girl once I didn't think I was good enough to paint. She encouraged me. She's the reason I applied to art school."

"Really? What happened to your plans for ethnic work?"

"I was afraid nobody would want it. I was just afraid."

"I haven't taken risks for a long time. I've wasted years in a bad marriage. I kept fooling myself. Today, on the road alone, I felt like myself again. Now I know it's over."

Tod's pulse raced and he spoke before he could change his mind. "Would you like to visit Boulder with me?"

"I'd like that," she said quietly. "And I can hardly believe I just said that. But it's just the moment, isn't it?"

"Sorry. I guess that was just a stupid thing to say."

"It was a sweet thing to say." She cocked her head, making her blond hair sway. "Tell me about a painting you never did."

Only one vision sprang from his memory. "I imagined a Chinese dragon in the mountains along the Central Pacific Railroad. Funny. I haven't thought about that in years." He looked into her eyes, searching but not believing.

She watched him for a long moment without speaking.

Lost in her blue eyes, Tod wanted the moment never to end.

At last she slid off her stool and came forward. "Would you do it for me?" She searched his face as though trying to see inside him. "Something that's really you?"

Tod ached to ask her questions that were so far-fetched, so ridiculous, that he just couldn't say them. Was it cause and effect or karma? This moment at the crossroads froze.

He remembered: *"When the moment's right for both of us. Wherever it has to be."*

"Promise me," she whispered.

Again, he stared deeply into her blue eyes. "I'll do it this time," he said. He felt a warmth, a confidence, a gift growing inside him, and the ache in his fingers became an ache to paint.

She kissed him on the cheek. Then she walked to the door, where she gave him a wistful smile. She turned and slipped out.

Through the window, Tod watched her walk to her car, the skirt of her blue suit twitching and her blond hair blowin' in the wind.

Two mature people, alone and lost in late middle-age, find their way when they find each other again. Are they brought together by karma, chance, or a promise made lightly, little more than a joke? No matter.

This is not about entwining lives, but living in the moment, as they travel on the road . . . through the Twilight Zone.

THE ART
OF THE
MINIATURE

Earl Hamner

Spencer Dowd, druggist by trade, devoted husband, loving grandfather, and model citizen, had no idea where it would lead when he became involved in the hobby of bonsai. He had never committed a violent act in his life, but when an employee transgressed on his hobby, Spencer was to commit an act so vengeful that it was shocking and bizarre even in . . . the Twilight Zone.

Spencer Dowd had everything he needed to make him happy: a patient wife, adoring grandchildren, good health, a reliable business, and a comfortable bank account. Yet, as he stood at the window overlooking the deck around his swimming pool, he was plotting a diabolical act.

For a long time he had suspected that Rusty, the pool cleaner, had been disturbing his bonsai plants. In removing leaves and other debris from the water, Rusty used a net or skimmer with a handle long enough to reach the deeper parts of the pool. Just a slight brush against one of the delicate trees was enough to sever a leaf, snap a small branch, or knock the whole pot over, spilling the contents and leaving the plant to suffer in the sun. Spencer had spoken to the man, warned him to be careful, but he was an oaf, and Spencer could tell that he had no idea that these trees were unique works of art, a disciplined combination of horticulture and sculpture, with strict requirements, worthy of respect and even awe.

Now, as he looked down at the deck, he had just seen Rusty swing his skimmer briskly out of the pool. As he did so, he hit and broke a major branch of Spencer's most treasured plant—a wisteria tree.

All appearance of symmetry, harmony, and balance that had made the tree a classic had been destroyed. Rusty looked about to see if he had been observed; deciding that it was safe, he picked up the broken branch and tossed it over the edge of the deck, where it would not be seen. An anguished cry rose in Spencer's throat and it took all his restraint to keep from rushing down and throttling the man right then and there. But Spencer bided his time, for he had already suspected that this day might come and he had settled on a far more satisfactory revenge.

Most of Spencer's life had been fairly uneventful. He grew up in the apple-growing region of Nelson County, Virginia. When he met and fell in love with a girl from Pasadena, California, he married her, and when her father died he inherited a small family drugstore. He kept regular hours, rarely took a vacation, voted the straight Republican ticket, went to church on Sunday, and was religiously faithful to his wife. He was the least likely person to commit murder, but he hit upon an even more imaginative vengeance.

His life had taken a dramatic turn after he illegally provided some medicine to one of his customers, an elderly Japanese American gentleman, whose prescription had run out and who was facing a long holiday weekend without his medicine. In gratitude, the old man had arrived with a present—a miniature crab-apple tree planted in a shallow, enameled blue bowl.

"It's a bonsai," the customer explained. "It means a plant in a pot."

The miniature tree evoked warm memories of earlier years. Spencer had never realized how very much he missed the warmth and grace of living in Virginia, where most everyone he knew had been gracious and thoughtful and well mannered. The tree reminded him of the contrast, of how distressing living in California had become. He had come to tolerate the fact that there was no appreciable change of seasons, the rudeness of people in their cars, the lack of any kind of connection to the past, the arrogant stride of pedestrians in Beverly Hills who would walk right over or into you if you did not move out of their way, the sounds of every language in the world except English in the shops and restaurants. It was all very unsettling.

Spencer cultivated the little crab-apple tree all winter long and was rewarded in the spring with pink and white blossoms that covered it. Spencer was enthralled. While he had never had a real hobby, he had always loved trees. He loved their silhouettes in the winter when their leaves were gone. He was refreshed each spring by the appearance of the buds, their swelling and unfolding into new green leaves, and finally their rich and exuberant colors that came with the fall.

The gift of the first bonsai sparked an interest that grew from curiosity to obsession. He learned there were shops that specialized in the hobby. Often the small trees had been imported from Japan and were for sale at staggering prices. A less-expensive way to build a collection was to find a small tree at the local nursery and miniaturize it oneself. His collection grew, and within a year Spencer was caring for fifty trees of various varieties. He had rarely exhibited passion, so his interest in his new hobby surprised all who knew him.

One of the bonsai Spencer bought was to become his most favorite plant. He found it in a nursery in the San Gabriel Valley, a wisteria vine that had been reduced in height to a foot and a half. From rugged, half-visible roots called the *nebari* by the Japanese, there rose a thick, gracefully curved trunk from which limbs extended, each of them fashioned according to the strict rules of the art, and each dripping with clusters of purple blossoms. It had been imported from Japan and he'd paid $250 for it.

"Do you think that was too much?" he asked his wife, Karen, that night when he brought it home.

"Of course not," she said. "It's very beautiful, and if it makes you happy, why not! You can afford it!"

Spencer's collection continued to grow. He specialized in deciduous trees—crab apple, quince, liquid amber, Japanese maples—but his prize specimen was always his wisteria.

Housing so many plants was a challenge. He built a greenhouse and filled it immediately. He created a space under the pool deck in a spot that received just the proper amount of sun and shelter from wind. He built benches. He bought oriental stools and stands and shelves to hold them and still he could not stop.

His life became a pleasantly demanding routine of pinching, trimming, watering, fertilizing, grooming, and shaping the little trees. If a frost threatened, he would move them all into the basement until the weather was friendlier. If he had to go out of town for longer than two days, he hired a specialist to do the watering and to keep an eye open for thieves, for there is a thriving black market for the better-specimen trees.

He joined his local bonsai club and learned more about the art. He learned that the practice of bonsai began many centuries ago in China. It then traveled to Japan, where it flourished. Following World War II, the practice was brought to America by returning soldiers, where it has become one of the fastest-growing hobbies of all time.

He won prizes for his trees and each spring when the wisteria was in blossom he showed it at the Desmond Gardens Bonsai Show and won First Prize in the Advanced Category.

One of his trademarks was the creation of small landscapes at the base of some of his plants. They usually represented a garden or a pond or a temple. Always the landscape was peopled with tiny oriental figures that he found at the specialty shops—a bench where two philosophers in deep discussion were sitting, a Buddha in the lotus position decorating the entrance to a temple, a lawn where two white cranes bowed each to the other, a kimono-clad female figure holding a parasol.

Spencer's preoccupation with his plants took over his life. He neglected his wife and let her go on trips without him. He hired assistants to run the drugstore, ignored his grandchildren, and stopped going to church. He thought of nothing but his trees.

His wife was tolerant. When friends made observations about his peculiar behavior she would say, "Oh, that's just Spencer! He's always been a tree hugger."

Spencer grew more and more obsessed. He traveled to Japan to study with a bonsai master. He enrolled in classes in horticulture at the local community college to improve his knowledge of the cultivation of trees in general. He studied cases of dwarfism in plants and humans and even read in-depth accounts of the Jiraco Indians in Brazil, who decapitated their enemies and miniaturized their heads. He learned how to cut off the sap to stunt the growth of selected limbs. He read extensively about mummification practices, the phenomenon of mind over matter, voodoo, and black magic.

After breaking the branch on Spencer's wisteria tree, Rusty, the pool man, disappeared. His truck seemingly had been deserted on the street outside Spencer's residence. The only thing missing from the truck was Rusty's skimmer. There was no body, nor were there witnesses or clues. There was an investigation, but everybody overlooked the evidence that was clearly visible to the naked eye.

In the mossy area surrounding the trunk of the wisteria bonsai there was recently installed a tiny, artificial pond. The miniature figure of a fisherman stood beside the pond, but if one examined the figure more thoroughly, he would discern that the face was not Oriental and that the object held in its hands was not a fishing pole, but a miniature pool skimmer. And if one moved in even closer and listened carefully, he could hear a faint little voice calling, "Help."

Persons seeking employment would be well advised to learn all they can about their potential employer's hobbies. Especially if that employer has a fondness for small trees and the practice of bonsai in the Twilight Zone.

BENCHWARMER

Mike Resnick
and
Lezli Robyn

There is a fifth dimension, beyond those that are known to man. It is a dimension as vast as space and as timeless as infinity. It is the middle ground between light and shadow—between science and superstition. This is the dimension of the imagination, where creations of air and darkness live on the sidelines, waiting to get back into the game of Life. It is an area that we call the Twilight Zone.

He'd been sitting on the sidelines, warming the bench, waiting, for almost seventy years. The winds of Time chilled him to the bone, and all he had to keep him warm were his memories, which got a little older and a little colder each day.

He wasn't an imposing figure. There were days he looked like Humpty Dumpty before the fall, and days he looked more like a teddy bear. It didn't make any difference to him. He had never seen a mirror, nor did he care to.

He could have chosen any name he wanted, but he stuck with Mr. Paloobi, for reasons only one other person would understand. It didn't have much dignity to it, but then, dignity was not his stock in trade.

He envied his companions. Not their grace, their easy athletic ability, or their infectious laughter, because those traits were unimportant him. No, what he envied was the fact that sooner or later they were all called back into action, they all returned to what he thought of as The Game. He wanted desperately to leave the bench, but he didn't know the ground rules. He couldn't even discern that there were any.

He'd been given two brief chances, but he hadn't lasted any longer than a sore-armed pitcher on the mound, a lame Thoroughbred on the track, or a tennis player with no racket. He had tried his best, had given it his all, but he hadn't been up to the job, and indeed had to face that fact that there was only one job that he was truly suited for—and that job had ended sixty-eight years, four months, and seventeen days ago.

It had happened on the last day that he was called forth from the limbo where he was born, where he existed now until he was needed again. It was a day filled with the same promise as the day before, the same exciting horizon to be approached, the same challenges, and the same goals. But there was one thing that was not the same.

On that day the Boy outgrew him, and nothing was ever the same again.

Even after all those years, he was still unable to remember that day without feeling a keen sense of loss, and the thought that he'd never be complete again. Day after day, year after year, he sat on the sidelines and watched as his companions came and went. And while he kept the bench warm for the others, he waited for his chance to do what he'd been born to do.

All he wanted was to be needed again.

Mr. Paloobi could hear the contented rumble of Lionel's purr long before he ambled out of the mist and made his way to the bench.

Looking more like a four-hundred-pound tabby cat than a true lion, Lionel nevertheless appeared quite impressive as he bounded onto the bench, the seat automatically changing shape to accommodate the gentle beast that now lay curled up on its surface.

Mr. Paloobi turned to look at him expectantly as the big cat nestled his head in among his forepaws and curled his tail around his body, softly purring a lullaby to himself.

Sensing his gaze, Lionel opened one lazy eye. "My boy is sleeping after our safari in Darkest Africa."

"Africa?" said Mr. Paloobi. "I thought he lived just outside of Wichita."

"He does," confirmed Lionel. "But his imagination doesn't. We tracked zebras down Maple Street, made a kill at the corner of Third and Main, and barely avoided a stampede of mad elephants on wheels over on Elm Street. There were spear-carrying natives whose witch doctors had made their spears appear like briefcases (though we knew better), and as we passed a brick hut with a huge screen, we saw hundreds of disguised hyenas laughing as they came out. Oh, yes, it was quite a safari. You have no idea how many scrapes we got into, how many hairbreadth escapes."

"And you enjoyed every minute of it."

Lionel's eyes softened perceptibly, glowing amber. "And I enjoyed every minute of our time together. I'll miss him—until my next charge comes along." He sighed contentedly, settling his head back down onto his forepaws. "I could sleep for a couple of months. That boy wore me out!"

"Try sitting on the same hardwood bench for decades and then complain to me," replied Mr. Paloobi bitterly.

"Try wearing this goddamned costume day in and day out," retorted a fairy princess who suddenly appeared before them in a burst of pink glitter. "Then you'd have something to really complain about. This corset is *killing* me." Her golden curls bounced, as if to emphasize her point. "A pox on the girl who designed me! Who in their right mind decides that princesses should wear such constrictive dresses?"

"So take it off, Sugarblossom," said Mr. Paloobi.

"It doesn't *come* off," said Sugarblossom. "You know that. And the worst part is the smell."

"The smell?"

"She heard they used whalebone stays, so it smells exactly like a dead fish."

Mr. Paloobi chuckled. "I'm sorry. But welcome back anyway. You were with your current charge longer than usual."

"Oh, yes, I was! And what a charming young lady she'll grow up to be," she said proudly, beaming at him, her smile more brilliant than the sequined dress, crystal tiara, and glitter-covered shoes combined. "It turned out my girl needed a substitute mother even more than she needed someone to play make-believe with." Her smile became wistful, her eyes getting a faraway look to them as she continued. "She lost her mother recently, and she was grieving. Her mother always used to let her dress up in her old fancy clothes, and so did I. I also took over the role as her confidante until she could adjust to the changes in her life." She paused, twirling her skirt around softly, absent-mindedly, with her hands. "Every child is a wonder, but this one was something special. She won't remember me when she's older, of course, but I truly believe I was able to help her."

"I don't help 'em," said Lionel. "I just play with 'em." He opened his mouth to roar; it came out as a squeak.

The bench adjusted to accommodate Sugarblossom as she sat down.

"Why does it supply *you* with pillows?" Mr. Paloobi asked, trying unsuccessfully to hide his exasperation.

"Because a princess needs her comfort," she replied with a smile. "Besides, *this* princess needs her rest. There is always a little girl somewhere in the world, with a teacup set or a fairy costume, that wants to play make-believe." She smoothed out the sumptuous velvet pillows with delicate little hands. "I think I deserve a little luxury in my downtime."

He didn't reply. Only the soft rumble of the slumbering cat broke the silence.

After a while Sugarblossom looked at him, the sparkles in her eyes softening. "I'm sorry. That was inconsiderate of me. How can I complain, when . . . ?" She let the words hang in the air.

"There's nothing to be sorry about," answered Mr. Paloobi. "If I'm to have my innings in The Game only once, at least I cherish every second I spent with the boy who called me forth."

"But it was so long ago," she said sympathetically.

Mr. Paloobi's hand reached up to his shirt pocket and felt the little object it contained, and his mind raced back across the decades to the day he was born.

As the Boy painstakingly placed the pewter pieces on the ornate chessboard his father had brought back from his last trip abroad, he wished that *someone* would teach him how to play the game. But his parents always seemed to be absent, even when they were there, and it was obvious that he was going to have to teach himself—and he had no idea how to go about it. It wasn't chess itself that appealed to him, anyway. The satisfying thing was to sit across the board from a parent, a sibling, a friend, even a stranger, and not feel so terribly, achingly *lonely*.

When he'd finally finished setting it up on the rickety little card table he had dragged from the spare room, he placed a chair on either side of it and sat down.

And then it hit him: he had no idea if he'd put the pieces on the right squares, and he *still* had no one to play it with. He closed his eyes as tears of frustration began to form. *I'm a big boy now,* he told himself, as little balled-up hands angrily dashed across his eyes, scattering his tears. *Big boys aren't supposed to cry.*

But he couldn't help it. He just wished for someone, *anyone*, to acknowledge that he was there.

"It's just a game," said a friendly voice. "It can't be *that* hard to play."

The Boy stopped crying, startled. He gingerly opened one eye, then both. He couldn't see anyone, blurry eyes or not. He sighed and closed them again.

"Surely if we put our heads together we can figure this thing out," the voice continued.

The Boy was startled again. This time the voice had sounded as if it came from the other side of the table. Someone else *was* in the room! He opened his eyes just in time to see a figure coalescing across the table from him.

It wasn't his father, he was certain of that, but he looked kind of tall and burly—just like his dad. And yet, he had sounded so affectionate. *The man must look cuddly,* the Boy reasoned. He rubbed his eyes again to clear them, and sure enough, he was right: a nondescript but definitely cuddly teddy bear of a man sat across from him, a gentle smile on his face. He was dressed like Dad, but that was where the resemblance stopped. He had fuzzy ears, warm brown hair, and even warmer eyes, the least threatening adult the Boy had ever seen.

Speechless, but remembering his manners, the Boy extended his tiny hand across the table, trustingly, to greet his new guest. A huge, furry paw of a hand encompassed his before pulling back to pick up one of the chess pieces. The stranger studied it for a minute, clearly curious, then looked up at the Boy. "So, shall we learn how to play chess together?" he asked.

"But you're a grown-up," the Boy replied somewhat petulantly. "Grown-ups *know* how to play chess."

"Well then, of course I do too," replied the gentle giant. Without preamble, he started moving all the pieces into their proper positions on the board while the Boy watched him, marveling at how such a huge man found it possible to balance on such a small chair.

Suddenly, the chair collapsed beneath the man, sending him sprawling. The Boy broke into a fit of giggles. When he finally got control of himself, he looked up, somewhat sheepishly, to see that the man was looking sheepish himself.

"Obviously the chair didn't like me," stated the man.

"Nope," the Boy agreed, and they shared a smile.

Suddenly the Boy's aunt walked in, carrying a tray laden with food, which she deposited on the toy chest beside the table. "Your parents have gone out for dinner," she said. "I'll be in again at eight, to make sure that you've put yourself to bed." She walked toward the door and then paused in the doorway, turning to glance quickly at the chess set and then down at the Boy again. "There's an extra dessert on the tray," she added with what she thought was a kindly smile. Then she was gone.

The Boy immediately looked across to the table to see a bear of a man leaning over to look at the contents of the tray with evident curiosity.

"She didn't even say hello to you!" the Boy exclaimed, indignant.

The man shrugged unconcernedly. "What difference does it make? *You're* talking to me, and that's all that matters."

The Boy looked at him for a long time before responding. "Well, as long as you're my friend, I'll never ignore you," he said with conviction. "I know what it's like to be invisible to other people."

Again they shared an understanding smile; and feeling happier than he had in a long time, the Boy hopped off his chair and scooted across to the toy chest to see what extra sweet had been put on his tray. He uncovered the first plate to discover meatloaf and veggies. Screwing up his face in distaste at all the green confronting him, he uncovered the second plate to reveal chocolate pudding and a slice of hot apple pie.

He was about to dig in when a slight movement caught his eye. He looked over at his new friend, who was delicately sniffing the chocolate pudding with interest, and he realized that the gentle giant didn't have a meal of his own. The Boy was torn. He *wanted* to share his meal—he'd never had anyone he could share with before—but he was rarely given chocolate pudding as dessert, and it was his favorite.

And then it dawned on him. Bears, even ones that were half man, wouldn't like chocolate; they'd like sweet foods like honey— or apple pie. "If you are going to be my friend," he stated with youthful certainty, "then friends share *everything*—even meals." And he handed over the apple pie, feeling quite pleased with himself.

They ate in companionable silence for a few minutes as the Boy mulled over what they were going to do after dinner. He'd never had a friend before; he didn't know quite where to start.

"Do friends play chess together?" came the muffled question from across the table, as the bear-man attempted to talk and eat at the same time.

"Yes, they do. Friends play *lots* of games. And they share food—except for chocolate—and they tell magical stories to each other and pretend to be warriors." He used his knife to mimic a sword fight, fatally spearing the meatloaf. "They also talk about *everything*, and . . ." He paused, not knowing how to say it.

"And they are always there when you need them."

"Yes!" the Boy exclaimed. He understood!

The huge man smiled. "Well, now that that's settled, why don't we play a game of chess?"

"That sounds like a great idea, Mister . . ." The Boy halted, realizing he didn't know the man's name. He considered the man's bearlike features with interest. "You know, you're kind of roly-poly, and you kind of look like Winnie the Pooh. . . ." His voice trailed off, and he bit his bottom lip in concentration. Suddenly he clapped his hands together enthusiastically. "I know! I'll call you Mr. Paloobi!"

Mr. Paloobi looked *chuffed*—there was no other word for it. His chest puffed out proudly as he repeated the name to himself, and then he beamed at the Boy. "Thank you," he replied. "I always *wanted* a name."

Mr. Paloobi was prodded back to the here and now—well, the here and *somewhere*—by a huge paw landing heavily on his arm. He turned his head to find himself looking directly into Lionel's eyes.

"I don't appreciate being awakened between safaris," the cat stated with a silky purr.

"Why tell *me*?"

"Your sighs are too loud."

"My sighs?"

"Like this," said Lionel, giving him an overblown demonstration. "It's been seventy years. Get over it."

Mr. Paloobi looked back down the timestream. "You don't get over something like that," he said wistfully.

He spent half an hour explaining the rudiments of chess to the Boy. But when the Boy started getting frustrated at being unable to remember all the different types of moves and suggested they give up, Mr. Paloobi changed his approach and performed a pantomime with the chess pieces instead.

As he moved the pieces across the board with gentle, furry hands, Mr. Paloobi told a tale of twin sisters married to kings who were at war with each other. "Both queens, each in love with her husband, devise a plan to infiltrate the enemy castle in order to get close enough to kill the enemy king," he stated in a conspiratorial tone. "It is a journey fraught with danger for them both, but their identical appearance gives them great range of movement in the enemy camp." He demonstrated by moving a queen around in all directions on the board. "Along the way there are male pawns to fight," he continued, picking up one pawn and pouncing it diagonally across one square and onto an enemy pawn, eliciting a giggle from the Boy when the defeated pawn went flying. "Female pawns also try to sneak across enemy lines and supplant them as queen." He made a show of another pawn creeping forward one square, all the while whistling innocently. "And even if the queen or her supporters get past the enemy watchtowers undetected," he continued, showing those pieces performing horizontal and vertical sweeps of the board, "what kingdom doesn't have a nosy clergyman or two trying to edge their way into the thick of things?" And he demonstrated by diagonally sliding a bishop into a position of power on the board.

Mr. Paloobi paused, making sure he still had the Boy's rapt attention. "Now, even when the enemy draws closer, the king tries to stay one step ahead of them at all times. But he's so heavily protected that he can only move so far," he continued, a furry hand demonstrating that a king could move only one square in any direction at any time. "If all his defenses fail, he has to rely on his knights and their valiant steeds to protect him, for they are well versed in tactics." He picked up a knight and made him prance one square over and then gallop two more in another direction, until he was in a better position to protect the king. "But will the queen get to the king before he flees to safety—or will she die in the attempt?"

The Boy waited for an answer, and when none was forthcoming he lifted his eyes from the chessboard for the first time since the story had started. "Don't stop now," he pleaded. "How does the story end?"

Mr. Paloobi grinned at him. "Well, to find out, you're going to have to play the game, aren't you?"

"Bright kid," said Lionel.

"A special kid," agreed the October Hare. He'd been christened the March Hare by his creator, but since he couldn't hold back the calendar, he had become the April Hare and then the May Hare, and now, in his eighth month of existence, he was the October Hare.

"Welcome back," said Sugarblossom.

"Thank you," said the October Hare. "But I can't stay long." He glanced at his wrist. "I'm late."

"You don't even have a watch," said Lionel in a bored tone.

"It doesn't matter," said the October Hare. "I'm always late. It's part of my nature." He made as much of a face as a white rabbit *could* make. "One of the things I'm always late for is dinner, and it's always gone. I wish my little girl would read something, anything, besides *Alice in Wonderland*." He turned to Mr. Paloobi. "I wish, oh, I don't know, that she played chess like yours did."

"He was more than a chess player," replied Mr. Paloobi. "He had the most inquisitive mind. He was reading when he was three, you know. I remember once when he was five, he had just seen a Sherlock Holmes movie on television, one of the old ones with Basil Rathbone, and I mentioned that according to Watson, Sherlock Holmes had neither any knowledge of nor interest in the Copernican system. Just that, nothing more. But within three days, this five-year-old boy had read the complete works of Copernicus!" A smile of pride crossed his face. "*My* boy did that!"

"Good thing it was Sherlock Holmes," said Lionel sardonically.

"If you'd quoted Johnny Unitas or Joe DiMaggio, he'd probably be the only boy who wouldn't have known who you were talking about."

"Then he'd have learned!" said Mr. Paloobi heatedly.

"Come on," said the October Hare. "We all admit he was bright, but when all is said and done, he was just a little kid."

"And you're just a bunny in a topcoat with a wristwatch," said Mr. Paloobi, still angry.

"I don't *have* a watch," complained the October Hare, getting up from the bench. "I'm heading off to find a carrot before they're all gone. No one can talk to you when you're like this. Lionel's right: it's time for you to wake up and smell the coffee."

"I *am* awake, and I don't drink coffee."

"That was just an expression," said the October Hare. "How can you be so literal-minded, especially when your mind is just a product of *his* mind?"

"You'll never understand," said Mr. Paloobi moodily.

"Enlighten me," replied the October Hare. "Pretend I'm the kid and explain it to me."

"You're not as smart as he was," said Mr. Paloobi. He looked up and down the bench. "None of you are."

His companions knew enough not to argue with him when he was like this. In fact, there was only one person who *could* argue with him, and they hadn't spoken in seven decades. . . .

"Doesn't it bother you that your parents don't seem to notice that you are a part of their life?" Mr. Paloobi asked, so annoyed on the Boy's behalf that he looked more like a grizzly bear than Winnie the Pooh.

The Boy simply shrugged. "I'm pretty used to it now."

"It's not something you *should* get used to."

The Boy looked up from assembling his toy train. "They ignore you too."

"Yes, but I'm not their son or their friend," Mr. Paloobi replied, exasperated. He sighed deeply as he watched the Boy go back to working on the intricate circuitry on his train.

After a long spell, the Boy spoke up. "Yesterday, when I asked Dad if I could buy a train track with my pocket money, he told me I should save it. And I told him I *had* to have the track, because playing with the train wouldn't be the same without it." He started screwing the last panel onto the side of the train. "And then Dad told me that a person can't miss what he's never had." He put the almost-finished train on the ground gently, and then looked up at Mr. Paloobi, his eyes sad. "Well, I've never really had parents."

Mr. Paloobi couldn't think of a response, so he remained uncharacteristically silent.

Then the Boy smiled, a youthful sparkle returning to his eyes. "You should be *happy* they're never here, because if they were, they'd never let you visit on a school night—even if you are my only friend."

And, as always, whenever the Boy mentioned their friendship, Mr. Paloobi found that he could not argue with him. So they played a game of chess, and when the Boy's aunt, who was filling in for his absent parents yet again, delivered his dinner, they divided it between them, as they'd been doing for almost two years now, and ate in companionable silence.

When the Boy uncovered his dessert tray to discover a generous helping of chocolate mousse, he looked at it as if it had suddenly grown antlers and tried to walk off the plate. He toyed with it for a few minutes. "Girls are so annoying," he suddenly blurted out.

"Oh?" Mr. Paloobi turned to him in surprise. "And why is that?"

"Because I got the last bowl of chocolate mousse in the cafeteria last week and Colleen wanted me to share it with her."

"You don't share chocolate with anyone," noted Mr. Paloobi. "I'm assuming you said no."

He nodded emphatically. "But then she kissed me on the cheek, real quick like, and then she said I *had* to share it with her now." He frowned, remembering the moment. "I told her that I never wanted her to kiss me, so why did I have to share my mousse with her?" He paused, fidgeting uncomfortably. "And then she cried." A puzzled frown. "She cried a *lot*."

"Why?" asked Mr. Paloobi, just as confused as the Boy.

"She said that if I liked her, I would have shared it with her after she kissed me," the Boy said. "Well, I told her I liked her just fine—for a girl—but I don't share my chocolate with *anyone*."

"And what was her response?"

"She asked me if I would share some chocolate with her when we're older."

"And you said?"

"I said maybe, because I didn't want her to cry again." He continued to push the mousse around the bowl with his spoon. "Now she smiles at me whenever I see her at recess and lunch."

"What's wrong with that?" asked Mr. Paloobi. "It's good to know that you didn't permanently hurt her feelings."

"But every time she smiles at me now, my stomach goes all funny inside, and I can't get any words out." He looked up at his at his friend. "Why?"

For the first time in their association, Mr. Paloobi was stumped for an answer. "Maybe you're worried that she'll kiss you again?" he asked finally.

The Boy shrugged. "It wasn't so bad."

"Well then, remind me never to ask you to share your chocolate with me if you're still this upset a week later," he said, forcing a very insincere laugh and trying to cheer the Boy up.

"It's not about the chocolate," he replied with certainty.

"Then maybe you're nervous about having a new friend," said Mr. Paloobi, grasping at straws. "You've skipped a year in school and you're still brighter than all the kids in your class. I know how hard it is for you to make friends—to feel as if you fit in."

This time the Boy shook his head even more emphatically. "We're not even friends. She hangs around with other girls, and I sit near the other boys." He paused, screwing up his nose in distaste. "Girls play with dolls and pretend they are fairy princesses. I don't even think I *want* to be her friend. . . ." His voice trailed off. "But I *do* kind of like her, so why does she annoy me so much? And why does it feel like an elephant is sitting on top of me every time she smiles?"

Mr. Paloobi walked down the bench to where Sugarblossom and Hawkmistress sat, the former shifting uncomfortably in her corset, the latter petting her hawk, which perched on her left shoulder.

"You look troubled," said Hawkmistress.

"Tell me about girls," said Mr. Paloobi.

"We're sweet and beautiful and delicate and we smell wonderful," said Sugarblossom. "At least, we'd smell wonderful if"—she raised her voice—"*someone would read a book and learn what whalebone does and doesn't smell like!*"

"I think you're very nice," offered Mr. Paloobi.

"Thank you."

"But I don't get all fidgety and nervous when you smile at me," he continued. "I don't spend endless hours thinking about you."

"Ah!" said Hawkmistress. "Your boy is growing up."

"What does that have to do with anything?" asked Mr. Paloobi. "I'm grown up and I just told you that I don't feel like that."

"You're two years old," said Hawkmistress, "and no matter what you look like, you are *not* a man."

"Certainly I am."

"You were created by a four-year-old who probably thought the only difference between sexes was that men shave," she said.

"Nonsense!" said Mr. Paloobi. "I'm every inch a man. A little bearlike, perhaps, and my eye color keeps changing to suit his moods, but I'm a man, all right."

"You think so, do you?" said Hawkmistress.

"Absolutely."

"Do you have . . . ?" she began. "Lean over. I'll whisper it to you."

He leaned. She whispered. He straightened up with a shocked expression on his round face.

"You're kidding, right?" he said at last.

"I am not."

"Sugarblossom, can she possibly be telling the truth?"

"I don't know what she said," replied Sugarblossom.

He placed his lips next to her ear and whispered.

"Oh, absolutely," she assured him. Then she slapped his face.

"What was *that* for?" demanded Mr. Paloobi.

"That's for talking about such things to a fairy princess."

"Well, what am I to tell the Boy about girls?" asked Mr. Paloobi, thoroughly confused.

"Tell him all will become clear in the fullness of time."

"That isn't the kind of answer that a six-year-old wants to hear," he said.

"The world—the *real* world—is full of problems," said Hawkmistress. "This, at least, is one that will solve itself."

"And in the meantime," added the hawk, speaking up for the first time, "watching a boy adjust to it is always good for a laugh."

"There is nothing funny about my friend being distressed," said Mr. Paloobi heatedly.

"There's nothing unique about it either," Hawkmistress assured him.

"Are you sure you're not putting me on?" asked Mr. Paloobi.

"Why do you think Prince Charming faces death in a thousand forms just for my kiss?" said Sugarblossom.

Mr. Paloobi was still thinking about that when both women were summoned back onto the playing field by their young charges.

This time it wasn't Lionel's insistent prodding that brought Mr. Paloobi back to the present, but a peculiar feeling that, despite nearly seventy years of absence, he recognized immediately. For a moment, the briefest and most blissful of moments, the Boy had somehow connected to him again. Before he knew what was happening, he was watching the Old Man that the Boy had become gently leaf through the pages of a leatherbound Sherlock Holmes book, and then slowly wrap it up and put it in one of the several cardboard boxes that littered the floor of his personal library.

"You know you can't take everything with you, Grandpa," a kindly voice pointed out. "There's simply not enough room where you're going."

"I know that," he replied, as he started painstakingly wrapping up one of the chess pieces on the table beside his recliner chair. "But I'd like to take as many keepsakes with me as I can."

"Well, surely you don't need to take that chess set with you," said his granddaughter. "I've never seen you play even a single game with it."

"I think I played once, maybe when I was a boy," said the Old Man.

"But not anymore," she noted.

"No, not anymore," he agreed. "Not in a long, long time."

"Then why take it? Besides, one of the pieces is missing."

He paused, looking at the bishop he held in his hand for a long moment. "I've taken it with me everyplace I've ever lived."

"But *why*?" she persisted.

He shrugged. "I don't know," he admitted. "And until I *do* know, I suppose I'd better keep taking it along."

"Maybe I'll ask Miss Juniper why you keep it," said the girl. "She knows *everything*."

"Who is Miss Juniper?" asked the Old Man.

"My playmate."

"Funny name for a playmate. Have I met her?"

"Only I can see her." She looked at him thoughtfully. "Didn't you ever have a playmate like that?"

The Old Man shrugged. "I suppose I must have."

"What was his name?"

"Damned if I know," he said as he began wrapping again.

With that comment, Mr. Paloobi felt the newfound tie between them start to dissipate. The Old Man's thoughts of the distant past began to vanish, his mind moved on to other things, and Mr. Paloobi felt the solidity of the bench starting to form beneath him again, as the coldness of the mist surrounded him once more.

He missed the Boy who had become the Old Man, missed him desperately, and painful as it was, he let his mind drift back to their last day together.

The Boy's interests were expanding apace with his intellect. He had less time for games of make-believe, even for chess. There were entire days when Mr. Paloobi was never summoned to the here and now. He didn't know what he had done wrong, but the Boy seemed content, indeed happier than ever, so he uttered no complaints. Besides, he knew somehow that they would do no good.

The Boy sat before his tray. His parents were out for the evening (some things never changed), and he separated the meal from force of habit, placing the greens and the nonchocolate dessert on a plastic plate, then pushing it to the other side of the empty table before rearranging his own plate.

"Could you please pass a spoon?"

The boy looked up to see Mr. Paloobi on the other side of the chess set, sitting on the little rickety chair that had broken countless times under the gentle giant's weight over the years, yet was always undamaged when the boy woke up the next morning.

Smiling, Mr. Paloobi reached out a furry paw, squeezing the boy's hand gently when he accepted the spoon. Then, instead of eating in quiet companionship as they usually did, the Boy spoke excitedly about his excursion to the planetarium the next morning.

After dinner the Boy pulled out an astronomy book he'd been given for his birthday, and they lay together on the floor, holding the book over their heads as they pointed out all the stellar constellations they remembered.

Then, just before bedtime, they played their first game of chess in a month, the Boy successfully protecting his king from the evil queen with one of his bold knights, their movements mirroring the story Mr. Paloobi had told when they first met. When the boy hopped into bed that night, the knight was still clasped tightly in his hand.

Rather than listen to a bedtime story, he told Mr. Paloobi about his day at school. His teacher had started to give him some extra work, so he was no longer bored in class, and he could now boast that he had four friends, not counting Mr. Paloobi. He had just started discussing the possibility of a camping trip with his friends when he noticed the sad smile on the Mr. Paloobi's face.

"You know I can't come, don't you?" asked Mr. Paloobi gently.

"I know," said the Boy, quietly.

"Perhaps we had better talk about it."

There was no response.

"Are you all right?" asked Mr. Paloobi.

Still no response.

He waved a huge hand in front of the Boy's open eyes. They didn't blink.

He spent another few minutes trying to get the Boy to react, to acknowledge that he was there. He was still trying when he was pulled inexorably back to the bench.

When the Boy woke up in the morning, he was no longer holding the knight in his hand.

Mr. Paloobi sighed, uncomfortably shifting his weight so that he wouldn't wake Lionel, who had rolled over sometime during his ruminations of the past and now lay curled up against his side. The benchwarmer smiled wryly to himself. If anyone could see them, they'd probably do quite a double take: an impeccably dressed man who looked like a bear, and a four-hundred-pound lion who looked like an oversized tabby cat.

He found Lionel's nearness comforting, his remarks amusing. But even after seventy years, Lionel's friendship couldn't fill the void the Boy's absence had made in his life. His two brief excursions with new charges seemed like failed job interviews. He felt lonely and incomplete.

And suddenly he knew that someone else felt the same.

He just had time to rub Lionel's head apologetically before he was called forth from the bench once more, hearing the discontented rumble of his feline friend as he left the limbo in which he had lived for so long.

The Old Man was having a difficult time of it. Yesterday he had forgotten his granddaughter's name—just for a moment, mind you; just once. And when the nurse had walked in, young and pretty, immaculate in her white outfit, he'd momentarily thought it was his wife, remarked that he didn't remember the white dress, and asked when she had bought it.

But he'd known who the nurse was when she came by with his dinner. She'd asked if she could turn the television on for him, and he'd thanked her and asked if it was time for *Maverick* yet. She had explained gently that *Maverick* wasn't on this week, and had left the set tuned to some mindless comedy with a bunch of actors he couldn't recognize.

The Old Man knew that these were just momentary glitches, but he also knew that the very best way to keep an aging mind sharp was to give it puzzles and problems to solve. He looked around the room for something to occupy him. It would have to be quiet; his wife was three months pregnant with their first child and he didn't want to wake her.

He got up and walked to a dresser, pulling open the top drawer. There was the first letter he'd ever earned, for making the baseball team. He ran his hand over it proudly. If he worked hard enough, maybe next year he could be a starter.

He heard a feminine laugh from somewhere beyond his door. He shook his head. Colleen was getting to be such a pretty girl these days. He still felt awkward and tongue-tied from time to time, but at least now he knew why.

He rummaged further, and then he came to the chess set. It had been a while since he'd played—maybe a week, maybe even a little longer.

He sat down at the same table he took his meals at, opened the board, and began painstakingly placing ivory and ebony pieces on it.

It took him a long time, because he had trouble remembering the specific placement of the pieces, but he was determined to get it right. When it was finally set up, he sat back with a satisfied smile on his wrinkled, grizzled face.

Then, suddenly, something on the board caught his attention. Or, rather, the *lack* of something. He leaned forward, frowning, as he realized that there was a piece missing. He stared intently at the chessboard, knowing that it was significant for some reason, but not quite certain *why*.

A furry hand reached across the table, gently placing a knight on the empty square where it belonged.

The Old Man looked up to see a man with warm, friendly eyes sitting across the table from him. He might have trouble recalling faces and names now, but he could never forget those bearlike features.

"So are we going to play a game?" asked Mr. Paloobi.

The Old Man smiled happily. "Welcome back." He reached into his pocket, then stretched his hand across the table. "Have a piece of chocolate before my queen conquers your kingdom."

And they spent the night playing chess, nibbling on chocolate, and talking about things that were of great import to very young boys and very old men.

It is said that friendship never dies. Case in point: Mr. Paloobi—a lonely being who has finally entered the game again after riding the bench for seven long decades in . . . the Twilight Zone.

TRUTH OR CONSEQUENCES

❂

Carole Nelson
Douglas

Sometimes life's highway insists on taking an unsuspected curve. Meet Miss Geraldine Purdy, en route to Truth or Consequences, New Mexico, named after a game show. And don't forget the "Miss." Miss Purdy has always lived the game of life by the rules. Is it possible she'll die that way?

The irregular Chihuahuan Desert sprawled over the surface of the map. Red and blue road lines made a varicose-veined jumble on the paper landscape. The knotted, dusty fingers of the Jarila, San Andres, and auxiliary mountain ranges fanned north from White Sands Missile Range, which nestled in the desert's ocher outline like the soft, padded palm of a gigantic hand.

Geraldine Purdy bent over the map spread across the front seat of her 1956 Ford Victoria sedan and squinted sun-blinded eyes in the car's heavy interior shade.

Now, she encouraged herself. Here's where I am *now.* Her narrow, joint-swollen forefinger tapped a dot at the eastern edge of the map's pale palm imprint, so like a hand opening to greet, or entrap, her.

"Green Tree, New Mexico, indeed." She snorted aloud, gazing through her parked car's tinted window at the weathered wooden houses surrounding a cheap café-tavern with one hot-red gas pump in front of it.

She'd seen the last "green tree" early that morning, when she'd left Roswell, twenty miles behind her down U.S. Highway 70. Why, Roswell was an *oasis* compared to *this* dusty speck upon the face of the earth.

Miss Purdy calmed her irritability, and sighed. She'd planned this trip for a long time, and she was going through with it, come hell or . . .

She giggled wickedly as her finger traced a red line westward to her destination. Come hell or . . . Truth or Consequences. Silly name! She'd liked the original one. Hot Springs. So much more natural. So appropriate. How strange that it had been fifteen years since her niece's letters had begun arriving postmarked with that absurd new town name, Truth or Consequences, New Mexico.

She'd heard the story from her niece when it happened in 1950. Host Ralph Edwards—of *This Is Your Life* TV fame later—had a radio program called *Truth or Consequences*. Mr. Edwards promised to broadcast the program from the first town that renamed itself after the show for the next fifty years. Hot Springs jumped at the bait and Ralph Edwards came to what New Mexicans now called "T or C" with a lot of hoopla—beauty contest, parade, and stage show. Edwards was out as host of the show by 1954, but the silly thing continued. She'd noticed only recently that *Truth or Consequences* was on TV now, hosted by some fly-by-night appropriately named Bob Barker.

Miss Purdy carefully refolded her fragile old map into a long rectangle and fanned herself with it, glancing again at the endless sandy terrain scarred by calloused mounds of cracked red earth. Far away, the low mountains looked olive drab from the scraggly mesquite bushes barnacled to their rocky sides.

She sighed again, delicately lifting short gray bangs from her damp forehead, and replaced the map in her glove compartment.

With a choking lurch, the dusty black Ford leaped forward from the road's gritty shoulder. It crawled like some shiny desert beetle onto the smooth black asphalt that snaked through the ocher sands ahead.

Green Tree disappeared behind her. The Ford cruised along at fifty miles an hour, five below the speed limit. Dry desert air flowed in through the rolled-down windows, stirring the short sleeves of Miss Purdy's beige printed voile dress and gently pushing up the brim of her cream-colored straw hat.

Stillness surrounded her. The entire desert seemed petrified, although she knew it was bustling with hidden buggy and snaky life.

I am the only person alive here, thought Miss Purdy, and the only sound in this wide desert is the *whoosh* of the wind against my little black car that's spinning along to Truth or Consequences, New Mexico.

She leaned back in the sticky vinyl seat and lifted her chin to the pale, hot horizon of bleached sky and dusty earth beyond her insect-crusted windshield. She smiled triumphantly and tingled down to her toes. The speedometer swung up to fifty-five.

My name is Geraldine Purdy and I am the only thing alive, and back in Roswell the library air-conditioning has broken down again and all the books, the stacks and stacks of books, are moldering and rotting and turning to dust and I don't care!

After all, why should she care? The library was no longer her concern. A round gold watch pinned to her left shoulder through the thin dress fabric and sturdy slip and brassiere straps proved that.

MISS G. PURDY was etched on the back in fine, old-fashioned script; *44 YEARS OF SELFLESS SERVICE*.

Forty-four years of rubber-stamping books—Melville, Faulkner,

Tom Jones (the naughty one), *Tom Sawyer* (the often censored one). Always changing the number of the day, or the month, or the year. Never thinking beyond three weeks at a time.

Then, unexpectedly, someone had stamped Miss Purdy herself—due to be returned and shelved.

It wasn't anyone's fault, really. Not the fault of the library board, certainly, those suit-coated solons who'd never failed to refer to her as "Our Miss Purdy." They hadn't done it.

Nor had Miss Purdy herself, who hadn't even noticed that her hair had grown gray, what with always looking at the books, their call numbers, and the library cards as they passed from her hand to the waiting hands on the other side of the desk, her desk.

No, it was time that had canceled Miss Purdy's circulation.

She smiled. How clever to think of herself as a book. She envisioned herself listed in neat Roman type in some huge bibliography: "Miss Geraldine Purdy, pub. 1900; hardcover and fine print; copyright expired, 1966; unavailable in paperback."

Not that she was bitter. Oh, no. She understood. She welcomed a change of scene. The library had become too much for her, infested with giggling gaggles of gum-chewing teenagers. She knew they called her "Old Pruney."

Anyway, her sister Hatty's girl, Evelyn, had long urged her to move to Hot Spri . . . to Truth or Consequences. So she had retired in ceremony, with a sheet cake and Hawaiian Punch reception. She bought the lovely gray suitcase set that now rested in the trunk and on the backseat, and left her small apartment on East Bland Street to begin a new life.

"There's a small garden, Aunt Gerry," Evelyn had written in her galloping scrawl, "that I really don't have time to tend. You'll find plenty to do, with the kids growing like weeds and me with a million errands to do. Naturally, we wouldn't expect you to *work* for us, or anything, but we know you wouldn't want to be bored to death by having nothing to do, either."

Poor Evelyn. Miss Purdy wondered how she really felt about her aunt coming to live with her family, though she had insisted. It was hard to tell.

The sun was almost directly over the car now, and Miss Purdy felt hungry. Only two miles to Tularosa, a sign said. She should find someplace decent to eat there. The growing outline of the town buildings shimmered in the noonday sun. Even the asphalt highway seemed about to melt, glittering as if wet where the road dipped.

Miss Purdy obediently slowed her Ford to thirty miles per hour at Tularosa's city limits, but her heart quickened unreasonably when she spotted a lonely silhouette standing on the road's sandy shoulder.

A hitchhiker.

How disagreeable! His very presence was so demanding. The landscape seemed to slide by in slow motion now, the hitchhiker's figure growing larger and clearer.

He wore blue jeans and a wrinkled white T-shirt. A duffel bag slumped at his tennis-shoed feet. He stood there in traditional hitchhiker's pose—arm and thumb crookedly extended—curly blond hair matted to his tanned forehead. His eyes squinted into the sun with an expression of hopeful cynicism.

His pose reminded Miss Purdy of that awful Marlon Brando in a movie she'd never seen, *The Wild One*, leering at passing women from that motorcycle that was cocked on its stand like his leather billed cap tilted above his sneering, smart-alecky face. Nasty boy. That Brando person had been even less appetizing in a film she *had* seen, *A Streetcar Named Blaze*, or something. Nasty film too.

As her car drew abreast, the hitchhiker's young, knowing face loomed in the passenger window, his squint drawn out to a leer as she drove past.

His face hung there for an agonizing instant.

Miss Purdy stared straight ahead, spasmodically pressing her foot down on the gas pedal, and finally felt him sucked behind her for good.

The heat still wove around her, a suffocating blanket. She released the breath she discovered she'd been holding. In the rearview mirror, she watched the figure diminish behind the dust of her acceleration. Finally, it bent to hoist the duffel bag and started walking along the shoulder of the road.

Oh! Her bangs were unpleasantly pasted to her forehead now, even as her hands loosened on the steering wheel. Tularosa streets flickered by. She was almost out of town before she spied a small café with an Air Conditioned sign in the window. The black Ford hesitated before pulling to the curb. Miss Purdy gathered her purse, gloves, and road map, then got out and locked the car.

Just before she entered the glass-doored café, Monte's Place, she glanced down the road behind her.

The hitchhiker was not in sight.

"It's hot. I'll just have an order of cinnamon toast and iced tea with lemon," Miss Purdy said briskly, closing the menu and placing it squarely on the shiny black Formica tabletop.

"Nothing else, ma'am?"

The skinny waitress was a bottle blonde, her eyes hollowed out by smudges of black mascara.

There was one thing Miss Purdy knew she wasn't going to get from such a disrespectful snip. Respect. Young people today were so judgmental and superior, like that hitchhiker, sneering at a lone woman for sensibly refusing to pick him up. Certainly, do a good deed, pick him up, and she could end up dumped in the middle of the White Sands, her car his, she left behind, robbed and ... raped, maybe. And killed too. No, thank you. Miss Geraldine Purdy of the Roswell Public Library System was not known for taking foolish chances.

The waitress stood, awaiting her decision, one hip cocked, and her bored face wearing the hitchhiker's same superior smirk.

"Well, perhaps a small dish of vanilla ice cream ... but we'll see."

As the girl ambled away, Miss Purdy brushed the tabletop to ensure that none of the waitress's bleached yellow hairs had fallen on it. Young people! Didn't even have the get-up-and-go to stand up straight anymore, thought Miss Purdy. Talk like slow syrup to your face, but just imagine what they say behind your back.

It was noon. High noon. No other customer was in the restaurant. Odd. Another waitress, idle, lounged against the deserted counter, filing her nails. Most unsanitary! From the kitchen came her waitress's lazy drawl, droning small talk.

Somehow, Miss Purdy felt conspicuous, watched, and commented upon. The girl behind the counter gazed out the window with the same unfocused squint as the hitchhiker's.

Miss Purdy unfurled her fold-frayed map and made a point of studying it intently. She was halfway there. Before her lay the White Sands Missile Base, and on the other side, Truth or Consequences, directly opposite Tularosa.

The mountain range had to be skirted, either by going north, or south. Her forefinger traced the thick red highway line northward to Oscura, Carrizozo, Carthage, and Elephant Butte. What strange, exotic-sounding names! And yet so logical. From Carthage, the name of Hannibal's ancient home city, to, of all places, Elephant Butte! Hadn't Hannibal's forces crossed the Alps with elephants to attack the Italians? She half expected to find Rome itself on the map.

Her finger darted back to the dot marking Tularosa and

meandered south through Alamogordo, then along the thin blue vein of country road that cut across the southeast corner of the missile base that was the White Sands National Monument before curving up through Radium Springs and Las Palomas to Truth or Consequences.

By the time the last piece of cinnamon toast had disappeared from her plate, Miss Purdy had decided on the southern route. It was, after all, shorter and less cluttered with cattle crossings than cactus-ringed junctions like Carthage would no doubt be. Still, how exciting to drive through Carthage—it would give her a sense of history, and the names to the north did intrigue her. . . .

Miss Purdy told herself firmly—as she so often did—that she had no right to be intrigued at her age. She paid her bill, left a fifty-cent tip and the café, receiving no notice but a lifeless flicker of sooty eyelashes from her heavy-lidded waitress.

Miss Purdy spread her voile skirt carefully as she eased into her hot car seat and checked her gold watch. It was 12:14 P.M. My, but time moved slowly in the desert. She'd have to be careful not to drive too fast. Evelyn didn't expect her until early evening. The plastic steering wheel was burning hot, so she pulled on her white cotton gloves and pulled into the street, glancing just once in the rearview mirror.

The hitchhiker was nowhere in sight.

Soon Tularosa, silly name, was no more than a narrow band of buildings in her rearview mirror. The voile dress stuck to the vinyl seat back as the heat circled around and around her. She could smell the rubber of the car's tires on the sun-softened asphalt.

Tall, dull-green yuccas edged the road here and there like trees. The sand between patches of sharp mesquite was getting whiter. Half past noon, the sky glowed white like hot lead, merging with the paling sand. The dun-colored wasteland still hung at her back like a cloud, but she was driving farther and farther into the heart of the gypsum dunes of the White Sands.

I'm off with the wraggle taggle gypsies, O! The old folk song about gypsies sang through her mind. She was a gypsy, free of workaday pulls and rolling along free.

Behind her, the tawny Alamogordo basin sand disappeared as the Ford climbed the road's gentle rises. In her rearview mirror, the basin receded until it curved and assumed the shape of a broad thumb, imprinted there in prehistory by some Titan hurled from the heavens.

My, this barren landscape made her fanciful. Miss Purdy adjusted her gloved hands on the steering wheel and thought about the map. Could the desert's strange hand shape be more than an accident? Who knew what mighty race of men could have once lived here and carved the earth to match their grandeur?

She saw herself as if from a helicopter or another planet ... Mercury, perhaps. That had a nice sound to it. She saw herself as a small, quick bug, scurrying in her shiny black shell across the hand of some tremendous being. Rushing from his thumb down his wide, grimy highway of a lifeline and, for all the 150 horse-power of her automobile, merely tickling that giant palm.

That thought tickled Miss Purdy.

I see, she chortled exultantly to herself, *I see!* I'm the only one who knows how things really are. That books are just so many tree trunks, and that air-conditioning is just so many rusty cogs. Miss Purdy felt a paean of joy rising inside her. I shall write a poem! she told herself. Heaven knows, she'd seen enough poetry in the past forty-four years to know what was being done nowadays.

Someone had always been coming to her desk, asking about some poet or other for a school paper. Wallace Stevens, T. S. Eliot, Rupert Brooke ... No, they didn't often ask for Rupert Brooke anymore. And he was such a nice poet, too. People think librarians don't remember, but they do. Miss Purdy remembered.

Her eyes slid down to the speedometer. Sixty miles an hour! What *had* she been thinking? She bit her lip and relaxed her foot on the gas pedal. Her ankle had been held quite . . . taut.

The Ford slowed and Miss Purdy gazed around her with wonder.

Everything was white. Sand dunes, like huge mounds of powered sugar, spilled onto the black asphalt, dusting it pale gray. The dunes towered above her little car, reflecting sun off one another and nearly blinding her. Everything shimmered and sparkled before her eyes. If it weren't for the dark, dead branches thrusting out here and there through the dazzling snowy sand, Miss Purdy would have thought she'd gone suddenly mad.

How utterly lovely, thought Miss Purdy. Like alabaster. Like monuments of some great race of beings wind-scoured to pure powder . . . all of them, temples . . . tombs. Strange that she had never traveled beyond Roswell before. Her little car held effortlessly to the steel-gray track of road. Miss Purdy stopped concentrating on driving and thought of milk, snow . . . oh, ermine . . . frosted sea spray.

Then, without warning, he was there.

Stark against the blanched dunes, standing as before—head cocked, eyes screwed almost shut, and thumb extended, carelessly, crudely—his white T-shirt blending into the dunes.

How? How had he gotten here *before* her? As if he was *waiting* for her.

Unless someone had picked him up . . . but who would leave him off here, in the middle of literally nowhere?

Miss Purdy's throat felt as if it were coated with cotton batting. Cotton is white, she thought absently. Her gloves were moist through and hugged her hands. And somewhere . . . someone was pressing a heavy, hot iron down on her. . . .

She was a woman alone. Always had been. The hitchhiker had noted that. He couldn't have walked this far this fast. Of course! He'd seen her stop at the café for lunch, then caught a ride and, and . . . had himself let out here, in the middle of nowhere! Waiting. Waiting for *her*. Wasn't there a famous story about someone who couldn't avoid someone else no matter where he went? "Appointment in Sahara"? Oh, she couldn't think!

Miss Purdy leaned back, away from the figure framed by her windshield, and steadily pushed, pushed, pushed the accelerator *down*.

The warm wind surged through the open window, blowing her bangs back against the brim of her straw hat, lifting her hat off her head and into the backseat. Her hat! A lady always wore a hat and gloves.

She wanted to clutch for her hat. She couldn't. Miss Purdy's hands were frozen to the hot steering wheel, which careened and swung as if granted a life of its own.

The hitchhiker whirled past her vision as the car wound around and around the glittering crystal dunes, caught in a maelstrom of white.

All at once, the car seemed to be turning over and over, like Dorothy's house in *The Wizard of Oz*. Miss Purdy's terrified mind seemed to be turning over and over, lofting up into the white, white clouds, caught in a tornado. Wherever she was heading, it wasn't Truth or Consequences. Maybe it was Oz. Maybe she and her little car were one of the passing airborne phenomena Dorothy had glimpsed in the tornado during the black-and-white part of the movie.

Maybe they were all heading for heaven, which would be a

much better place than silly old "T or C," as the residents called it.

And that would be fine with her.

Still, Miss Purdy felt she might be sinking again into a giant bowl of white sugar frosting below, spinning around to the slowing hum of an electric blender as the wind's sound crescendoed into a shrill, evil scream, like that modern music the kids loved. The wind and an alien shrillness whirred like a thousand furies with high-pitched, mechanical madness.

But the car was not moving. Everything was level, and Miss Purdy felt as if she had stopped safely at last. Even her heartbeat was slowing down, despite the racket. She felt utterly alone.

So why had the shriek increased to a screech as a dark shape slid out of the whiteness and attached itself to her car like a huge black fly?

Miss Purdy frowned to see a black arm gesturing, a great pair of buglike dark glasses staring sightlessly at her. Oddly, she didn't feel menace. She blinked.

Oh . . . no wonder! It was a . . . a . . . motorcycle policeman, the lone woman motorist's guardian angel, albeit in Brando black leather.

Thank God! She wasn't alone and at the mercy of that horrible hitchhiker anymore.

She didn't remember stopping the car or hearing a siren behind her. Yet she must have braked, for she saw in the rearview mirror that her car had left black tire tracks like a dotted line on the whitened asphalt along the road's sandy white side.

She was finally, really, and truly safe. And she was *so* embarrassed.

The officer pulled to a stop behind her, his siren whining into silence. She saw his huge black motorcycle. Miss Purdy clenched and unclenched her gloved hands. They suddenly felt freezing cold, and her cheeks felt searingly hot.

The officer strode to her open car window.

"It's a good thing you stopped, ma'am."

Miss Purdy watched him wrench off one black leather glove and pull a thick notepad out from somewhere. The sun gleamed on his white helmet, glancing off the big, dark sunglasses and his black leather jacket.

He might take off his sunglasses, sniffed Miss Purdy to herself. Doesn't he know that the reflection hurts my eyes?

A pen appeared and the policeman strolled around to the front of her car, marking something down in his notebook, probably the license number. He looked so young and strong and tall. Miss Purdy eyed the huge black gun holster at his side as he walked back to her, leather jacket and holster squeaking in the dry air.

She hadn't thought to find her driver's license in her purse. She'd never before—

"Your name is?" he asked.

"Purdy. It rhymes with 'birdie.' Geraldine Purdy. *Miss* Geraldine Purdy." She was so glad she could answer promptly and crisply. "Oh! You're not going to . . . to write this . . . me . . . down? Really, it's not necessary, I—"

"Standard procedure, ma'am."

"It won't go into my—my record, will it? And must you write it in ink? Couldn't you—?"

"Afraid not, ma'am. May I see your driver's license?"

"But, I assure you, officer, I've never had a record of any kind . . . not one accident in fifty years of driving. I was always so *careful*."

She fumbled through her patent-leather purse. What would Evelyn think when she found out? A lady her age, *ticketed. Arrested even, maybe!* Evelyn might think she was, well . . . unreliable. Nobody had ever thought Geraldine Purdy was unreliable. Then Evelyn wouldn't want . . . Oh, the newspapers!

Her name might even be listed in the newspapers! How awful. To be avoided at all costs. Oh, dear.

Miss Purdy's hand pulled her license out of its clear plastic berth in her money clutch with a snap. She passed it triumphantly through the window. The officer looked down at her hand for a long moment, then took the license and began copying parts of it down.

"You always drive with gloves on during the summer, ma'am?" he inquired without looking up, as if that would matter with those dark glasses on. So disrespectful, young people today. She had expected more from an officer of the law, but he looked young, too. Everybody did, nowadays.

She stared at her white-gloved hands and shook her head. "No, I just happened to wear them driving today because the steering wheel was so hot, you see."

"Wheel could slip, you know, with gloves on. You could lose control of your car and have an accident. Wearing cotton gloves while driving isn't a good idea."

Miss Purdy nodded miserably.

"Any excuse for speeding, ma'am?" He took in the '56 Ford's dusty black shell. "This car isn't a youngster. I'm sure a lady like you must have had a reason."

"Why, thank you, officer. It was foolish, I suppose, but that hitchhiker unnerved me, turning up like that from nowhere."

"Hitchhiker?"

"Why, yes. The disreputable-looking one back down the road, black as the Devil against all that white sand, the one who *shouldn't* have been there. Surely you passed him if you caught up with me?"

The policeman turned his sunglass-shaded eyes to scan the winding asphalt trail through the White Sands gypsum dunes behind him.

"No, ma'am. I didn't."

Miss Purdy heaved in an indignant breath. How dare he stand there and claim he hadn't seen the hitchhiker? Marking her down in his little notepad and smirking over her gloves and "ma'aming" her up and down, just like that snip of a waitress back in Tularosa.

Well, she wouldn't stand for it. The moment she got to Truth or Consequences she'd report him to his superiors, that's what she'd do. Everybody had superiors.

She leaned out the window. "Young man," she demanded, "what's your name?"

The officer, who was walking down the road to peer beyond the bend, muttered something the wind picked up and whirled away across the dunes. Something about Sahara, or was it Samarra?

"What?" demanded Miss Purdy.

But the officer had disappeared beyond a white mountain of sand. She pursed her lips and sat back against the Victoria's hot vinyl upholstery.

Moments later, the policeman was back, apologetic.

"Sorry, ma'am. There's a hitcher, all right. Down the road a bit, walking this way. Don't you worry. Someone will pick him up eventually."

"He's *coming*? *This way?* Oh, but he mustn't! He mustn't catch up with me!"

"Ma'am?"

"Don't you see? I've got to keep ahead of him. I've a feeling that . . . that . . . it's like a black cat, you know? So, if you've got all your information, please let me go on. I'm all ready to move on now, *see*?" pleaded Miss Purdy, pulling off her gloves and showing her thin, blue-veined hands in readiness.

The policeman pocketed his little book in silence.

In the rearview mirror Miss Purdy saw a small black speck growing with each second into the forebodingly familiar figure of the hitchhiker.

She looked pleadingly at the motorcycle policeman. He seemed to have become taller and thinner in his head-to-toe black.

"Please, officer. Please! I must go. Is there a fine? I'll pay it now." She milled desperately through her purse.

"Ma'am, I'm sorry, but you'll have to come to headquarters with me."

"But I'm going to my niece's to retire. My niece, Evelyn Taggert's house in Truth or—"

The policeman's helmeted head shook firmly. "No, ma'am. This is according to regulations."

"Isn't there any other way?"

The hitchhiker was growing in her rearview mirror. She couldn't take her eyes off him. He became bigger and clearer and terrifyingly close.

"No, ma'am. There isn't any other way."

The moment she bowed to authority and said, "Yes, I see that. Yes, of course," the hitchhiker . . . vanished.

When the New Mexico newspapers reported the accident in their morning editions, the only witness was identified as a young hitchhiker, Eugene Menides of Carthage. He stated that the 1956 black Ford Victoria sedan had abruptly accelerated as it passed him on U.S. Highway 70 in the middle of the White Sands.

The car had braked violently on a sharp curve, as if the driver had encountered an obstacle, Menides said, and spun out and rolled over several times. He had seen no cause for the car to either speed up or brake. He had rushed to assist the driver, but it was too late. Menides had walked back toward Tularosa until he met a trucker, who had driven him to the nearest gas station to phone the state police.

The car's sole occupant, Geraldine Purdy, sixty-six, of Roswell, was dead on arrival at Mercy Hospital, Truth or Consequences, New Mexico.

Those of a mind to meditate on mortality might consult an ancient Persian tale about fate called "The Appointment in Samarra," as told by Somerset Maugham. The inescapable Angel of Death has a long history of taking many forms, and his henchman is always Fear—and nowhere is that more true than in the Twilight Zone.

PUOWAINA

Alan Brennert

Her name is Nani—not "Nanny," but "Nani." An exotic name, perhaps, though not where she comes from. And her home? A place some call paradise, while others know it simply as another far-flung outpost . . . of the Twilight Zone.

O h, so you want to talk story? Chicken-skin-kine story, makes you shiver? All right, here's one I've never told before, in all my years—maybe I've been afraid to, afraid no one would believe. No, it's not about the Marchers of the Night (though I did see them once, at Ka'ena Point, and ran like the wind before they could abduct me into their spirit ranks). It happened a long time ago—back in your old auntie's small-kid time, when I was just a skinny little Hawaiian girl, ten years old. Yes, I was skinny then! My sisters used to joke that "even *poi* won't stick to Nani's ribs," and it was true. America had entered the First World War the year before, and the sleepy little Honolulu of my childhood suddenly woke up one day to find it had become a bustling seaport. Anchored in the harbor were the dreadnoughts of many navies—American, British, Japanese, Australian—and the once-uncrowded streets were now filled with servicemen on the prowl for bathtub gin and bedroom eyes. (Never you mind what that means!) My mama volunteered as part of the ladies' food-conservation committee, and as a good Victory Girl I gave up my weekly nickel to see the movies and pledged it to the war effort; but my parents had only daughters, no sons, so this was the closest the Great War came to knocking on our door.

We lived up on the furrowed slopes of Punchbowl Hill, in a big plantation-style house necklaced by a white picket fence, overlooking the green taro fields and glistening silver rice paddies of the Pauoa Valley. Mama was *kanaka maoli*, pure-blood Hawaiian; Papa was a *haole* from St. Louis, Missouri, who'd come to Hawai'i as a young man and found success as an engineer for the Hawaiian Electric Company. When I think of my father, I think of fire: he had an Irishman's red hair and florid complexion. When I think of Mama, I think of cooled lava: her hair, black as the volcanic ash of the hill we lived on, was usually piled like stones atop her head, but sometimes tumbled in a rockslide down her back. My two sisters favored my father, with light complexions and russet manes; I was my mother's daughter, tawny skin and black hair, only worn shorter.

Your auntie was a bit of a tomboy, you see, and long hair got in the way when I'd scale the heights of Punchbowl's craggy ridges. All the neighborhood *keiki* climbed it, cutting our own trails that wound their way up to the five-hundred-foot summit. Sure, there was a road for cars to go up, but where was the fun in that? Leave that for the tourists and the soldiers on leave, come to take in the view. Back then, the view was just about all there was up there: the inside of the crater was a brown plain, sparsely decorated with lantana scrub, *koa* trees, the prickly *panini* cactus that flourished like a weed, and balloon plants, whose blossoms were round, hairy, and seemed to strike the neighborhood boys as hysterically amusing. But usually I'd go up alone—though I was never completely alone at the top. As I'd hike across the crater, I'd pass poor Hawaiian families squatting in sad little shacks and lean-tos, wives doing laundry in buckets as their children played with yappy little *poi* dogs. They might be stringing shell-and-seed *leis* for sale to tourists at the wharves, but otherwise had no jobs, nowhere else to live; when I could, I brought them fresh fruit from our garden.

On the southern rim of the crater there was a lookout, a tiny spur of land jutting like a raised eyebrow from Punchbowl's massive crown. I'd sit on the edge of the lookout and gaze down at the city spread out below me, dollhouses scattered amid orchards of toy trees. It was hard for me to imagine that thousands of years ago, rivers of fire had spilled down these slopes to the sea. I'd try to picture the molten lava boiling away the ocean, but the scene was just too peaceful from up here—from Punchbowl's equally placid volcanic sister, Diamond Head, on the left, to the slumbering mountains of the Wai'anae Range on the right, and across the ocean to mysterious Moloka'i wrapped in clouds on the horizon.

One day as I was sitting on the brow of the crater, I had a feeling—not a start or a fright, just a simple awareness—that there was someone standing behind me. I'd had this feeling a lot lately: I'd be alone in our backyard when I'd *know* that my sister Moani was standing in the doorway, and when I'd look up, there she was, asking me if I wanted to come in and play jacks. Or I'd sense that my teacher was going to call on me to answer a question a split second before she did. It happened often enough that I was beginning to accept it as routine. I turned to see a man— Hawaiian, maybe twenty years old—standing behind me, wearing the drab, olive-colored uniform of the United States Army. He had a round, gentle face and smiling brown eyes. "*Aloha*," he called out to me.

I returned the greeting.

"Some kine view, eh?" he said as he approached. "Mind if I share?"

"Sure, no boddah."

He sat down a few feet away and extended a hand, something most adults didn't bother to do with a little *keiki*. "John Kua. Friends call me Johnny."

I shook his hand, feeling very grown-up. "I'm Nani. MacGillvray."

"You know why I like this side of the crater best, Nani?"

"Why?"

" 'Cause I can see the house I grew up in from here." He pointed into the middle distance, toward the crowded tenement neighborhoods of the Pālama district. "Right down there, on Cunha Lane. Little white-frame house sitting under a monkeypod tree."

I squinted into the distance. "I can't make it out."

"Eh, neither can I." He laughed. "But I know it's there." Despite his good humor, there was something sad in the way he said it.

I asked, "You just get home from the war?"

He shook his head. "No, I'm stationed here on O'ahu. Schofield Barracks."

"How long you been in the Army?"

"Oh, I joined up even before we declared war. Saw the writing on the wall, figured we going get into it eventually. You come a lot to Puowaina?"

I was confused by this. "You mean Punchbowl?"

"Punchbowl's the name the *haoles* gave it when they came," he told me. "The old Hawaiian name is Puowaina—means 'hill of sacrifice.' "

"Why did they call it that?"

He hesitated for a moment, then explained, "Long time ago, there was an altar up here—like in a church, yeah? Except on this altar, people were put to death for violating the *kapus*—the rules—laid down by the chiefs. Or they might be offered up as a sacrifice to the gods in exchange for something, like to end a drought."

My eyes popped at that. "Honest-kine?"

"Honest! Not for long time, though." He winked. "We know better now."

"How do *you* know that's what happened?" I said dubiously.

"My *tūtū*—my gramma—used to tell me stories about the before time, back when the slopes of Puowaina were covered with *pili* grass." He took proper note of my skepticism. "You want to see where it happened?"

Well, what *keiki* wouldn't? He got up and led me over to a large, impressive pile of perpendicular stones that looked, if not like an altar, then definitely like something that used to *be* something. "The chiefs would bring the victims up from the town," he said with an expansive wave of his hand. "Sometimes they'd drown them in the ocean before they brought 'em up here . . . and that's when they were feeling *kind*. Other times they'd bring 'em straight up and put them in that fire oven, over there"—he pointed to another, smaller pile of rocks not too far away—"built especially for burning men alive."

I gasped. To think that a place like Punchbowl, which I thought I knew as well as the back of my hand, could have such a hidden, and bloody, history! Needless to say, I was thrilled.

Johnny went on to tell me a few other legends about Puowaina—how the side of the crater had once opened up and poured fiery lava on a band of warriors who had cruelly destroyed a helpless village on Kaua'i—but, as fascinating as I found it all, eventually I looked at the fading sunlight and said, "I better go, I'll be late for supper. Nice meeting you, Johnny."

"Yeah, same here. Maybe I see you again sometime. *Aloha*, Nani."

. . .

Well, after that, I saw Punchbowl in a whole new way. Kine scary way, to tell you the truth. I'd think about climbing it, then look up at the brooding summit, imagine men burning in fire ovens, and think, *Eh, maybe I stay home*—and I'd go play in my own back-yard. That was where I was, late one afternoon, when I looked up from my game of hopscotch and noticed something funny-kine in the sky above a neighbor's house. The sun was already behind Punchbowl, throwing its dying light onto a big cloud, making it glow like embers. But it was the shape of the cloud that was funny: a long "body" thinning at one end into a curved tail, and at the other end fattening into a diamond-shaped head. It looked exactly like a *mo'o*, a lizard, breathing fire into the sky above the home of Mrs. Fereira, a widow who lived across the street.

Then my mother called me in for supper, and at the table I happened to mention what I'd seen. Mama seemed unusually in-terested in what I'd said.

"The cloud looked like a *mo'o*?" she asked me. "Are you sure?"

"What's a *mo'o*?" my little sister, Moani, asked.

"*You* are," my big sister, Cynthia, taunted.

"Am not! I don't think."

My mother hushed them both. I told her, "It was lit up like it was on fire!"

"And it was directly above Mrs. Fereira's house?" Mama said.

"What's so all-damned fascinating about that?" my father asked, finally looking up from his bowl of clam chowder.

Mama instantly seemed to regret her interest in the subject. She explained, reluctantly, "In the old days, the appearance of a *mo'o* was thought to be an ill omen, for women especially. It au-gured the worst kind of misfortune."

Father let out a derisive snort, as we all knew he would.

"Superstitious claptrap," he declared. "There are thousands of lizards on this island, and what do they do? Augur? Portend? No.

They stick to ceilings, leave their droppings everywhere, and womankind is none the worse off for their presence, unless it's to clean up after them." He shook his head disgustedly and returned his attention to his soup.

In fairness it must be said: Papa would have been equally likely to pronounce as "claptrap" a sighting in the clouds of the Virgin Mother. He had no patience for any kine religion, whether it was Christianity or the old pagan Hawaiian beliefs. My mother gave me a look that told me, Subject closed.

Father believed in science, especially as it was represented by his beloved 1915 Ford Model T Roadster—the first model to feature electric headlights. Each morning he would patiently hand crank its engine, then proudly—and, it must be admitted, a bit speedily— drive it down the steep hills of the Pauoa Valley to the offices of the Hawaiian Electric Company on King Street. And nearly every day he would inquire of his daughters, "Who wants a ride to school?"— but because so few of our classmates' families owned automobiles, we feared being seen driven to school, lest our friends accuse us of being stuck up.

Sometimes, though, Papa would smile devilishly at me and whisper, "C'mon, Nani—I'll let you drive," and my hesitation would disappear like the new moon. I would sit in his lap as he disengaged the parking brake and opened the throttle, and we would hurtle down Pauoa Road as if on a roller coaster. Then, when we reached level ground, Papa would turn off onto a quiet side street with no traffic, carefully place my hands on the steering wheel, and allow me to "drive" the Tin Lizzie for an entire block. (His hands rested lightly but reassuringly on the top of the wheel, in case he needed to take control.) It was always a thrill for me, and well worth the occasional stink-eye I might get from a jealous classmate.

"Mum's the word, eh?" Papa would say as he dropped me off at school, and as I nodded readily he would race off, with a squeal of his transmission, to work.

Two weeks after I saw that fiery cloud above her house, Mrs. Fereira died unexpectedly of influenza. It was very sad; she was a nice lady, still young, and her Portuguese sweet bread was divine. But I didn't really think of it as having anything to do with what I'd seen in the sky. I'd almost forgotten about what Mama had said about bad luck and *mo'o* lizards.

I don't think Mama forgot, though. After she learned the news about Mrs. Fereira, Mama gave me the strangest look all day.

It wasn't long after that I had the most awful nightmare. It started out nice enough: I was soaring like a gull over the sea, though the shadow I seemed to cast on the water was much bigger than a bird's, the wind raking pleasantly through my hair. But then night and fog darkened both sky and ocean, and soon I felt myself dropping like a stone, unable to see a thing in the foggy dark . . . until the very last moment, when the fog blew away to reveal tree-tops looming up below me, and I crashed into them with a sound like crumpling wood and metal. Suddenly my whole body was drenched—not with water, but with what smelled like gasoline. Its acrid odor filled my lungs and stung my eyes.

I yelled so loudly it woke me up.

Cynthia and Moani tried to quiet me but couldn't. I was a dervish of anxiety. Only Mama, hurrying in from her bedroom, could quell my night terrors. "Sssh, sssh, it's all right," she said, taking me up into her arms and rocking me. "It was just a bad dream."

"I *fell*," I told her breathlessly. "I was flying and I *fell*. . . ."

"You fell into bed, safe and sound," Mama said with a smile. "See?" As I calmed down, I told her a little more about what I'd dreamt, and she reassured me that I was home and safe. But though I felt better when she finally left, I still didn't get much sleep the rest of the night.

By the time I got to school the next morning I'd mostly forgotten about it. But the teachers were all talking to each other about a story in that morning's newspaper about two aviators named Clark and Gray, who had just made the first interisland airplane flight in Hawai'i. The pair had taken off from O'ahu in a seaplane, landed briefly on Maui before heading for Hilo on the Big Island—and then promptly disappeared, and were feared to have crashed.

When I heard this I began choking again on gasoline fumes, so overwhelming that I had to flee into the bathroom, where I gagged over the sink.

When I got home that afternoon, Mama was looking at me strangely again. "Nani," she said, "tell me again about your bad dream."

I repeated what I'd told her last night, then said I wasn't feeling well and asked if I could be excused from supper and go straight to bed. She put a hand on my forehead, said, "Yes, of course," and tucked me into bed. Once she left the room, I wasn't so sure I *wanted* to go to sleep, after all; but eventually I did.

That night I dreamt calmer, though still exotic, dreams: I found myself walking through a jungle of algaroba trees and *maile* vines, feeling hot and sweaty and hungry, but oddly unafraid. There were no jarring crashes, no smell of gasoline; just heat, humidity, and a dull ache in my belly. This time I didn't wake up from it with a shout, just drifted out of it into other, less interesting dreams.

The next morning, over my breakfast *poi*, I calmly told my mother, "It's all right, they're alive. They're walking out of the jungle, that's all."

"What? Who?" my father said.

"The two men in the plane," I replied casually.

Mama looked stricken.

"It's nothing," she told my father. "Just a story Nani made up."

"That's nothing to be spinning yarns about," Papa chided me. "Those poor devils are probably lying at the bottom of the ocean."

But Papa was wrong. That day, against all odds, Harold Clark and Robert Gray emerged unharmed from the thicket of the Kaiwiki Forest on the eastern slopes of Mauna Kea, where their seaplane had crashed two nights before. They had walked away from the crash and then kept on walking through the jungle, without any food, for the next two days.

I thought Mama would be happy to learn this, but when I got home she took me aside and told me, sternly, "Nani, you must stop doing this."

This was the last thing I expected to hear. "Doing what?"

"*Seeing* things. In the clouds, in your dreams."

"But I'm not *doing* anything," I protested.

"You're telling your father things you can't possibly know! He won't understand."

"He will if I explain it to—"

"No!"

Mama seldom raised her voice to me, and it stung. "You asked me about my dream and I told you," I said. "I didn't do anything wrong!"

"No, you didn't, I know that," she said, softer. "But from now on I won't ask you any more questions, and I don't want you to tell me anything about what you—see. You understand?"

"But what if I have another nightmare?"

My mother looked pained at the thought, but said nothing.

Angrily I turned and ran out of the house, without any real idea of where I was going. Then I glanced up at the slopes of Punchbowl and I sensed, somehow, that if I went up there now I would find Johnny Kua. I picked some mangoes from our tree, put them in a sack, then began climbing the trail to the summit, baffled as to why Mama was scolding me for things I didn't have any control over—what I saw in the clouds, or dreams that came to me in the night. I ate one of the mangoes on the way up, then when I reached the top I gave the rest to one of the squatter families and hurried across the crater to the lookout. Sure enough, Johnny was standing there, once again gazing down at the city.

He turned, saw me, smiled. "Well, if it isn't Nani MacGillvray. *Aloha.*"

"Hi," I said, sounding pretty glum.

"What's wrong?"

I was suddenly reluctant to tell him for fear that he might have the same reaction as my mother.

"Come on," he prodded gently, "what is it, what kine *pilikia* you in?"

We sat down and I told him everything: the *mo'o* in the clouds, Mrs. Fereira's death, my dream about the two aviators. To my relief, he didn't laugh or even look at me cross-eyed, but seemed to accept my story at face value. I told him about Mama scolding me, half afraid he'd scold me too. But he just smiled.

"Nani, there's nothing the matter with you," he assured me. "What you dreamt is called a 'revelation of the night.' You have a gift. Your mama knows it too, even if it scares her."

"A gift?" That wasn't the word *I'd* have used to describe it.

"We Hawaiians live in two worlds, Nani," he said gently. "This world you see around us, that's just the first layer, like the skin covering our bodies. There's another layer underneath, like you and I have blood and bones beneath our skin. My *tūtū* said the ability to see this second layer of reality is called *'ike pāpālua:* it means 'twice knowing.' Seeing events that haven't happened yet—or things happening now, but at a great distance—that's a special gift you have, Nani. The *haoles* call it 'second sight.'"

"So I'm . . . not being bad when I see things?"

He laughed. "No, just the opposite. Your gift is *pono*—a very good thing."

"It doesn't feel good," I said.

"That's because your mama is afraid of it, or she's worried your father will be afraid. The important thing is, don't *you* be afraid of it."

"Johnny, do *you* have—'twice knowing'?"

He shook his head. "No, I joined the Army early on a hunch, not a vision. I'm not like you."

I thought about that a moment, and as I did I could see Johnny glancing down at the city again, and I knew he was looking at his family's house in Pālama.

"Johnny?" I said. "Can I ask you something?"

"Sure. Shoot."

"Why do you look so sad when you look down at your home?" I didn't need second sight to see it.

He smiled sheepishly. "Long story. Maybe I tell you sometime."

"Can't you go back there and visit your *'ohana?*"

He smiled and said, "I think maybe you're the one needs to go home . . . your mama's probably worried."

We got up, and then he squatted down and put his hands on my shoulders. "Just remember, Nani: it's *pono.* Don't be afraid of it, no matter what happens."

But something in the way he said that only made me feel more afraid.

For the next few weeks I tried not to remember my dreams, and I even did my best to avoid looking up at the clouds. One weekend

Papa took us all for a Sunday drive to Kailua, though this was not as restful as it sounds: Papa took the hairpin turns at his customary brisk clip up the windward side of the island. But we did have fun, stopping to watch the geyser of water erupting out of the Hālona Blowhole, and later Papa bought us all ice cream cones at the Elite Ice Cream Parlor.

The following day, I was playing tag in the schoolyard when I got tagged by Annabel Lucie—a girl I hardly knew—her fingertips just barely grazing the skin of my arm. All at once I had a familiar feeling—kine like when I was in the ocean, bodysurfing, and a wave pulled me under. It felt like I had a wave sitting on top of me and I didn't have more than a single breath in my lungs, but I didn't dare open my mouth to take another. The air of the playground actually began to thicken, to *liquefy*, as if it were turning to water all around me. I could still see the other girls playing tag, but now they were running in slow motion in the water, their hair floating up from their faces, oblivious to what was happening around them. I felt the sting of salt in my eyes; I couldn't hold my breath much longer and was on the verge of taking in a deep swallow of ocean when . . .

"Nani? You okay?"

It was my friend Beverly's voice, and the touch of her hand on my arm caused the water to evaporate, just like that. I was no longer bursting for breath.

"Nani? What's wrong?"

"Eh . . . not'ing," I lied and returned to the game, though steering clear of Annabel after that.

I went to bed that night with the salty taste of the ocean still on my lips.

The next morning, as my classmates and I filed into the schoolroom, I cautiously skirted past Annabel as she settled in at her desk, two rows behind me. I didn't touch her, didn't come close, but in my nervousness I bumped into her desk as I passed, and that was apparently enough to trigger it.

With the same absolute clarity that I'd dreamt of falling like a meteor from the skies above the Big Island, I now found myself treading water off Waikīkī—I could see Diamond Head off to my right, and some dozens of yards in front of me, a line of surfers rode a break I recognized as the one called Castle's Surf.

But the fact that I could see the surfers' backs meant that I was too far out. My leg cramped suddenly; I flailed in the water like a fish without a fin. I tried to call out to my family on the beach—not *my* family, I knew, but Annabel's—and to her older brothers, swimming closer to shore. I didn't know if they could hear me, couldn't tell whether they saw me frantically trying to wave and get their attention. A wave suddenly slapped me in the back, knocking the wind out of me as it pushed me under water and held me there. I knew I had only a single breath in my lungs, and I started to panic as I fought the reflex to open my mouth, and . . .

A boy's hand clasped my arm, pulling me up to the surface.

No—a boy jostled me as he passed me in the classroom, startling me from my trance. I was no longer drowning, I was back at school, in my classroom.

I took a deep gulp of air and hurried to my desk.

I sat there wondering what had happened. Had—would—Annabel be saved by someone, one of her brothers, maybe? Or had it just been me who'd been rescued, by that boy's brief contact? And should I warn Annabel, tell her not to go swimming at Waikīkī—or at least not to swim beyond the surf break?

My first instinct was to do just that. But then I worried: What if she didn't believe me? What if she told the teacher I was trying to frighten her? What if the teacher told my mother, or, worse, my father?

Paralyzed with anxiety, I fretted over the question all week and into the next. And that Monday morning, Annabel came to school breathless with the news that she had nearly drowned in the surf off Waikīkī and had only been saved at the last minute by a surfer paddling by on his board.

She had certainly not been saved by me, and, as relieved as I was that she was all right, I was also angry at myself for doing nothing.

I thought of what Johnny had told me: "It's *pono.*" But I knew that what I had done, or failed to do, was not *pono.*

That night, alone on the slopes of Puowaina and hiding behind some *kiawe* brush, I wept in frustration. I was just a little *keiki,* why did I have to make such important choices? I didn't want to see these terrible things! *Go away, dreams,* I commanded them. *Go away and leave me alone!*

To my relief and amazement, this actually seemed to work, at least for a while. The dreams and visions of other places, other people's lives, all stopped—as if my conscious mind were stubbornly refusing to take messages from my unconscious. Weeks went by without anything odd or disturbing happening to me. My dreams were all placid, benign: clouds that looked like clouds, not lizards; flying that didn't end in a tailspin; frolicking in the ocean, but not drowning in it.

So at first it seemed typically peaceful to find myself dreaming one night that I was on the beach, building sand castles as I listened to the rumbling sigh of the surf behind me. As in any dream, there were things that made sense only *in* a dream, so it didn't surprise me when I looked up to see a group of tanned young Hawaiian men wearing old-style *malo* cloths walking up the beach—and carrying lit torches, though it was the middle of the day. I heard drums, too; when I turned around to see where they were coming from, I saw instead an outrigger canoe coming ashore. And the young men were now carrying something else—a long bundle, about six feet long, wrapped in tapa cloth. They stopped in front of me and lowered their burden for me to look at.

I was startled to see that it was my father bundled up in tapa cloth, his eyes closed, his skin looking unusually pale. But there was such a peaceful calm on his face, it didn't bother me. I asked him, "Papa, are you sleeping?"

"Yes," one of the young men said with a nod, "he sleeps the *moe 'uhane.*"

I had no idea what he meant by this but somehow didn't think it important enough to ask.

The men lowered Papa into the hull of the canoe, now bobbing in the shallows, then pushed it away from shore. In moments the canoe bearing my father was being paddled out to sea, where the sunlight sparkling off the ocean made it seem as if the canoe were riding waves of white fire. It was beautiful to see, and though parts of this dream may have puzzled me, I didn't find it at all frightening, and awoke with a feeling of serenity and peace.

After breakfast, Papa again asked, "Anybody need a ride to school?" —and when Cynthia and Moani shook their heads, all he had to do was look at me with that devilish smile and I replied eagerly, "I do!"

I climbed into his lap and the Tin Lizzie took off down Pauoa Road. As usual, Papa took us onto a quiet little side street where I could steer, but this time I reached up and gripped the wheel in my hands—

And suddenly the car was spinning sideways—lurching off the road and down a steep embankment, though the street we'd been on a moment before had been flat as a board. The world literally turned upside down as the automobile rolled over with a crunch, jolting me out of Papa's lap. I fell, my head banging into the roof,

which was now below me—and only inches from where a huge
rock had torn a hole in the vinyl. I screamed as we kept on rolling
and I was thrown like a beanbag around the passenger compartment. Then I heard a sound like tearing metal under me, and the
whole world exploded in an angry roar. Flames were everywhere
but we were still rolling, a fireball encased in metal. I continued to
scream—even as I found myself suddenly, safely, in Papa's arms
again.

"Nani, what is it, what's *wrong*?"

We were stopped in the middle of that quiet, level little side
street—the car no longer tumbling end over end, no longer in
flames. But the sudden normalcy and safety were anything but
reassuring. My screams died in my throat as I looked around me
and realized that what I'd seen hadn't really happened.

Not yet.

I started to cry. Papa held me tightly against him. "It's all right,
baby, everything's all right. . . ." But it wasn't, because as I turned
my tear-streaked face into the crook of his arm, I caught one last
glimpse from inside the burning car—a man's hand lying limp on
the crushed steering wheel. And though I dearly wished I didn't,
I knew for certain whose hand it was, or would be.

When I finally stopped crying, Papa asked me again what was
wrong, what had happened. I told him I'd just gotten scared. It
didn't sound convincing even to me, but in the absence of any other
explanation, Papa took me home . . . and, after he had reassured
himself I wasn't injured, he left me in Mama's care. She put me to
bed, stuck a thermometer in my mouth, and left to make me some
tea. I lay there terrified to tell her what I'd seen, yet terrified not to.
I thought of Annabel—but that had turned out all right, hadn't it,
even though I'd said nothing? Maybe this would too. How did I
know what was the right thing to *do*?

Mama came back into the room to find me crying again. She sat down on the bed, took me in her arms, and asked, "What did you see, Nani?"

I looked at her fearfully.

"I know I promised I'd never ask you that again," she said gently, "but never mind that. What was it you saw in the automobile?"

"You won't be angry at me?"

"No. I swear."

I told her. She listened, looking concerned but not angry, even when I told her of the last image I'd seen, the man's hand—the hand I knew belonged to Papa.

"You—you never saw your father's face?" Mama asked hopefully.

"Not this morning," I said.

"What do you mean?"

"I . . . I had a dream last night." I went over every detail: playing on the beach; the Hawaiian boys carrying torches; Papa sleeping as they carried him. . . .

Mama was looking increasingly agitated. "But he was—just sleeping?"

"Yes. I asked one of them, and he said, 'He sleeps the *moe 'uhane.*'"

She nodded. "'Spirit sleep.' Hawaiians believe that when someone is deeply asleep, their soul travels outside of their body. What happened next?"

"Then they put Papa into a canoe and took him out onto the ocean."

She could not have looked more horrified had I said that Papa had been stabbed with a knife in the back.

My heart was racing now. "Mama? Did I say something wrong?"

She sat, pale and silent, for the longest while, then finally worked up the nerve to tell me: "A dream of a canoe is a dream of death. Your father was sleeping *the* spirit sleep, and was making the final journey . . . to the next world."

"Are you sure?" I said. "Maybe the canoe was just going to—to Maui, or the Big Island. . . ."

Tears filled her eyes.

"A dream of a canoe is a dream of death," she repeated, and began to weep.

Now it was my time to comfort her, holding on to her, offering her hope. "There's still time, Mama! We can warn him about what's going to happen. . . ."

She shook her head. "He would never believe us, Nani. He would deride it as—'Hawaiian mumbo jumbo.'"

"But we have to do *some*thing, we can't just let him die! What can we *do*?"

She looked more shaken and afraid than I had ever seen her.

"I don't know," she said miserably. "I don't know."

Later, trusting an instinct I wished I didn't have, I hiked up the trail to the Punchbowl lookout, where of course Johnny Kua was again waiting for me. "Funny how you're always here when I come," I said.

"Or maybe you only come here when I'm here," he pointed out. "You're the one with second sight, 'ey?"

But I really was glad to see him. I told him about what had happened in the car, the terrible fate that seemed to await my father, and I desperately sought his advice. "Johnny, can I—can I change the things I see?"

He considered that. "Sometimes, I've heard, you can. Sometimes, what's seen in the *'ike pāpālua* is just what's *possible*, not inevitable."

"So I should warn Papa? Tell him not to drive so fast, to be more careful, or he'll . . . he'll . . ."

Gently, he put a hand on mine. "Tell him."

I tried to hold back my tears of worry and hope. "I can save Papa?"

"You can't if you don't try."

"Are you sure?"

"Yes. *Tell* him."

I thanked him and scrambled down the hill in record time.

When I got back, my father was already home—he'd left work early out of concern for me—and so I couldn't speak freely to Mama. When Papa tried to give me a little kiss on the cheek, I couldn't help myself, I flinched a little, afraid that his touch might plunge me into another vision of his death. This only made him fret more about my own health, and over supper he stole worried glances at me; I could see a similar worry in Mama's face as she gazed at Papa.

After supper I insisted on helping Mama wash the dishes, and once alone with her in the kitchen I could tell her that we had to do something to warn Papa, we had to *try*. She had apparently come to the same conclusion, because she said, "I know we do. I could never forgive myself if I didn't."

"Do you want me to go tell him what I saw?"

"No, you leave that to me. I'd rather he be angry with me than with you. I'll talk to him after you leave for school tomorrow."

I went to school the next day filled with excitement and hope that we would be able to prevent this horrible future from coming to pass. I could barely keep my mind on my schoolwork, and when we were dismissed for the day I ran like a banshee—one of Papa's favorite expressions—all the way home. As I neared our house I could see Mama sitting on our *lānai* in a big wicker chair. I pounded up the steps and onto the porch and asked her breathlessly, "Did you tell him?"

Only now that I was so close did I notice the distant look in her eyes.

"Yes," she said, her tone flat as a broken piano. "I told him."

She wasn't looking at me so much as past me.

"You told him about the car accident?"

"Yes."

"Did you tell him about Mrs. Fereira?"

"Yes."

"And the two pilots? And Annabel Lucie?"

She said tonelessly, "Coincidence."

I blinked. "What?"

She sighed like a balloon losing the last of its air. "Your father says that was all just coincidence."

"But I *saw* his car go off the road," I said. "I could *feel* the flames!"

"It doesn't matter what you felt." There was a bleak surrender in her voice that I had never heard before.

"Did you tell him about the canoe?"

She broke into a short, sour laugh. "Oh, yes. The canoe. He especially liked that."

She looked straight at me now, and I saw the exquisite, unbearable hurt in her eyes.

"He told me I was acting like a . . . 'superstitious native whore,'" she said, and though I didn't know the word, I could feel the shame in her voice as she spoke it aloud. "That I was filling my daughter's head with ignorant pagan nonsense . . . making her throw a fit in the car. He said if I didn't stop it, he'd leave me, and he'd take you and your sisters with him."

I was shocked not just by Papa's cruel words but by the fact that Mama had even repeated them to me. It was the first time in my life that an adult had shared such a thing with me . . . such a raw, adult pain.

I went to her and hugged her, and she held me to her for a long while as we sat there on the *lānai*. Then finally she said, sadly, "There's nothing more we can do for him, Nani. We did our best."

That night, Papa sat me down and explained to me the laws of physics and the inviolate rules of science. He didn't scold me, just warned me not to let my imagination get the better of me, and never to credit any of Mama's "fairy tales."

After that, he also stopped offering me a ride to school. I think he was afraid that being in the car would trigger another "wild burst of fancy," as he put it.

Two months later, Papa was on his way to work, driving too fast down a steep hill, when he lost control of his beloved Model T and plunged into a ravine. The last of the series of rolling impacts punctured the ten-gallon fuel tank under the front seat, which exploded, killing him instantly.

When I think of my father, I think of fire.

Those were sad days for our *'ohana*. Papa's body was burned so badly that his casket had to remain closed during the services at the Nu'uanu Funeral Parlor. I had never heard a Hawaiian *kanikau* before, a lamentation chant; the mourners cried the traditional wail of *'Auwē! Auwē!*"—"Alas! Alas!"—as I stared helplessly at the coffin, unable even to kiss my papa goodbye. But this was so much harder for my sisters, because Papa's death had come as such a complete shock and surprise to them. Mama and I had been more prepared, and shared our own secret sorrow, our inability to prevent what we'd known would come to pass.

But in addition to my grief, I also felt a budding anger at one who'd given me, I felt, false hope.

After Papa's burial I didn't even bother to change out of the black dress I was wearing before I went charging up Punchbowl

Hill. I got my dress torn and dirty, black ash soiling black lace, but I didn't care. I raced across the crater's desolate face to the lookout, where, of course, I found a uniformed solider standing with his back to me. Johnny turned as I approached, his eyes sadder than the saddest *kanikau*. "I'm sorry, Nani," he said.

I ran at him and began pummeling him with my fists, screaming, "You *told* me I could save him!"

He winced, but it wasn't from my blows, I'm sure. "I told you to *try*."

I kept pounding at him, ineffectually, with my little fists. "What's the good in seeing what's going to happen," I cried, "if I can't change it!"

"Nani, listen, listen to me." He squatted down, took my hands in his, and closed his big fingers around my balled fists. "You *did* change something."

"I didn't change anything!"

"You did. You *did* save someone."

"Papa's dead!"

"But you're not. You saved *yourself*, Nani."

I stared at him, not comprehending. He let go of my fists. I let them drop helplessly to my sides.

"I swear, it's true," Johnny said. "After your mama told your papa what you saw, he stopped asking you to ride with him to school. Didn't he? And if he hadn't, you would've died with him in that car."

Disbelievingly, I said, "Me?"

"He's thanking you for it, Nani. Can you hear him? He's thanking you for telling him, so his little girl didn't die with him."

I couldn't hear Papa, and I didn't know how Johnny could, either.

"You—said you didn't have 'twice knowing.'"

"I don't. But I know, in a different way, that there are some things in the future you can change, and some things you can't. What happened to your papa was one you couldn't, I'm sorry—but there'll be others that you can. Don't give up, Nani. Your gift saved you—it can help save lots of other people too."

He stood up, and as he did, I heard a kind of low thunder rumbling in the distance behind us.

"You hear them, don't you?" Johnny asked.

"Yes," I said, baffled. "What is it?"

"Something else you can't change," he said sadly.

In moments there were dozens of airplanes—more than I'd ever seen, in strange unfamiliar shapes—roaring above us. They were flying so low that I could see the markings on their sides—a bright red circle, like a burning sun at daybreak. They thundered on, swooping low over the harbor, where they began dropping torpedoes on the ships at anchor there. The explosions were deafening, even from here, and they turned mighty destroyers into flaming wreckage within minutes. Columns of thick black smoke rose from the ships like grave markers. Wave after wave of planes came, until there were so many they almost formed a cloud that resembled the *mo'o* lizard I'd seen in the sky—but this was more like a dragon breathing bursts of fire onto the land.

Johnny stood there on the lookout, as flames leaped and smoke rose behind him, and smiled his gentle smile.

"There's nothing you can do for me, either," he said, adding fondly, "*Aloha*, Nani. Use your gift wisely."

And then I blinked, and he wasn't there any longer. Neither were the airplanes, or the burning ships in the harbor. Not knowing what was real and what wasn't, I walked slowly to the edge of the crater and peered down at the city. Honolulu—the Honolulu of 1918—lay dozing peacefully below me, as if what I had just seen were only a bad dream the city was having while it slept.

I would see this carnage again, of course . . . though not for another twenty-three years. But I never saw Johnny again.

As Honolulu's day of destiny approached, I did try to warn the authorities about the Pearl Harbor attack, even though Johnny had said that it couldn't be prevented. I wrote letters to the Navy, but they all went unanswered. In the months leading up to the bombing, it seemed as if every other week the local newspapers were full of speculation that the Japanese might attack or invade Hawai'i, so I'm sure I appeared to be just another vocal alarmist. The few officials I managed to meet with in person dismissed me as well, and even had they believed me, they were at such a low level in the chain of command that they probably could not have made any difference. The Japanese planes came, and the rising sun breathed its *mo'o* fire onto Honolulu. All I could do was to warn people I knew personally, and try to get them to safe havens where they might survive the aerial assault.

This is what I've tried to do all my life, what Johnny wanted me to do: to use my gift wisely. He was right: if there were some things I couldn't change, there were others that I could. Sometimes that meant warning a friend away from a certain place at a certain time, avoiding an accident that would have claimed his life; sometimes it was telling a neighbor family that a fire would break out in their apartment the following day, or warning a pregnant woman that her baby was backward in her womb and would need special medical attention if it was to be delivered safely. Some people heeded my advice; some didn't. I've never counted the number of lives that have crossed mine in this way, but I imagine it would be nearly a thousand over the long course of my life, and I am proud to say that a majority of those lives were improved for having touched mine.

I'm grateful, now, for this gift I've been given, as well as for the young man who crossed so huge a gulf to help me understand it. Once a year, in his honor, these old bones of mine make a solitary pilgrimage up Punchbowl Hill. Of course, it looks considerably different than it did when I was a girl: today the crater is graced with lush green grass and tall white monuments to the thirty-five thousand fallen souls who now abide there. One of the most beautiful of these monuments bears an inscription—a quotation from Abraham Lincoln—with words I've always found ironic in this place that was once known as Puowaina:

THE SOLEMN PRIDE THAT MUST BE YOURS
TO HAVE LAID SO COSTLY A SACRIFICE
UPON THE ALTAR OF FREEDOM

When this National Memorial Cemetery of the Pacific was first dedicated, the many graves were marked with thousands of small white crosses, each like a tiny sapling whose life was cut short too soon; but today these have been replaced with simple flat head-stones. I make my way slowly across the serene expanse of lawn, carrying a plumeria *lei* to one particular grave located not far from the lookout where I first met my old friend, in sight of his onetime home. And now, as I bend down, tears fill my eyes, as they always do, and I drape the *lei* across a granite marker that reads:

JOHN ROBINSON KUA
HAWAII
PVT 25 INFANTRY
WORLD WAR II
MAR 2, 1920   DEC 7, 1941

Call it, if you will, "the time element"—and across that bridge of years is passed a torch of friendship, hope, and valor—no finer gifts to be bequeathed anywhere, in or out of the Twilight Zone.

TORN AWAY

Joe R. Lansdale

Consider one Mr. Wilson. A tired man in a wrinkled suit, driving an old car, wearing a haunted expression like an ancient dueling scar. A man forever traveling and watching nervously over his shoulder for something that, in the words of baseball great Satchel Paige, might be gaining on him.

He was a young man in an old black car, parked out by the railroad tracks near an oil well that still pumped, pulling up that East Texas crude. I got word of the car from Mrs. Roark, who lived on the far side of the tracks. She called my office and told me that car and man had been sitting there since late afternoon, and from her kitchen window she had seen the driver get out of the car once, while it was still light, and walk to the other side, probably to relieve himself. She said he was dressed in black and wore a black hat, and just the outfit spooked her.

Now, at midnight, the car was still there, though she hadn't seen him in a quite a while, and she was worried about going to sleep, him being just across the tracks, and she wondered if I'd take a look and make sure he wasn't a robber or killer or worse.

Being Chief of Police of a small town in East Texas can be more interesting than you might think. But, not my town. It had a population of about three hundred and was a lazy sort of place where the big news was someone putting a dead armadillo in the high school principal's mailbox.

I had one deputy, and his was the night shift, but he had called in sick for a couple of days, and I knew good and well he was just spending a little extra time at home with his new bride. I didn't tell him I knew, because I didn't care. I had been married once, and happily, until my wife died suddenly in childbirth, losing the baby in the process.

Frankly, I've never gotten over it. The house seemed too large and the rooms too empty. Sometimes, late at night, I looked at her photograph and cried. Fact was, I preferred the night shift. I didn't sleep much.

So, when Mrs. Roark called and told me about the car, I drove out there, and sure enough, the car was still there, and when I hit my lights on high, I saw that it looked like it had seen a lot of road. It was caked in dust, and the tires looked thin. I bumped the siren once, and saw someone sit up in the seat and position his hands on the steering wheel.

I left the light on to keep him a little blinded, got out, and went over and tapped on the glass. The driver rolled it down.

"Hello, sir," I said. "May I see your license?"

He turned his face into my flashlight and blinked, and took out his wallet and pushed his license out to me. It said his name was Judah Wilson. The license was invalid by a couple of months, and the photo on it looked somewhat like him but it was faded and not reliable. I told him so.

"Oh," he said. "I should have noticed it was out of date."

"This is your picture, here?" I asked.

He nodded.

I thought about giving him a ticket for the problem with the license and sending him on his way, but there was something about him that made me suspicious; the photo not being quite right. I said, "I tell you what, Mr. Wilson. You follow me to the station and we can talk there."

"Is that necessary?" he said.

"I'm afraid so," I said.

At the station, I found myself a little nervous, because the man was over six feet tall and well built and looked as if he could be trouble. His hat and suit were a bit worn, and out of style, but had at one time been of good quality. He shoes needed a shine. But so did mine. I had him seat himself in front of my desk and I went around to my chair and, without thinking about it, unfastened my holster flap where he couldn't see me do it. I studied the photo. I said, "This looks like you, but . . . not quite."

"It's me," he said. "I'm older by a few years. A few years can make a difference."

"I just need to make a call," I said. I wasn't able to go somewhere private and call, since I was the only one there, and yet I was not in a position where I felt comfortable locking him up. I made the call and he listened, and when I finished, I said, "I guess you heard that?"

"The owner of the license is dead?"

"That's right. That means you have another man's out-of-date license."

He sighed. "Well, it wasn't out of date when I first got it and it's not another man. Exactly. It's just that I can't duplicate another person completely, and some less than others, and this man was one of the hard ones. I don't know what the difference is with one and then another, but there's sometimes a difference. Like you buy a knockoff product that has the same general appearance, but on closer inspection you can tell it's not the real deal."

"I'm not sure I understand," I said, "but I'm going to ask you to stand up and walk over to the wall there, and put your hands on it, spread your legs for a pat down. I got reason to hold you."

He did what I asked, sighing as he did. I gave him his Miranda rights. He listened and said he understood. I marched him to one of the two cages we had in the back. I put him in one and locked the door.

"You really ought not do this," he said.

"Is that a threat?"

"No, it's a warning."

"You're behind bars, sir, not me."

"I know," he said, and went and sat on the bunk and looked at a space between his shoes.

I was about to walk away, when he said, "Watch this."

I turned, and his body shifted, as if there was something inside him trying to get out, and then his face popped and crawled, and I let out a gasp. He lifted his chin and looked up. Inside his black suit, under his black hat, he looked almost exactly like me.

I felt weak in the knees and grabbed the bars for support. He said, "Don't worry, I can shift the way I look because I do not have a core, but I can't turn to smoke and flow through the bars. You've got me. And that ought to worry you."

There was a bench on the outside of the bars for visitors to sit and talk to their friends or loved ones on the other side, and I sat down there and tried to get my breath. I kept staring at him, seeing my face under that black hat. It wasn't quite right. There was something missing in the face, same as the one he had before, but it was close enough.

A long moment passed before he spoke. "Now watch."

He closed his eyes and tightened his mouth, shifted back, and looked the way he had before, like Wilson. Or almost like Wilson.

"It's best you let me out," he said.

I shook my head.

He sighed. "I'm not like anyone you've dealt with before."

"I don't doubt that," I said, and took my pistol out of its holster and laid it on my knee. He was behind bars, but the whole thing with his face, the way his body shifted under his suit, I couldn't help but think I might have to shoot him. I thought I ought to call my deputy and have him come in, but I wasn't sure what he could do. I wanted to call someone, but I couldn't think of anyone to call. I felt as if every thought I had ever possessed was jumbled up inside my head, knotted up and as confused as Alexander's Gordian knot.

I made myself breathe slowly and deeply.

He took off his hat and placed it on the bunk beside him and stared at me.

I said, "Tell me who you really are. What you are. Why you're here."

"You wouldn't understand."

"Try me."

"It wouldn't make any difference," he said, and smiled at me. The smile had about as much warmth as a hotel ice machine.

"Are you . . . are you from somewhere else?"

"You mean am I from Mars? From somewhere out there?" He pointed up to give his words emphasis.

"Yes."

"No. I'm not. I'm from right here on earth, and I am a human being. Or at least I once was."

I bent forward, overwhelmed, feeling light-headed and strange.

"What I can tell you is there is something coming, and when it gets here, you won't like it. Let me out."

"I can't do that."

"Because I'm not who I say I am?"

I nodded. "And because the man you look like is dead."

"Don't worry. I didn't kill him. He died and I took his identity. It was simple, really. I was in the hospital, for a badly sprained wrist; had to have a kind of support cast. Accident. Silly, really. I fell off a ladder working in a bookstore. But I was there, and Wilson died because of a car accident. It was time for me to move on anyway. I can't stay anywhere very long, because it'll find me."

"It?"

"Just listen. His family was in his room, and when they left out to do what was needed to be done about having the body dismissed, I went in and found his pants and looked through his pockets and took his wallet. I pulled back the sheet and studied his face. I became him. It was okay until tonight, long as I kept on the move and didn't have trouble with the law. But tonight, me being tired and you checking me out . . . It's come to an end."

"You could be me if you wanted to?"

"I could. If I killed you and hid the body, I could go right on being you. But not here. I wouldn't know your ways, your mannerisms, your experiences, but I could use the face and body and move on; become you somewhere else. Or use the face and not the name. There's all kinds of ways to play it. But I'm behind bars and you're out there, so you've got no worries. Besides, I don't kill. I'm not a murderer. Thing is, none of it matters now; I've lost time and I've lost ground. It's coming and I need to put enough miles between me and it to give myself time to truly rest."

"You're crazy?"

"You saw me change."

"I saw something."

"You know what you saw."

I nodded. "Yeah. Yeah, I do." I got up and slipped the gun into its holster and took hold of the bars and said, "Tell me about yourself. Tell me now."

"If I do, will you let me out?"

For a moment I didn't know what to say to that. Finally I said, "Maybe."

"Ha. You're pulling my leg. You're the law. You're dedicated."

"I don't know if the law covers this," I said. "I don't know what I might do. I know this: what you got is a story, and I got a gun and you behind bars, and you say something's coming, so it seems the problem is yours."

"Something is coming all right, and if you're in the way, it could bother you. It could do more than just bother. Look here. Listen up." He stood up and spread his arms and stood under the light on the ceiling.

"What do you see?"

"A man."

"Yes. But what is missing? What do you not see?"

I shook my head.

"Look at the floor where you stand. What do you see?"

I looked. I saw nothing, and said as much.

"No. You see something all right. Think about it . . . Here. Listen. Move to your right."

I stepped to my right.

"What moved with you?" he asked.

"Nothing moved with me."

"Look at me."

I looked. He stepped right. "Look on the ground. What do you see?"

"Nothing."

"Correct. Now follow me when I step left."

He stepped left. "What do you see now?"

"Still nothing."

He nodded. "Look at your feet again. Step left."

I did.

"Step right."

I did . . . and then I got it. I had a shadow and it moved with me. I jerked my head toward him and saw that where he had stood there was nothing. No shadow.

He stepped right, then left. He spun about like a top.

"My husk is empty," he said. "I am without shadow."

I took hold of the bars again, stood there trembling. I said, "Tell me."

"Will it matter? Will you help me out?"

"Perhaps. Tell me."

He sat down on the bunk again. "All right," he said. "I will."

"My troubles began during the War Between the States. For me that was a year or two after the war started. Eighteen sixty-two."

"The Civil War?"

"That's what I said."

"You're a time traveler?"

"In a way we all are time travelers. We travel from our date of birth until our date of death. We travel through time as it happens. Not around it, but through it. I am like that, same as you. But I have traveled farther and longer. I was born in 1840. I fought in the Civil War. I was killed in 1864."

"Killed?" I said.

"I was struck by a musket ball, during . . . Never mind. The where and how of it is unimportant. But I was struck dead and laid down in a shallow grave, and I was uncovered by wild dogs who meant to tear at my flesh. I know this because she told me."

I took my seat on the bench again. I didn't know what to think. What to feel.

"An old woman chased the dogs away and finished digging me up and took me home and I came alive again on her kitchen table, stretched out there naked as the day I was born, my chest and legs covered in designs made in chicken blood. Standing by the table with a big fruit jar full of something dark was the old woman. And she told me then I was hers. She was a witch. A real witch. She had rescued me from death and brought me to life with a spell, but she had kept my shadow; had torn it away from me with her enchantments. If I had it back, she said, after being brought back from the dead, I would die as others die, and I would not have the powers that I have now."

"The shape changing?" I said.

Wilson, for I knew no other name by which to call him, nodded. "That, and my ability to live on and on and on."

"And the jar of shadow?"

"She kept it on a shelf. My shadow was small at first, minuscule, like a piece of folded cloth. As time went on, it swelled and filled the jar. The jar could only hold my shadow for so long, and when it swelled enough, the jar would break, unless moved to some larger container, but once it was free, it could never be contained again. Even then, as long as I stayed away from it, I would remain ageless, be able to change my shape. But, if it found me, it would take me and I would age the way I should have aged; all the years that had passed would collect inside me, turn me inside out."

"Why didn't the witch use the spell on herself, to keep from aging?"

"Because you had to be young for it to work, or so she told me. But perhaps it was because she knew that eventually, no matter what it was contained within, it would get out. You had to worry about it forever pursing you, forever fleeing.

"As time went on, my shadow grew, and the old woman placed the jar in a crock, and one day we heard the jar crack inside the crock, and we knew the shadow was growing. During the day I did her bidding. I chopped and gathered wood. I worked her garden. I cooked her meals and washed her clothes. At night I lay on the floor in the thin clothes she had given me, shivering or sweating, according to the weather, unable to move because of the magic marks the old witch had made on my body. And my shadow, I could hear it moving around inside the crock, like insects in a hive.

"Then, one morning I awoke and nothing held me. The spell was broken. In the night the old woman had died. I buried the crock deep in the ground inside the floorless cabin and I set the place on fire and burned it and the old woman's body up. I went away then, walking as fast and as far as I could go.

"All I could think about was my shadow. When I lay down at night I felt as if I could hear it swell inside that crock, under the ground, and that it was breaking free, and coming up through the earth, taking to the wind, moving deliberately after me. I knew this as surely as if I could see it. I knew this because it was part of me and it was missing. I knew it traveled only at night, and found dark places during the day, for it had lost its host, and without me, it couldn't stand the light of day. I knew all of this instinctively, the way a chicken knows to set a nest, the way a fish knows to swim or a dog knows to bark.

"I moved across the land, year after year, ahead of my shadow, moving when it moved, at night, sleeping during the days, sometimes, but often driving day and night until exhaustion took me. The decades ticked by. I grew weary. That's why I was in the car during the night when I should have been moving. I slept the day and planned to move on when night came. Kept telling myself, You're too tired to drive. Just a few more minutes. A half hour. And then you can go. It's only just dark. Thoughts like that; the kind of thoughts an exhausted man thinks. I had been that way before, all tuckered out, and it had almost caught me. I was down with some disease or another. Down for three days, and I awoke, some kind of internal clock ticking louder and louder, and I knew it was near. This was over a hundred years ago, that near catch, and I still remember it sharp as a moment ago. The air turned cold in the dead of summer, and the world felt strange and out of whack, as if something had tilted. I took a horse and rode out. As I rode, I looked back, and there it was, a dark swirl of gloom tumbling toward me, dead as a distant star.

"I whipped that horse and rode it until it keeled over. I whipped it to its feet, rode it until it fell over dead. I ran on foot and found a barn and stole another horse, rode it for miles. I caught a train and just kept going. But it had been close. I had felt it coming, and that had saved me. I feel that way now. In this damn cell I'll meet my Waterloo, and there you'll stand, watching it happen."

I stood there for a long moment, and then I got the cell key and opened the door. I said, "Not if you run."

Wilson stood up and adjusted his hat and came out of the cell, showed me a thin smile. "Bless you . . . By the way. The real name, it's Elton Bloodline. Thank you, thank you."

"Go!"

I followed as Bloodline moved swiftly to the door, opened it, and stepped out. The wind was chill and Bloodline stopped as if something wet had crawled up his spine; he went white under the overhanging light. He turned his head and looked, and I looked too.

Way down the street, the darkness pulsed and moved toward us on the breeze; it twisted and balled and sometimes resembled a giant dark and faceless man, running.

"It's found me." Bloodline seemed frozen to the spot. "Torn away, and now it's coming back."

I grabbed his arm. "Come. Come with me. Now!"

He came alert then. We darted to the police car. He got in and I got behind the wheel and started up the engine and drove away in a roar and a squeal of tires.

I glanced in the rearview. And there it was, a shadow man, maybe ten feet high, passing under streetlights, pulling their glow into its ebony self. It ran swiftly on what looked like long, wide, black, paper-wobbly legs, and then its legs fluttered out from under it and it was a writhing wraith, a tumbleweed of darkness.

I put my foot to the floor and the car jumped and we put space between us and it, and then I hit something in the road, a pothole maybe, but whatever it was it was a big bad bump and the right front tire blew. The car swerved and the back end spun to where the front should have been. As it did, through the windshield I saw that the shadow looked like an inkblot, then I saw lights from the streetlamps, and then the car flipped and bounced and I didn't see much of anything for a while.

I couldn't have been out longer than a few seconds. When I awoke, I discovered that I was hanging upside down. Through habit, I had fastened my seat belt. Bloodline, in his haste and fear, had not; he was wadded up on the ceiling of the car and he was starting to move. I unfastened my belt and managed not to drop too hard or too fast by bracing my hands on the ceiling of the car and twisting my feet around to catch myself. I glanced about. The front and back glass were still intact. The glass on the driver's side was knocked out and the passenger's side was cracked in such a way that you couldn't see out of it.

Bloodline sat up, shook his head, and looked at me. I saw the hope drain out of him and he began to shake. "You tried," he said, and then the car was flung upright and we crashed together, and then I heard glass break, and a big dark hand jutted through the shattered windshield. It grabbed at Bloodline. He tried to slide backward, but it stretched and followed and got him around the waist. I grabbed his legs and tugged, but the thing was strong. It pulled him through the glass, cutting him with jagged shards stuck together by the windshield's safety goo, and then it pulled so hard that he was snatched from my grasp.

I wiggled through the busted-out driver's window, and on my hands and knees I crawled along the street, glass sticking into my hands, the reek of spilled fuel in the air. I got to one knee and looked; I saw that Bloodline's shadow was completely in the shape of a large man. It had grown from only moments ago, standing now twenty feet high and four feet wide. It lifted Bloodline high into the air, tilted its head back, and carefully swallowed him.

The shadow swelled and vibrated. There was a pause, and then it throbbed even more. With a sound like metal being torn, it grew smaller, rapidly. Smaller and smaller, and then, there it stood, a shadow the shape and size of a man. It looked at me, or would have had it had eyes. The darkness it was made of began to whirl in upon itself. The shape grew pale, and finally it was Bloodline standing there, the way I'd seen him before, but nude, his suit and hat and shoes all gone; his nude body shivering in the wind. He looked at me and a strange expression ran across his face, the kind you might have when someone points a loaded gun at you and you know he is going to pull the trigger. He turned his head and looked to his left, and there, poking out from him, framed by the street-lights behind him, was his shadow.

Then he withered. He bent and he bowed and his skin creaked and his bones cracked, and his flesh began to fall in strips off his broken skeleton. The strips fell into the street and the bones came down like dominoes dropped, rattled on the concrete; the skull rolled between my feet. When I looked down at it, it was grinning, and shadows moved behind the sockets, and then even they were gone and the darkness that replaced them was thin. The skull collapsed. I stepped back, let out an involuntary cry.

Then all of it, the skull, the bones, and the strips of flesh, were caught up on the chill wind, and then they were dust, and then they were gone, and then the air warmed up and the night brightened, and the lights all along the street seemed clearer and I was left standing there, all alone.

So the journey of Mr. Wilson, aka, Mr. Bloodline, ends with a splash of darkness and a scream, emphasizing that no one can outrun fate. He and his pursuer have become one, and in the wink of an eye they have been hurtled across a great void, into that narrow yet diverse and shadowy region of unique sight and sound . . . called the Twilight Zone.

VAMPIN' DOWN THE AVENUE

◉

Timothy Zahn

Within every human heart lies the desire for fame. The need to have one's achievements praised, one's stature and skills applauded, one's name and face recognized by an admiring public.

But fame, like her cousin wealth, is a capricious lady. Even as she smiles upon her chosen ones, she deftly weaves golden chains into their lives, chains that grow ever thicker, stronger, and harder to remove. Chains that remain as long as those who wear them count the lady as their traveling companion.

Some revel under the weight of those chains. Others end up crushed beneath them. Others seek a way to cheat the system, to eliminate the chains without giving up the glow of the lady's smile.

Sometimes, they succeed.

Rusty Lanford had always considered himself a reasonable enough man. But when a particularly audacious paparazzo named Browser tried to take a shot up Natalie's skirt at the restaurant, he'd finally had enough.

The cop who arrested him was sympathetic enough. So was the sergeant who booked him.

"Can't really blame you, Mr. Lanford," the latter said apologetically as he rolled Lanford's fingers over the ink pad and then onto the arrest form. "If those guys hounded me like they do you, I'd want to take a swing at them, too. But we've got laws say you can't do that."

"There must be something you can do," Lanford insisted in the persuasive baritone he'd used to such effect in *Return from the Sierra*. "What about Ms. O'Keefe? *She's* not a public figure. Can't you give her protection from this kind of harassment?"

"Wish I could, Mr. Lanford, wish I could," the sergeant said regretfully. The baritone was clearly not having any effect on the man, Lanford saw. Maybe he should have used the resonant bass from *Day of the Dark* instead. "You can wash up over there, and then we'll take you back to post bail. By the way, love your work."

The upside was that the L.A.-area police departments had long since gotten this thing down to a science, and Lanford was back on the street in less than an hour. The downside was that the paparazzi were waiting out there for him when he emerged. He walked stolidly through the gauntlet of electronic flashes, giving them nothing but the impassive expression of his deaf-mute in *A Scream from Within,* and made it to where Natalie was waiting with his car.

A few of the more-adventurous vermin were also waiting in their cars, and gave chase as their targets headed off into the night. But Lanford knew the city, and he knew a few tricks, and within two miles he'd lost them.

It was only a temporary victory, of course. They all knew where he lived.

Natalie knew it too. "If you don't mind, I'd rather skip the night-cap and just go home," she said as he left a tangle of winding residential streets and turned back onto the boulevard. "It's been a long night."

"Sure," Lanford said in his soothing, sympathetic voice, even as he privately ground his teeth in frustration. Tonight was supposed to be the night where he turned up the charm and got her under the sheets. "I'll call you tomorrow, okay?"

He parked the car two blocks from her apartment building for their good-night kiss, just in case any of the vermin were hanging around her place, then drove her the rest of the way. Sure enough, a couple of flashes went off as she got out of the car, stopping only when it became clear that Lanford wasn't going to get out with her.

He drove back to his house, cursing under his breath as once again he had to drive through a barrage of flashes to get inside the community's gate. *A water cannon,* he thought as he parked the car in the garage and trudged inside. *A nice water cannon with a remote control I can hose them down with. No law against giving people a free shower, is there?*

But there probably was.

He was undressing for bed—alone, dammit—when he found the card in his jacket pocket. Frowning, he peered at it.

"You didn't see me put this in your pocket," it read in neat, precise letters. *"The paparazzi won't see you, either. Call me anytime."*

He turned the card over. The only thing on the other side was an embossed name—Janick Winsley—and a Beverly Hills phone number.

It was a joke, obviously. Someone must have slipped the card into his pocket while he was punching Browser's lights out, or maybe planted it later at the police station.

But Lanford was pretty good about keeping his personal space personal. He should have noticed if anyone got that close.

He looked at the bedside clock. It was nearly two in the morning. Still, the man *had* said "anytime." Picking up his cell, he punched in the number on the card.

It was answered on the second ring. Apparently, this Winsley character was a night owl too. "Hello?" a smooth tenor answered.

"This is Rusty," Lanford said, suddenly unwilling to give his full name. "I, uh, have your card here."

"Yes, Mr. Lanford," Winsley said, his voice brightening and at the same time turning briskly businesslike. "If I may say so, you're definitely a man in need of my services."

"And what services would those be?" Lanford asked. "Security?"

"Oh, please," Winsley said with a chuckle. "The paparazzi and their telephoto lenses laugh at large men with guns and frowny faces. No, what I'm offering is the chance to get the paparazzi off your back forever. Well, after dark, at least."

"After dark?" Lanford echoed.

"But then, from what I've seen in the tabloids, most of your trouble comes at night anyway," Winsley continued. "Harassing you and your lovely female companions. Was tonight's a new one, by the way?"

"You mean Natalie?" Lanford asked. "No, I've been seeing her for a couple of weeks."

"Ah," Winsley said. "I've been a little out of touch, I'm afraid. Anyway, are you interested in hearing more?"

"I suppose," Lanford said cautiously. "When?"

"Why not now?" Winsley said. "You have security cameras outside your front door, don't you?"

"Yes, of course," Lanford said, feeling rather like he had that time the raft broke loose while they were filming *Jeremiah* and he'd been dragged two miles through raging whitewater before they finally got to him. This was all happening way too fast.

"Go downstairs and turn on the cameras," Winsley instructed. "I'll be there shortly."

"Wait a—"

"See you soon." The phone went dead.

Lanford closed the phone, muttering a Romanian curse he'd learned back when he did *Ill Bit by Moonlight*. Pulling on his jacket again, he stalked downstairs and turned on the monitors.

The well-lit driveway was empty. So was the equally well-lit portico outside the front door.

He was still gazing at the emptiness, wondering what in the world he was doing, when there was a knock at that same front door.

Lanford stared. This was impossible. The entire door was visible on the screens. Yet the knock *had* come from the door, not from somewhere along the wall that might somehow be out of the cameras' range.

Could someone have fed a tape loop into the system while he was out, as he himself had done in *Ten Seconds to Treason*? But his system was all digital and didn't use tape. Would that make a difference?

"Mr. Lanford?"

Lanford jerked. Winsley's voice had definitely come through the door. Right from a spot where the cameras were showing empty air.

"Mr. Lanford?"

Lanford squared his shoulders. If this was one of those stupid practical joke shows, he was not going to go all twitchy just for their amusement. He turned the dead bolt, and then, watching the monitor carefully, he slowly turned the doorknob.

The knob turned in exact sync with how he was turning it. So it wasn't a loop, after all.

Which meant that it was some sort of ventriloquism gag, instead. Throw the knock, throw the voice, and see if you could scare good old he-man actor Rusty Lanford for a loop of his own. Muttering the Romanian curse again, he twisted the knob the rest of the way and swung open the door.

To find a young man standing in front of him on the mat, all calmness and pleasant smiles. "Good evening, Mr. Lanford," he said briskly. "I'm Janick Winsley."

For a long minute Lanford just stared at him. Then, almost unwillingly, he looked back at the monitor.

The screen showed the door opened wide, and Lanford standing there with his mouth hanging open. Of Winsley himself there was no sign. None.

"No, I'm not a ghost," Winsley said into the silence. His professional voice had a hint of amusement in it. "May I come in?"

Moving like a man in a slow-motion dream, Lanford stepped back. Winsley walked inside and closed the door. His footsteps, Lanford noted distantly, made just the right amount of noise, and he could feel the slight vibration of the floor through his own shoes.

On the monitors, the door appeared to close by itself.

"Why don't we sit down?" Winsley continued, gesturing toward the living room. "Maybe have a drink, too. I know this is a lot to take in one gulp."

Lanford took a deep breath. Whatever was going on here, he was *not* going to crack for some hidden camera's benefit. "What did you mean about being a ghost?" he asked, ungluing himself from the floor and heading to the living room.

"What?" Winsley asked as he followed. "Oh—that. A lot of people think I'm a ghost, that's all. It sometimes helps to clear that one up right from the start."

"A lot of people?" Lanford asked, his frozen brain finding a section of dialogue he could get a handle on. "You've done this before?"

"Oh, many times," Winsley assured him as he settled himself into one of the recliners. "Shall we get to business? Or—sorry—did you want that drink first?"

"Business first," Lanford said, sitting down on the couch on the other side of the coffee table.

"Excellent," Winsley said approvingly as he crossed his legs. "Well, then. I presume you've got some questions. But first, would you like another demonstration?"

"Demonstration?" Lanford asked, a bit lamely.

"Yes," Winsley said. "You could get a camera and—" He broke off, took a close look at Lanford's face, and sighed. "Maybe it would be easier if I just laid it out for you. As you just saw, I'm invisible to all cameras. I can give you the same—"

"To TV cameras, anyway," Lanford put in.

"To *all* cameras," Winsley said, a slight edge to his voice. "TV, movie, film, digital, infrared—if it takes in light and creates an image, I'm invisible to it." He smiled suddenly. "I also don't show up in mirrors. Does that remind you of anything?"

Lanford frowned. Then, abruptly, that scene from *Ill Bit by Moonlight* flashed to mind. "You mean you're . . . you're a . . . a . . . a *vampire?*"

"Very good—you got it out," Winsley said with a grin. "Actually, no, I'm not. Or rather, not completely."

This was all coming *way* too fast. "What do you mean?"

"I mean I don't turn into a bat or drink blood or any of that other stuff," Winsley explained. "The only vampiric trait I have, actually, is that I don't show up on cameras." He gestured to Lanford. "And I can make it so that you won't, either."

"You mean *ever?*" Lanford asked as another piece surfaced that he could understand. "But I'm an *actor.*"

"Of course you are," Winsley said soothingly. "Don't worry, my technique works on a strictly temporary basis. That's why I specified you'd only be invisible after dark. After all, we have to let you make a living during the day, don't we?"

"So I *will* be visible when I'm being filmed?" Lanford said, just making sure.

"Yes," Winsley said. "Of course, that means the paparazzi will still be all over you during those times, too. Nothing I can do about that, I'm afraid, unless you're looking to change careers."

"No, thanks," Lanford said. "So how does it work?" He frowned suddenly, remembering something else from that vampire movie: "You don't have to *bite* me, do you?"

"Oh, please," Winsley said, looking pained. "No. Fortunately it's much simpler than that."

Reaching into his pocket, he drew out two white containers the size of aspirin bottles. One of them had a thin blue line around the edge of the cap, the other had a red line. "Blue pills; red pills," he said, hefting them one at a time. "You take a blue pill after sundown, ten minutes before you plan to go out. Then you take a red pill before sunrise the next morning. Nothing could be simpler."

Lanford eyed the bottles suspiciously. It was simple, all right. *Way* too simple. "And the vermin won't be able to see me?"

"They'll *see* you just fine," Winsley said patiently. "They just won't be able to take your picture."

"And there are no side effects?"

"Not as long as you follow the instructions," Winsley said. "What do you say? Shall we give it a test run?"

Lanford was still staring at the bottles. They seemed to have an almost hypnotic effect. "What do you mean? Take a pill and go find some paparazzi?"

"Actually, I was thinking more of you taking a pill and getting out your camera," Winsley said. "But if you want to go whole hog, sure, why not? It's not like you'll have to go very far—there was still one sitting out front when I came in."

Waiting there on the chance that Natalie would try to slip in on her own, no doubt. "Vermin," he growled.

"Indeed they are." Winsley raised his eyebrows slightly. "As a matter of fact, I believe it's the same man you punched in Sadie's tonight."

"Is he, now," Lanford said, standing up as his brain finally started to unfreeze. Browser outside his house, and unable to get photographic evidence of anything Lanford did? "Give me those."

Winsley tossed the blue-rimmed bottle across the coffee table. "Shall I get you some water?"

"Don't bother." Lanford twisted off the blue-edged cap and looked inside.

He'd expected something exotic-looking, like the deadly muscle enhancers from *Man and a Half.* But they were just plain blue tablets the size and shape of over-the-counter pain medicine. Shaking one out into his palm, he tossed it back in his throat and swallowed.

For a few seconds he stood motionless, feeling the lingering sensation of the pill in his throat, waiting for something dramatic to happen. But nothing did. He felt just fine, and not very vampiric at all. "Nothing's happening," he said.

"It takes ten minutes, remember?" Winsley reminded him. "Actually, you might want to watch it this first time. You have a mirror somewhere handy?"

"Over here," Lanford said, and led the way to the guest bathroom.

And over the next ten minutes he watched in a combination of horror and fascination as his image in the mirror slowly faded away into nothingness.

"It's temporary, right?" he asked one last time as he shifted his attention between his completely solid hand and the blank mirror.

"Just take a red pill," Winsley said. "Shall we see if Browser's still out there?"

"You stay here," Lanford said, heading for the front door. "Help yourself to something from the bar."

When Lanford slipped through the gate, Browser was sitting in his car, studying his bruised cheek and eye in his rearview mirror. "You're up late, Browser," Lanford greeted him as he strode up to the paparazzo's car.

"Well, well—the big he-man himself," Browser said sarcastically as he turned to Lanford. His eye was already starting to puff up, Lanford saw, with the promise of being a spectacular shiner by morning. "'Smatter, big man? Conscience bothering you?"

"I'm surprised you even know what a conscience is," Lanford said. "No, I just came out to deliver a warning."

Browser raised his eyebrows, though only one of them actually moved. "Really," he said, his hands dropping casually to his waist. Readying his camera, no doubt, in hopes of getting a juicy candid photo. "I'm listening."

"Leave my dates alone," Lanford said, stopping a few feet short of the car and giving Browser the intimidating glare and full-bodied voice he'd used as chief heavy in *Sicily*. "You want pictures of me, fine. Come by the studio, catch me at lunch—knock yourself out. But leave my girlfriends alone. You hear me?"

"I hear you," Browser said. "And here's a little something for you." He lifted his left hand, middle finger extended.

Lanford suppressed a smile. It was an old, old trick, trying to goad your subject into responding in kind to an obscene gesture. The tabloids loved pics like that, which was why he never took the bait.

Until now. "Right back at you," he said, lifting his own middle finger in response.

Quick as a rattlesnake, Bowser's right hand came up from his lap and a flash burned into Lanford's retina. "Ha!" the ghoul gloated.

"Oh, you want candid?" Lanford said, holding his finger out for one more flash. "Here's some candid for you."

Browser was still flashing madly away as Lanford re-formed his hand into a fist and hit the vermin right in the center of his bruise. "There you go," he said over the other's howl of pain. "Have a good night."

Turning, he strode back to the gate. He opened it, locked it behind him, and then took a moment to look over his shoulder.

Browser was sitting in his car, bathed in the faint glow from his dome light. One hand was pressed against his newly injured cheek; the other was rapidly thumbing through his camera's memory. And what Lanford could see of his face looked confused, alarmed, and furious, all at the same time.

Winsley was back in his recliner when Lanford came in, a small drink in his hand. "Enjoy yourself?" he asked as Lanford headed to the bar.

"Immensely," Lanford assured him. "I even got to hit him again, right in the middle of his bruise."

"So that he won't have anything new to show the cops," Winsley said, nodding. "Nice."

"Actually, I was thinking that it would hurt more there," Lanford said. "But you're right, too." He took a deep breath. "Okay, I'm sold. How much?"

Winsley gestured at the pill bottles sitting on the coffee table. "You've got a week's supply there, assuming you take a pair every night. This first batch is free."

Lanford frowned. "Oh?"

Winsley smiled faintly. "Don't worry, I'm not going to toss any hidden strings at you. I've just learned that it takes a week or so for the paparazzi to finally give up on those evening shots and go away. Hence, those few days are free. The next batch will cost twenty thousand a week."

Lanford smiled to himself. That was probably less than half of what one of those vermin could get for a really juicy photo of him. "Deal," he said.

"Excellent," Winsley said, setting down his drink and standing up. "You've got my number. Let me know when you're ready for more."

Lanford spent the next hour with his four cameras, including his old classic Polaroid, taking endless photos of the empty space where he should have been. Then, almost reluctantly, he decided it was time to call it a day. He wasn't due at the studio until ten, but if he didn't get at least a few hours of sleep, Jenny or Randall in makeup would chide him about the dark circles under his eyes, which they would have to cover up.

Before he crawled into bed, though, he made sure to take his red pill.

The next week was heaven on earth.

The very first day, his assistants fielded eight separate calls asking oblique questions about his health. They assured everyone that, yes, Rusty Lanford was fine, was hard at work on his next film, and that they were welcome to come by to see for themselves if they wanted.

At least two of the calls, as near as Lanford could tell from the voices on the tape, were from Browser himself.

The vermin were heavily in evidence when Lanford went out clubbing that night, throwing enough flashes at him to spark a Sierra wildfire. A few of them got right up in his face, risking the same violence that had happened to Browser the night before. Lanford let them get away with it this time, and waited for the inevitable reaction.

It came about two hours into his club crawl, when the flashes suddenly went dark for nearly half an hour while the vermin apparently got together, compared notes, and tried to figure out what was going on. The respite was followed by a fresh surge of activity, accompanied by a lot of cursing and shouted demands.

Unfortunately for them, Lanford had carefully chosen that final club because it was owned by a friend of his. After ignoring two warnings to keep it civil, the whole lot of them ended up in the nearest police station's holding cells.

The second night was much like the first, except they'd learned to keep it civil. The third night, only a few hopefuls showed up and hung around for only about an hour before heading off to hunt more promising and profitable game.

Midway through the third night, Lanford felt confident enough to call Natalie and ask her out for the next evening.

Pictures of Rusty Lanford with his latest *femme du jour* were always in demand, and he and Natalie had to suffer through a few opportunistic flashes as vermin stalking other targets caught sight of them. But, as on the previous evenings, the harassment stopped very quickly.

He had a bad moment the next day when a couple of Web sites proudly displayed some photos of him and Natalie together. But the studio's legal department—and Lanford's own legion of fans—were right on top of it, and by lunchtime they'd conclusively proved that his image had been Photoshopped into the pictures. The Web sites quickly took them down, and Lanford spent most of his free time that afternoon daydreaming about the conversations that probably went on between the sites and the offending vermin. Presumably, considerable sums of money reversed direction, as well.

The next night, no one showed up at all. No matter what the paparazzi saw, they got paid only if there were photos; and even if they couldn't figure out how Lanford was doing it, it was abundantly clear that he was no longer going to be a cash cow for them.

At least, not after dark. They still could—and did—hound his footsteps during the day. But that was all right. Lanford was, after all, a media personality, and the free publicity those shots provided were all to the best. As long as they left him alone on his nights out, he was happy to handle the daylight stuff.

The effect of the unspoken truce on Natalie was like magic. With the disappearance of their unwanted entourage, her tension faded and she started genuinely enjoying his company. Lanford pressed his advantage, working the sequence he'd used in *Countdown to Love*, as he wore down the last of her lingering resistance to his charm.

Six days after Winsley had not shown up on his security cameras, he finally scored.

His first warning that something was wrong was when he was jolted awake the next morning with the terrifying sensation that the house was on fire. He jerked upright in bed, throwing off the blankets, his eyes blurring momentarily as he tried to get them open and focused.

Only, nothing was wrong. In the hint of sunlight peeking through the blinds, the bedroom looked just the way it always did, except for the tangled trail of clothing leading back to the door.

But while there weren't any flames, there *was* a hint of an odd smell coming from somewhere. Had Natalie lit some incense after he'd nodded off?

He looked down at her, still sleeping peacefully on the other side of the bed. At least his sudden movement hadn't awakened her. It was just after six, he saw by the bedside clock, five minutes after his alarm should have gone off. Was the sound of the buzzer what had sparked his waking nightmare about fire?

Five more minutes, he told himself. Five minutes, and a quick shower, and he could still make his makeup call. Blinking his eyes again, he lay back down.

His head had just hit the pillow when a sudden, burning pain flashed through his cheek.

"*Ow!*" He gasped, snapping back up into a sitting position and grabbing for his cheek. *What the hell—?* His eyes fell on the pale beam of sunlight crossing the pillow.

And the awful truth flooded in on him.

In the heat of passion and the languid drowsiness afterward, *he'd forgotten to take the red pill.*

He threw off the blankets, still clutching his throbbing cheek, and made a mad dash for the master bathroom, the only room in the house without any windows. Along the way he crossed two more errant sunbeams, picking up two more slashes of pain across his thigh and shoulder. He made it through the bathroom door, slammed it behind him, and grabbed a towel to jam under the door. Breathing hard, he flipped on the lights.

His first impulse was to go to the mirror to see what sort of damage the sunlight might have done to his famous cheekbones. But all the mirror showed was the Jacuzzi tub behind him. Cursing under his breath, he instead twisted around to see the back of his throbbing leg.

The burn looked nasty, a bright red welt across the skin. And that was just the diffuse light that had managed to get through the blinds. God only knew what would happen if full-bore sunlight got him.

Luckily, God was going to get to keep that knowledge to Himself. Popping open the medicine cabinet, Lanford twisted the top off the red-rimmed bottle and popped the second-to-last pill.

"Rusty?" Natalie's voice came faintly through the door. "You all right?" The doorknob rattled and started to turn.

"No!" Lanford snapped, leaping back to the door and grabbing the knob to keep it from turning all the way. "I mean no, I'm not well. I think I'm going to be sick."

"You mean sick as in . . . *sick?*"

"Very sick," Lanford said. "Those, uh, probably that shrimp cocktail. I think I'm going to be in here awhile. Sorry."

"That's okay," Natalie said, sounding both concerned and disappointed. "Can I get you anything?"

"No, I've got everything I need," Lanford assured her, glaring into the mirror. He'd never watched the magic process in reverse and had no idea how long it was going to take. But surely it couldn't be more than the ten minutes it took going the other direction. "You can use the bathroom downstairs if you want to shower."

"Okay," she said. Her footsteps faded away, and Lanford went back to standing in front of the mirror. Nothing was happening. *Shouldn't* something be happening?

He frowned, cocking his head. Some sort of faint scratching sound was coming from somewhere outside the door.

He caught his breath as the sound abruptly clicked. *Natalie was opening the blinds!*

No! Ruthlessly, he choked back the impulsive shout. Of course she was opening the blinds. *Everyone* opened the blinds in the morning. If he ordered her not to, she'd only want to know why.

The bedroom had been dangerous before. Now, Natalie had unknowingly turned it into a death trap.

For the next half hour he paced across the cold marble floor, looking into the blank mirror each time he passed, listening to the faint sound of running water from downstairs. Midway through Natalie's shower, with still nothing happening, he swallowed the last of his red pills. Maybe a double dose would do the trick.

Natalie finished her shower and presently he heard the sound of footsteps outside the door again. "Rusty? How are you doing?" she asked.

"Still sick," Lanford said. "I'm sorry."

"That's okay. I understand." There was a brief pause. "Uh . . . how am I going to get to work?"

Lanford winced. Telling her to call a cab would be incredibly tacky. But the alternative . . . "I guess you can take the Vette," he said between clenched teeth. He *hated* letting other people drive his cars. "Keys are on the hook by the garage door."

"Oh," she said, an odd tone to her voice. "Okay. Thank you."

Lanford ground his teeth in frustration. Natalie knew about his love for his cars, of course. Everyone in the Western Hemisphere and parts of Europe knew it. Which meant she was undoubtedly swelling her view of their relationship into something way beyond anything justified by a simple one-night stand.

But there was nothing he could do about it. Not until he could get out of this damned bathroom. "I'll call you later," he added.

"Okay," she said. "Bye."

"Bye."

A minute later came the hum of the garage-door opener, followed by the throaty roar of his Corvette. He strained his ears, wincing, as she ran awkwardly through the gears on her way down the driveway.

And then she was gone, and he was alone.

He looked around the bathroom, too emotionally drained even to swear. No phone. No food. Plenty of water, but so what?

And meanwhile, his career was about to go straight down the tubes. Kendall Fornier was one of the world's most demanding directors, and Lanford was already late. If he didn't figure out something, and fast, the phone in the bedroom was going to start ringing.

Right on cue, it did.

Lanford looked around the bathroom again, trying desperately to think. Still no phone. He couldn't throw a note out a window— no window. The sunlight that must be blazing across his bedroom by now would cook him like an Argentine steak if he tried to get to the phone.

But if he *didn't* do something—if he didn't get out there and answer that phone—Tom or Bonnie or one of his other assistants would eventually get worried and send someone to check on him. When he also didn't answer the door, they would probably call the paramedics, who would probably break down his door and stomp upstairs and probably ignore his protests that he was fine and break down the bathroom door, too.

At which point he would probably flash cook into a mound of greasy ashes. The vampire in *Ill Bit by Moonlight* had done that, though it had taken the FX people three takes to get it right.

Lanford would probably get it in one.

The bedside phone stopped ringing. Five seconds later, his cell phone began chirping the studio's personalized signal.

He winced. So it wasn't one of his assistants calling. It was one of Fornier's people, calling on Fornier's orders, which meant the damn director didn't have anything better to do than watch the clock and count heads.

Come on, Lanford, think! *Think of something!* This was ridiculous—he'd played the master improv craftsman in three separate Ennis McKenzie movies. Surely he'd picked up *something* of the technique along the way.

And then, finally, he got an idea.

The bedside phone had started up again, its ring making a nice counterpoint to the cell's chirping, by the time he had the eight huge Turkish bath towels wrapped around him. Sweating inside his new cocoon, wondering if he was going to suffocate before the sunlight even had a chance to cook him, he awkwardly turned the doorknob with his elbows and shuffled out into the bedroom.

There was no possible way to pick up his bedside phone without exposing his hands to the burning rays he was sure he could feel right through three layers of towel. Fortunately, his cell was still in his jacket pocket on the floor somewhere near the bedroom door. Waiting until it started its chirping again, he homed in on the sound and pushed the whole jacket along the rug in front of him like a penguin trying to get its egg up on its toes.

He'd known that nature documentary he'd been conned into narrating would come in handy someday.

The cell had rung twice more by the time he made it back into the safety of the bathroom and got the door closed and sealed again behind him. Ripping off the towels, he dug the phone out of the jacket and punched in Fornier's private cell number.

There was no answer. He must already be on the set, where any phone left on was subject to instant demolition. A quick scrolling through the missed-calls list showed that two of them had been Bonnie, and he punched for a callback.

The assistant answered on the first ring. "Mr. Lanford!" she said, sounding breathless. "I've been trying to reach you all—"

"I know—I've been listening to the phone ring," Lanford cut her off. "Listen, I've come down with something and I can't come in today."

"What sort of something?"

"You really don't want to know," Lanford told her, trying to straddle that thin line between the vague and the suspiciously implausible. Still, he'd had lots of practice doing that in *Keefer at the Races*. "Let's just say I'm leaking badly. At both ends."

"Oh," Bonnie said, her voice suddenly going a little queasy. "Is, uh, that what you want me to tell Mr. Fornier?"

"Tell him to take Acapulco and multiply it by about ten," Lanford told her. "If he wants details, he can call me now that I've managed to get the phone in here with me."

"Okay, I'll tell him," Bonnie said. "Anything I can do for you?"

"No, this is just something that has to run its course," Lanford assured her. "Hopefully, I'll be fine by tomorrow."

"Okay, Mr. Lanford," she said. "If you need anything, just call."

"I will," Lanford promised. "You and Tom might as well take the day off. I'll talk to you later."

Lanford's next call was to the studio wonk who'd called him, feeding him the same line and assurances he'd just fed Bonnie. The wonk wasn't nearly as easy to convince, but Lanford had been brushing off people for years and he got rid of the man quickly enough.

His third call was to Winsley.

"Good morning, Mr. Lanford," Winsley said cheerfully. "I presume you're calling about a new supply—"

"It won't shut off," Lanford snapped.

There was a brief pause. "What?" Winsley asked more cautiously.

"It won't shut off," Lanford repeated. "I forgot to take the red pill last night, and now I'm stuck this way. I took the pill—both of them, actually—and nothing happened."

The pause this time was longer. "Okay," Winsley said at last. "First thing to do is not panic."

"Not *panic*?" Lanford echoed. "Can't you fix this?"

"Of course I can," Winsley said. "It's happened before. You got drunk or something, right? Or you were with a woman—this Natalie or whoever—"

"Never mind what I was doing," Lanford ground out. "Just *fix* this."

"I'm on it," Winsley promised. "Where are you now?"

"In my bathroom," Lanford said. "No windows, and I've got towels stuffed under the door."

"Sounds good," Winsley said. "Just stay there. I'll get back to you as soon as I've got an answer."

"Any idea how long?"

"Not really," Winsley said. "It's different every time it happens."

Lanford felt his eyes widen. "What do you mean *every time*? I thought you said there were no side effects."

"As long as you follow the instructions," Winsley said patiently. "But sooner or later you Hollywood types always— Never mind. Like I said, I'm on it. Just stay there, at least until eight-o-three, and I'll call you."

"Eight-o-three?"

"Sundown," Winsley said. "*Don't* leave before that."

"Don't worry," Lanford growled. "Just hurry it up, will you?"

"You got it." The phone went dead.

Lanford spent the next hour on the phone, talking to his assistants, his housekeeper—no, no need to come in today—more of Kendall Fornier's studio wonks, and finally Fornier himself.

The Great Man wasn't happy. In fact, judging by the level of cultured civility in his voice, he was furious. Lanford tried every calming trick he knew, but he could tell that none of them was helping. Promising to be back on set as soon as possible—and also promising he'd see a doctor if his supposed ailments hadn't cleared up in two days—he wished Fornier well and hung up.

The rest of the day he spent brooding.

You Hollywood types, Winsley had said. How many of his fellow actors, Lanford wondered, had tried this same antipaparazzi stunt and run into this same problem? The big names in the business were always going into seclusion or sneaking into some high-priced rehab facility somewhere. How many of those were actually hiding from nothing more exotic than sunlight?

Or was it even worse? Lanford couldn't even name all the actors he'd known through his career who'd suddenly quit the business and retired into complete obscurity in some backwater like Fresno or Oregon. Had all of them simply been tired of the phoniness of the movie business? Or had they quit because they'd become permanently invisible to cameras?

Or had Winsley been lying about his vast client list? Was Lanford simply the guinea pig in this particular technique?

In which case, Winsley might not have the faintest idea how to reverse it.

He spent the last hour pacing restlessly back and forth, his heart thudding with dread and anger and a sudden surge of claustrophobia. Finally, at exactly eight-o-four, he kicked the towel out from under the door, twisted the knob, and escaped.

The first order of business was to close all the shades in the house, as tightly as he could get them. The second was to get dressed. Food and drink—*real* drink, not just tap water—were next on the list.

The smart thing would have been to stay home, out of the public eye. But the claustrophobia that had hit him in the bathroom had extended itself to include the whole house, and he had to get out before he went completely crazy. There had to be *some*place in the L.A. basin, some seedy neighborhood bar and grill, where they wouldn't recognize the famous Rusty Lanford. Or at least where they wouldn't believe it if they *did* spot him. Putting on the shabby jacket, hat, and glasses he'd swiped as souvenirs from the *Jackson's Way* wardrobe, he got into his still not-quite-restored 1985 Mustang and headed off into the gathering dusk.

He landed in Pomona, or possibly Montclair. The place was no great shakes, but the extra-rare steak he ordered was cooked properly, the beer was acceptable, and—best of all—there was no mirror behind the bar.

He had just finished the steak and was working on his third beer when the door opened with a rattle of small bells and Browser walked in.

Lanford ducked his head, rubbing vigorously at a pretend itch over his eyebrow. But Browser wasn't fooled, or else he already knew Lanford was here. He glanced around the bar, then headed straight across to Lanford's table. "Well, well," he said as he helped himself to a chair. "Fancy seeing you here."

Lanford sighed and gave up on the eyebrow rubbing. "What do you want, Browser?"

"What I *want* is to know how you're doing this," Browser said. "But none of the others would ever tell me, so I don't suppose you will, either."

So Winsley hadn't been lying about his client list. Even a ghoul like Bowser had apparently heard of at least some of them. "You're right, I won't," Lanford said.

"Didn't think so." Browser cocked his head. "By the way, did you know I was fired today? Oh, no, of course you don't. Silly me. You spent the day hiding from everyone, didn't you?"

"No, I spent the day being sick," Lanford corrected him stiffly.

"Ah," Browser said. "Remarkable recovery."

"Don't count on it," Lanford said, frowning as his brain belatedly caught up with his ears. "What do you mean, you were fired? I thought you people worked freelance."

"Some of us also have retainers," Browser bit out. "Or we did. I don't. Not anymore."

"Let me guess," Lanford said, permitting himself a smile. "You were the one who sold those Photoshopped fakes."

"They weren't fakes," Browser snapped. "You were *there*. I just put you back in where you belonged."

Lanford shrugged. "Still constitutes fraud."

"Yeah, so they tell me," Browser growled. "They also tell me my credibility is shot to hell." He smiled thinly. "So as long as *you've* ruined *me*, I thought I'd return the favor." He waved dramatically at the door.

Lanford looked over at the door, feeling his stomach wrapping a little tighter around his dinner. But nothing happened. "Really?" he said.

Browser snorted. "People," he said with a sniff. "Don't any of you know how to hit cues anymore?" Abruptly, he stood up. "Oh, well, it's still too late for you. See you around, Lanford. Maybe."

With a nod, he strode away from the table and sat down at the bar. Lanford watched as he muttered something to the bartender, wondering what all that had been about.

And then, with a horrible jolt, he understood.

Snatching out his wallet, he dropped three twenties onto the table beside his plate and slid out of his chair, jamming his hat back around his ears as he made for the door. He had to get out of here, and fast.

He was still three paces away when the door swung open and Kendall Fornier strode into the bar.

There was nowhere for Lanford to run. Nowhere for him to hide. Nothing to do but look Fornier straight in the eye as if he had nothing to hide and nod a greeting to the Great Man. "Good evening, Mr. Fornier," he said, forcing calmness into his voice. "I'm surprised to see you here."

"As am I, Mr. Lanford," Fornier replied, running his eyes up and down Lanford's seedy outfit, urbanity fairly dripping off the man. That was a very bad sign. "I gather your, ah, illness has passed?"

"For the moment, anyway," Lanford said cautiously.

"Yes." Fornier's eyes flicked around the room. "And yet, fresh from stomach trouble, you go out to dine? You don't stay home with tea and a simple broth?"

"I was asked to meet someone," Lanford said, improvising desperately. "This was the place he specified."

Fornier's eyebrows lifted fractionally. "What a coincidence," he said. "I, too, was invited."

"Yes, I suppose you were," Lanford said under his breath. *Damn* Browser, anyway.

"I shall expect to see you on set promptly at six tomorrow morning," Fornier continued calmly. "If not, you're off the picture." His eyes bored into Lanford's with sudden intensity. "Do I make myself clear, Mr. Lanford?"

"Yes, sir," Lanford said with a sinking feeling.

"Excellent," Fornier said. "Until tomorrow, then." With a polite nod, he turned and left.

Slowly, Lanford turned around, a sudden white-hot rage burning inside him. Browser was sitting at the bar, swiveled around on his stool to face Lanford, a satisfied smirk plastered across his face. He caught Lanford's eye and lifted his glass in mocking salute.

And suddenly, Lanford had had enough.

He started across the bar, oblivious to the other patrons and the curious eyes now following him. He could kill Browser, he knew. He could kill the man right here, right now.

Sure, there were witnesses. But who cared? He'd been in enough crime dramas to know that witnesses were vague and contradictory and the next best thing to utterly useless. What mattered these days were security cameras and cell phone photos.

And Lanford was invisible to all of them.

He was halfway to Browser now, and he could see the other's smirk starting to slip a little. Maybe he was belatedly realizing that he'd pushed Lanford too far. Realized that death was coming for him.

None of the witnesses would even really focus on his face, Lanford knew. They would all rely on their precious cameras, or else count on everyone else to remember the details. He could kill Browser right here in front of them all and walk right out and never be caught. And maybe after he killed the little swine he would rip open his throat and suck his blood out, draining him like the ghoul he was—

Lanford stopped short, his anger evaporating into sudden horror, his own blood running icy cold.

Suck his *blood* out?

For a long moment he just stood there, all of it rushing back through his mind. Invisible to cameras. Eating an extra-rare steak, though he invariably ordered medium-well. Murder and mutilation on his mind.

He ran his tongue over his upper teeth. Had his canines always been that sharp?

What the hell was happening to him?

He focused on Browser again. The paparazzo's face had gone gray, his earlier smirk completely gone.

And the bar had suddenly gone very quiet. Slowly, his muscles trembling with emotions Lanford couldn't even begin to identify, he backed away through the tables, his eyes darting back and forth between the patrons now staring openly at him. If someone tried to stop him . . .

No one did. He reached the door, took one final look at Browser, and escaped.

Winsley was waiting on his doorstep when he finally arrived home. "*There* you are," he said reproachfully as Lanford opened the door for him. "I don't suppose it occurred to you—"

He broke off with a choked gasp as Lanford grabbed him by the shirt and roughly pulled him close. "What the hell is happening to me?" he demanded, his face inches from Winsley's.

Winsley's face settled into something set in granite as he reached up and effortlessly pried Lanford's fingers off his shirt. "Don't ever do that again," he said quietly.

Lanford swallowed hard. "Sorry."

Winsley nodded, a simple acknowledgment. "I have your anti-dote," he said. Reaching into his pocket, he pulled out another of his small white bottles, this one with a bright yellow ring around the cap. "One pill. You can take it now."

Grabbing the bottle, Lanford crossed to the bar and poured half a glass of water. The pill was also bright yellow, he noted as he washed it down. "How soon before it takes effect?" he asked, heading for the guest bathroom and the big mirror there.

Winsley hesitated. "About three weeks."

Lanford braked to an abrupt halt. "Three *weeks*?"

"That's the best I can do," Winsley said. "I'm sorry."

"No, no, no," Lanford bit out. "You don't understand. I have a job. I have to *be* at that job tomorrow morning."

"So you'll get bounced off a film," Winsley said, a touch of im-patience in his voice. "So what? Actors get bounced all the time."

"*I* don't," Lanford ground out. "Ever. *Especially* not by Kendall Fornier."

"Well, I guess there's a first time for everything," Winsley said, stepping over to the door and taking hold of the knob. "Maybe you can talk him into doing a remake of *The Invisible Man*. Then you can be as invisible on-camera as you want."

Lanford took a deep breath, forcing down the red haze of fury shimmering across his vision. Browser would have been easy to kill. He wasn't so sure about Winsley. "Get out," he said darkly. "And never come back."

"As you wish," Winsley said stiffly. "Oh, and that last blue pill you still have? Keep it. With my compliments."

Pulling open the door, he strode out into the night, closing the door gently behind him.

"Damn," Lanford muttered, sinking down onto the couch and pressing his palms against his throbbing temples. No, Winsley didn't understand. How could he? It wasn't just the work, or the hit his reputation would take if Fornier kicked him off the film.

He needed the *money*, dammit. His houses, his cars, his wine cellar, his girlfriends—none of it came cheap. If he didn't work— if that money didn't come rolling in from somewhere—he was going to be in trouble. Serious trouble. Probably within two weeks.

Only there wasn't going to be any such windfall. The next project after Fornier's wasn't even scheduled to start shooting for another ten weeks. *If* it was on time, which it probably wouldn't be.

What could he do? Take out a loan? Sell off one of his cars? Or two, or even three of them? He winced at the thought. The only thing that got the tabloids salivating more than a new girlfriend was the suggestion that someone was having financial problems. No, he would simply have to find some other way to make a quick couple of bucks.

He stared at the water glass sitting on the bar, the glass that wasn't reflecting his image, an odd thought nagging at the back of his mind.

Why not just *steal* the money?

It would be simple, even simpler than murdering Browser in front of a bar full of witnesses. Every security system in the world relied on cameras, none of which would register him. Even laser systems might not work—he was invisible to mirrors, after all. He could go through the jewelry stores of Beverly Hills like a ghost.

Or just go into Fornier's office and grab some of the piles of cash the old neurotic always kept on hand.

He sighed. And while he was dodging cameras and lasers, some off-duty cop would probably stumble across him and shoot him dead. Wouldn't the tabloids have a field day with *that* one? Lying there in a satin-lined casket, unable even to speak up in his own defense.

To speak in his own defense . . .

Abruptly, he snatched out his phone and punched in his agent's number. "Don, this is Rusty," he said. "Sorry to call you at home."

"No problem," Don assured him. "What's up?"

"You remember that e-mail you sent me a couple of weeks ago from Frank Reynes at FlickerCell Productions? He had that upcoming animated film he wanted me for?"

"And I told him you were booked solid for the rest of the century," Don said. "Why?"

Lanford gripped the phone tightly. "Actually, it looks like I'm going to have a sudden opening in my schedule."

"Oh, no," Don groaned. "You haven't honked off Kendall Fornier, have you?"

"Never mind who I may or may not have honked off," Lanford snapped. "Just set it up, will you?"

The phone hissed a sigh. "Whatever you say, buddy. I'll do it first thing tomorrow. Talk to you later."

Lanford closed the phone. An animated film. Voice work only. No cameras, no film, no paparazzi.

No problem.

"See?" he said aloud to the room around him in his *Return from the Sierra* baritone. "There's always a way. You just have to be smart enough to find it."

Frank Reynes hung up the phone, smiling harder than he'd smiled in weeks. "You, my friend, are a miracle worker," he said to the man sitting across the desk from him. "How in the *world* did you ever convince Rusty Lanford to sign on? And not just one film, either, but the next one, too." He lifted a hand. "No—never mind. I really don't care how you did it."

"I'm glad I could be of service," his visitor said. "You have my check?"

"Right here," Reynes said, pulling the cashier's check from his top drawer and handing it across the desk. "Tell me, would you be interested in another job?"

"At the same price? Of course."

"Here's the thing." Reynes leaned conspiratorially across the desk. "Dame Edith Hartwell would be absolutely perfect to do the three cats in the next film. I've been trying to get her on the phone for weeks, but she's so busy with the ramp-up to *Eden's Fall*—not to mention that new boy-toy of hers, too—that I can't get her to sit still long enough to even listen to my pitch. You think there's anything you can do?"

"Could be," Janick Winsley said, smiling a secret sort of smile. "I'll get back to you."

Lady Fame has always smiled on Rusty Lanford. Now, for a brief moment, she has winked.

It has been said that everyone will someday have their fifteen minutes of fame. When your time comes, bask in the lady's smile if you wish. But beware of her golden chains, for those chains are not easily broken.

And they stretch all the way to the Twilight Zone.

A CHANCE OF
A GHOST

Lucia St. Clair
Robson

Life is a gamble. To win or lose at it depends on what hand Fate deals. But when love was in the cards, Sophie Swensen, a real-life queen of hearts, bluffed death itself. She proved it's never too late to take a chance on romance in the Twilight Zone.

His presence haunts this room to-night,
A form of mingled mist and light
From that far coast.
Welcome beneath this roof of mine!
Welcome! This vacant chair is thine,
Dear guest and ghost!
　　　—HENRY WADSWORTH LONGFELLOW

The postal truck turned off the highway and headed for an adobe ranch house set amid a tumble of boulders. The truck bounced and shimmied down a quarter mile of unpaved driveway barely distinguishable from the high Nevada desert stretching to the mountains around it. The postman rapped twice with the horseshoe hanging from a hook on the battered oak door. When Sophie opened it, he tipped his nongovernment-issue Stetson. He handed her a long cardboard box in which a window shade once had been shipped from the factory. Now it contained a shade of a very different sort.

Sophie carried the package into her parlor. The walking stick inside included instructions for the care of the ghost who came with it, but Sophie didn't notice them in the brown envelope under the shredded paper packing material. She probably wouldn't have opened the envelope if she had. She already knew the cane's story from the auction posting on eBay. An old man living in his daughter's house had recently died at home. Now the daughter's young son was terrified that his grandfather's ghost still lurked in every room.

The boy's mother decided that if she sold the ghost she could convince the child the old man was truly gone. She offered to send his cane along as something tangible. She also asked that the highest bidder write to her son and tell him that his grandfather was happy in his new home.

The description on eBay had said the ghost's name was Gabe, short for Gabriel. It included a grainy, thumbnail-size picture of him as a young man wearing an army uniform from the Truman era. It also featured a photo of the hand-carved cane, but details were impossible to make out.

The real thing was more exotic-looking than Sophie had expected, and certainly worth the seventy-three dollars charged to her credit card. The artist had incised MADE IN HAITI into it, but neglected to add his own name. He had carved the ebony wood into a sinuous snake so realistic it might have frightened someone of less hardy pioneer stock than Sophie. Only on closer inspection did she notice the delicate tracery of wings folded against the creature's back. It was a dragon, not a snake.

Its saw-toothed tail curled up along the length of its belly, with the tip dangling from its mouth. Its eyes were claret-red glass marbles. The sleek head served as the handle. It had been rubbed smooth by the ghost's hand in the years before death made him but a memory of his former self. When Sophie picked up the cane, it warmed to her touch. The curve of the dragon's head seemed to settle into her palm like a weary kestrel coming home to the nest.

Seventy-five years of hard work and harsh weather could have a withering effect on inhabitants of moister climes. In Nevada it turned ranch women like Sophie into living examples of how a human being is supposed to age—erect, strong, fit, tanned, and topped off with horse sense and a generous dollop of kindness.

She knew that the woman's story about her frightened son might be bogus, but it touched her. Besides, an old mule-inflicted knee injury had just now gotten around to bothering her. She could use the cane. More than that, it would make a good yarn to entertain her poker pals.

Sophie's eyes were the crystalline blue of arctic glaciers, courtesy of her Viking ancestors. The beauty she once had been was still evident in the abundant waves of her silvery hair and the strong lines of her jaw and cheekbones. Men had proposed to her—dusty cowboys, laconic ranchers, and even a few hairy prospectors in the old days. She had gracefully declined. She said no man could abide her ornery ways. Truth to tell, she hadn't met a man who seemed worth the effort of explaining herself, not even a little bit.

Sophie remembered that the name of the ghost's six-year-old grandson was Cody. With the side of her hand she swiped a clear surface in the windrow of unopened mail, work gloves, small tools, books, and keys on the kitchen table. In large block letters, with a felt-tip pen, she wrote a letter to Cody, as requested. She printed the boy's return address—a post office box on Deer Isle, Maine— then threw the empty cardboard box into a utility closet.

Before she went to bed that night she leaned the cane against the entryway wall by the front door. The next morning she found it in her recliner. It stood upright on the seat with the dragon's head resting on the chair's back and facing out into the room.

Sophie paced the perimeter of the house, checking every window to make sure all were still locked. No one had broken in last night. She stared at the cane, waiting for it to twitch the tip of its tail or blink its red glass eyes. It remained motionless and noncommital.

She was puzzled, but not alarmed. She had grown up in Paiute country. Most of her childhood friends were Indians. She had heard their grandparents tell stories about shape-shifters. Still, a shape-shifter in a campfire yarn was not the same as one staking a claim to her furniture.

She considered driving the cane into town and lobbing it into a Dumpster, but she wondered if she had the courage to risk its reaction to rejection. Besides, the situation was beginning to intrigue her. She reached out to move it, paused, and pulled back. What if the cane decided to spit out its tail and chomp down on her hand?

Sophie believed that when all else failed, she could fall back on reason. Feeling six kinds of foolish, she stood in front of the chair with her feet planted and her fists on her hips. She made eye contact with the cane, but she spoke to Gabe, the spirit she was beginning to believe inhabited it or at least hung around with it.

"You're a guest in this house, sir. I assume you have the breeding to act like one." She didn't expect a reply, but she paused a few beats while she thought of what to say next.

"I will set you by the fireplace. From there you can see the living room, the dining room, and the kitchen. If that spot doesn't suit you, take over the couch or find a window with a good view. But this chair is mine."

She took a deep breath and picked up the cane. She stood, holding it at arm's length, waiting for it to do something. It stayed as still as a stick of wood should, but when Sophie crossed the room, she felt a chill around her ankles, as if a draft had blown in under the front door.

The next morning the cane was standing next to the recliner, leaning against the arm. While Sophie worked around the house, she kept a wary eye on it. In the evening, she approached the chair as cautiously as she would a horse with a reputation as a biter.

She settled into it, clicked on the television, and absentmindedly laid a hand on the cane. She was astonished by the rush of affection and gratitude that shot like electricity up her arm. It tingled in her fingers. It spread through her chest in a warm wave. She watched her prime-time shows with her palm resting on the smooth curve of its handle.

At bedtime she left it by the chair, but walking away she felt as if she were wading through a cold puddle. She turned around and faced it.

"You can come with me," she said. "But no hanky-pank."

She carried it into the bedroom and leaned it against the nightstand. Fully dressed, she lay down on top of the comforter and pulled an afghan over her. When she turned out the light, she saw a glowing red ribbon around the cane, like a band of neon. It was better than a night-light.

She slept more soundly than she had in years. Gone were the leg cramps and the jittery muscles that forced her to pace through her dark house. Gone was the insomnia that kept her playing solitaire for hours at the kitchen table.

In the morning she found the cane where she had left it. No hanky-pank, although she couldn't imagine what that would have entailed. By now, relief on discovering that Gabe and his walking stick were gentlemen came naturally.

Sophie didn't bother wondering if Gabe's ghost inhabited the cane or merely kept it company. For all the human spirit's faults and shortfalls, it was nothing if not adaptable. A wooden dragon that took midnight rambles and a spook as a roommate had become the norm. But she was curious about the cane's neon glow. She googled auras.

Clear red indicated a powerful, energetic person, competitive, passionate, and sexual. Sexual? She didn't have to look in the mirror to know she was blushing. Could Gabe see her cheeks turn red? For that matter, exactly what could Gabe see?

In the days that followed, Sophie took the cane to the barn when she fed the chickens and goats. She leaned it against the stall while she milked the cow. She had always sung when she worked. Now she felt as though she had an audience, and an appreciative one at that. She started talking to the cane as she did her chores around the house. She told it things she never had told anyone.

One morning she found an anthology of poetry lying open on the floor. It had fallen out of the tall bookcase next to the fireplace. When she picked it up, the English translation of a poem by Heinrich Heine caught her attention.

> *Your eyes' blue depths are lifted*
> *With love and friendship stirred.*
> *They smile, and, lost in dreaming,*
> *I cannot speak a word.*

"I wish you could speak a word," she whispered. "I wish you could tell me everything about youself."

That night, she left the television off and read aloud. She chose a Travis McGee mystery. She had a feeling Gabe would find common ground with John D. MacDonald's gangly, suntanned knight in tarnished armor. If he preferred to hear something else, he would find a way to let her know.

The next day she made her first trip into town with the cane. When Sophie's grandparents had homesteaded this ranch, the nearby hamlet of Hardpan had been a former stage stop. It had consisted of a livery stable, general store, saloon, and an unassuming but piquant little bordello in a whitewashed clapboard cottage with a picket fence.

Traces of gold dust brought a temporary boom. When the traces didn't amount to more than that, Hardpan teetered on the rim of ghost-town status. Even the ladies of the evening closed the shutters of their clapboard cottage and moved on. The old-timers who sat rocking on the porch of the ranch supply store started referring to Hardpan's collection of boarded-up windows as Deadpan.

The promise of jobs in the new metropolis of Las Vegas, an hour's drive to the south, lured away what was left of Hardpan's youth. Sophie's nephew, Skip, was one of them. He and his law school diploma went to work for a firm with offices in a building close enough to Las Vegas Boulevard to reflect the neon glow on its windows at night. If casinos were the primary method of getting rich quick in Las Vegas, litigation was the secondary one.

Lately, however, not even Las Vegas could contain all the people who wanted large quantities of money, and wanted it fast. Two of the three blocks that made up Hardpan's business district each had a new minicasino with a hotel appended. At the edge of town, an eighteen-hole golf course formed a bile-green blot on the desert landscape.

Workmen had pried the plywood off most of the plate glass windows on Main Street. Many of the new shops were boutiques, or bootie-cues as the locals called them, but Sophie didn't mind. She figured gambling and bootie-cue revenue was better than no revenue at all.

Hardpan's only grocery store called itself a supermarket. It was mistaken about the "super" part, but its warped shelves held whatever Sophie needed. After she checked out she put the strap of her purse over her head and adjusted it at an angle across her chest.

She left the store with a brown paper grocery bag tucked in the crook of one elbow and the cane in her other hand. She stopped beside her truck and hooked the dragon's chin over her arm. She was fumbling in the pocket of her jeans for the key when a wild-eyed individual leaped out from behind a dented Dumpster. The word *addict* radiated like sparks from every magenta tip of his spiked hair.

He waved a salad fork at her. A salad fork? He obviously had not thought this heist through carefully.

"Give me your purse."

"I can't." Sophie glanced down at the strap across her chest. "My hands are full."

The logistics of snatching a purse with an old lady still attached to it further befuddled her mugger, which was not a good thing. The look in his eyes grew more feral. Sophie was about to try reasoning with him when the cane leaped straight up off her arm. Had it decided to flee, to abandon her? Sophie dropped the bag of groceries and made a grab for it, but flight was not its plan.

Sophie held on with both hands while it whacked her attacker on the head and shoulders. Gabe must have been in good shape when he died. The speed, force, and solid thunks of the blows made Sophie wince. They would have knocked out anyone not stoked by angel dust, but they didn't faze this boy. He took off running.

The cane chased him across the parking lot and pulled Sophie along much faster than she ever had moved as the star of her high school track team. The cane went horizontal, as though to hit a line drive. It yanked Sophie's arms back, then landed one final clout across the saggy seat of the lad's filthy chinos.

The force of it whirled Sophie around. It sent her attacker fly-ing off the edge of the asphalt and onto a shaggy carpet of cholla, prickly pear, and a sprinkling of horse-crippler cacti that had es-caped the ranchers' wrath and backhoes. Horse-cripplers were aptly named. Their thorns could puncture a truck tire without half trying. The boy picked himself up and hightailed it through them as though they were dandelions.

The cane came to rest at a jaunty shoulder-arms position. Dazed and panting, Sophie headed for the truck. Over the rasp of her own breath she heard someone whistling the "Colonel Bogey March" in the sounding box of her skull.

She didn't remember gathering up the groceries, turning the key in the ignition, or putting the Chevy into gear. She must have done it, though, because fifteen minutes later she pulled into the shed that served as the truck's garage.

With a wrenched shoulder, a skinful of ache, and the theme from *The Bridge on the River Kwai* still resonating in her braincase, she put the groceries away. She had to admit that the situation with the cane had gone beyond a little harmless telekinesis. Was she harboring some psychopath's ectoplasm? She needed more infor-mation about Grandpa.

She booted up her laptop and looked for the eBay posting about the ghost for sale. It had been removed. She consulted the online white pages for the daughter's phone number, but without a last name she had no success. She found Deer Isle, Maine, in her atlas. It seemed small enough for people to know one another by their first names, but when she called the library and the post office, no-body had heard of anyone selling a spook. They told her that even if they knew who the person was, they couldn't release personal in-formation.

She pulled the cardboard box out of the closet and rustled through the paper excelsior in search of information about her

knight in shiny ebony. She found the brown envelope with a letter and a faded black-and-white photo inside. The photo must
have been the original. One corner was creased, and the edges
were worn.

Sophie stared for a long time at the young man in the uniform
with sergeant's stripes on the sleeve. His was not the face of a
psychopath. He had kind eyes, a square jaw, and a carefree smile
on his generous mouth. He looked like just the sort to sport a
Corvette-red aura.

She touched the smile with the tips of her fingers and felt them
tingle. She realized then that this particular electricity was far
from static. Its arc formed a bridge between the past and the present. It connected the living and the dead, a man and a woman.

"You're a handsome one, soldier." Tears stung Sophie's eyes.
"Where have you been all my life?"

She had never been one to waste time on regrets, but she could
not help wishing his path had crossed hers while he was still alive.
How cruel of Fate to introduce them to each other now, when it
was too late. A life together was tricky enough, but a life and a
death together? Impossible.

Maybe Fate knew what it was doing. Maybe the handsome
young sergeant would have been less appealing alive than he was
dead. After all, defunct guys could do no wrong, whereas living
ones screwed up all the time. Sophie stared into those smiling eyes
and knew that Gabe would not have been perfect. No one was. But
he would have been close enough to ideal to suit her.

She rooted through the stack of old picture frames in the closet
until she found one that fit the photo. She set it on the mantel and
sat in the recliner to read the letter.

It started with a thank-you to the ghost's new owner for helping
to ease a young boy's fears. It promised anonimity for the transac-

tion, and assured Sophie that the cane did not have a voodoo curse on it.

A voodoo curse? The description online had said nothing about a curse.

The daughter went on to summarize her father's life, without divulging enough information to track down herself or any other kin. Gabriel was born in Maine in 1933, which made him Sophie's age. As a sergeant in the U.S. Army he had earned the Silver Cross for "valor in the face of the enemy."

When the Korean War ended, he became his family's fifth generation of lobstermen off Maine's rocky coast. Fifteen years ago Gabe's wife had died. His daughter went on to say that when her own marriage broke up five years ago, her father invited her and her ten-month-old son to live with him.

"Dad was a reader and a thinker," the daughter wrote. "A regular philosopher in a lobsterman's galoshes. When I asked him why he would surrender the tranquility of his home to a smelly, squalling baby, he quoted some dead poet, 'There is too much beauty upon this earth for lonely men to bear.'

"As for the cane, Dad said that a dragon eating its own tail is called Ouroboros. It represents the cycle of birth and death. It's an ancient symbol for eternity."

Eternity. Sophie had never spared much thought for mortality, and even less for eternity. Now she was sharing her home with someone who had finished with the former and was facing the latter. That raised a host of questions, not the least of which was: what did he want of her?

That night she changed into her cotton nightshirt, then she fetched the photo and cane from the living room. She set the photo on the nightstand and laid the cane on the other side of the double bed with the dragon's head on the spare pillow. She pulled the covers over her and turned off the lamp. The strip of light around the cane radiated a shimmery red halo onto the white cotton pillow case. Sophie floated into the deepest, most tranquil sleep she had ever experienced.

She was washing the breakfast dishes the next day when the phone rang. The caller ID flashed UNKNOWN NAME, UNKNOWN NUMBER. Sophie went on guard. A person who refused to say who or where he was had something to hide.

A woman's crisp voice instructed her to "please hold for Mr. Smith." While Sophie waited, she was sure she heard in the background the faint chime of slot machines ringing the changes. She didn't like strangers telling her what to do anyway, and when Mr. Smith had kept her on hold a few seconds too long, she hung up.

The phone rang again. "Mrs. Swensen?" This time Mr. Smith had managed to dial the number for himself. Sophie would have congratulated him on his initiative and manual dexterity, but she wasn't in a good enough mood for sarcasm.

"There's no *Mrs.* Swensen living here." Sophie returned the phone to the cradle with more force than necessary.

The phone rang again. Sophie glared at it before she picked it up.

"Am I speaking to Sophie Swensen?"

"Who are you and what do you want?"

"My name is John Smith. I'm a collector of oddities. It's a hobby of mine."

"That answers my first question."

"I want to buy the cane from you."

So much for the promise of anonymity. Sophie wondered how much Mr. Smith had paid Gabe's daughter for her name.

"What cane?" She wanted to ask how he knew about it, but that would tip him off to the fact that she had it.

Sophie could tell from Mr. Smith's tone that he usually got

what he wanted. His voice was warm maple syrup poured over chunks of concrete.

"The cane would make an interesting addition to my little collection, Ms. Swensen. I'll give you . . . three hundred dollars for it."

Sophie was a horse trader and a poker player. She heard the almost imperceptible hesitation between "you" and "three hundred dollars." She figured that if he knew she had bought the cane, he also knew what she had paid.

She could guess his train of thought. He had assumed he would be dealing with a local yokel, a hick who'd be tickled to unload the trinket for the princely sum of a couple of hundred dollars. Instead, she had flipped him a verbal bird, so he had upped the offer to three hundred.

"No, thank you. Good day, Mr. Smith." She heard, "Four hundred dollars . . ." emanating from the receiver on its way back to its base.

John Smith called the next day and each day after that. Their conversations were cordial, but they became a game for Sophie. She was curious to see how much Mr. Smith would pay to own her oddity. When the amount jumped from five thousand to fifty thousand dollars, he mistook her stunned silence for another rejection of his offer.

"One hundred thousand." For the first time, his voice revealed the concrete under the maple syrup. "That's my final offer. I suggest you take it, Ms. Swensen."

"If that's your final offer, then I can count on you not calling here again, Mr. Smith." Sophie laid a little concrete herself, and laced it with gravel. "If that much money is burning a hole in your pocket, why don't you consider donating it to charity?"

Her hand shook as she hung up. She had come to assume that the cane would protect her. Now she had the feeling that she must protect it. She took her grandfather's old six-shooter and holster from the bottom of her sock drawer and cleaned it. She buckled it on when she went to the barn to do her chores. At night, she loaded her father's sawed-off shotgun and stood it next to the bed.

Her mental state of seige went on for most of a week. For five days she jumped whenever the phone rang, but Mr. Smith must have decided to pursue other oddities. Even so, she didn't want to risk someone snatching the cane on the street. Before she drove into town for groceries she leaned it, with apologies, between the broom and the mop in the kitchen closet. She even locked the front door after her, something she'd never bothered to do in the daytime.

She returned home to find the lock jimmied and the house a shambles. The cane was gone, but it had put up a fight. The disarray indicated combatants, and not mere burglars in search of jewelry and spare change. Furniture had been upended, pictures knocked off the wall, and a mirror shattered; but the television, stereo, and computer were still in place.

Sophie called to report the break-in. A slim-hipped young policeman arrived with his hat under his arm, a clipboard in hand, and military creases in his uniform. Sophie didn't recognize him, which proved that Hardpan was indeed growing. Time was when she knew everyone in town.

He surveyed the damage and asked what had been stolen.

"A wooden cane carved in the shape of a dragon."

"What else?"

"That's all."

"Are you sure, ma'am?"

"I'm sure."

"Was the cane valuable?"

"It was to me."

"What would you estimate it was worth, ma'am?"

Sophie wanted to say a hundred thousand dollars, but he wouldn't have believed her. What had made her think she could send the police on a goose chase, searching all the casinos in Nevada for a haunted cane?

"I paid seventy-three dollars for it." She sounded foolish even to herself.

He was polite in that big-sky-eyed "yes, ma'am" way western policeman have. He advised her to file an insurance claim. He told her to call 911 if she saw or heard anything suspicious. He helped her right the furniture. He said "yes, ma'am" a few more times, tipped his hat as he put it on, and left.

Sophie sat in her recliner, stared at the dark television screen, and considered her next move. There certainly would be a next move. Mr. Smith had not seen the hind end of her.

He had sounded too big-time, too wise-guy to be connected with Hardpan's penny-ante casinos. But where in Las Vegas should she begin to search for a collector of oddities named Smith? That would be like looking for one specific sequin in the Old Elvis's entire wardrobe of jumpsuits.

In desperation she called her nephew, Skip. Eyes the pale blue of a Nordic fiord were the only things he had in common with her. He was always nice to her, but she suspected his motives. As her only living relative, he expected to inherit her house, outbuildings, and the eighty acres of desert on which they sat. The house didn't merit the two or three sticks of dynamite required to blow it up, but at the rate Hardpan was expanding, the land would be worth tens of millions one day.

Skip had what was politely called a gambling problem. When he wasn't in his Las Vegas law office or chasing ambulances, his secretary knew to page him in a casino. He might have some idea about Mr. Smith's identity.

Sophie didn't have to spend as much time explaining the situation as she'd expected.

"You bought the ghost that the woman auctioned off on eBay so he wouldn't frighten her son?"

"Yes."

"*You* bought Grandpa's ghost?"

"Yes."

"Then I'm not surprised the cane is gone."

"What do you mean?"

"Aunt Sophie, the auction of the ghost and his cane are all over the Internet. It's been on television and in every newspaper. If you weren't always watching *Jeopardy!* at news time, you'd know that."

"The news is depressing. *Jeopardy!* is educational."

"You're famous. Well, not you exactly. No one knows who the sucker . . . I mean, who the highest bidder was."

"One man knows who the highest bidder was. He said he wanted to buy the cane for his collection of oddities. I wouldn't sell it so he stole it. I want it back."

"Who tried to buy it from you?"

"John Smith, but if that's his name I'm Sophia Loren."

"How much did he offer?"

"A hundred."

"A hundred dollars?"

"A hundred thousand."

"He offered you a hundred thousand dollars?"

Sophie was too upset to enjoy the effect this must be having on her nephew. First he learned that a hundred grand had almost been added to his inheritance. Then he heard that some bastard had stolen what, within a split second, he had come to think of as his own.

Skip's ego was a black hole of self-interest. The light of altruism could not escape it. Sophie was counting on that to set him baying on Mr. Smith's trail like a bloodhound after a pork chop on the lam.

"What's Mr. Smith's phone number?"

"He blocked it on caller ID, but I heard slot machines in the background."

"I'll bet he's the owner of that new casino, the Milagro. He has a display case full of stupid stuff. He paid fifty-eight thousand for a pizza with the image of the Virgin Mary in the cheese. He even bought Napoleon's penis, for chrissake. He keeps it in a pickle jar."

The fact that Mr. Smith might have a sense of humor about Napoleon Bonaparte's personal gherkin was lost on Sophie. The last thing she wanted was for her nephew to hear her cry, but the full impact of the theft finally hit her.

"I want him back."

"What do you mean? Who's 'him'?"

"Gabe."

"Gabe?"

"The boy's grandfather."

"Gramps came with the cane?"

"Yes."

Technology for videophones had been around for decades, but there was a reason why they'd been slow to catch on. Sometimes a person doesn't want to be seen, and not just because he's taking the call in the john.

Sophie's nephew wouldn't have wanted her to see the grin on his face when he heard that she thought she had bought a real-dead ghost. Now he wouldn't have to wait for her to die, which, given her tough-as-toenails constitution, could take another twenty years. He could have her declared mentally incompetent and seize control of her land and considerable savings, plus whatever sum he would wring from the owner of the Milagro.

When large amounts of money were involved, Skip was very

good at bluff and persuasion. He would go to the Milagro and take a photo of the cane. It probably still had Aunt Sophie's fingerprints all over it. In return for telling his aunt that some anonymous Atlantic City mogul had bought it, he would demand a cut of the hundred grand Mr. Smith had saved with his sticky-fingered discount.

He was confident that Mr. Smith would agree. Men like him had as much ego as money invested in whatever their particular obsession might be. What was the use of scoring the cane if he couldn't display it without some old lady making a fuss and getting her picture in all the papers?

"I'll look for Mr. Smith, Aunt Sophie, and I'll call you in the next couple days."

Sophie hardly slept that night and she spent the next day pacing. When her nephew didn't get in touch the second day, she called his office. His secretary said no one had seen him and he wasn't answering his pager.

Still wearing the clothes she had put on to clean the barn that morning, Sophie drove over the mountain pass to Vegas. Usually she steered her old Chevy into the slow lane and stayed there. Today she passed everything on the road, including the owner of a Cadillac convertible who was taking his ratty gray ponytail for a spin with the top down.

She arrived at the casino to find the entrance ringed by police cars, utility vehicles, and media vans with rooftop satellite dishes sprouting like mushrooms. A large crowd of spectators and casino employees had gathered in the parking lot. Most looked merely curious, but a few held signs advising the unsaved to prepare for the Apocalypse.

Sophie walked unchallenged past the barricade of yellow tape. Computer geeks, security guards, policemen, and executive suits swarmed inside. The geeks hovered among ranks of slot machines that were silent for the first time ever. The security personnel tried to look in charge of a situation that was clearly out of control. The police were interviewing a gaggle of hysterical women, slots players by the look of them. The suits stood in a worried clot, their cash-register brains calculating the losses from the unplugged one-armed bandits.

Sophie wondered if Mr. Smith was among them. She hoped so. Slot machines once had been gambling's stepchildren. Now they accounted for 70 percent of casino profits. When slots players weren't happy, nobody was happy. And Sophie could see that at least some of Milagro's slots players were very unhappy indeed.

The casino's main hall was as big as three football fields. Sophie walked to the far end where a glass display case spanned the wall from side to side and from floor to ceiling. It contained oddities alright. The Holy Mother of Pizza, a two-headed snake, and a stuffed, five-legged calf were only a few examples of the bizarre, the grotesque, and the downright screwball. There was even the pickle jar with what looked like a piece of blackened shoelace suspended in a vitreous substance. The label claimed it was Napoleon's penis. If that was true, it explained a great deal about the man. Poor Josephine.

Sophie saw only the long mahogany case, lined in red velvet, propped upright with the lid open to reveal the cane inside. She stood with the palms of her hands pressed against glass that had to be bulletproof. She wanted to take a swing at it with one of the wrought iron bar stools, but she was sure that whatever hit it would bounce off. Also, she could not be of any use to Gabe if she was in a jail cell.

She decided to go in search of Mr. Smith's office. Maybe security would mistake her for a cleaning woman. Maybe the key was in Mr. Smith's desk drawer. Maybe the drawer was unlocked. Maybe everyone would be too busy with the defective slot machines to notice her take it.

She wouldn't have wagered a plug nickel on the success of the plan, but it was the only one she had.

As she turned to go, her sweaty palm stuck to the glass. She felt it move sideways ever so slightly. The sliding glass panel was unlocked. What was it the old sage had said when an earnest pilgrim asked him for the key to the universe? "The bad news is, there is no key. The good news is, it isn't locked."

Sophie slid the panel open enough to reach in. She took what she had come for and closed the door again.

Pretending to lean on the cane for support, she headed for the front of the building. When anyone got in her way she gave the dragon a subtle wave and they moved aside without appearing to see her. She felt like Moses parting the Red Sea with his staff.

She stopped at the two slot machines that were preoccupying a dozen techies with gizmo belts slung low on their hips. The machines had levers for the nostalgic players to pull, but since the innards were computerized, a button served just as well. The repairmen had taken off the machines' back panels and were poking at the circuitry, the reels, and the random-number generator inside each one.

From the front, the slot machines looked like all the others. Then Sophie took a closer at one of them. It had a picture of a sprig of cherries in the left-hand window, but the watery blue eyes of Sophie's nephew stared, terrified, from the other two.

Sophie stood transfixed. She didn't know if Gabe had had anything to do with this, but she would have to figure out a way to ask him. Maybe she could persuade him to use his influence on the Other Side to spring the poor sap's soul from slots hell.

She turned around to see what was wrong with the machine

across from her nephew's. It displayed one lemon and two eyes as dark and bitter as cold coffee grounds. They stared at her without fear or remorse. The Devil had better watch his back.

"Mr. Smith, I presume," Sophie murmured. She lifted the cane in salute. "*Arrivederci*, wise guy."

No one saw her leave and walk out into the crowded parking lot. Among the protesters, gawkers, ranters, and exhibitionists gathered there, no one thought it odd when a silver-haired woman in faded blue jeans, a flannel shirt, and manure-smeared sneakers began to dance a jig around her cane. No one noticed her pick it up and waltz away with it among the flashing blue and red strobes of the police cars' lights.

Sophie's nephew and Mr. Smith learned the hard way that they couldn't beat the odds in a game of good and evil. Treachery and avarice don't stand a ghost of a chance in the Twilight Zone.

THE STREET THAT FORGOT TIME

Deborah Chester

Corporate employee Nick Penby is a workaholic in a modern, fast-paced world. Caught in his daily grind, he lives alone, a solitary, hardworking man cast adrift from friends and neighbors, and far too busy to slow down. Eager to streamline his life, he's recently moved into a new, attractive community that promises every convenience and amenity. Yet, Nick Penby is about to discover that his dream of a quiet neighborhood may just turn out to be his worst nightmare when he moves into . . . the Twilight Zone.

I f it hadn't been for the dog, Nick Penby might not have noticed anything seriously wrong with his neighborhood.

It was dusk. He was driving home almost on autopilot after a long day at the office, his mind numb from hours of battling figures. A light, drizzling mist was falling, and there, glimpsed between sweeps of the wipers, sat the dog, hunkered down in his driveway, its eyes shining in the car headlights.

"Christ!" He slammed on the brakes.

Bedraggled and wet, of no particular breed, the dog didn't run.

Wide awake now, Nick rolled down his window, letting the drizzle come in, and flapped his hand at the animal. "Shoo! Get out of the way!"

It didn't move.

Grumbling to himself, he thrust open his car door and marched up to the dog. "Go home! You don't belong here. Get out of the way, you stupid mutt!"

The dog stood up, took one limping step, and sat down again, holding up its front paw. Looking into its gentle eyes, Nick felt some of the day's pressures ease from his tense shoulders. He blinked against the pelting rain, and crouched beside the dog to let it sniff his hand.

It didn't seem to be afraid of him. With dignity, it gave his fingers a quick lick, then went back to staring at him with that same beseeching gaze.

Nick found himself petting the dog. "How'd you get hurt, huh?"

His fingers dug through the dog's wet fur for a collar. None. He felt a spurt of irritation. "So what's wrong with your owner, letting you go out on a night like this without your tags?"

Nuzzling his hand, the dog whined softly.

Nick went back to his car and raised the garage door. Then he ran his hands gently over the dog's body, testing for any sore spots that might make the animal snap in pain, and gingerly picked it up. He was going to have dog hair all over his new suit. Again, he felt a spurt of irritation before dismissing it. Didn't matter. Free pickup and delivery to the dry cleaner's was just one of many conveniences in Haven Estates.

Carrying the dog into his utility room, he put it on top of the washer to look at its paw. The pad was badly cracked and bleeding a little. A sharp sandbur was stuck into it as well. It took a while to pick the burr out. The dog flinched a little and whined, but didn't object, as though it realized he was trying to help it. By the time he finished, Nick had managed to stick the burr into his own finger, which meant some awkward work with the tweezers and a liberal dose of antiseptic for both of them.

Wagging its tail, the dog gave Nick a quick slurp on his chin.

"Hey!" he said in sharp protest, then smiled, enjoying the dog's wiggling gratitude. "You're welcome, old buddy. I guess that sticker was really hurting you."

He hadn't owned a dog since high school. In college, no time or money; since then, too busy with the fast-lane trajectory of his career. But tonight, he found himself enjoying the little chores of filling a bowl with water and spreading out a couple of towels and an old blanket on the floor. The dog drank thirstily before curling up, licking its paw, and resting while Nick parked his car in the near-empty garage that held only a dusty set of unused golf clubs and an equally unused toolbox. Normally he ate takeout, but he wasn't sure the dog would like Chinese food. Earlier that week, he'd ordered groceries online, and his refrigerator was well stocked. Finding some hamburger meat, he hunted through his cupboards for a skillet to cook it in, and ended up scrambling enough for both of them.

Usually, by this time of night—almost eight—he was back on his laptop, putting in some extra work. That had been his routine since moving here: up at six, on the commute to the city by seven-fifteen, home by six or seven, dinner, a couple of beers, and back on the laptop until bedtime. Four months ago, he'd accepted a promotion and job transfer, moving into this quiet, spanking-new neighborhood that was close enough to the city to work but gave him a complete change. He'd done the hip urban scene: the downtown loft with an edgy vibe of cement and exposed pipe, lots of parties, even the trendy, live-in girlfriend. Now Whitney was gone, the loft was gone, and the parties didn't matter anymore. All he wanted was peace and quiet so he could work. He'd found it here in Haven Estates, on a suburban street called Ladybrook Lane, and until tonight he'd been grateful for the numbness of his routine that gave him no reason to think or bother.

Now, however, he found himself restless, unwilling to settle down at the computer and bored with the thought of TV, even one as amazing as the superwide, superhigh-resolution flat panel hanging on his wall. Compliments of the builder when he moved in, it was calibrated for amazing picture quality and plugged into the latest, newest, highest-tech wiring currently available for the residential market. In fact, he lived in a so-called Clever Home. He could program the lights and the sealed, gas-log fireplace to come on, the oven to be preheating, and his preselected on-demand movie to be playing the moment he walked in the door.

When he'd first moved in, he'd loved all the gadgetry. Now he took it for granted and didn't use half the features. After all, when he wasn't working, he was sleeping.

Except tonight. He checked on the dog, now snoring. It hadn't left the utility room to venture into the rest of his house, as though it sensed it might not be welcome.

Leaning against the doorjamb, Nick frowned at it. Now that its coat was dry, it had turned into a cute, gray-and-white fluffy dog with expressive eyebrows and a beard, all packed into a medium-size package.

Wouldn't cost much to feed, he found himself thinking.

Alarmed, he started figuring out how he was going to find the dog's owner. Some little kid somewhere was probably crying for it right now.

Slipping on a jacket, he walked to the house next door. The lights were still on. He heard the muffled sounds of a television playing. During the four months he'd lived on this street, he'd yet to meet the couple. Until now, he hadn't been interested in them. He'd probably transfer out next year anyway. Why get involved?

Nobody answered the doorbell beneath the small plaque that said ANDERSON. Shivering a little in the cool March night, Nick fidgeted on their porch before ringing the bell again. Then he knocked. No one came.

Muttering to himself about people who fell asleep with their lights and TV going, he headed across the street. No one answered the door there, either. As for the two-story house on the other side of him, the one that must have little kids because now and then he saw small bicycles and scooters lying in the driveway, all the lights were out. Besides, he didn't think the dog was theirs. He'd never noticed one barking in their backyard.

So he went home, and, instead of watching the late news, he made flyers to post in the neighborhood before he left for work in the morning.

A week later, Nick figured he now owned a dog. No one had called in response to his flyers. Maintenance had cleared them so quickly that he wasn't sure anyone had seen them. No one had answered the Found ad he ran in the newspaper. No one had advertised for a lost, gray-and-white dog, either. He had carried the dog up and down Ladybrook, knocking on doors, but no one had answered, and he'd never seen any kids out playing whom he could ask.

"I've done my best," he said as Buddy reared up on his knees and wiggled all over. "I guess you dropped in from outer space, because no one seems to think you're missing."

As strays went, Buddy was a gem. He was housebroken and well-mannered. He didn't bark excessively, dig holes in Nick's backyard, or steal food. As soon as his paw healed, however, he began to pester Nick every evening whenever Nick picked up the TV remote. He either brought Nick his squeaky toy for a game or he would bark and run to the front door, begging for a walk.

So Nick bought a leash and collar on his lunch hour, and left work promptly at five, instead of lingering an extra hour or two like usual. He turned through his neighborhood gates, smiling with anticipation, and saw a handful of people strolling the sidewalks. Cars were pouring home. Ladybrook Lane looked livelier than he'd ever seen it since he moved in. He rushed inside, greeted an ecstatic Buddy, fastened on the new collar, found his old sneakers, and headed out. He figured he could meet his neighbors, start learning his way around, maybe even make an acquaintance or two.

But something strange was going on. Nick frowned, looking in all directions. Ten minutes before, the street had been a beehive. Now it was deserted. Except for him and Buddy, there was not another individual to be seen. Just rows of neat houses in small yards, lined up in perfect formation.

The same thing happened the next evening. And the next.

Nick and Buddy explored every street in Haven Estates, all eight of them, and saw not a single individual. No one out working in his garage with the door up. No kids playing on front lawns. No dogs barking when he and Buddy walked past yard fences.

It was eerie, unnatural. Like walking through a ghost town.

Okay, sure, maybe his timing in getting home was out of sync with everyone else's, but not every time. In a planned neighborhood of 352 houses with a 90 percent occupancy, the law of averages said that eventually he had to meet at least one other person outdoors, but he didn't.

Nick was a commercial real-estate insurance adjuster, so the more hours he billed, the more commissions he earned. Normally, he worked on weekends, too, but when Saturday rolled around, he opted to stay home, and opened the front blinds of his house so he could watch his neighbors.

"This is it," he said to Buddy. "I'm now my grandfather, officially nuts, with nothing better to do than spy on people and make up stories about them."

Anderson, from next door, walked out to his mailbox.

Nick shot outside with a big, goofy smile. "Hi, neighbor!" he yelled, waving.

Anderson, tall, slightly bald, and middle-aged, hesitated for a long moment before lifting his hand perfunctorily. Without another glance in Nick's direction, he walked back into his house.

"Friendly type," Nick said, frowning. He settled down in his chair to stare out the window, but aside from a couple of cars that drove by, nothing happened.

Bored, he wondered what Saturday chores he could do. Cleaning and yard work were provided by the maintenance staff. Sighing, he gave Buddy a bath.

Through the thin walls of his house, he heard the people on his other side talking as they walked out to their driveway, and the muted chatter of children. Tossing the wet towel at Buddy, he hurried outside again.

Just as they slammed their white SUV doors and drove away.

Standing in his front yard, Nick looked up and down his street. At the south end he saw a woman picking up her newspaper like a sleepwalker. At the north end, he heard children shrieking and yelling, although he didn't see them. A normal Saturday, he thought.

His frown deepened. There was something wrong, though. He couldn't put his finger on it, but something about his street was off-kilter.

Exactly eighteen minutes later, the white SUV returned. For the rest of the day, it left every two hours, returning each time exactly eighteen minutes later. Nick was baffled. He'd once clocked the distance to the nearest shopping area, and about all that was possible in eighteen minutes was to buy a newspaper at a corner convenience store and come straight back. But no one would do that multiple times in a single day.

Anderson, he noticed, walked to the end of his driveway and back at equal intervals. The man didn't look around, wave at anyone, or change expression.

That afternoon, Nick planned to take Buddy out right after lunch. But a phone call from his boss tied him up. He prepared a report, with a ball game playing in the background, and the afternoon flew by. Before he knew it, twilight was darkening the windows and Buddy was lying by the front door with his head morosely on his paws.

"Hey, I'm sorry," Nick said, genuinely penitent. "I lost track of time."

He grabbed his jacket and Buddy's leash, and they headed outside. It was nearly dark, darker than Nick preferred. But the breeze was mild and balmy, very damp as though a storm might be brewing. No one was outside at this hour, although when he was a kid Nick and his friends would have been jumping hedges and trying to shine flashlights at possums to make them freeze and hiss. Times had sure changed, Nick thought, and laughed at himself for thinking something his father used to say.

As he and Buddy walked along, they saw yellow lights shining from windows, but all the blinds were drawn and all the garage doors were down. Not like old Mrs. Gregor, who lived on the street where he grew up. Every night, she left the drapes of her dining room window open to show off her highly polished furniture. And Nick's dad was always phoning the old man across the street, who regularly forgot to close his garage door after smoking there in the evenings.

But here, people didn't seem to forget anything. Probably because their Clever Homes sounded a low, pleasant chime when they failed to lower the garage door within a certain number of minutes. Nick drew in a deep breath of the pleasant spring air, musing about how he might disconnect that feature. He felt tempted to mess up some of the relentless perfection around here. Let grass grow over a flower bed, leave the curtains open, put a lawn chair on the roof, plant those plastic pink flamingos in the front yard, blast his stereo at three in the morning . . . something to loosen this place up a little.

Down on Crestmont Court, he thought he heard a woman

screaming in one of the houses, but the noise faded before he could be sure. By the time he reached the end of the cul-de-sac, he decided he'd imagined it.

The light wind died, leaving air so still and moist that Nick thought it might rain. Even so, he didn't turn back. Crestmont Court was one of the newest streets at the very edge of the neighborhood, and still had several vacant lots. The streetlights were set far apart, and they were growing dimmer as the fog closed in.

Without warning, Buddy suddenly yelped and jumped sideways about two feet, nearly yanking the leash from Nick's hand. Nick was strong enough to keep him from running away, but the dog stood cringing with his tail between his hind legs, staring at something Nick couldn't see.

"Easy, boy. What's wrong with you?" Nick asked. When he ran his hand over Buddy he felt the tension in the dog's neck and down his spine. Buddy was trembling, and he edged closer to Nick.

Petting the dog in reassurance, Nick looked around.

Only one house had been built down here at the very end of the cul-de-sac. Empty lots lay on either side of it. The house was dark, whether empty or simply no one at home, Nick couldn't tell. FOR SALE signs weren't allowed by the HOA. The place looked innocuous enough: bricked single story with a tidy row of spiky bushes in the basic landscaping package. Nothing, not even the crickets, made a sound.

"I don't see anything here to scare you, Buddy. Let's go home."

Buddy finally took a few frightened steps, dodging a place on the pavement that had nothing visibly wrong with it. The farther they got from the dark house, the more Buddy relaxed, until he was once more trotting along. But his tail stayed down, and now and then he looked back apprehensively.

Partway along the street, a cement drain channel ran between two houses, feeding into Ladybrook, which ran behind Crestmont Court. Buddy abruptly dragged him toward the channel. A sign was posted there: NO UNAUTHORIZED PERSONNEL.

"Stop, Buddy," Nick said firmly, holding him back. "No prowling expeditions tonight. No unauthorized shortcuts. Let's stick to the sidewalk."

Buddy dug in, pulling harder, and the reawakening imp in Nick surrendered. He hadn't thwarted authority this harmlessly since high school, when he'd made it his mission to enter every area marked KEEP OUT. The drainage channel ran maybe three feet lower than ground level. Paved, clean, and dry, it made an efficient shortcut home.

When they emerged on Ladybrook, Buddy planted all four feet and locked his attention on something Nick couldn't see in the fog. Nick tugged on the leash, but Buddy took only a step or two before turning around again. He whined softly.

Alone on the deserted, fog-shrouded street, Nick wasn't sure he wanted to know what was approaching. He heard footsteps, and glimpsed a pale figure approaching through the mist. Squinting, he made out a woman in a light-colored raincoat, walking a small, white terrier.

Buddy danced with excitement, still whining.

Nick felt excited, too. Suddenly all his recent speculations seemed foolish. "You see?" he said to Buddy. "We're not in a ghost town after all."

Buddy strained at the leash again, and this time Nick went along, stopping under the nearest streetlight and waiting politely where the woman and her West Highland terrier could see him clearly. Wagging his tail, Buddy uttered a short, happy woof.

The woman seemed startled, and stopped a safe distance away.

"Hello," Nick said with casual friendliness. "Sorry to look like I'm lurking. I live on this street, that way." He pointed, while Buddy strained to sniff noses with the Westie. "My dog's dying to meet your dog, so we waited here. Your dog's pretty."

"Thanks."

The woman was maybe thirty, with smooth, dark hair cut chin-length. He couldn't see her well in the gloom, but her voice was pleasant. "I just moved here," she said, sounding wary. "Cotton and I are trying to learn our way around."

"Well, great! Welcome to the neighborhood! I'm Nick Penby. And this is Buddy." He was conscious of his voice sounding too loud and hearty. "When did you move in?"

"Today." She shortened her dog's leash, as though ready to go on.

Nick pulled Buddy back. "A pleasure to meet you, uh . . ."

"Erin. Bye."

She walked on briskly. Nick watched her appreciatively, taking note of the gray brick house that she went into. There was a U-Haul parked in the driveway. He hadn't noticed a FOR SALE sign in the yard, but then there never were any. People moved in and moved out without fanfare, much the same way he himself had done a few months ago. The corporate life, he thought with sudden dissatisfaction. This rootless, transitory existence was no way to really live. And this so-called perfect community he'd moved into wasn't a real community at all. At least, not until now. He felt immeasurably cheered by having finally talked to a neighbor. Especially a good-looking one.

"Very nice, Buddy," Nick said happily. "Good job, boy. I guess this place is improving, huh?"

Buddy panted contentedly.

The next two evenings, Nick and Buddy prowled the neighborhood in hopes of seeing Erin and Cotton again. No luck. They were back to the same old deserted emptiness, and Nick's uneasy feelings about Haven Estates returned.

Then he saw Erin standing in her front yard one afternoon as he was coming home from work. She was wearing jeans and a bright pink sweatshirt, and she was trying to cut down and flatten a pile of cardboard boxes.

He pulled in along the curb and jumped out. "Hi! Need help?"

She stared at him for a moment, looking unsure.

"I'm Nick. Our dogs met the other night."

"Oh, the guy with Buddy!" she said, smiling now. She crossed the small yard to him, holding out her slender hand. She shook firmly, and he liked her pretty, dark brown eyes. She wore minimal makeup—very unlike Whitney's elaborate maquillage—and he liked the faint dusting of freckles on her nose.

She laughed, a bit self-consciously. "Sorry. I guess you think it's rude, me remembering the dog's name instead of yours."

"Getting settled in?" he asked.

She nodded. "Almost. I start my new job on Monday, so I've been pretty busy." She hesitated. "Do—you said you live here on Ladybrook, right?"

"Yes." He pointed. "Down that way. Number 3501. Red brick, white shutters. Classic fake neo-nonstyle Colonial."

When she laughed, he felt encouraged. All the while, his gaze was taking in the details . . . the small number of boxes still unpacked in the garage, along with a kitchen table and chairs . . . only one car parked in the driveway. She was single, he hoped.

He decided to take a chance, give her an opening if she wanted it. "If there's anything you need help with, don't hesitate to ask."

"Well . . ."

He grinned. "Name it! That table over there?"

"I'm getting rid of it because it won't go through the doorway. No, I can't figure out my breaker box. I called maintenance, but they want to schedule a training session on how to customize my Clever Home settings." As she spoke, she rolled her eyes.

Nick laughed. "Part of the package."

"Yes, but I want to understand my breakers, in case of an emergency."

"We don't have emergencies in Haven Estates," Nick said, imitating the sales pitch featured on the HOA's Web site.

She wrinkled her freckled nose at him, looking stubborn. "My dad taught me to always be prepared."

Grinning, Nick dealt with the breakers, flipping them and listening for her to call out from inside the house. As the breakers were sorted out, he labeled them for her, and realized he was enjoying himself. After months inside his smooth-running Clever Home, he'd almost forgotten how much satisfaction a simple household chore could provide.

"Thanks," she said, smiling, when they were done. "I could have handled it by myself, but it was going to take forever, running back and forth."

"Maintenance should have identified everything for you before you moved in."

She shrugged. "I'm not used to all the service they provide here. I bought this place online. You know, visual tour, new construction, too much in a hurry to look in person." She hesitated. "Very enticing incentive package."

He grinned. "The flat panel with all the bells and whistles?"

"Right. And it interfaces with my computer like you wouldn't believe. Only . . ." She hesitated, frowning.

"Problem?"

"Did you get one of these?" She handed over a letter.

It was from the HOA, listing rules for using the park, pool, and small clubhouse.

"I looked up the full set of association rules online before I purchased the house," Erin said. "I was okay with it. Then this letter is waiting in my mailbox the day after I move in. Did you read this part?" She pointed at one line.

"No dogs allowed?" A strange feeling blossomed in his chest. "No way."

"I read the rules," she insisted, looking near tears. "There was nothing mentioned about not having pets. I mean, I wouldn't have moved here if I'd known."

Angrily, Nick was shaking his head. He wasn't giving up Buddy because of some stupid rule. "I didn't get one of these letters." He read it again. "Weird."

"So I e-mailed the HOA president and was told it's a new policy." Scowling, she tossed her dark hair. "We're owners, not tenants. This isn't right. Cotton is my baby. We just got here, and I start my new job on Monday, and now—"

"Hey," Nick said, trying to reassure her. "I don't think they can enforce this. I think we have to vote on it or something for it to go through."

Her face still looked stormy as she crammed the letter back into its envelope. "It's a mean trick. Some kind of bait-and-switch tactic."

"They can't make you get rid of your dog. Don't worry about it. These HOA things move slowly. Maybe a neighbor complained or something—"

Next door, a car door slammed, and they watched a sleek black Nissan with dark-tinted windows pull away.

Erin made a face. "I tried to meet those people, but no luck as yet."

"Wouldn't answer when you knocked?" Nick asked in sympathy.

She shot him a puzzled look. "Yeah. In fact, you're the only person I've met all week. In my last place, I barely backed my U-Haul in the driveway and the neighbors were all over me, inviting me to supper and bringing me casseroles and brownies." The worry returned to her face. "Now I've got someone complaining about my dog."

"I'll let you know if I get one of those letters, too."

She tried to smile, but it didn't quite work.

He stared at her for a moment, with his head cocked to one side. "Want me to see if I can move that table into the house for you? Seems a shame to throw it out if I can get the top to come off."

So, once the table was reassembled in her spotless little kitchen, she ordered takeout and offered him supper. Nick dashed home and fed Buddy, then spent a pleasant evening with Erin, cutting down boxes for her while she unpacked. She didn't have a lot.

"Divorced?" he asked, hoping she wasn't going to think him too personal.

She nodded, but didn't say anything else, and he let it drop. Clearly the hurt was fresh, and he wasn't going to poke at a sore wound.

She didn't invite him again, and Nick was okay with that. He waved when he saw her walking Cotton or planting flowers in her small front yard, and gave her space. But as the days went by, he saw her less and less. Assuming she was busy with her new job, he shrugged it off. But he was disappointed, too, and he knew from the way Buddy perked up when they passed Erin's house that the dog was hoping to see Cotton. It was as though Haven Estates had swallowed them up, and Nick and Buddy were back in ghost town. Even the flowers she'd planted disappeared one day, and Nick figured maybe she was so busy she'd let them die.

One of the letters containing the no-dog policy appeared in his mailbox, but Nick didn't call her about it as he'd promised. He tore up the letter and threw it away. Buddy was a quiet, well-behaved dog that didn't bark excessively in the backyard. Nick had put a padlock on the yard gate to further secure Buddy, and he told himself these HOA bozos had no say in what he did on his own property.

Then, the first big thunderstorm of spring hit. There was a black, evil sky with storm clouds roiling overhead when Nick got home that evening. Out here on the prairie, where houses were built on flat, open ground and tornadoes sometimes churned everything into splinters, spring storms could get very fierce. Glad to be off the interstate before the pyrotechnics hit, he drove into his garage just as the first fat drops began to pelt down. Thunder rumbled overhead, and a flash of lightning made the power flicker, jamming the garage-door opener.

Grumbling, Nick fiddled with the switch, trying to get the thing to shut. On the other side of the utility door he could hear Buddy scratching and barking. Finally the garage door whirred and started lowering. Relieved, Nick opened the utility door to go in, but Buddy shot past him and streaked through the garage and outside just before the door came down.

"Hey!" Nick shouted.

He pushed the button to lift the door again, but the opener jammed, squealing as the motor burned out. Cutting it off, he tossed his keys and briefcase aside, grabbed Buddy's leash, and ran out the front door.

The rain was coming down at an angle, soaking through his suit. He looked in all directions, but Buddy was already out of sight.

"Buddy!" he yelled, suddenly scared. "Buddy, come back!"

He had the awful feeling that Buddy might have done this before. Maybe that's how the dog had come to be lost in the first place. Now he might never see Buddy again, and the idea of being back in that lonely, dronelike existence he'd been living before Buddy had come along drove him out into the street. He started running, wincing every time lightning forked across the sky. He could imagine the headlines: MAN KILLED BY LIGHTNING WHILE CHASING DOG.

"Buddy!" he yelled. "Hey, boy! Come on!"

His next-door neighbor's white SUV came down the street toward him. Nick waved, hoping the driver would stop. He wanted to ask the family to be on the lookout for his dog. But the vehicle drove straight for him, never veering.

Astonished, Nick barely jumped out of the way in time. Without stopping, the SUV pulled into its driveway and inside the garage. The door came down before anyone got out of the car. No one ran out to see if Nick was hurt or even waved in apology.

Fuming, he went on searching for Buddy, taking care now to use the sidewalk. He was halfway across the driveway of Erin's neighbor when the black Nissan zoomed into sight. Instead of pausing to let him cross the rest of the way, the Nissan pulled in, clipping him hard enough to spin him off his feet. Sprawling, Nick lay there, half stunned. His leg hurt like blazes.

Sheer anger propelled him to his feet. "Hey!" Nick shouted. Furious, he pounded on the dark-tinted window as the car paused there, waiting for its garage to open. "You bastard! Are you crazy or something?"

The driver, unseen behind dark windows, didn't respond. As the Nissan pulled into its empty garage, Nick decided he wasn't going to let this guy get away with it.

He ducked inside the garage just as the driver's door opened. Nick grabbed it from the driver's hands as the man got out. "Now see here, you—"

He found himself staring into a pair of dead eyes. He'd never looked into a gaze so void of personality or feeling. The guy was maybe in his forties, with thinning hair expertly trimmed. His green eyes were bloodshot and red rimmed. And as they stared into Nick's they held nothing at all.

The man didn't speak, just went on staring through Nick. Creeped out, Nick balled his fist and socked the guy in the jaw, making him stagger. "Think about *that* the next time you run down a pedestrian, you stoned son of a bitch."

Limping outside, he stood on the driveway in the rain as the garage door closed.

"Jerk," he muttered.

Worry about Buddy sent him hobbling onward. As soon as he found his dog, though, he would be sending complaints to the HOA and the cops.

All eight streets of the neighborhood later, and still no sign of his dog. Exhausted, soaked to the skin, hurting as his leg stiffened more and more, Nick kept on searching. It was dark now. The worst of the thunder and lightning had moved on, rumbling to the east, but the rain was still pounding down so hard that he could barely hear his voice every time he shouted. He just hoped that poor Buddy would come to him.

A dog's yelping cry caught his attention. He was on Crestmont Court by now, and the street was ankle-deep with water the storm drains could not handle.

"Buddy!" he bawled at the top of his lungs.

A bark answered him.

Down at the end of the cul-de-sac, he saw a pair of men by the isolated house. They were struggling to put a gray-and-white dog into the trunk of a car.

Nick never stopped to think. "Hey!" he shouted angrily. "You there! That's my dog!"

They ignored him, one raising the trunk lid higher as the other man tried to shove a struggling Buddy inside.

"Buddy!" Nick yelled anxiously. "Come here, boy! Buddy!"

With a snarl, Buddy squirmed free. He came streaking to Nick, who knelt and caught him in relief, clutching the panting, shaking dog tight.

"There's my Buddy," he said breathlessly. "There's my good boy."

A car engine roared to life, and tires squealed as the dognappers' automobile peeled from the driveway and gunned straight for Nick. Half blinded by the headlights, he felt himself frozen by sheer astonishment, but only for a split second.

Grabbing Buddy, he flung himself to one side, rolling over as the car swept past, missing him by inches. Lying there as the rushing water gurgled into the swollen storm drain, Nick tried to catch his breath. Being nearly run over three times in one evening was no coincidence. In his arms, Buddy was trembling. After a moment the dog gave him a small lick on his chin.

Nick's heart was pounding so hard that he thought he might pass out. Finally, he managed to sit up. Still clutching Buddy, he fumbled around, intending to clip the leash securely to his dog's collar before he stood. But Buddy's collar was gone. In its place was a too-tight nylon strap with a small plastic box affixed to it. A short, blunt wire like an antenna poked out of the box.

"What the hell is this?" Nick asked, while Buddy whimpered and rubbed his head against Nick's chest. The dog pawed at his ears, whining harder, and scratched violently at the strap.

"Okay. Hold on. Let's get this thing off."

Nick fumbled with the strap until he finally succeeded in pulling it free. He turned it over in his hands, curious about what it might be, but Buddy was still whining and shaking his ears.

On impulse, Nick tossed it into the storm drain, letting it disappear in the swirling water. As though some signal it was emitting had shorted out, Buddy stopped whimpering and jumped at Nick, licking his face with joy.

"Good boy," Nick said, rubbing his ears until Buddy winced. "Got a problem there? Want me to look?"

Buddy shook his head violently, making his ears flap, and whined softly.

"Okay," Nick said, scratching Buddy's chin instead. "Don't run away from me again, promise?"

Just to be safe, he made a slip knot in the leash and put that on Buddy before he stood up.

Pain shot through his ankle and burned up his leg. Crying out, he staggered and barely managed not to fall. It hurt so badly that he couldn't catch his breath at first. If he had been able, he would have screamed. Finally, the agony faded, leaving him sweating and exhausted.

Drawing several deep breaths, he gritted his teeth and gingerly eased his weight onto his left foot. Pain lanced through his ankle again. Gasping, he patted his pockets for his cell phone. It was smashed. He thumped it to be sure, but the casing was cracked and it wouldn't even light up.

That meant dragging himself somehow to the nearest house.

Only, the nearest house was the dark, unlit one that Buddy was afraid of. Staring at the place, Nick thought he saw a shadowy figure walk past one of the front windows. A cold chill that had nothing to do with the rain ran up Nick's spine. *Okay*, he thought, *not there*. Next house, then.

But as he looked up the street, the lights in that one went out. As did the lights in the next one, until all the lights were out on Crestmont Court.

It wasn't a power failure. Nick could see lights still burning fine on the other streets. All of Haven Estates ran on the same power grid with backup generators. It was unlikely that one street would lose power while the rest kept going.

The garage door opened at the isolated house. A vehicle backed out without its lights on. Buddy pressed against his injured leg and growled, making the prickles run up Nick's spine again.

Instinctively he turned toward the shortcut, hobbling along in the rain and putting as little weight on his left foot as he possibly could. Every step was excruciating, but he had only to glance at Buddy, cringing as close to him as possible, to keep going. Buddy's fear was contagious.

The only way to get himself into the drainage channel was to drop onto his butt and slide in. He did so, gasping and wincing, and crouched in the rushing water with his head below the top edge of the drain. As the vehicle drove by, Nick clutched the dog to him and held his breath. It was moving slowly . . . too slowly . . . as though searching. The beam of a powerful flashlight swung above Nick's head. His fear grew hot and tight in his chest, but he forced himself to remain absolutely still. If he didn't move, they couldn't see him.

Finally, the car drove on, still without headlights. When he could no longer hear it, he crawled through the water rather than get to his feet again.

Emerging onto Ladybrook, he straightened slowly and tried not to feel discouraged by how far it still was to his house.

Only, the car that had searched for him on Crestmont Court was now sitting in his driveway, the engine running.

This time, he was more angry than scared. "What are they, the dog police?" he muttered. He wanted to confront them, but this wasn't the time.

Erin's lights were shining brightly close by, and he struggled in that direction. It took an eternity to reach her front door. Shivering, he knocked, but she didn't answer.

Frustrated, he rang the bell, but she didn't come and Cotton didn't bark from inside. "Don't be gone," he whispered.

He limped around to the side of her house, trying to look in a window. All the blinds were drawn. But a gap in the curtains next door drew him to it.

Desperately he peered inside, and saw a man and woman sitting in the living room. Their TV was playing, but the woman wasn't watching. Instead, she was staring off into space with a vacant look on her face. A bowl of popcorn had turned over in her lap, spilling kernels onto the floor.

He thought at first that she'd suffered a stroke or something, but the man on the sofa was eating popcorn. His hand moved regularly to his mouth like an automaton.

Something about the two of them made Nick think of the Nissan's stoned driver. He backed away, tangling himself in the shrubbery for a moment and nearly falling. That saved him, for, as he crouched, leaning against the house for balance, he heard a car moving slowly along the street, very slowly as though searching for something.

Me, he thought with a shiver.

It was crazy, but he didn't waste time rationalizing anything. Pulling himself up, he opened the gate to Erin's backyard. He was careful in case Cotton was out there. He didn't want her escaping, too. But the Westie wasn't around.

"She's a smart girl," he told Buddy, who was whining again. "Safe and dry inside with her mommy."

At the back, Erin's windows were open under a covered patio, letting the rain-washed breeze into her house. Erin was sitting on her sofa with the TV on, muted. Her laptop was running on the coffee table, but Erin wasn't typing. Instead, she was sitting there slumped with her hands in her lap, staring vacantly at nothing at all. The laptop's screen saver was on, so Nick knew she'd stopped working several minutes ago.

"Erin," he called softly, not wanting to scare her. "Hey, Erin, it's me!"

She didn't move. She didn't seem to hear him.

"Erin!" he called again. "Hey! Wake up!"

Like a sleepwalker, she turned her head slowly in his direction. He couldn't imagine what he looked like, clinging to her window like some kind of ax murderer with his clothes torn and wet. But her expression didn't change. Her face was slack, as though she'd taken a drug and couldn't quite wake up.

"Erin!" he said sharply. "For God's sake! It's Nick. I need help."

Buddy barked sharply.

She flinched and blinked, lifting her hands to rub her face. Only then did she seem to notice him. Fear flashed in her eyes. "Who's there?"

"Nick Penby! Please, Erin. If you don't want to let me in, call a cab for me, okay? I need the emergency room." He felt a wave of agony run through him, as though all his strength was draining away, and pressed his palm to the window screen. "My cell phone is broken. I think I've busted my ankle. Buddy ran away in the storm, and a car hit me."

"My God."

At last she was running to the back door. Throwing it open, she helped him inside. Buddy ran in circles around them, tangling his leash and getting in the way.

"I'm sorry," she said breathlessly, struggling to support Nick's weight. "I must have been half asleep, or something. What happened?"

He didn't have the breath to tell her. She started to put him on the sofa, but he protested, not wanting to ruin it. So he ended up on one of the kitchen chairs that he'd helped move in. It felt so good to sit down that he wanted to cry.

Instead, he swallowed the water and aspirin she brought him. When he could, he told her everything, while she sat holding Buddy on her lap, toweling him dry.

The more Nick talked, the stranger her expression became. Her glassy brown eyes, he noticed, were red rimmed as though she'd been crying. And her hands moved slower and slower across Buddy until they weren't moving at all.

"Erin?" Nick said sharply.

She didn't seem to hear him. Her gaze strayed to the television.

He turned around, wincing as he moved. The commercial that was playing vanished, and Nick saw instead a black screen filled with jagged, spiky colors flashing rhythmically, like a badly designed screen saver.

When he blinked, it became the commercial again. Puzzled, Nick flexed his leg, deliberately making it hurt. The TV image wavered, and he saw the jagged, spiky lines.

"Erin!" he said loudly. "Wake up!"

She blinked and looked at him.

"Turn off your TV, please."

She sat there as though drugged and didn't move. Finally, Nick pushed himself to his feet and limped over to click off the TV. When Buddy wiggled on her lap and licked her face, she blinked, cradling his whiskery face in her hands and smoothing back his eyebrows. Tears welled up in her eyes.

"They were trying to steal you," she said, as though the conversation hadn't been interrupted. "You silly dog. Why did you let the storm scare you into running away? You might have been lost forever."

Suddenly she was crying, clutching Buddy and weeping into his coat.

Nick watched her in concern. "Where's Cotton?" he asked.

"Gone!" Erin wailed.

"When? Tonight?"

She shook her head. "Three days ago. I came home and she

wasn't in the backyard. I—I thought she'd run away. I looked everywhere."

Nick stared at her, not sure what to think. "Why," he asked finally, conscious of feeling hurt, "didn't you ask me to help? You know I would have."

She wiped her face, refusing to look at him. "Sure, I—I guess I knew that. I put up flyers right away. No one called me, no one. When I got home that night, all my flyers had been taken down." Her eyes flashed with dull anger. "Who would do that? What kind of place is this, where they won't even help you find a little dog?"

Thinking of the men who had tried to steal Buddy tonight, he was beginning to have an idea.

"Erin," he asked, "do you play your TV a lot?"

She shrugged. "I guess so. I don't watch it. It just comes on, and I leave it going for company. You know how it is."

"You know about subliminal messages, right?"

She frowned at him. "Why?"

"And your TV just comes on? You don't turn it on?"

"I don't know." She thought for a moment, as though still in a fog. "No, it comes on every evening just before I get home. It's set to have my news program running when I get here." She brightened. "Neat, right?"

"Why don't you turn that function off?"

"Why should I? It's nice, like—like someone waiting here for me, you know?" Then she reddened. "I—"

"Hey, it's okay to feel lonely, living like this. I was, until Buddy came along."

Buddy woofed proudly.

"And you've got Cotton waiting for you, or you did," Nick continued. "Have you called the pound, or your vet's office?"

"What?" Erin's voice was spacey and faraway again. She stared at the screen saver on her laptop.

Angrily, Nick slammed down its lid and unplugged its charger.

"Hey!" she said. "What are you doing?"

"I'm talking to you about your sweet little dog that's missing. The one you keep forgetting to look for."

"I wouldn't do that."

"You just admitted that she's been gone for three days, and you haven't even made the basic phone calls."

"But—"

"Was the gate open or shut when you got home that day?"

"What?"

"Answer me!" Nick said. "The day she disappeared. Was the gate open or shut?"

Erin closed her eyes, lifting her hands to her ears. "I don't know! I don't know!"

"Think about it."

"Open . . . no, shut." She lowered her hands. "It was shut! My God, you think she was stolen?"

"Maybe. Some men were trying to steal Buddy tonight."

"Like . . . like a—"

"Like maybe our HOA now has its own animal-control officer," Nick said grimly. "To enforce this no-dog policy that's recently popped up. Since I got Buddy. Since you moved here with Cotton. We're the only residents that walk our dogs. I wonder if that's why we got the letters."

Erin looked bewildered. "I don't understand."

"I think I do. Dogs keep us active and alert. They entice us outdoors, where we see, and feel, and think. Don't they, Buddy?"

Buddy wagged his tail.

"When did you quit walking Cotton every day?" Nick asked.

"I—"

"After your TV started coming on every evening?"

Erin shook her head. "Why are you asking all these questions?"

"Because something strange is going on here." He started to tell her his whole theory, but stopped because she looked too confused. Sighing, he said in a quieter, weary tone, "Would you call me a cab, please?"

The emergency room patched him up, strapping his ankle that was badly sprained but not broken, and giving him a pair of crutches, a prescription for painkillers, and the advice to stay home from work to elevate and ice his foot. Out in the cab, Buddy greeted him with anxious affection, as though they'd been parted for days. The dog was whining again and pawing his ears in obvious discomfort, so Nick asked the cabbie to drive them to the animal emergency clinic. The vet on duty was a young guy, with very gray intense eyes behind a pair of glasses and long, gentle fingers that probed Buddy expertly.

"He's got a microchip implanted in his ear," the vet said, frowning. "Badly done. It's bleeding, and it shouldn't do that. You don't live in Haven Estates, do you?"

"Yeah. Why?" Nick asked warily.

"What is it with you people? This company that's selling you these invisible fence systems for dogs is taking all of you for a ride. I've removed several of these chips from dogs that lived there, nearly all of them runaways." The vet shook his head. "There's usually a collar with a transmitter that goes with the chip. It's badly designed, set on a wrong frequency. It drives dogs nuts. It's inhumane. These people don't know what they're doing."

Nick frowned, deep in thought. He figured they had a very good idea of what they were doing, and it wasn't to keep dogs safe at home. It was to drive them away.

"You want me to remove this chip?" the vet asked. "He's going to be suffering extreme discomfort until I do."

Not liking the censure in the vet's voice, Nick started to explain but held back. It would sound too crazy. "Yes, get it out," he said.

And when Buddy was bandaged and given a treat, Nick asked, "You haven't removed one of these chips from a runaway Westie, have you?"

The vet had. Two days before, a female Westie had been brought in by a Good Samaritan. She wasn't wearing any tags, just her transmitter. She was half crazed from the frequency it was set on, and exhausted and dehydrated from running.

"Obviously she came from a good home. She was clean, no fleas, had her nails trimmed properly, showed regular brushing and exercise. But that damned collar . . ."

"Is she still here?" Nick asked, amazed at such luck.

"We can't board dogs here. The animal shelter picked her up."

"Thanks!" Nick shouted, already heading outside on his crutches.

He tried phoning Erin to tell her the news. When she didn't pick up, he left a message on her voice mail. In the morning, he called the shelter, but Erin hadn't gone there to rescue her dog. So Nick went to retrieve Cotton. The Westie was thinner and a bit unsure of things, but soon she was romping with Buddy in Nick's backyard. He called Erin's work number and finally reached her with the good news.

Sounding flustered and emotional, Erin thanked him, offering to walk both dogs that evening when she got home. But as five o'clock came and went, she didn't show.

Worried, Nick phoned her repeatedly that evening, without success. He wanted to go by her house and check on her, but the prospect of trying to wedge his swollen ankle, his crutches, and two dogs into his car to drive half the length of the street was daunting. Still, he kept imagining Erin sitting on her sofa, zoned into space.

"This place is turning us into zombies," he muttered to the dogs, and resolutely kept the TV off, as he had all day.

In the middle of the night, he woke up, courtesy of his aching leg, and couldn't go back to sleep. He hadn't filled his prescription of painkillers, telling himself it was too dangerous to be zonked on something when the dog nazis might show up, demanding Buddy. Now, lying there in the dark with his ankle throbbing, he wished he hadn't been so macho about the pills.

Until he heard a stealthy sound at his yard gate. He froze under the blanket, his ears straining. Just when he thought he'd imagined it, he heard another soft scrape along the brick side of his house.

He sat up, all senses on alert. The gate was padlocked, so no one was getting into the backyard without climbing over the fence. Buddy and Cotton were snuggled together in a comfy doggy bed in Nick's bedroom, completely safe, so he didn't have to worry about them. Still, was it burglars or dognappers prowling around his house?

Nick heard a quiet rattle of the latch and then the sharp *snick* of bolt cutters.

He rolled out of bed in a tangle of blankets and crutches, finally gaining his feet. Buddy sat up, watching him uncertainly.

"Shush," he whispered, hoping Buddy wouldn't bark.

Easing himself over to the window, he peered out and saw three men in dark coveralls moving quietly across his small backyard. One was roaming around as though searching. He crouched to shine a penlight inside Buddy's doghouse and shook his head at the others. Another opened the phone box in Nick's yard and fiddled inside it.

"Hell," Nick whispered, wishing he still had a cell phone.

He could hear the third man working quietly at the side of the house, as though he was messing with the security system . . . or the cable box. In his corner, Buddy growled. Cotton sat up, panting nervously.

At the other end of the house, in the living room, the unmistakable sound of the TV's activation mode powered on. Nick felt an almost imperceptible sensation crawling across his skin, followed by the sudden urge to go watch something. He wondered what kind of electromagnetic fields were being emitted by the high-tech wiring in his house and what it was really being used for.

Clad only in his boxer shorts, he stood listening in the shadows, barely breathing, his heart racing. He feared the men in dark coveralls would be coming inside the house next, like alien invaders in old B movies. Maybe they were going to carry him out of there to their spaceship and dissect him. Would anyone on Ladybrook Lane notice that he was gone? Would anyone care?

Not the clown with the white SUV that had nearly run over him. Not Anderson, who wouldn't say hello. Not the stoner in the black Nissan that had left him bruised black. He wasn't even sure about Erin, who'd blown him off. He didn't know whether to be worried about her or mad.

His gate eased shut, and he peered out, watching one of the men fit a new padlock in place. Nick had the awful conviction that it would be identical to the one they'd cut and his key would fit perfectly. When he heard them walking away, he swung himself through the shadowy house on his crutches, but by the time he reached his front window, there was no sight of them. He heard no vehicle, either. But someone had placed a kid's soccer ball in the yard next door. It hadn't been there earlier. And Nick realized that although he heard the kids out playing sometimes, he'd never actually seen them.

He hobbled to the front door, checking the dead bolt to make sure it was secure, although now he realized that there was nothing secure about his house. Maintenance knew his security and house codes. They let the cleaners in. If they wanted to come in there and get him, they could.

On the living room wall, the flat-panel TV was glowing gray, and its green power light was on, meaning it was once more standing by to switch on with his preselected morning program at six o'clock, giving him the early headlines, the weather forecast, and a good dose of whatever message was being sent subliminally.

But *why*? What did they want? Why were they doing this to people?

There were no answers.

After a largely sleepless night, he was up again at dawn, gritty-eyed but determined. Buddy and Cotton watched him with their heads cocked quizzically as he struggled around his bedroom, pulling on an old tracksuit and tossing clothes into a small duffel. He'd bought this house online. He'd sell it the same way, but he and the dogs were getting out of there now.

In the living room, the TV blared suddenly, making Nick nearly jump out of his skin. He hesitated for a moment, then finished his hasty packing and looked around. There was nothing there that he couldn't abandon if he had to, or leave for professional movers to pack up for him later. That might be a sad commentary on how he lived, but at the moment it was damned convenient.

He fed the dogs, clicking the TV off without looking at the screen. Even so, during the short time it was on he developed a headache and a feeling of lassitude that made him wonder if he shouldn't put this off until he felt better.

Watching coffee drip through the filter into his cup, he sagged a little, letting fatigue and strain wash through him. Maybe he was overreacting. The maintenance guys had to work in their yards at some time, and it was nice to have them stay out of sight, wasn't it?

The dogs came scampering through the kitchen, pretending to chase each other. Cotton leaped at his injured leg with a happy little bark before tearing off after Buddy. Pain flashed through the entire left side of his bruised body, making him lean over, gasping for breath.

His head cleared, and he realized that if he didn't get out of there—right now—he really was going to become a zombie, maybe forever.

Using one of his crutch tips, he pushed his duffel into the utility room, then sacked up dog food and bowls.

"Buddy!" he called. "Bring Blue Wuzzy, okay?"

Buddy came running to him, but without the toy. Nick was looking for it when the TV came on, loud and bright. He stopped, his ears and eyes assaulted by sounds and flashing colors. A corner of his mind told him not to look, not to wait, to get out of there, but he couldn't move.

A dog pawing at his injured ankle snapped him out of it. Gritting his teeth, he leaned over through a haze of pain and punched the remote. The TV went gray again, leaving the room in deafening quiet. Sweating, Nick sucked in several deep breaths.

The sun was streaming in his east windows now, puzzling him until he glanced at his watch and saw that a half hour had gone by without his realizing it. A half hour of standing in his living room like a statue while the TV blared at him.

"Oh God," he whispered.

The dog toy ceased to matter. He felt the panicky need to run. Fumbling with his crutches, he nearly lost his balance until he forced himself to slow down. The dogs bounced happily around him, excited when they saw their leashes. Buddy ran to the front door and back several times, while Cotton wiggled until he could barely snap her leash to her collar.

He tried to be patient and keep his voice calm. But Buddy was being goofy. He ran to the back door and pawed it, then ran to the front. Obviously he needed to go outside, but there was no time . . . no time.

The sound of loud, anxious barking snapped Nick back to consciousness. He looked around, befuddled, and realized that the TV was on again. Both Buddy and Cotton were prancing at the back door, and another half hour had slipped by.

Nick's brain was foggy. He didn't want to move, but Buddy kept barking. Nick blinked slowly. He had to let the dog out. No. He needed to get into the car. He couldn't remember why.

Struggling to recall what he'd been trying to do, he reached out with a wavering hand and tried to push the remote. The TV stayed on.

Fear gathered inside him, but he couldn't remember why he was afraid. He thought that maybe he should do something, something very important. Only, he was so tired. He wanted to sleep.

Buddy barked again.

"Okay," Nick mumbled. "I'll take you out. Can't you let a guy sleep?"

Forgetting his crutches, he took a step forward. The moment his weight landed on his injured ankle, the pain woke him up as though he'd been branded with a hot iron. He yelped, nearly fell, and caught himself on the kitchen island. Hanging on to it desperately, he threw one crutch at the TV, and heard the sound of shattering glass. It went mercifully black and silent.

A viselike force that had been gripping him released, and Nick sagged to his knees. When he realized he was making soft little whimpering sounds, he forced himself to stop. At least that damned TV wasn't digging into his brain anymore.

Then the security-control pad at the utility door began to flash a red symbol, and a soft chime sounded, warning him that he had an error in the house system.

They know, Nick thought in desperation. *They'll be coming.*

He lurched forward, abandoning his other crutch, and threw himself at the utility door. He managed to fling it open just as the dead bolt tried to lock. One second slower, and he would have been locked inside his house, unable to escape. *Good old burglar-capture system*, he thought. It had nearly captured him.

"Buddy! Cotton! Come on!" he called. He loaded the dogs into the car and yanked on the manual release of his garage door, grateful now that the lightning spike had burned out the opener. They couldn't control this, he thought, rolling up the overhead door.

A man in coveralls was standing in his driveway with a toolbox and a grim expression. "I'm here to fix that, Mr. Penby."

Nick jumped into his car, bumping his swollen ankle in the process. He wanted to swear. He wanted to weep. There wasn't time for either. He locked the car doors just as the man thumped on his trunk lid.

"Hey!" the man shouted.

Starting the car, Nick roared out of his garage, making the maintenance guy jump for his life. Shooting into the street, Nick barely avoided hitting the white SUV that was also backing out. It braked sharply, and the driver's window lowered. A puzzled face with red-rimmed eyes peered out at him as though not knowing who he was.

From the opposite direction, a maintenance vehicle was coming down Ladybrook Lane. Nick's heart was pounding so hard that he thought he might hyperventilate, but he gunned his car up the street, not slowing when the maintenance truck flashed its headlights at him. It veered as though intending to smash into him. Nick swerved through a front lawn, sending chunks of sod flying in his wake, as he wrestled his bouncing, lurching car back onto the pavement and went rocketing on.

Not until he passed Erin's place did he slow fractionally. It was past time for her to be at work. Had she gone, or was she sitting in her living room, still staring blankly? He dared not stop to check. Next door to her house, the black Nissan was gone, and a red Ford sedan was parked in the driveway instead. A little blond girl he'd never seen before was playing hopscotch in the driveway while her mother unloaded suitcases and boxes from the trunk.

"Angie!" the mother called. "Come and help me, please."

Nick couldn't believe new people were already moving in. Where had the stoner gone? How could new residents be in place so quickly? Something inside him didn't really want to know the answer.

He shot out through the neighborhood gates and drove across town before finally finding a gas station that still offered a pay phone. Dialing Erin's work number, he counted the rings impatiently.

Finally she picked up.

"Erin!" he said, grateful to hear her voice, even if it sounded slightly slurred. "Thank God. I thought they'd got you. Don't worry about Cotton. She's safe and—"

"Who?"

"Cotton," he said, slowing down. "Your dog."

"Oh." She paused. "I'm sorry. Who did you say was calling?"

"It's Nick. Your friend on Ladybrook. Listen, Erin, for your own good, don't go home tonight. Are you listening, Erin? Do you hear me?"

"I'm sorry. Who did you say was calling?"

"Don't hang up," he said desperately. "You have to move out of Haven Estates. Don't go home after work. Do you understand me? There's something crazy going on there. It's not safe for you to go home. Stay with a friend or get a hotel room. As for Cotton, meet me at Eastside Park at Twelfth and Main to get her."

Erin didn't speak.

His frustration grew, making him grip the phone so hard that his hand was shaking. "Erin! Remember Nick? Remember your dog? That cute little white number you said was your baby? Remember taking her for walks? Remember planting flowers, and how I helped you take your kitchen table apart so it would go in? Come on, Erin! You have to shake this off! Meet me at Eastside Park as soon as you can."

"Eastside Park," she said slowly.

"Yes. Go straight there on your lunch break, and I'll explain everything I've—"

She hung up, leaving the phone buzzing in his ear.

He frowned, bowing his head before slowly replacing the receiver. Beside him, Buddy panted, staring at him with complete trust. Cotton stared at him, too, her bright little eyes less sure. He reached out and sadly scratched her white ears as he drove away.

At noon, an unmarked panel truck circled Eastside Park, checking all the vehicles parked under the trees. The driver called in. "Nick Penby's not here. No sight of him."

"Acknowledged. We'll put a new family in 3501 Ladybrook tonight as soon as the repairs are finished. Keep watching the park in case he turns up later."

"Will do."

The panel truck turned right onto Rickman Avenue and sped away, only to return ten minutes later to circle the park slowly once more.

From a nearby side street, Nick watched bleakly from his parked car. He knew then that Erin wouldn't be coming. And whatever purpose was being served by experimenting on the inhabitants of Haven Estates, Erin was now a part of it, sucked deep into a place where not even her former love for her dog could save her.

Unlike Nick, who recognized in time the perils lurking in today's high-tech world—where people increasingly sacrifice human contact for online chats, where they sleep in houses but don't live in them, where they live and play in virtual reality without realizing they have forgotten how to live in real time—Erin couldn't unplug enough to regain her balance.

Even the simplest values, such as a dog's unquestioning love or the friendship and trust between two people, can cease to have any meaning, once an individual moves into the Twilight Zone.

THE WRONG
ROOM

◉

R. L. Stine

The tall man in the pinstriped suit is Mr. Samuel Mechling. As Mr. Mechling pulls his suitcase through the hotel lobby, he has a lot on his mind. Mechling is a salesman, and he's thinking about sales brochures and new contacts, marketing meetings and business dinners. As he steps up to the front desk, there's one thing he hasn't thought about. He hasn't considered the startling fact that he's about to sign the register . . . for the Twilight Zone.

Mechling rolled his suitcase into the hotel lobby and glanced around for someone he knew. Behind the concierge desk, a young man with carrot-colored hair and a cadaverously pale face dabbed a paper towel over a stain on his white jacket.

Two young female clerks in gray uniforms stood stiffly behind the wide, mahogany reception desk, staring straight ahead. The only occupants of the lobby were two middle-aged men, huddled together with cell phones pressed to their ears. One of them wore white tennis shorts and a sleeveless, blue T-shirt stretched over a bulging beer belly.

Mechling caught himself frowning. A few years ago, no one would have been seen wearing shorts in the lobby of the Fraser-Carleton.

"You're starting to sound like your father."

He heard Joanna's voice in his mind. "A few years ago, we had *real* snowfalls, snow up to our waists. . . . A few years ago, we survived *without* carrying water bottles everywhere we went. . . ."

Well, it was his tenth convention, his tenth stay at the Fraser-Carleton, so he had a right to feel like an old-timer. And anyway, what was wrong with noting the declining standards? It wasn't like he was complaining unjustly.

That was an argument he'd never win with Joanna. She was always so much more accepting than he was. After all, she accepted him and all his faults and quirks. Most of the time.

Mechling pulled his suitcase to the front desk and set his briefcase down beside it. The young reception clerk watched him approach. She was Asian, pretty, perfect makeup, short, straight bangs over almond eyes that reflected the bright overhead light. He read the brass name tag on her lapel: MIA.

She blinked at him. Was his smile too broad? He always felt a little giddy checking into hotels. Maybe it was the possibility of something unexpected happening.

"Welcome to the Fraser-Carleton," she said. A little-girl's voice. But she had to be in her thirties. So hard to tell women's ages these days.

"I'm checking in," he said. Obviously. "For the convention."

She clicked some keys on the keyboard beneath the desk. How could she type with those long, purple fingernails?

"Mechling," he said.

She nodded and typed some more.

He raised his eyes to the tall, dark portraits on the wall behind her. Two somber-looking men in dark pinstriped suits, faces slightly to the side to show off their profiles. "Did you change the paintings?"

She stopped typing. "Excuse me?"

He pointed. "Those paintings. Are they new?"

The old ones showed stern-looking Mr. Fraser and bloated Mr. Carleton in Colonial finery—lacy, ruffled shirts under serious waistcoats. Even powdery, white wigs. Insane paintings. Added a little humor to the staid lobby.

"I don't know," Mia replied. "I'm new here, Mr. Mechling."

Mechling squinted at the dull portraits. New management, maybe. "Do you need my credit card?" He reached for his wallet.

She tapped a final key, then raised her eyes to his. "No. It's all been taken care of."

Really? That's odd.

Well, don't argue.

She slapped the silver bell on the desk. The carrot-haired dude came hurrying over, trying to hide the round, wet stain on his valet coat.

"Show Mr. Mechling to his room. You've been upgraded, sir. Enjoy your stay."

The valet took the key-card folder and grabbed the handle of Mechling's suitcase. His name tag read: ANGEL. "Y'all follow me, sir." He glanced at the number scribbled on the key folder. "This is a good room."

And it was. Twenty-third floor. A junior suite, Mechling figured. Living room with standard but pleasing decor. Flat-screen TV. A full desk. A generous minibar. Ice already loaded in the bucket. No hotel-room smell. The air fresh, almost sweet.

Angel set the suitcase down. Mechling stepped to the window. He gazed down on downtown Atlanta—office towers, hotels, condos with penthouse terraces.

"Nice," he murmured. Great to be up so high. Almost like an aerial view.

"Glad y'all like it." Angel set the key card down. "We change the view every day."

"Huh?" Mechling wasn't sure he had heard that right. "What do you mean?"

The door closed behind the valet.

Mechling stretched his arms, his back. Long flights tightened him up for days. He filled a glass with ice, then found a Diet Coke in the minibar. He unzipped the suitcase and lifted the lid.

The envelope on top made him smile. A note from Joanna. She always slipped a note in after he'd packed. He set it aside to read later.

He found the remote next to the TV and clicked the power on. Then he clicked from channel to channel until he found a sports channel. "The Vengers have tied it up!" an excited announcer screamed. "The Vengers have come from behind to tie the Red-Marvins!"

Who?

What sport were they playing? Mechling squinted at the screen. Tall, skinny men in loose-fitting yellow and white uniforms were running back and forth an indoor court. Were those hurdles on the court? Why were they ducking *under* them?

Must be a foreign channel, Mechling thought. He clicked off the TV. Finished unpacking. Checked his black suit for the banquet. Had it survived the plane ride, or should he have it pressed? Seemed okay.

He pulled out his BlackBerry and punched Joanna's office number. He always called to tell her he'd arrived safely. The call didn't go through. He tried it again. No. He checked the phone. It said: NO SERVICE.

Weird. He'd never had reception trouble at the Fraser-Carleton.

He tried to send her a text message. No service. *Okay.* He picked up the room phone. Punched 9, then Joanna's office number. Busy signal.

He felt his back muscles tighten. A wave of heartburn rose in his chest. Mechling didn't like frustration. He was a salesman. He had to be in touch. In touch. In touch all the time.

He gripped the receiver tightly. Punched in Joanna's cell phone number. Busy signal. *How can that be?*

One more try. Busy signal.

Mechling downed the Diet Coke. Then he punched 0 on the room phone.

Four rings . . . five rings . . . six . . . seven. And then finally, a soft, man's voice: "Operator. This is Barry. Can I help you, Mr. Mechling?"

"Yes. I can't seem to get my call through."

"That's no problem, sir."

"Well, yes it is." Mechling couldn't hide his impatience. "My BlackBerry doesn't have service. And the hotel phone keeps giving me a busy signal."

"That's no problem," Barry insisted.

"Well, can you dial the call for me?"

"That's no problem, sir."

Mechling heard a definitive click, and the line went silent.

He uttered a groan and pressed 0 again. This time, a busy signal. He slammed down the receiver. Picked it up. Listened for a dial tone. Pressed 0. Busy signal.

Slammed it down again and heard a knock on the door. Someone to help him? That was fast.

He pulled open the door and almost gasped at the shock of the beautiful woman. White-blond hair falling over her shoulders, red midriff top that revealed a lot of creamy skin. Tight, red miniskirt. Green eyes. Red lips in a generous and, yes, sexy smile. A red cloth bag over her shoulder.

Wait. Not as young as Mechling had first imagined. Crow's-feet.

Some lines under her green eyes. Makeup covering some skin flaws. She smelled of oranges and cigarette smoke. Stiletto heels about a foot high.

"I'm here," she said, breathing the words. "I'm Mindy. Aren't you going to let me in?"

"Excuse me?"

She raised a finger and slowly ran it down Mechling's cheek. "You sent for me, honey. I'm going to make you happy." She edged past him into the room, tilting a little on the high, pointy heels.

"No, wait—"

She started to pull up the midriff top. He caught a glimpse of her breasts, very round and full. Not real, he thought.

"I . . . didn't call for you." He was forty-five years old. Why was he stammering?

She leaned forward and kissed him on the cheek, a very soft, wet, lipsticky kiss. "Your office called my service, hon."

"My office?" He stepped back. Sorenson called an escort service? Not very likely. He inhaled the tangy orange perfume of her. Yes, he could feel himself aroused. "No, I don't think so—"

Joanna's face popped in front of him. Married fifteen years, he'd been tempted, of course, but had never strayed.

Mindy put her hands on his shoulders and brought her face close. She brushed her lips over his ear. She breathed softly. The tingle started at the back of his neck and trickled down his back.

"They said they wanted to give you a good send-off," she whispered.

"Send-off?" He pulled away from her with such force, he stumbled into the wall. "I'm up for a promotion. Are you telling me I'm being laid off?"

She giggled. "No, honey. You're being laid."

She reached for his hands and started to pull him into the bedroom.

The green eyes must be contacts, he thought. What did she mean by *send-off*?

"Oh, wait." Mindy let go of his hands and rummaged in the red bag. She pulled out a yellow paper. "You have to sign this first, Mr. Romero."

"Romero?" He blinked. "My name isn't Romero."

Her expression went flat. She aged about twenty years. "You're joking."

"No. I'm not Romero. Really."

She tapped one foot. Made an unattractive face. "What's your name?"

"Mechling."

Her eyes ran down the piece of paper. "Sorry, babe. I have the wrong room."

She pulled the top back down over her breasts. "Just when I start to think I'm a pro . . ." she muttered, shaking her peroxided hair.

Mechler felt confused and a little dizzy. Now he really wanted her.

"Wait. Maybe you could stay and—"

"Sorry, honey. Really sorry." She waved the paper at him. "I've got my orders. See?"

"But you could—"

She ran her finger again down his sweating face. He winced as the fingernail scratched his cheek. She swung the bag over her shoulder and swept out the door. Mechling took a deep breath of oranges and cigarette smoke—and held it.

What did she mean by send-off?

She was talking about Romero—not Mechling—right?

No Internet service in his room. When he tried to call the front desk, no one picked up. *Joanna must wonder where the hell I am. I'm cut off. Totally cut off.*

What time was it, anyway? His BlackBerry said seven o'clock. Impossible. He'd arrived at the hotel at seven. The clock radio on the bed table was dark. Unplugged, he quickly discovered.

This used to be a four-star hotel.

The next morning, he pulled the stack of sales brochures from his briefcase. They looked good, he decided. Clean and easy to read. With the new prices, competitive to anyone.

Mechling hoped for a good convention. After the cutbacks, there were only three salespeople left in his division. Beller, Leeman, and he. He was a survivor—but for how long? Yes, there was talk of a promotion. But he had never been Sorenson's favorite.

Schwartzman popped into his mind. Again. The look of pain on Schwartzman's face when he got the goodbye notice and realized he'd wasted nineteen years of his life.

Mechling shook his head hard, trying to shake that picture away.

He stopped at the front desk to complain about the phone and the Internet. But there was no one there. No one at the concierge desk, either. He pounded the bell two or three times before he saw the little sign: WILL RETURN SOON.

He realized his jaw was clenched, neck muscles straining. No way to start a convention. He needed to be relaxed, amiable, bright-eyed and bushy-tailed. Who always used that awful phrase? Schwartzman?

The convention was always held in the ballroom of the hotel. As he made his way down the long, carpeted hall, in and out of the chandelier brightness, he heard a clamor of voices. It cheered him up. He neared the long line at the registration table. Lucky he'd gotten his badge at the office. He pulled it from his inside jacket pocket and, tucking the brochures under an arm, pinned the badge to his lapel.

His eyes moved from face to face. He didn't recognize anybody. Did they seem younger than usual? Or was he just getting older?

Loud, barking laughter from inside the ballroom. Voices shouting over the blare of music. Mechling stepped inside, into the labyrinth of tables and booths, posters and video screens, stacks of brochures and giveaways, samples and demonstrations, firm handshakes and arm-tugging pitches.

He had that giddy feeling again, hands suddenly moist, a little fluttering in his chest. He was the one who enjoyed these conventions. Beller and Leeman barely tolerated them: "Too crowded, too noisy, no way to conduct real business." Blah blah. Excuses, Mechling thought. Beller and Leeman hadn't been around long enough to be so skeptical and down.

Where *were* they, anyway?

His eyes slowly surveyed the faces, all pale under the unforgiving chandelier light. None looked familiar. Someone in an enormous brown-bear costume was handing out DVDs. An embarrassed-looking young blond woman in a skimpy majorette's uniform was having baton trouble—one rubber bulb had come off the end.

Mechling straightened the brochures under his arm. Where was his booth? Beller and Leeman were probably waiting for him. He started down one aisle, dodging a large woman pulling a wheeled backpack. And found himself in front of a table and a sign: WEDG-STREAM.

A balding man with a brown, push-broom goatee, in a shiny gray suit with shoulders way too loose, grinned at Mechling like an old friend. "Good morning, partner." Yes, a Texas accent.

"I . . . I'm looking for my booth," Mechling said, eyes down the aisle.

The man nodded, his grin frozen. "What forums do you use? It's organized by forums this year. Someone had a crazy idea."

Mechling squinted at him. "Forums?"

"Mort Boyer." The man was suddenly pumping Mechling's hand. "You're not with MarketStretch, are you?"

"No," Mechling said, trying to free his hand. "My name's Mechling. I—"

"You seen our product?" Boyer asked, not letting go. "I don't care what forum you use. We're the compatibility kings. No joke, son. We're compatible with all forums. Even the new SG-2s."

He pulled Mechling into the booth. He was surprisingly strong. He slapped his hand against a poster on the booth wall. "See? All forums. We can integrate it with a flash drive if you want. Faster that way. Or, of course, you can keep it in the clouds. Nice and simple. What's your forum?"

"I . . . I don't know."

"Well, what's your company, Mechling?" He grasped Mechling's badge in two fingers and lifted it toward his face. Mechling got a strong whiff of Old Spice. Coming from the man's beard?

"Flash-Freez?"

Boyer let go of the badge. His eyes traveled up and down Mechling as if memorizing his suit. "That's like something to do with flash drives? Is it for servers? Servers are in the other hall. Upstairs, I think."

Mechling shook his head. "No. It's not a computer thing. You know. Flash-Freez. Frozen food delivered to your door every morning. It's ready to eat by dinnertime. You know the commercials, right? *It Freez-up Your Life and it Freez-up Your Time.*"

Boyer tossed back his head and gave a hearty laugh. Mechling glimpsed several gold teeth. "Don't mean to laugh, partner. Aren't you in the wrong convention?"

"I don't think so."

"This is Streaming and Storage," Boyer said, slapping the poster again, so hard that the flimsy wall shook. "No food companies here, that's for sure."

"But, I know—"

"Look at your badge, dude." Boyer fingered it again. "It's green. Look around. All the badges are red."

Mechling felt his face grow hot. He knew he must be blushing. "Weird," he muttered. He still wasn't convinced. He gave Boyer a wave and began walking the aisle, taking long strides. Up and down the rows of booths ...

CLOUDCOVER.ORG.... MAXIM-EYES LTD.... FLASHFORWARD ...

I don't know any of these companies. I'm in the wrong room.

He shifted the stack of brochures to his other arm. He saw that his sweat had soaked through the ones on top. The flutter had left his chest, replaced by a heavy feeling on top of his stomach.

He trotted down the long hall to the front desk. Someone behind it now. The young woman who had checked him in. Mia. She fiddled with the collar of her white blouse.

"Good morning, Mr. Mechling. How are you enjoying your stay?"

He didn't answer her question. "I went to the wrong ballroom," he said, tugging at the green badge. "Which ballroom is this convention in?"

She studied the badge. "There's only one group meeting at the hotel this weekend," she said.

"But it's the wrong one!" Mechling realized that he sounded overwrought, maybe even a little crazy. But how much frustration could one man take?

"You can check the listing board, Mr. Mechling." Her tone grew colder. "That's the only meeting scheduled."

"Am I in the wrong hotel?" He hadn't meant to ask it out loud.

She tapped a few keys and studied the screen. "We have your reservation right here."

Mechling chewed his bottom lip. "How many nights am I here?"

She lowered her gaze back to the screen. He glimpsed two yellow enamel butterflies clipped to her hair. "It says *indefinitely*, Mr. Mechling. You're staying here indefinitely."

"That's IMPOSSIBLE!"

"Please don't raise your voice, sir. I'm just reading what we have here."

"No! No way!"

He felt himself lose it. He even pictured an ocean wave, tall and roaring, sweeping him away, his arms and legs flailing helplessly in the bubbling froth.

"I have to get out of here!"

Was that *him* shouting at the poor woman?

"My BlackBerry will work outside. I'll call Joanna. I'll call the office. I'll get in touch. I have to get in touch."

He let the brochures fall to the floor. Spun away—and ran. Grabbed the handle of the glass door. Pushed hard. And bumped the glass with a jarring *thud*.

Startled, he spread his palms against the glass and pushed again, leaning a shoulder into it.

"The door is locked, sir." Angel, the carrot-topped valet, stepped up silently behind him.

Mechling stumbled back. "Locked? It can't be."

The young man stared straight ahead. "It's always locked, see."

Mechling's chest heaved up and down. A bleating sound escaped his throat. A trickle of hot sweat ran down one temple.

Angel took his arm gently and led him away from the door.

"It's not a problem, sir. We're going to change the view in about an hour."

Back in the room, Mechling understood it all.

He was a smart man, and well read. As a boy, he'd devoured science-fiction and fantasy books. He'd had a huge comic book collection. He and his brother had gone to every horror movie they could find.

And now, he knew what had happened to him. Yes, he was shocked and dismayed—no, make that *terrified*. But he understood it clearly.

"I died—and this is Hell."

He had never taken the cholesterol thing seriously, even though Joanna had tried to change his diet. And he'd ignored all the blood pressure warnings.

It must have been a heart attack. He'd died in his sleep.

And here he was in Hell. It was so obvious. Hell was being in the wrong room.

It was all so perfect. The details added up so clearly. He had to smile. He thought of the hotel greeters who had welcomed him on his arrival. The woman behind the desk—her name was Mia. *Missing in Action?* And the valet was *Angel.* Of *course* he was.

Missing in Action? Angel?

Could it be any more obvious?

The names came at him in a flurry. The hotel operator—his name was Barry. *Bury?* And the escort woman . . . What was the name of the guy she was supposed to see? *Romero.* Mechling knew that name, the name of the horror director who'd done *Night of the Living Dead.* Perfect.

And the obnoxious guy in the convention booth? Yes. His name was Mort. Mort Boyer. Mort. Mort. *Mort.*

Is that enough clues for you, Mechling?

The convention floor. All the wrong people . . . all the wrong products . . . No phone connection. No text messaging. No Internet.

The salesman's worst nightmare. The salesman's Hell!

Why hadn't he figured it out even sooner?

Mechling wiped sweat off his face with his hand. He needed fresh air. He walked to the window and pushed it open. A gentle burst of cool air greeted him.

He stared down at the roofs of the apartment and office buildings below. He leaned out, taking breath after breath. The air had no fragrance at all.

Suddenly shivering, his teeth chattering, he turned back into the room and dropped onto the couch. He hugged himself, trying to stop the shakes.

I can jump out the window, he thought, *and it wouldn't matter. I'll end up right back here in the wrong room. I can take a knife and plunge it into my heart. I can drown myself in the bathtub. It wouldn't matter.*

I'm dead. I'm in Hell. Salesman's Hell. No matter what I do, I'll be back in this room . . . indefinitely.

Indefinitely, that's what Mia had said. Indefinitely. Right, Mia, Mia, Mia. I'm Missing in Action. Indefinitely.

Beller, the tall one, and Leeman (nicknamed The Leprechaun for obvious reasons) stopped outside the room door. Beller sniffed. He had a cold. "You want to be the one to tell him?"

Leeman snickered. "Tell him it was all a joke? We'd better make sure he isn't near a weapon. He'll kill us both."

Beller laughed till he coughed. "It's not a joke. It's a *test*, remember?"

"Sorenson is a sadist." Leeman frowned and tugged at his jacket sleeves. "Only a sadist would come up with this kind of test. So elaborate and expensive. Why not just give the guy his promotion and see what he can do? Why put him through all that crap?"

Beller nodded, sniffed again. "Mechling handled himself okay, I think. He didn't freak until the locked-door thing."

"Nerves of steel," Leeman said, only half joking. He sighed. "Let's get this over and get down to the bar. Drinks on Mechling."

He didn't answer their knock. Beller tried the knob, and the door swung open. They stepped into the living room. Briefcase open on the coffee table. A red necktie crumpled on the couch.

"Hey—Sammy? Sammy? It's us!"

Bathroom door wide open. Into the bedroom. Not there, either.

"Hey—Sammy? Where are you hiding?"

Beller tapped Leeman's shoulder. "Hey, look. The window's open."

Well, sometimes even the best salesmen jump to the wrong conclusion. Mr. Mechling will be getting a promotion—but not the one he expected. He has just been promoted to a top position in . . . the Twilight Zone.

GHOST WRITER

◎

Robert J. Serling

A tired, harassed president. His frustrated, unhappy speechwriter.
Not a particularly exciting situation . . . Right? Well, maybe. For
both are about to emerge from history's own Twilight Zone.

The minute Victor Deming entered the Oval Office and
saw the president's haggard, tired face, he almost turned
around and left.

His second impulse was to hand him the few sheets of paper
he was carrying, place them gently and almost reverently on the
mahogany desk, and tell him: "Great speech, Mr. President. Exactly what I hoped you'd say, and what needs to be said."

Which would have been one huge, cowardly lie. What Victor
Deming really thought was that the speech had been flat, feeble,
totally inappropriate, and dull: a boring collection of punchless
banalities and platitudes. He wondered, not for the first time,
how this inarticulate simpleton could have won reelection in the
middle of a seemingly endless, bloodletting war.

Deming was a short, rather pudgy man with shaggy, unkempt
hair framing a sour-featured face that gave him the appearance of
a dyspeptic undertaker. Yet, when he smiled, it dissolved what
seemed to be a perpetual frown that had been glued onto his
mouth. The effect was like seeing glass shatter. Deming was not
smiling now, however. He resisted the temptation to toss the suggested remarks—God knows they didn't deserve to be called a

speech—toss them onto the president's desk with contemptuous force. He compromised by handing him the pages with an expression of regret that barely managed to hide a disapproving frown.

Deming sat down in the stiff-backed chair that faced the chief executive.

"I'm sorry, Mr. President," he said, "but I think you should use what I wrote for you. Your, uh, effort really doesn't say anything. Beautiful sentiments, I'll admit, but that's not what the country wants or needs to hear right now."

"And what do you think the country wants or needs to hear, Victor?"

"What I suggested you say. Some assurance—no, *some factual evidence* that we're actually going to win, so the slaughter of our brave men will stop, and that the enemy will pay for their heinous crimes against the freedom we cherish."

He hesitated, cognizant that his next remarks might well be construed as blatant disloyalty. In his job, Victor Deming reported to no one except the president himself. But in this case, his disappointment in what the president had written numbed all feelings of disloyalty.

He cleared his throat, mentally cursing himself for even this tiny sliver of nervousness.

"Mr. President, I took the liberty of showing your . . . your speech to a few cabinet members, four in all. I wanted their reaction to make sure I was not being unfair in my negative opinion."

"A most fair-minded jury," the president observed with a sardonic little smile. "I take it the verdict was not one of thunderous approval."

"No, sir. The four members I consulted all felt as I do: much stronger sentiments are needed. I hope you will forgive my frankness, Mr. President, but some of the things you've said and done during this conflict have been most controversial, and have even caused outright resentment, let alone understandable concerns."

He cleared his throat again, only this time it felt as if he were on a ship clearing for action. "I fear I'm being disloyal, but you told me to be honest with you when you hired me as an experienced journalist who could help you with your public addresses and advise you on, well, I suppose you might call it possible public reaction."

The president nodded. "And you have performed well in that task, Victor. I appreciate honesty and frankness—there's too damned little of it in this political cesspool we call the nation's capital. So tell me, which words or actions of mine do you think have created the most resentment?"

Deming didn't bother to clear his throat this time; he was back in the mode of a journalist.

"Using the war as an excuse to tamper with civil rights, for one thing. I believe many Americans, and certainly not a few members of Congress, felt such drastic measures were unnecessary and in violation of the Constitution itself."

"There are very few sentences in the Constitution that are permanently engraved in stone, Victor. We have been facing a determined and formidable foe, and sometimes strong measures had to be taken regardless of their unpopularity. But please go on. I have a very thick skin, as you undoubtedly know. You need one in this damned job."

"I understand, sir. However, I must point out that the remarks you've prepared for next week's appearance seem to contradict the strong measures you've espoused previously. And that is why I also took the liberty of showing those four cabinet members what I had prepared for the forthcoming occasion. Frankly, sir, they expressed their strong approval."

The president smiled wryly again "Victor, you do not have to answer this question if you prefer not to, but I'll ask it anyway. Would you care to identify the four cabinet officers who are in agreement with your views on what I should or should not say next week?"

Deming was sorely tempted to refuse and take everyone including himself off the hook, but there was something about this particular practitioner of executive power and political maneuvering that invited at least admiration, if not agreement. If there was one unpleasant quality the man lacked, it was vindictiveness. He decided to answer the question honestly.

"The secretaries of treasury and interior, the postmaster general, and the attorney general. They were the cabinet members willing to talk to me. I should add, however, that they praised your intent. They merely urged a less conciliatory approach. Stronger measures of retribution toward an enemy responsible for starting the war in the first place. We had to attack them, sir. We had no other choice. You've said that yourself many times."

The president nodded sadly. "Yes; although I do regret the price we've paid, not just in lives, but in this case national unity also was a casualty. We've become a nation of polarized beliefs and prejudices. Of hate for anyone holding different opinions and beliefs."

He rubbed his eyes wearily. "Victor, I am so damned tired. I realize only too well the wisdom of one of my most illustrious predecessors. How Thomas Jefferson once described this job I now have the dubious honor of holding. He called it 'a life of splendid misery.' And by heaven, Jefferson was quite right. God, how I hate this damned old house!"

Guilt mixed with pity invaded Deming's mind. He wished now he had not raised the whole issue. The occasion for a presidential appearance had seemed appropriate and timely, but it certainly couldn't be called mandatory, not with this war against oppression far from won.

The military leaders who were fighting the war had been warning that it might take another two years to achieve a decisive triumph, with a crushed, completely vanquished foe prostrate in defeat. Yet here was the president waving premature olive branches and implied forgiveness.

Is the president so naïve as to expect forgiveness toward an enemy whose very way of life we've abhorred and sworn to destroy? Whose beliefs and practices we've denounced as blatantly cruel and even barbaric? The very thought renewed his conviction that what the president intended to say was inappropriate and almost defeatist.

"Sir, once more I implore you to use my much stronger language. You *hired* me as a confidential adviser on precisely such matters as public appearances, occasions requiring you to make utterances of future policy and intentions. To defend the past while enunciating how you envision the future. I mean no disrespect, but the future as you see it is not one in which I take much comfort. Nor will anyone else."

Deming pointed to the pages of oratory that the president had composed. They lay on his desk like fallen leaves from a dying tree. "What is the point of paying me good money if you are bent on ignoring my advice and suggestions?"

"I pay you to advise and suggest, Victor. That does not mean I have to follow all your advice and accept all your suggestions."

Deming expelled a sigh of surrender. When this man made up his mind, he was harder to budge than a five-ton boulder.

"I take it then that you are definitely going to use your words instead of mine," he said in a tone of petulance.

The president chuckled. "Take that frown off your face, Victor. You look like a child who's had a toy taken away from him."

The good-natured jab forced Deming to smile slightly, but he could not resist firing a last salvo.

"Then may I venture to make one final suggestion, Mr. President?"

"Of course."

"Your speech is rather brief. Too brief, if you will permit that observation, which I assure you is well intentioned. There will be other speakers there, of course, but what the President of the United States has to say will draw the most attention."

The president nodded. "I agree with you on its brevity, but I believe I told you once that I always thought a speech should be like a woman's skirt: long enough to cover the subject but short enough to be interesting."

This time Deming permitted himself an audible chuckle. He had heard the president use that metaphor before and had borrowed it himself on more than one occasion. He rose and bowed.

"Then, with your permission, I shall take your leave and return to my own desk."

"No hard feelings, I hope."

"None, sir, I assure you."

The president shook his head, a gesture Deming sensed was one of sympathy, and his instincts were right.

"Tell you what, Victor. As you already know, we'll be taking a special train to the speech site. I'll bring your proposed speech with me, which I'll study again thoroughly and objectively. And while I'm not promising you anything, I might incorporate some of your suggestions into my own remarks."

"That would be very acceptable, Mr. President, and I'm grateful."

Outside the Oval Office, from which he emerged with his head down, he almost bumped into the attorney general, who was on time for a scheduled meeting with the president.

The cabinet officer studied Deming's expression, one of obvious frustration and disappointment, and shook his head understandingly.

"I gather you got nowhere with him, Mr. Deming. Otherwise you'd be grinning from ear to ear."

Deming nodded. "He did promise to review my contributions during the train trip, and make any changes he agrees are necessary. Personally, I'll wager a month's salary his own revisions will be in punctuation."

"I'm not surprised. At any rate, I suggest that you dress warmly for next week's solemn occasion. We shall be into the month of November, and Pennsylvania can be quite chilly at this time of year. Personally, I'm not looking forward to it one bit. Gettysburg itself is a cold, rather dreary little village."

You've undoubtedly heard the adage, "History has a habit of repeating itself." Adages usually are one-line sermons, brief words of advice often written by unknown, even nameless philosophers. Never mind the author of the homily you've just read, whether famous or anonymous. We suspect that its real source was one of those students of ironic coincidences who inhabit the capital of ironic coincidences, more commonly known as . . . the Twilight Zone.

THE SOLDIER
HE NEEDED
TO BE

Jim DeFelice

Courage under fire. A seemingly simple concept, defined more by action than by thought. It is a product of some internal impulse, an emotion beyond our ken. But there are places where those definitions do not hold—where courage may not be simple, where the boundaries between internal and external constantly shift, and where the delicate balance of impulse and action are forever changing. Places where good intent may mix with coincidence and chance to produce results not quite expected . . .

Two hajji on the trail! Brownie!" hissed Gimme over the team radio. "What the fuck?"

Private Michael C. Brown jerked up from his spot in the rocks to get a better view of the trail snaking out of the tan hills below. Two men were walking along it, homemade packs on their backs and AK-47s slung on their shoulders. They were coming from the direction of Pakistan and were almost certainly Taliban infiltrators.

Brown froze for a second, unsure whether to answer or to shoot. By the time he decided he should do both, one of the men saw him and began shouting. Before Brown could raise his M4 to fire, the guerrillas began peppering the rocks around him with bullets.

The rest of the fire team began shooting back. Gimme ran down the slope, firing his M249 SAW. The bullets from the light machine gun blew the guerrilla's skull apart as if it were a pumpkin.

The second man got away, running quickly back up the path and climbing across a small saddleback hill to escape. Jobbers, north of Brown and on the same side of the hill, began circling around to try to follow. But Corporal Gutierrez, the team leader, called him back. The Taliban knew the mountains much better than the Americans did, and it was too easy to be ambushed here. With their position exposed, he pulled them all back to a small plateau about a half mile away, where he could regroup and call in the exchange to the company commander.

Brown had the company radio. He knelt down next to Gutierrez, feeling like a kid making a confession as the corporal called in.

Neither Gimme—Private James Reston—nor Jobbers—Private Dante Wood—said anything to Brown when they saw him. In their eyes, Brown had screwed up big time. Not only had he failed to see the Taliban soldiers as they walked past him, but he'd then alerted them to the fact that the Americans were nearby. Brown knew what they were thinking: if he was going to miss seeing them, he could have at least waited until they cleared the curve where Gimme was; at that point, both could easily have been killed or, better, taken prisoner. There was also the fact that the two might very well have been scouts for a larger unit, following behind.

Standing up was dumb, but it could easily have happened to anyone; it was impossible to be GI Joe Perfect in the Afghan hills, especially at the tail end of a long, mostly boring operation. But Brown had already developed a reputation as a screwup. Everything he did was viewed through that prism.

Corporal Gutierrez didn't say much of anything about it. He never did.

"Floater'll pick us up in four hours up the road," he told the others, referring to the helicopter that had dropped them off two nights before. "Let's get up there."

. . .

There were some snickers back at the camp. Brown pretended not to hear. When that didn't work, he pretended he didn't care. But each glance, each whisper out of earshot, killed him inside.

Being a screwup was new to him. He'd been a good soldier—a *great* soldier—from the day he'd reported to basic training. Brown had aced every class he'd been in. He'd scored a perfect 100 in every section of the APFT, the Army's physical fitness test. He had a nine-minute time in the two-mile run, a phenomenal showing even if he hadn't been six foot four and pushing 180. In his brief career prior to Afghanistan he'd received glowing reviews and the highest possible ratings from everyone in a position to pass judgment on him, formally and informally. He was, on paper, a perfect soldier.

But in the field he just seemed to fall apart. It was always something different. One day he couldn't focus. Another day his finger froze when he needed to pull the trigger. His eyes went fuzzy. He found it hard to breathe. He dropped stuff he needed to carry. A thousand little things multiplied into an avalanche of trouble.

Brown didn't want to feel sorry for himself, but he did. A couple of times he tried talking about what was going on with Corporal Gutierrez. Gutierrez was old for a corporal—he'd enlisted when he was nearly twenty-eight—and by reputation was the best fire-team leader in the company. He tried to be encouraging—Brown could see him straining sometimes to find kind words—but that just made it all harder to accept.

Brown finished eating and headed out of the mess. He figured he'd catch up on his sleep. Corporal Gutierrez was just coming in to get something to eat. Brown felt as if he should say something, but didn't have any words. Gutierrez nodded at him as he passed by, his face calm and stoic. Brown could tell that he meant it to be reassuring, but it only made him feel worse. For the first time since he was maybe seven or eight, he could feel tears starting to well behind his eyes.

I'm not a screwup, he thought to himself as he trudged back to his barracks, but the fact that he had to say it argued directly against its truthfulness.

He bit his lip, trying to pull himself together. Mostly, he was just tired, he thought; a tired guy feeling sorry for himself. If he could get some sleep—real, uninterrupted sleep, days, not hours—he'd be better, back on top.

He'd be lucky to get a few hours of sleep, let alone days, but the idea that it was all he needed gave him a little hope. He was feeling somewhat better when he sat down on his bunk and started to pull off his boots. It wasn't until then that he noticed the package.

"Gotta be a mistake," he muttered to himself—nobody sent him packages. But the name was the biggest thing on the label: PVT. MICHAEL C. BROWN. It even had the *C* for Constantopoulos, his father's best friend's name when he was born, a name he'd never used.

The package had come through an APO box service that the company commander had set up. It was wrapped extra tight in tape, and Brownie had to use his combat knife to get it open. He couldn't imagine who would have sent it. He was even more surprised when he tore open the yellow mailing envelope it was packed in and discovered a small iPod Shuffle, complete with earphones and a USB charger.

"Who the hell sent this?" he said aloud, holding the player up. "Jeez."

There was no return address on the padded envelope; Brown figured that it had probably been inspected somewhere and the original envelope had been battered and then replaced. The only paperwork related to the service company, not the sender.

Suspicious, he flicked the little switch at the side. The light came on green. It was fully charged.

Brown stuck the earphones in, then pressed the button. "Looks That Kill," by Motley Crüe, blasted into his eardrums.

Brown had never been much for heavy metal or hard rock, especially older groups and songs. But he liked the beat, and the edge. Megadeth's "Sleepwalker" played next. Brown was hooked.

Three days later, the company was assigned to backstop a task force operation on the border. The helicopters picked them up at 0200, the big rotors clubbing the dark sky. Brown had his iPod with him, but he kept it in his pocket through the flight, staring at the floor of the chopper as it skipped over the mountainous terrain. There was no moon that night, and when the team landed, Brown thought he'd been deposited in a mine shaft. Even the night scope on his rifle seemed to have trouble with the dark, as if the mountains were sucking in every bit of energy around them.

The team moved along a narrow trail built along the steep edge of the mountain cliffs. Brown walked behind Corporal Gutierrez, struggling at times to keep up, even though Gutierrez was nearly a foot shorter than he was.

"We'll have some breakfast," said the corporal after they'd been walking for nearly three hours.

They sat down in the rocks. Jobbers and Gimme joked about some girl they'd seen on the Internet who posted pictures of herself half nude. She had to weigh two hundred pounds, and she called her blog "Notes from the Nude Porker."

When Brown laughed, the other soldiers didn't seem to notice. He took the hint that they didn't really want him in the conversation, and got out his iPod.

Gutierrez reached over and stopped him.

"Just make sure you can hear what's going on, right?" said Gutierrez.

"Yes, Corporal, I will."

"Good."

When the sun rose they were working their way across a scramble of rocks that had taken out nearly two hundred yards of the road. Gimme said it had to have been done by B-52s, claiming the big planes had dropped tons of ordnance here during the early stages of the war.

Brown was too busy trying to keep his balance to figure out if that was true or not. He went down to all fours, but the rocks shifted so badly that he felt as if he were swimming. By the time he reached solid ground, he was soaked with so much sweat that he wouldn't have been surprised if it had gone all the way through his body armor.

The iPod had turned off. He reached down and clicked on the button as he straightened himself out. A new song came on, something he didn't remember hearing.

It was a punk-rock tune, something similar to what The Clash had played during the late seventies and early eighties, though the band wasn't The Clash. He reached into his pocket and put his thumb and forefinger on the player's anodized aluminum shell, as if touching the device might explain who was singing.

When he looked up, he saw two figures moving across the rocks in the distance, trying to hide in the shadows.

"I got two men across from me, on the side of the valley," he said over the team radio. He raised his rifle. Then, realizing he hadn't been spotted, he flattened himself against the ground, watching the men walk cautiously across the slope. Both had AK-47s; one had an RPG slung across his back.

The RPG—rocket-propelled grenade—left no doubt that these were Taliban soldiers.

Gutierrez tried to maneuver the team into position to capture the two guerrillas, but they spotted Gimme as he started down the slope. The Taliban guerrillas weren't nearly as brave as those the team had seen the other day—rather than fighting, they started to run back in the direction they had come. Gutierrez jumped up and shouted at them to stop and drop their weapons, first in Pashto and then Arabic. But seeing him blocking their way, they squared to fire. Jobbers cut both of them down.

The intelligence that had led to the sweep proved to be a bust, and the fire team's encounter turned out to be the only one of the whole operation. The dead men didn't have any papers and were poorly equipped, but one of the intelligence officers had made a fuss, praising the team for locating the enemy in the jumbled terrain.

Brown felt good about it. For the first time, he hadn't been a screwup on patrol. Gimme and Jobbers didn't ride him at dinner, and the next morning after PT, Corporal Gutierrez told him he'd done well.

"That's the sort of attention you have to give," Gutierrez told him. "Keep at it."

It wasn't much of a compliment, maybe, but Brown felt like he'd just won a Bronze Star. It seemed to him that his luck had changed for the better; he'd gotten the iPod, and now he'd stopped being a total screwup.

He still wasn't sure where the iPod had come from. His mom knew nothing about it. His best theory was that it had come from his half brother Stephen, whom he very rarely saw. He'd lost Stephen's e-mail address, so he had no way to thank him. Several times he thought he might try to find it by contacting someone else in the family, but either he got interrupted or just became shy, somehow unable to actually reach out.

A few days later, their platoon was assigned as part of a sweep through the hills to the south, traveling along a dirt trail that passed for a road here. Brown and the rest of the fire team secured the road leading into a small village as the company CO and two battalion officers met with the village "mayor." The word aggrandized both his title and the settlement—there were only seventeen houses in the entire town, and the man they met with was simply the oldest resident. While they were Pashtun, the villagers seemed to have almost no connection with any of the other people in the province, regarding even their nearest neighbors with some distrust. The Americans, in their eyes, could just as well have stepped off a flying saucer.

Brown knew nothing of the subtleties the officers had to deal with as they tried to establish a connection with the village. His job was to provide protection, and if it wasn't an easy job in the Afghan badlands, it was at least easy to summarize: watch everything, check everyone, trust no one.

The afternoon passed quietly. There was no traffic on the road, and the only person who came close enough to stop was a boy around ten years old, carrying clay bricks he'd gathered from the ruins of a building about a mile and a half away. The bricks were a daub brown, each about eight inches long and three high—heavy for a child, Brown thought, especially a skinny one. But the kid didn't seem to think he was doing anything out of the ordinary. He smiled when they stopped him, let them see everything he had in the bucket, and gratefully took a candy bar as a reward.

They were about halfway back to camp when the first shot rang out, a sniper's bullet that dinged off the Hummer at the lead of the column. In less than a minute, the Americans were involved in a

full-blown firefight with half-a-dozen Taliban fighters. Helicopter
gunships and reinforcements were routed to assist as the unit ma-
neuvered to pin down the would-be ambushers and capture them
in their own trap. Brown and the rest of the fire team were sent
eastward, part of the anvil that the commander hoped to smash
the rebels against. They dismounted from their Humvee a few
hundred yards from a narrow pass through the far side of the hill,
squeezing up into the rocks.

Brown flattened himself against the side of the hill, worming into
the loose rocks. The trail that led down from the western side of
the hill was only fifty yards away. His breaths were hard and close
together; he tried to slow his heart, knowing he had to relax if he
was going to be any good.

The gunfire on the other side of the hill had sputtered out.
The helicopters were circling the area in ever-widening circles, a
sign that the rebels had somehow managed to slip away.

Suddenly Brown heard an odd sound behind him. He turned
quickly, not knowing what to expect. There was nothing there.
He turned back, spooked, off-balance.

Then he realized that it was music from the iPod headphones,
which were dangling from his collar. He'd left the player on as he
scrambled from the Humvee.

He reached down to turn the music off, feeling for the player
clipped to the side of his pocket while keeping his eyes on the
trail. He couldn't find it. Finally, he had to look down.

A new song came on, different from the Megadeth tune that
had just been playing. It had a rockabilly beat, 1950s' revival style.
Brown held his thumb over the arrow button, listening for a few
bars.

A low mumble behind the slope brought his attention back to
the trail.

Quickly, he got his hand back on his M4. Seconds later, one of the rebels appeared, trudging down the hill. He had his AK in his hands. Blood dripped down his arm from a wound near the top of his shoulder, and he moved drunkenly, exhausted by the battle and the blood he'd lost.

Brown glanced to his left. A few yards farther uphill, Corporal Gutierrez had his hand up, indicating that he should wait to fire. There were more men coming.

He aimed his gun and squeezed the breath from his lungs gently, trying not to make a sound. Three more Taliban soldiers appeared, two carrying the third between them.

"Darawem!" yelled Gutierrez, ordering them to stop in Pashto. He jumped up. Brown did so too, pointing his gun at the man who had come down ahead of the others.

"Stop! Stop!" yelled Gutierrez, using phrases he'd memorized. "Give up! You are my prisoners!"

The two soldiers with their wounded comrade took a few steps backward, then dropped the man and began retreating up the hill. Corporal Gutierrez fired two short bursts. His bullets struck both men in the back, but neither went down.

The man opposite Brown hesitated. A million thoughts and emotions flew through Brown's head—panic, fear, hate, confidence, anger, all speeding through in an adrenaline-filled rush. They went so quickly that they were impossible to separate or distinguish.

If the Taliban soldier had raised his rifle even an inch, Brown would have fired—he was ready, his finger heavy on the trigger. But the man dropped his gun.

Brown took a slow step forward. He tried desperately to remember the Pashto words he'd been taught to use to accept a surrender, but they wouldn't come.

"Up," he said in English. "Hands up. Up!"

The command was obvious enough. The rebel raised his arms.

Gimme ran out from behind the boulders farther down on the trail. Brown kept his gun aimed point-blank at the enemy's chest.

"Good, good, good!" yelled Gimme. Then he switched to Pashto, telling the rebel to get down on the ground, away from his gun. The man started to kneel, then collapsed.

"Watch him," said Gimme, running past to cover Corporal Gutierrez and Jobbers, who'd gone after the other two Taliban.

Brown went over and kicked the rifle away. His heart pounded wildly. A rush of sweat poured through him, making him feel as if he were swimming.

He saw something moving on the trail out of the corner of his eye. The wounded man who'd been carried down the slope rolled over and started to rise. He had a grenade in his hand.

"Down! Down!" Brown yelled. But rather than take his own advice, he fired his M4, emptying the magazine into the man. Then he threw himself onto the rebel who had just surrendered.

The grenade exploded in the Taliban soldier's hands. Brown felt a rush of hot air, incredibly hot air.

He couldn't hear.

Brown pushed up, expecting to find that he was wounded, or maybe dead, that this was what it felt like to die. But as he got to his knees he realized that he was alive, and unwounded, covered with dust but fully intact. The rebel had fallen on his own grenade, crumpling under the weight of Brown's bullets.

Gutierrez and the others ran down to him a few seconds later. The other two rebels had collapsed farther up the trail, mortally wounded.

"Brownie, you okay?" asked Gutierrez.

Brown held his hand to his ear. He could hear some of the words, but not very clearly.

"I—I kind of blew out my ears," he said.

"Shit, man, you did good," said Jobbers, pounding him on the shoulder.

"You're really turning yourself around, soldier," the company commander told Brown after they returned. "Good work."

"Sir. Thank you, sir."

Brown stood ramrod at attention, then saluted. He felt his cheeks buzzing red with embarrassment. The CO returned his salute, smiled just a bit, then walked away.

Jobbers and Gimme were nearby, snickering.

"Sir. Thank you, sir," mocked Gimme.

"You turned yourself around," said Jobbers, deepening his voice to mimic the CO's.

"Sir. Thank you, sir," said Gimme, raising his voice to a falsetto.

"Come on," said Brown. "Cut it out."

"You turned yourself around." Jobbers stretched out the words. "Now you ain't Taliban bait anymore."

Brown laughed. Had they made fun of him a week before, he would have felt like retreating to his bunk. But now he didn't care. If anything, their mocking meant he had turned himself around. He wasn't a screwup any more.

It was the iPod that had done it. It had changed his luck entirely.

Brown developed a routine over the next few weeks as they patrolled. He'd leave the iPod earphones down around his neck, tucked tight against his collar, with the volume just high enough so he could hear the music. Then he'd turn his attention entirely to the patrol, concentrating on what he was doing. Twice, he heard strange music coming from the headphones. Exactly at that moment, he would drop to his knee, or press himself down, or do whatever he had to, to be ready for something to happen.

Both times, something did—the first time, he spotted a pair of

Taliban soldiers on horseback in the distance, too far for them to attack. The second time, he noticed a truck careening down the road toward their roadblock before anyone else did. The driver turned out to be a would-be bomber. Gimme shot through his magazine, wiping out the motor and the driver before the bomb exploded.

No one made fun of him after that. Brown had gone from being the company screwup, from being maybe the worst soldier in the entire battalion, to being someone the NCOs could use as an example. He'd always *looked* like a good soldier; now he was acting like one. He felt as if his strides were longer when he walked.

Brown knew, though, that the real credit wasn't due to his own abilities, or even to Corporal Gutierrez's patient, almost wordless counseling.

"It's my iPod," he told some other soldiers in the company one night in the mess while they were eating. He didn't feel embarrassed to admit it. If anything, it was easier to credit it. "I know something's going to happen when I hear a song I've never heard before."

"Get out," said one of the soldiers, a specialist from the Bronx. "No way."

"Really."

"Let me see it."

Brown took it from his pocket—the iPod was never far from him now, even when he was showering.

The other soldier turned it over in his hand, looking at it. There was nothing special about it—silver anodized aluminum, white plastic on the sides and the dial.

"You're telling me this is magic?"

Brown reached to grab it back, but the specialist pulled it away.

"Magic?" said Bronx. "I think you're loony."

"Fuck you," said Brown.

"What's the problem here, boys?" said Corporal Gutierrez, walking over to the table. He'd just come from the food line.

"No problem," said Bronx. He handed the player back.

Gutierrez sat down across from Brown. Everyone ate in silence. Bronx left a few minutes later; soon, only Brown and Gutierrez were at the table.

"How you doing, Brownie?" asked Gutierrez. "You feeling good?"

"Yes, Corporal, I'm feeling real good."

"Relax, Brownie. Take it easy."

Brown nodded. "Yes, Corporal."

"You can call me Ray," said Gutierrez.

"Yeah, okay. Thanks."

Gutierrez picked up the cola he'd brought over with his dinner. "What's with the iPod?"

"Oh, you know. Nothing really."

"You think it's good luck?"

"I told you, Corporal."

"Yeah, I know. You really think it's good luck?"

"I hear all these songs that I never heard before, and it's right then that something happens."

"What do you mean, you never heard them before?" Gutierrez asked. "You listen to that iPod twenty-four/seven."

"I know, Corporal, but they're always songs I never heard before. And very different, too."

Gutierrez smiled.

"I don't know if I'd give the player too much credit," he told Brown. "You're working hard."

Brown nodded.

"I'm just saying, take a little credit, that's all."

.   .   .

A week later, Brown was sleeping in his bunk when the ground began to shake. He rolled out of bed with the second thud; by the third, he realized that they were under attack.

Gimme, Jobbers, Van—everyone else in the barracks was up and scrambling outside. One of the platoon sergeants shouted at Brown as he came out of the building, yelling at him to get up to the northern perimeter. Brown, boots still untied, ran as fast as he could. The area beyond the fence line flashed with white explosions, the sound coming a quarter-beat later, as if they were part of a mistimed sound track. There were gunshots and screams— the Taliban were trying to rush one of the machine guns.

Brown ran to the HESCO barrier—a large earth-filled wall at the camp's perimeter. He jumped on a large wire spool so that he could see over the seven-foot wall and began firing wildly at the flashes in the distance. He went through his magazine in seconds, flipped in another, and fired again.

He was in panic mode—heart crazy, unable to properly aim— but until the M4 was out of ammunition he couldn't stop himself.

Two other soldiers ran up behind him. One had fresh ammunition. Reloading, Brown rose and aimed at the dark clump in front of the machine-gun post. Once more he emptied his magazine, though this time as part of a plan, somewhat more calmly. Still, he couldn't tell whether he'd hit anything or not.

The machine gun was firing furiously at the Taliban, who seemed determined to overwhelm it with sheer numbers. Brown decided he'd fire where it was firing.

As Brown ducked down again for yet more ammunition, two soldiers ran up from the barracks area to help the machine gunner. Another private jumped up onto the spool next to Brown and began firing. The camp's defenders were rallying, stiffening their resistance.

The mortar fire stopped, and for a moment it seemed as if the

Taliban had given up. But then a fresh wave of rebels came out of the hill opposite the camp, renewing the attack on the machine-gun post. Two rocket grenades slammed into the dirt barrier near Brown. Then a half dozen, almost at once, hit the wall in a line that extended on either side of his position.

The paralysis Brown had banished only a few minutes earlier returned. He grabbed at a magazine to reload, then froze with it in his hand, unable to load. It was as if he'd forgotten how. The fury of the attack had driven all his confidence away.

The iPod, he thought. I have to put it on.

A mortar round came over the perimeter and landed behind him. Most of its force was contained by an interior HESCO wall, saving Brown and the men nearby, but fragments caught two soldiers on the other side. They screamed with their wounds.

The agonized yells pushed Brown into action—he reached into his pocket for the player and turned it on. He started to pull the earphones out, but before he could insert them, one of the soldiers near him began firing madly. Brown jumped up and saw three Taliban guerrillas within four feet of the wall.

He shook with the gun as it fired, his body seeming to punch each bullet out. The rebels fell into the darkness of the earth.

And still the Taliban kept coming. It was as if the soldiers were springing from the rocks themselves. Artillery began raining on the area beyond the perimeter, then suddenly stopped. Their explosions were replaced with the beat of helicopter rotors, pounding the air. Salvos of rockets screamed from the sky. Then the artillery returned again.

Brown reloaded, then peered over the berm. The flood of black streaming toward the walls had disappeared. The attack had been repulsed.

.   .   .

From that night on, Brown knew that the iPod was more than just good luck. It had a certain power in it, something that would protect him and keep him from harm.

He finally got the courage to call his half brother. He denied sending him the iPod. That only made it seem even more powerful.

Magic?

Brown didn't care what the mechanics of the thing were. He only knew it worked. He kept it with him all the time, fully charged.

Two weeks later, the company joined another sweep near the Pakistan border, this one a large operation involving French troops and Afghan commandos. Brown's fire team was assigned to move up a valley about two miles, hold the area for twenty-four hours, then return.

"So now we just twiddle our thumbs," said Gimme after the helicopter had dropped them off.

"Don't be bitchin'" said Jobbers. "I'd hate to be with the Frenchies. They're walking into heavy shit."

"Better than sitting on the goddamn bench, half a million miles from the action," said Gimme. "But shit, I'd hate to be with the French. Because you know they're going to screw it up."

"I wouldn't mind a fight," said Brown.

"Junior's rarin' for a rumble," laughed Jobbers.

"Let's get walkin', boys," said Gutierrez. "Separate. Don't take anything for granted."

They covered the two miles in under an hour, cutting their own path across the rock-strewn terrain. Afghanistan here looked more like the moon than the earth, a cold and arid vacuum where no human could thrive. But there were villages sprinkled all through the hills, places that had been settled for thousands of years. Smoke curled up from a crook in the peaks to their west, and the ruined bricks of a long-abandoned hamlet sat on the near side of a hill not two miles away.

They climbed up a ridge that cut like a scar across a low mountain. The view was as breathtaking as it was unworldly. After they reached the GPS point they were assigned, Corporal Gutierrez called in and got an update on the overall operation. Things were moving well, he was told, but so far there had been no contact with the enemy. The fire team should just sit and wait, as assigned.

Brown settled behind some rocks, relaxing a little as he began scanning the valley below. When he'd first come to Afghanistan, a two-mile trek with a full ruck would have left his thighs sore and his upper back cramped. Now he barely noticed the difference when he took his backpack and gear off.

By midafternoon, everyone on the team knew their end of the operation was going to be a bust. Nothing was happening here, not today, not tonight, not tomorrow.

The hours dragged. They split up the watch to sleep, even though no one could. Finally, at 0200, the sky to the east began to light up with explosions. They were so far away that they couldn't hear the rumble of the shells and bombs hitting.

The show continued for nearly two hours. The silence returned; the only sound Brown could hear was the distant whine of a jet engine, and his own labored breathing.

They started for the chopper at 0800, giving themselves about two hours of cushion to get there. Just as they neared the landing zone, Corporal Gutierrez received a change in orders—the operation they were supporting was continuing; they were to take a new position about three miles farther east of the one they'd held the night before. Things were fluid; they should be ready for anything.

.   .   .

Brown trudged up the ridge, Metallica pounding into his skull. His stomach felt as if it were stretching—the first sign of hunger.

"We have another mile to go," Corporal Gutierrez announced.

Before Gimme could make any of his usual jokes about who or what was waiting for them there, the ridge above percolated with rounds from a .50-caliber machine gun.

Brown threw himself flat. Through the dust he spotted some boulders four or five yards from where he was. He scrambled to them, pushing in against the biggest as the ground percolated. Lead and dirt mixed in a mist around him, so thick that he started to cough.

His first thought was that they were taking friendly fire—the machine gun was across the valley somewhere, and the staccato as it echoed sounded exactly like the sound of an American M2 heavy machine gun. But he knew there weren't any other Americans nearby.

As the gunfire continued, Brown slipped off his backpack. He curled around, trying to see the others. Corporal Gutierrez was in a ditch about five yards ahead of him. Gimme was behind him, a little farther down the slope. Jobbers, who'd been at point, was lying on the ground, writhing in pain.

The music in the iPod changed. Nickelback came on, playing a song from *Darkhorse* he'd never heard.

"Cover me!" he yelled to Gimme and Gutierrez. Then he jumped up and ran to Jobbers. As soon as he realized what Brown was doing, Gimme raised the M249 and began firing in the general direction of the enemy machine gunner, hoping to draw his fire. Brown stooped down and ran to Jobbers, pushing down and sliding his right arm under the private's chest. He pulled up, then lost his balance as the gunfire turned back in his direction. As he started to fall, he managed to pitch his weight toward the shallow ditch where Corporal Gutierrez was waiting. The corporal caught him and Jobbers, falling backward against the side of the rill but breaking their fall.

Jobbers groaned. He'd been hit in the right leg as well as his armored vest. The vest had taken a beating, but the ceramic inserts had managed to deflect most of the bullets' force. His face was pockmarked with blood from rock splinters.

Gutierrez ripped off the bottom of his pant leg with his knife and used it to stop the bleeding. Brown squirreled back around and tried to figure out where the machine gunner was.

"Bastard has to stop soon," said Brown. "His frickin' barrel's gonna melt."

"Grenade him," said Gutierrez.

"Yeah, yeah," said Brown. But his grenade launcher was back with the rest of his gear near the rock.

"You take this," the corporal told him. "I'll do it."

The grenades seemed to make the machine gunner more determined.

"I gotta go get the radio so we get support," Brown told Gutierrez.

The corporal shook his head.

"Just wait. He's going to have to stop. His barrel's going to melt down to nothing."

But the machine gunner didn't stop.

"I'm going," said Brown.

"Next lull," said Gutierrez, grabbing his arm.

Brown eased down off his haunches. The music had faded, and for a moment he felt a twinge of panic rising in his chest—what if the battery had died? But it was just a pause before changing songs.

The player dished up a gospel song by Johnny Cash, old and obscure.

He'd definitely never heard that.

"Now!" said Brown, leaping to his feet.

Gutierrez tried to stop him, but he moved too quickly.

The machine gun stuttered and then stopped firing abruptly. By the time the enemy gunner got the weapon unjammed, Brown was back with the radio and his gear.

Command said that the main units were still engaged some miles to the east, but promised artillery. The barrage started a few minutes later. Within three or four shells, the machine gun stopped firing.

They had to get Jobbers out, but the helicopter would be an easy target if the Taliban across the way were simply hiding in the rocks or a cave.

"I'll check it," said Brown.

"No, I'm gonna go," said Gutierrez. "You and Gimme stay with Jobbers."

"I can do it, Corporal." Brown tapped his iPod. "Nothing's gonna happen to me."

"That thing ain't magic, Brown. You stay here."

There was no arguing with Gutierrez this time. The corporal trotted away.

Brown leaned against the side of the ditch, eyeing the area where the machine gunner had been. He touched the volume on the iPod, amping Megadeth but leaving the earphone out of his ear.

"How's Jobbers?" asked Gimme, trotting over.

"I think he's going to be okay," said Brown.

"Yeah."

Gimme leaned down to his friend.

"You're going to be okay, man," he told him. "We're getting you out."

Jobbers grunted. His breathing was normal, but he was going in and out of consciousness.

"You okay here with him?" Gimme asked Brown. "I want to back up Guts."

"Yeah, I'm okay."

Gimme rose and began trotting down the trail.

The Taliban gunner had been splattered by an artillery shell. Only pieces of him were left, scattered around the small rift in the hills that he'd used as a nest.

He'd been using an American-made M2, old and battered but obviously still deadly. The shells had smashed the body on one side and blown off the barrel. Even so, Gutierrez took away the belt feed, cartridge stop, and some of the rest of the guts, worried that it might somehow resurrect itself.

The corporal stayed on the other side of the valley when the chopper came in, making sure there was no possibility of an ambush. The Black Hawk popped over the ridge, hovering so close to the hill that it looked like its blades would scrape the rocks. The basket it lowered for Jobbers swung and bashed Brown in the face as he grabbed it; he pushed down on it, settling it next to his comrade. He reached over and scooped Jobbers into it, closing his eyes as grit kicked off from the hill peppered his face. With one eye closed, he pulled the straps tight, then leaned back.

"Take care, Jobbers," he said as the winch began hauling him away.

The pickup took less than ninety seconds. Brown didn't draw a breath the whole time.

Adrenaline spent, the fire team began making its way back to the original pickup point. The operation to the east had petered off. Like many, it had been successful and frustrating at the same time. Three dozen Taliban had been killed, and one taken prisoner, but at least another dozen had managed to escape into Pakistan, where they couldn't be pursued.

Corporal Gutierrez didn't think that there'd been only one gunner on the hill when the fire team was ambushed—a lone machine gunner would have been unprecedented—but at this point it made no sense to look any further. They were all tired, they'd used a little more than half their ammo, and the best thing to do was go back and regroup.

The team stopped about a half mile from the pickup, climbing into some rocks that gave them a good view of the landing zone and the area around it. The chopper was about an hour away; Gutierrez decided they'd wait until it was nearby to descend.

"I can't shake this feeling we're being tracked," said Gimme, scanning the valley behind them.

"Maybe I should swing back," said Brown. "I can get behind the hill over there, go around. You guys see if I'm followed."

Gimme laughed. "Who do you think you are? Rambo?"

"No, I can do it."

"Relax, Brownie," said Gutierrez. "You don't have to prove yourself anymore."

"I'm not trying to prove myself. Shit. I just think we can do that. I can do that."

"Don't push it."

"You're crazy," said Gimme. "You went from being, like, yellow, to now like Superman."

"I'm not Superman," said Brown. "But I have the iPod."

Gimme smiled, then got up and walked a few feet away to take a leak.

"It's not the iPod," Gutierrez told him.

"It *is*," said Brown. "It's—I know you think I'm nuts. But it's got some special power. And it came from nowhere. I thought my half brother sent it, but he didn't. It came out of nowhere. I think God or some part of the universe sent it. Whatever—it's turned everything around."

"I gave it to you," said Gutierrez. "I was trying to cheer you up."

Brown stared at him in disbelief.

"I did," said the corporal. "You were so depressed. Your butt dragged every morning, every night. I wanted to get you going."

"Where'd you get it?"

"I've had it. I just never used it after I got the Nano."

"I don't believe you."

"Why would I lie to you?"

"I don't know." Brown stood up.

"I can name every song on it."

"How do you explain the songs that don't play until the hajji show up?"

"That's your imagination. All the songs are there."

"Bullshit."

Gimme came back. "What's up?" he asked.

"Nothin'," said Brown. He pulled the earphones up and slipped them in. Wherever the iPod had come from, there was something about it—call it magic, a miracle, God—call it whatever.

It was *special*. It could last forever on a charge, for one thing, much longer than any other MP3 player by far. And then there was the music, which he *knew* couldn't be explained.

Brown began walking along the hill toward the east, thinking about whether to cross over the valley and look for any Taliban following them. He couldn't disobey an order, though.

Just then he saw a glint in the hill opposite them.

"There!" he shouted, pointing.

There was a puff from the slope. A mortar shell whistled through the air.

. . .

Brown knew instantly what he had to do. He didn't think about it. He started to run down the hill, in the direction of the valley. He would swing around, come at the bastards from the rear.

It was the right thing to do. He should have done it earlier.

Corporal Gutierrez yelled at him, but his words were drowned out by the explosions. Brown guessed he was telling him to stop, but that made no sense, and he didn't. He ran as fast as he could, welcoming the tightness in his chest and the burn in his thighs.

It wasn't until Brown had gotten across the valley and onto the far side of the ridge that he realized how stupid his idea was.

Corporal Gutierrez had called in for support, and as Brown climbed the slope, a pair of F-16s doused the Taliban position with five-hundred-pound bombs. The explosions sounded like cracks of thunder, shaking the hill and bringing up a cloud of smoke that turned gray as it rose over the ridge. But there was no stopping now—Brown kept moving, locked in the course he had set. To turn back would be to deny everything that had happened over the past few weeks, to once more become a coward.

And to deny the power that was guiding or at least helping him. He believed, he simply believed. It had no logic; it might have no rational explanation, but he knew that the iPod was definitely saving him, was definitely helping him be the soldier he needed to be. Maybe Gutierrez *had* given it to him—there really was no reason for him to lie about that—but what the iPod did could not be explained.

The back of the ridge flattened to a gentle slope as Brown moved east. The scrub vegetation was sparse; there'd be little cover if the Taliban fighters were still alive. He trotted forward, then started to run, heart pounding.

Megadeth gave way to Slayer.

Then silence. Then a song that sounded like something from Jane's Addiction's early years, something he'd never heard.

Brown dropped to his knee, M4 raised. He held his breath.

Two, three, five Taliban came across the side of the hill, scrambling down.

Brown waited a beat, wanting them all to appear first.

The second man in line turned.

Bullets ripped from Brown's gun. He swept up in a line, swept back. His fingers flew to the mag. He reloaded, fired again. And again.

They were dead, all dead, every one of them. Dead.

A song by Starkweather began blaring in his earphones.

Corporal Gutierrez and Gimme were waiting at the bottom of the hill when Brown came down. The chopper was approaching in the distance.

Gimme's face was a smile, an entire smile.

"You da man." Gimme laughed. He hugged Brown, squeezing him. "You da fuckin' man."

"How many?" asked Gutierrez.

"Five, Corporal."

"Relax, Brownie. It's all right. I ain't mad. Much." Gutierrez laughed. "It's okay."

Brown nodded. He felt—"solid" was the only way to describe it, as if he were a building and every nail, every screw, every bolt had been tightened and perfectly adjusted. He was not a coward. He might not be a hero—he couldn't quite see himself fitting into that definition—but he was definitely a soldier, and a solid one.

"It ain't magic," said Gutierrez. Then he hugged him.

"Thanks, Corporal," said Brown.

He smiled.

The chopper was close.

"Let's get the hell out of here," said Gutierrez.

Brown pushed the earphones into his ears. He smiled. "Looks That Kill" was playing, the same song that he'd heard when he first listened to the iPod. He'd heard it dozens if not hundreds of times.

He fell into line with the others.

"Watch for snipers," said Gutierrez.

"Nothing to worry about," said Brown. "I chased them off. Ain't nothing going to happen now—I got the iPod."

He pulled off his helmet and wiped some of the sweat from his hair. The day had gotten hot.

"Yo, watch for snipers," barked Gimme.

"Relax, man—ain't nothin' happening to us," said Brown.

The chopper was coming in low on the other side of the hill, drowning everything out. Brown couldn't hear the music.

Then he realized that it had stopped.

"What the hell?" he said, looking down at the player.

A single shot flew from the hill behind them. Brown heard it—a long, sleek whistle, the sound of a guitar string breaking under stress.

Then he fell to the ground, killed by a bullet through the back of his head.

Alerted by the Black Hawk, another F-16 came in and dropped a fresh bomb load on the hill where the sniper had fired from. Gutierrez and Gimme picked up Brown's prostrate body and carried him between them all the way around to the other side of the hill, where the chopper was waiting.

Gutierrez unclipped the player from his dead soldier's body, holding it in his hand as the helo took off.

The iPod had turned Brown around, there was no question about that. It had made him a good soldier, the soldier he'd needed to be.

It seemed to have stopped playing. Gutierrez put his thumb on the switch and turned it off, then back on. The little power light remained off.

"Broke?" asked Gimme.

Gutierrez flipped it over in his fingers. He pushed the large dial, turned it on and off again, but couldn't get it to play.

"Battery ran out," said Gimme.

Gutierrez nodded. He closed the player in his hand. He couldn't help but think he was responsible for Brown's death. The kid had needed something to believe in, magic, and Gutierrez, by accident, had given it to him.

Was that wrong? If he hadn't, Brown would never have become the soldier he was capable of becoming. But he wouldn't have gotten stupid, either; he'd never have removed his helmet, or made himself such an easy target. Really, it was a miracle he hadn't been killed earlier.

"What you told him was the truth, Ray. That player was just a player," said Gimme, who was staring at him. "There wasn't anything special about it. Just a player."

"Yeah."

Gutierrez felt a sudden impulse to throw the iPod out the open door of the helicopter. He reared back.

"Hey, Corporal, what are you doing?" asked the door gunner.

Gutierrez stopped. He opened his hand, revealing the iPod.

"You're not going to throw that out, are ya?" asked the gunner.

"Yeah."

"Shit, I'll take it."

"Battery's dead or it's busted," said Gimme.

"Hell, you can get batteries for these things online cheap," said the gunner.

"But if it's broken—"

"I'll take a shot. What do you have to lose?"

Gutierrez handed it over. Then he sank back on the bench.

When they landed, the gunner jumped out with him and stopped him on the tarmac.

"Hey, you sure it's okay I take this iPod?" he asked. The player was clipped to his vest, and the phones were in his ears.

"Yeah. It's busted."

"No way, man, listen." He pulled out one of the phones. " 'Looks That Kill,' man. Motley Crüe. You got good taste."

Gutierrez glanced down at the iPod. The power light was green. Fully charged, fully functional.

He stared for a full five seconds. Maybe there was something about that iPod after all. Maybe he should take it back. Destroy it.

He raised his hand to take it.

"Gotta go," said the gunner, turning back and hopping into the Black Hawk. "Thanks."

The helo roared upward before Gutierrez could say anything else.

Corporal Ray Gutierrez. A good soldier, an excellent leader. A brave man. But he will spend the rest of his life thinking about courage and foolishness, and wondering where the boundaries lie. More critically, he will ponder his own responsibility for the death of a brave soldier, and wonder what role he played in the fates of others as they met their fears, battling chance and destiny in . . . the Twilight Zone.

ANTS

Tad Williams

Everybody knows someone like Karl Eggar, a man with the right answers for everyone else's problems—or at least so he thinks—but who never gets as much respect as he thinks he deserves. This weekend, though, that's all about to change for Karl. He's going to be proved right in a way even he couldn't have expected. . . .

I t feels good to swing hard, to feel his muscles flex and the blade of the ax bite deep into the wood. It feels even better that it's the old apple tree, the one whose apples have never been any damn good, puny and sour. *But the blossoms,* she always says, *it blossoms so nice—it makes the whole yard look pretty!* Yeah, and who gives a crap about that?

Well, today he's made his mind up. If there's one upside of having lost his job down at the salvage yard, it's that he doesn't have to pretend to care about anything around here that isn't pulling its weight. The apple tree is a perfect example: a few useless blossoms versus the need to bring down the heating bills next winter equals the tree is history.

As he finishes setting the cut wood onto the pile, which is getting impressively high, he sees her watching from the window. Oh, God, that face. Like he was killing a family dog instead of just taking down an old eyesore of an apple tree. He gives her a mocking smile and wave, a little twiddle of the fingers. She turns away.

He married her. He must have—everybody tells him so. But

he doesn't really remember it happening and certainly doesn't remember why. Sometimes, listening to her complain about all the things that (according to her) he should have done and hasn't, or shouldn't have done but did anyway, he has a sudden fantasy of just taking a big old swing at her with his fist, like something out of a Popeye cartoon, hitting her so hard she just flies away and he never has to hear that voice again.

He even sees it with a caption, like one of those rumpled, xeroxed cartoons they used to pass around at the yard in the days before the Internet: "Bitch in Space."

"That's just great, Karl," she tells him as he comes in and sets the ax in the corner of the kitchen. It needs to go out to the garage to be oiled and resharpened and put away properly, but he's going to have a beer first because he goddamn well deserves it. He wipes sweat from his face and the back of his neck. Maybe two beers. He's had only a couple today so far and it *is* Saturday. Is there some law that says you have to have a job to enjoy a few beers on Saturday?

"What the hell are you talking about?"

"Just great. Spend an hour chopping down a harmless tree for firewood in the middle of July instead of doing something useful. It's ninety goddamn degrees outside—what do we need firewood for?"

He ignores her, feels the beer sliding down his throat, icy and perfect. If only there were a way to pour cold beer over his whole life. Yeah, drown the bitch with it . . . or at least drown her out.

"Have you done any of the other things I asked you to do? Did you call the exterminator?"

"We don't need any goddamn exterminator. Do you know what those cheating bastards charge? It's just a few ants."

"Just a *few*?" She stares at him like he's crazy. "If you were ever in here for any longer than than it takes to open another beer, you might have noticed that we're being overrun by the creepy little things. Look. Look!" She's waving her arm like her turn indicator is broken. He rolls his eyes, which just makes her more pissed off. "Look in that sink, damn you!"

He takes a long swallow of his beer, hitches his pants up, rubs some sweat from the small of his back, and ambles over to the sink. It really would be nice just to plant her one, a shot in the nose to straighten her right up. Yeah, he'd probably go to jail, that's the way things are nowadays, but oh my God it would be like a dream come true. . . . "So what?"

"Do you happen to notice about a thousand ants in there?" She points at them like he's stupid—like he really doesn't see them. "And in the cabinets, and on the table, and all over the floor. It's *gross*, Karl, it's goddamned gross and disgusting! I can't walk across the kitchen without stepping on hundreds of the things!"

"So why do you want to pay an exterminator if you're doing it yourself?" A good one. He laughs.

She slaps him stingingly on the arm. "You're not funny, you mean bastard!"

For an instant—just an instant, but it rushes through him like a wildfire—he almost does hit her. Things go a little bit upside down, like when he sometimes gets up too quickly, gets dizzy, and almost falls. "Don't . . . don't you ever do that again," he tells her, with enough of his true feelings in his voice that she backs away a few steps, like a dog trying to decide whether to bolt.

"I want those things out of here, Karl," she says, but whining now like a stuck-up kid. "They're disgusting."

"Oh, they're in the sink, isn't that too bad," he says, mocking her. "Did it ever occur to you, you lazy bitch, that all you have to do is turn on the water and wash 'em down the drain?" He does, using the rinsing hose to send all the little, leggy black creatures sliding and swooshing away to a watery death. "Bye-bye, you little fuckers." He turns to her. "See? Problem solved."

She's gone pale now, her face cold and hard. She hates it when he calls her "bitch"—as if it wasn't the best possible name for someone like her, someone who was pretty damn cute in high school but has long since gone fat and mouthy, just like her chain-smoking, vodka-gargling mother, but who also puts on airs like she's too good for him because she watches Oprah and reads an occasional book.

"Why are you so hateful, Karl? It's not just ants in the sink." Her voice starts to rise. "What about the ones on the floor? What about the ones on the counter, and in the damn cabinets, and in the goddamned *sugar bowl*, Karl? Huh? What about that?"

Why don't they think? he wonders. Why *can't* they think? Because all this Oprah, Dr. Phil, everything's-about-feelings bullshit clouds their minds, that's why. Not a one of them can think about things logically, make a plan, solve a problem.... "Oh, Jesus, shut your mouth for just a minute, Norah—I know it's hard for you, but try—and I'll show you what to do with the goddamn sugar bowl."

The ants trek across the table in a wavering line. You have to admire their focus, if nothing else, he thinks. They're like him, in a way—small, maybe, but tough and strong and well organized. They're carrying little grains of sugar from the bowl across the table and down onto the floor, then off to their nest or hive or whatever they have. It's kind of funny, really. If you're an ant, finding that sugar bowl must be like winning the lottery.

He puts his hand under the sugar bowl to lift it. The plastic table cover is sticky and it grabs at the hairs on the back of his hand. Something hot and red flares in him again. "No wonder we got ants everywhere. This place is filthy. Now, pay attention, stupid, and I'll show you something. Ants in the sugar bowl, big problem? I don't think so." He goes to the sink and dumps out the sugar, stands for a moment, sweat on his face and his heart beating strangely as he watches the little black shapes dig out of the pile of white crystals on the floor of the basin. Then he sluices them away with the rinsing hose.

"Empty the sugar bowl," she said. "Real clever, Karl. God, it's just like you always say, men are just *smarter*. I wonder why I never thought of it? And when I want to put sugar in my coffee, or on my cereal, why, I'll just go scrape it out of the drain. Brilliant."

He isn't going to look at her because if he does, he's probably going to smack the shit out of her. He only ever did it once before, when they were first together. She came back from her mother's after two weeks and they didn't talk about it again. She hadn't seen Oprah in those days.

"Just because *you* don't use sugar doesn't mean I don't want to use it, Karl." She was still using that voice, the one that made his hairs stand on end. "They're into the sugar bag in the cabinet, too, but I'm sure you thought of that already with your superior male logical intelligence. So tell me, Mr. Spock, am I just supposed to give up sugar entirely?"

Wouldn't do you any harm, you fat bitch, he thinks. His head hurts and he doesn't really want to talk anymore. He wants another beer, maybe two—shit, maybe four—and then he wants to go sit in the living room and watch the baseball game, or wrestling, or anything that means he won't have to think about any of this.

"Shut up and look," he tells her. "Just . . . shut up. I'm warning you." Mr. Spock, huh? Compared to the crap that fills her head, he *is* an alien genius. His teeth are clenched so hard now that it's making the headache worse. He rinses the sugar bowl, dries it off with a paper towel, then refills it from the sugar bag after flicking off a few six-legged explorers. It's the hot weather. The ground gets dry and the little bastards come in looking for water, but then find out where all the good stuff is. *Little shits.* His moment of identification with the ants is long gone. Just somebody else who wants to rip him off.

When the clean, dry sugar bowl is full of clean, dry sugar, he takes it to the dish cabinet and rummages around until he finds a bowl large enough for it to sit in comfortably. Then, with it nesting there like a small boat in a bigger boat, he fills the outer bowl with water and holds the whole arrangement out for Norah to see.

"Get it?" He points to the inch-wide span of water now ringing the sugar bowl. Karl is pleased to get the last word for once—he couldn't have proved his case against her lazy thinking more completely if he'd had a chance to prepare in advance. There's absolutely no way for her to refute this evidence. "It's like a moat around a castle, see? The ants can't get to the sugar bowl. They try to cross the water, they drown. No ants in the sugar. Get it, Norah? *Get it?*"

He's about to set the sugar bowl back on the table when he remembers the stickiness that had sucked at his arm. He wipes the sweat from his forehead. Bad enough the heat, but the whole goddamn house is sticky, too. Ants? The way she cleans, they probably have roaches. . . . Karl puts the sugar bowl up on top of the refrigerator, then pulls the plaid cover off the kitchen table and holds it out toward her. "Go on, make yourself useful. Clean this shit up, the ants won't even *want* to get on the table. It's only because you keep this place like a pigsty. . . ."

He picks up his ax and starts toward the garage. The headache is beginning to ease.

"You . . . you *bastard!*" she shrieks. "You stupid, ignorant bastard! Those damn ants are *everywhere!* What am I supposed to do, bring in the hose and just fill the house with water? Is that what you're saying?"

He's not going to argue anymore. He showed her—he *shut her up*—so why won't she stay that way?

"Don't walk out on me!" She's screaming louder now, that voice like a dentist's drill—he swears he can feel it buzzing in his fillings. *"Don't you dare!"*

"Shut your damn mouth or I'll slap you silly." He tries to get the garage door open but she's blocking his path. He grabs her arm and yanks her out of the way. The garage beckons like a cave, dark and cool, quiet and safe. Then he feels her fingernails in the skin of his neck, burning, sharp, and her other hand in a rude little fist, smacking away at the back of his head.

"Don't you dare turn your back on me, Karl Eggar, you ignorant pig! Don't you dare! Don't you . . . !"

And suddenly something just expands inside him, a great, hot plume like the blast that leveled Hiroshima. He can feel it blaze up through the whole length of his upper body, out of his guts and up his spine and out the top of his head, rising like a mushroom cloud. He has the ax in his hand and suddenly everything has turned hot; the very air is blazing like an oven. Everything is flow, and noise, and movement, and all of it is glowing red—a single, hot, moving, expanding thing, with him helpless in its midst, helpless but laughing as the ax rises and falls, over and over again. Each time it strikes it makes a sound—*skutch, skutch, skutch*—as satisfying as sinking a steak knife into a thick porterhouse. He can't stop laughing. Heat and the glorious pounding—the pounding! He feels like he is hammering the world in half.

For a long time after he has finished swinging, Karl only stands, the ax now hanging in his hands, heavy as an iron girder. His limbs tingle; even his scalp prickles. He is drained, as bonelessly weary as if he has just had a ten-minute orgasm. But there is a . . . thing . . . on the floor. No, many things, one big and the rest in all kinds of sizes and shapes. It's hard to make out details because the kitchen is very messy. The walls are spattered and dripping red. Red everywhere.

The exhilaration is beginning to wear off. He sinks into a crouch in the middle of one of the larger scarlet puddles. The strangest, thickest, saltiest smell is in his nose. He's trying to think, staring at what's left of his wife. Call an ambulance? No point. No ambulance in the world is going to do any good. All the kings horses and all the king's men aren't going to put . . . that . . .

He wretches up what is in his stomach, a slurry of beer and less identifiable components. The smell combines with the blood and suddenly he is on his side in the warm red goo, unable to do anything further until he has emptied his stomach to its lining, until he is gagging out air and streams of mucus. Then, numb and unable to think about much of anything, he staggers to his feet, drops his shoes and clothes where he stands, then steps carefully over the abstract red splatters as he leaves the kitchen.

He stands under the shower for what seems like hours, hoping in a hopeless kind of way, like a superstitious child, that if he waits long enough and lets enough water run over him, when he goes back to the kitchen, things will be . . . different.

But, of course, they are not. He stands shivering, looking down at the bloody meat and bone, the scatter of pieces that had seemed so inevitably connected once, but now seem as random as an emptied bowl of stew. His stomach lurches again but there is no longer anything in it to throw up.

Think, he tells himself. Think. Don't panic. That's when people make mistakes. Don't think with your emotions. Be a man. Be . . . logical.

First things first. The shower was a mistake. He shouldn't have left the room. The police, they have all this equipment now, special lights and chemicals to detect bloodstains, even stains that are so small or so old you can hardly see them. He'll put his shoes back on and stay in the kitchen, and if he has to go anywhere else, he'll leave the shoes here so he doesn't track any blood.

But he has to leave the room almost at once because the blood is pooled everywhere across the floor, right to the baseboards. He doesn't think it will soak through the vinyl flooring, but at the edge of the floor it will definitely get into the gaps between the flooring and the walls, and that will be that. So he goes to the garage and gets a big plastic tarp left over from camping, and then, back in the kitchen, he gingerly lifts the largest piece up onto it—it is surprisingly heavy for only part of a person—then begins piling the other decent-size chunks onto the plastic as well. He has to stop several times to gag again, but after a while he gets used to the smell and a sort of gray haze covers his thoughts and he can work without thinking too much about what he's doing. Still, the discovery of a finger with a wedding ring still on it makes him pause for a moment. It's not that he loved her, or even gave a damn about her, but this . . . this is so . . . final. Not to mention the fact that he'll spend the rest of his life in jail if he gets caught, and that's if he's lucky. And now he's cleaning up. He's trying to hide what he did. That could get him the death penalty.

Karl pauses for a moment, then gives a sort of shrug. Too late now. The bitch drove him to it. Admitting that he did it, calling the police, going to jail—that would be giving her the last word. That would be Norah having the last laugh as he spends the rest of his life, maybe fifty years or more, suffering for what *she* did to *him*.

But how will he get it all clean? He's seen it all on television cop shows. Eventually, they'll come, and he'll be the first suspect.

Karl surprises even himself by laughing. Of course he should be the first suspect. Because he did it! He's sitting naked in his kitchen in a pool of his wife's blood!

No, think, he tells himself. Look. There are red splatters

everywhere, and dozens of pieces flung all over the room still to find. And on top of everything else, ants, hundreds of the little bastards still crawling everywhere, oblivious, and if they aren't already doing it, they'll soon be tracking thousands of little bloody ant footprints everywhere. The ants are searching for food—they'll head right for the blood and bone chips and bits of meat. And even if he keeps them off the body, how will he find all the pieces of Norah and get this kitchen clean?

The idea, when it finally comes, is so good that he begins to laugh again.

You dumb bitch, he thinks. You could have watched Oprah for a hundred years and you'd still never have an idea as good as this!

He gets to work.

Once he has every visible piece collected on the plastic tarp, some of them already crawling with tiny black insect bodies, Karl begins to scrub. He concentrates on soaking up blood first, as quickly and thoroughly as possible, using paper towels and rags from the garage. It takes a couple of hours, and after a while he realizes he is dizzy with exhaustion and hunger, so he stops to stand naked in the middle of the kitchen and eat corn chips from the cupboard. While he is getting them out, he notices a few random droplets of red on the cupboard door, six feet above the ground. There must be hundreds like that, he knows. Still, he has a plan.

When he has finally mopped up all the blood he can see and mopped the whole floor with rubbing alcohol to kill the traces, he takes the red rags and the ruined torso and the forlorn, bloody pieces, even the ants climbing on them, and wraps them all together in the plastic tarp and tapes it shut. Then he sits down on the floor to wait. He has blotted up every ant he could find, mashing them into the bloody rags now wrapped inside the tarp, and for the first time today the kitchen is antless. Norah would be pleased, if she weren't dead.

The sky is darkening outside and the sounds of the empty house give him the strangest feeling that he should finish up soon because his wife will be coming home from work soon—but, of course, she won't. Besides, it's Saturday. The weekend. Tomorrow's Sunday. He stares at the huge tarp swathed in duct tape. Day of rest.

His laugh, this time, is raspy and hoarse.

He opens a beer, but doesn't have to wait long. Within ten minutes the first scouts of the ant army return to the kitchen. Karl sits, sipping on his beer, and lets them walk past him—hell, they can walk over him for all he cares. He's smeared in blood again, so why wouldn't they? But he's waiting for something else. At last he sees a trail beginning, leading from the entry point in the sink cabinet out to the wall beside the trash can, then looping back again. The trail becomes an orderly line. The ants are at work in earnest now. After a few more minutes, Karl moves the trash can. There, stuck to the wall down by the baseboard, is a sliver of something pale—bone, fat, it doesn't really matter. He wipes it up with a piece of alcohol-soaked tissue and throws the tissue into a trash bag, then goes back to watch some more.

It becomes a weird sort of sport, following the busy ants as they do his work for him, locating with their ant senses all the body pieces and blood spots too small or too well hidden for him to have found on his own. They find what looks like a tiny slice of eyelid and eyelash stuck to the refrigerator-door handle—how did he miss that? More shockingly, they locate an entire toe that bounced out of the kitchen and into the hallway. That would have been a bit of a giveaway, wouldn't it? Karl laughs again. He's beginning to enjoy this, despite the mute presence of the bundled tarp.

It goes on throughout the night. The blood gets sticky, dries, and when he finds hidden spots he has to scrub harder and harder to get them clean. He brings his spotlight out of the garage to help him see better. The ants themselves are repaid for their searching by being wiped up along with whatever they have found. It doesn't quite seem fair, but hell, they're only ants.

At last, sometime around ten the next morning, his eyes red and his head ringing with exhaustion, he sees that the ants are all walking aimlessly. There is nothing left to find. No pieces, no spatters, nothing. The tiny, mindless creatures have done their work. They have saved his life.

Logic, he thinks as he drags the tarp to the garage. He'll deal with the rest tonight, when it's dark. Cold, hard, logic, that's how to do things. Mr. Spock? Damn right.

Sunday has its share of struggles, too. He empties her car trunk and glove compartment, files the vehicle identification number off the engine, removes the plates, then puts what's left of its former owner in the trunk and, when nighttime comes, drives it down to the salvage yard where he used to work. He certainly hadn't imagined anything like this when he copied the old man's keys before they got rid of him, but it just goes to show the quality of ideas Karl Eggar has.

As he closes the gate the dogs come at him, growling, hackles raised, but he knows them both, calls them by name, gives them the remains of his lunchtime cold pizza. They wag their tails happily as he drives the car into the crusher. The salvage yard is out by the bay, and the landfill next door is closed. Nobody to hear when he fires up the crusher except for maybe a few migrant fishermen out in their boats. No car lights coming down the bay road, either, so with rising confidence he gets into the crane and pulls out Norah's car, which looks like a wad of metal gum; then, after swinging it over onto one of the piles of wrecks, he drops a few of the other smashed cars on top of it so as much of her car as possible is buried. It'll all be gone to the smelters on Monday night. If not . . . well, since they're right beside the landfill, it's not like the place doesn't already smell like wet garbage.

He walks home, careful to keep to the shadows and enter the house through the back door. No, he thinks, we don't want surprise witnesses telling how he went out with Norah's car and came back on foot.

You the man, Mr. Spock, he thinks as he takes a well-deserved beer out of the refrigerator. He's suddenly single, the house is quiet, and with all this cleaning he's managed to drive the ants out of the kitchen, too.

Oh, yeah, you the man.

He calls them himself, of course—it doesn't make any sense to wait. Waiting is like a little kid covering his eyes and hoping he's turned invisible. Karl calls them Tuesday morning, tells them his wife hasn't come back since she drove away on Sunday night.

When he opens the door he's immediately reassured to see two young officers, the kind of square-jawed, just-out-of-the-academy types that always say "sir," and "ma'am," even to half-naked lunatics they're arresting for drunk and disorderly. Probably neither of these fellows has even *seen* a dead body.

"Come in, please." He tries to sound both pleased to see them and properly worried. "Thanks for coming so soon."

"No problem, Mr. Eggar," says the shorter of the two. He's freckled and has the wide-eyed look of one of those born-again Christian kids in Karl's old high school, the ones who always studied and never cheated. "Please tell us when you realized your wife was missing."

"Well," he says with a humble sort of laugh, "I'm not sure she *is* missing. To tell the truth, she was pretty pissed off at me when she left. Argument, ya know. I called her sister in Trent to see if she was there, but she hasn't heard from her." Of course she hasn't, unless she can hear all the way to the scrap heap at the salvage yard, but he called her late the night before to make the timeline look good. Thinking, always thinking. "Hey, come on into the kitchen. I'm just making some coffee."

He leads them in, holding his breath as he does, although he knows there's nothing to see. Even a county forensics team wouldn't find anything, he's been that thorough, so what are these two bowling-leaguers from the sheriff's department going to see except a clean kitchen? And not even *too* clean: he's given it a bit of a temporary-bachelor look, cereal out, bowls unwashed. He gestures them to two of the chairs at the small table, then lifts the pitcher out of the coffeemaker and pours himself a hot, black cup full. "Can I get you some?" he asks. They shake their heads.

"Tell us more about what happened Sunday," the one who hasn't spoken before says. He's tall, mustached, slightly familiar. Maybe he worked in the Safeway or something when he was a kid. That's one of the funny thing about small towns, the way you keep seeing faces and features. Karl has never liked the idea of other people knowing his business, but Norah, well, you'd have thought it was her own soap opera to hear her go on all the time about everybody else's private lives.

He works his way slowly into his story about the argument, although now it's a story about a guy who just wants to drink a beer and his wife who keeps nagging him to chop some firewood.

"I told her, 'Jeez, it's the middle of summer, Norah,' but she's all, 'It's going to be a cold winter, Karl. You always put things off to the last minute.' All I wanted to do was watch the ball game. Anyway, I guess I sorta called her a name—the *b* word, if you know what I mean—and went off to do it. Better than having her riding my back all day, I figured. But when I came back in the house, she was gone. Figured she was just letting off some steam, but then she didn't come back. When I got up the next morning and saw she'd never been home, well, I called you guys. Do you think she's all right? I hope she's all right. It was just a stupid argument."

He can tell from their expressions, which are already glazing over, that they think this is a waste of their time. A fight, they're thinking, maybe a bit worse than he's telling. She's got a boyfriend—that's what they're also thinking—and now she's shacked up with him, deciding whether to come back to ol' Karl or not.

Oh yeah, he thinks, and almost laughs. She's shacked up, all right. But it's kind of a small apartment. . . .

"Look," he says to Officer Born-Again while the tall one is writing the report, "you sure you won't have some coffee? I just made it."

The small, freckled one shrugs. "Sure, I guess. Been a long morning already."

"There you go." He pours it out, hands the officer a steaming cup. "How about you?" he asks the other. "Change your mind?"

The one writing the report shakes his head. "No, thanks, I'm off caffeine. Doctor's orders."

Karl nods sagely. "Yeah, it's probably not good for any of us, but I figure, hey, what's life without a few risks?" He's ready to have a good long chat, actually. He's all but in the clear and it feels good. His new life starts now. Maybe there's even a way he can collect Norah's insurance. . . .

The smaller cop looks around absently. "Uh, sorry to bother you, but you got cream and sugar?"

"Milk, hope that's okay. It's not expired or anything." He takes it from the fridge. The sugar he can't immediately find. "Never use it myself," he explains, but just then he spots the edge of the

sugar bowl. It's sitting, for some reason, up on top of the refrigerator.

It is only as he grabs it and something wet slops onto his wrist
that he realizes it is still sitting in the dish of water he placed it in
to keep the ants out of the sugar. The bowl has been sitting up
there all this time, ever since . . . since . . .

That day. The day he was right about everything—even the
sugar.

Because the moat around the sugar bowl has definitely worked.
The ants never got near it. Karl can see that clearly as he sets it
down on the table in front of the freckled cop, because there, in
full view, perched on a mound that is snowy white except for the
crusted bit of sugar at the top that has gone brown with dried
blood, lies the severed tip of one of Norah's fingers, nail and all.

Ants never take a day off and they always get the job done, but
not everyone appreciates their diligence. Just about now, Karl
may be wishing he'd chosen a slightly less hardworking insect
than the ant to help him out. The grasshopper springs to
mind. . . .

YOUR LAST
BREATH, INC.

John Miller

In the course of a long and happy life, seldom do any of us give a great deal of thought to those final seconds of sentience, that all-too-brief interregnum in which we realize that death has arrived. We may have a will, but what of last-second changes of heart? A desire to clarify a point, a sudden wish to make an apology or right an old wrong? We would need only a few seconds, a last breath, to set right an error in judgment, or to speak words by which we can long be remembered.

Unfortunately, as any newspaper reporter can tell you, no such final opportunities exist. But what if a reporter were to stumble upon a story too good to be true—a small shop suddenly appearing out of thin air, an elegant couple, and a mysterious, rather sinister marmalade cat—a story that leads him to a place where that most precious of commodities may indeed be for sale? A place one enters at one's own risk, where unforeseen consequences often prove quite unpleasant. A place called the Twilight Zone.

Nobody could say, with any certainty, when the little shop on upper Union Street, not terribly far from the stone wall guarding the old Presidio of San Francisco, first opened for business. In and of itself, that touch of uncertainty wasn't particularly surprising, given not only the shop's location at the very cusp of where the street changed in character from exceedingly high-rent commercial to absurdly overpriced residential, but also its lack of any sort of eye-catching signage. In fact, the only indication that it was a business at all was the understated gold-leaf lettering on the front door: YOUR LAST BREATH, INC. And the only indication that the shop was open was the appearance one day of a marmalade cat sleeping in the picture window fronting the street. Beyond those two admittedly rather opaque clues, the gold-leaf lettering and the sleeping cat, passersby, whether shoppers on the far periphery of the commercial district or neighborhood residents out for a stroll, were provided with little concrete evidence of much of anything.

"What, exactly, do you sell here?"

The shop had been open, or, perhaps more accurately, the cat had been in the window, for two days before the first person, a woman, expensively clad in designer athletic wear and pushing a baby carriage the size and heft of a small automobile, opened the door. Keeping one hand on the baby carriage, she aggressively thrust her head and shoulders through the doorway, leaning forward somewhat precariously as she did so. Standing in the center of the room were a man and a woman, to whom, jointly, the visitor addressed her question.

"I beg your pardon?" the man responded, his tone of voice distinctly formal and carrying a hint of an accent that neighborhood pundits, after much thought and discussion, would later conclude was Eastern European. Tall, thin, and elegantly handsome, he was dressed in a white linen suit accessorized with a mauve Egyptian cotton shirt, white silk tie, and patent leather shoes with, of all things, white spats. He had emerald-green eyes, short blond hair shot with a hint of gray, and could have been anywhere between thirty-five and sixty.

"Sell," the woman in the door repeated, sudden irritation evident in her voice. "What do you sell here? I mean," she looked from the man to the woman, out to her baby carriage, and then back to the man again, "this is a business of some sort, isn't it? You must sell something."

"I'm sorry to disappoint you," the man said, "but I'm afraid we don't actually sell anything here." He looked at his companion and smiled. "Do we, my dear?"

"Technically speaking, we do not," she confirmed, returning his smile with a look of affection. Almost as tall as her companion, she wore a simple, black satin sheath dress with three-inch black pumps and, at her throat, a necklace bearing an eight-carat rose-colored diamond. High cheekbones and a deep tan gave her face a vaguely Amerindian look, her exotic beauty heightened by luxuriously thick black hair that fell straight to her bare shoulders. "And certainly not in the mercantile sense to which you," she turned her head to look directly at the woman with the baby carriage, raising a single eyebrow as she did so, "are alluding."

Craning her neck, the woman in the doorway could see that the room contained only, in addition to the couple with whom she was speaking, and, of course, the cat in the window, a nine-foot Bösendorfer concert grand piano, a leather-upholstered love seat, and a matching leather club chair.

"And in any event," the man continued, smoothly stepping forward and slowly but firmly closing the door on the inquisitive woman, "in order to better serve our existing clientele, we are able to accept very few," he paused a beat and looked over at the cat, now awake and watching the proceedings with obvious interest, "*very* few," he reiterated, "new customers."

Suddenly possessed of an inexplicably urgent need to learn more, the woman waved her free hand even as the door was closing. "But," she cried out, "you don't understand. I just want . . ." Her voice trailed off as she realized that she was talking to a closed door and that other passersby were giving her sidelong glances.

Over the course of the next several days the same scene was repeated any number of times as word began to spread about the mysterious shop with the decidedly exotic couple and the cat in the window. Many were annoyed about being given a rather genteel version of the old-fashioned bum's rush, but most laughed it off, repeating the all-encompassing Bay Area mantra, *only in San Francisco.*

"My name is Roger Sims and, as you can see from my card, I'm a reporter with the *San Francisco Chronicle*."

An intense young man in his early twenties, Sims wore brown corduroy trousers, a rumpled and somewhat threadbare Harris Tweed jacket, and a polyester Hawaiian shirt. He sported wire-rimmed glasses, a Mickey Mouse watch, and badly scuffed white tennis shoes.

The woman, dressed in a sleek gown of pastel green shantung silk with matching heels, took the proffered business card and, without so much as a glance at the information printed thereon, passed it to her companion.

"Say, my girlfriend's got a cat," Sims informed them, putting forth a hand as if to pet the marmalade cat in the window. The cat quickly extended its right paw, exposing a fearsome-looking set of claws in a warning no less graphic than the weaving, flattened head of a cobra about to strike. "Damn," Sims exclaimed, snatching his hand out of harm's way, "that's not a very friendly cat."

"Do *you* welcome the uninvited touch of complete strangers?" the woman asked. "Furthermore," she continued after an instant's pause, "I can assure you that Grace is not merely a cat."

"Oh, really?" Sims replied sarcastically. "What is she then?"

"She owns this business," the woman said in a matter-of-fact tone of voice. "Laszlo and I are her employees."

The man, Laszlo, nodded his head. He wore a bespoke navy

silk-and-wool-blend suit, a crisp white shirt that seemed to gleam with an inner light, a blood red raw-silk tie, and mirror-polished cordovan wingtips. His voice, when he spoke, was deep and layered with over- and undertones that gave it an almost choral quality. "We, Clarissa and I, are in fact Grace's *only* employees."

Sims looked at them for a second before nodding his head and smiling. "Whatever." His smile faded. "Which brings me to the point of my visit here this morning." He looked from Clarissa to Laszlo. "What exactly *is* your business?"

Laszlo moved gracefully toward the door as if to show the newspaperman out. "I doubt your readers would have the least interest in what it is that we do," he said. "But we, Grace, Clarissa, and I, nonetheless thank you for your kind interest."

"No, no," Sims said, sidestepping neatly to avoid being herded back out to the street. "Something interesting is going on here and I intend to get to the bottom of it." He reached into the pocket of his sport coat and took out several photographs. "For instance, ever since you opened you've refused to tell people what you do, and yet you've had some very interesting visitors, such as," he handed them the first photograph, "Mrs. Ralph Johnson." The photo showed an elderly and frail woman being helped into the shop by her uniformed chauffeur. The widow of the late scion of San Francisco's oldest banking family, Mrs. Johnson was widely reputed to have a net worth somewhat in excess of one billion dollars. "And," he handed them the second photograph, "Roscoe Wilson." Roscoe Wilson, a legendary investment banker and Silicon Valley venture capitalist said to be worth almost as much as Bill Gates, was also a much respected and not-a-little-feared political power broker in Sacramento. "And there's three more here," Sims continued, handing them the rest of the photos, "all financial pillars of the community, so to speak, and all," he retrieved the photos and put them back in his pocket, "elderly. Now, I'm going to get this story, one way or the other, so wouldn't it be better if I got it firsthand, so to speak?"

Laszlo and Clarissa looked at each other, then at Grace, the cat, then finally back at the young reporter. "Please sit down, Mr. Sims," Laszlo said, indicating the club chair next to the piano with a slight wave of his hand.

"Tell me," Clarissa asked when they were seated, "what would it be worth to you to have one final breath of life?"

"Come, come, Mr. Sims," Laszlo interjected upon seeing a look of confusion on the reporter's face, "as one who asks questions for a living, you should certainly be able to answer one as simple as this." He paused for a second and smiled at Clarissa. "Imagine, if you can, that death has somehow, say by the occurrence of a stroke or heart attack, as it does for most of us, taken you by surprise. A sudden pain in the chest, a flash of light, and," he snapped his fingers, "off you go. No opportunity to utter, for example, a long-delayed apology to a loved one you somehow wronged in the past, no chance to issue, perhaps, heartfelt gratitude for a kindness rendered, no final words of wisdom through which you might be remembered by the world at large. Just," another smile, together with a very Gallic shrug of the shoulders, "an instant of regret followed by eternal darkness. Now, under those circumstances, circumstances, I hasten to remind you, under which the vast majority of us exit this soi-disant veil of tears, we, Clarissa and I, ask again, what would it be worth to you to have one final breath?"

"Do I really look that stupid?" Sims asked, annoyance apparent in his tone of voice.

"We have no reason to believe that you are possessed of anything approaching a below-average intelligence," Clarissa replied innocently. "Although," she smiled brilliantly, "I must say that your clothing choices hardly inspire confidence in a business setting."

"My clothing choices?"

"One seldom sees corduroy worn with Harris Tweed," Laszlo gently pointed out.

"And for good reason," Clarissa confirmed. "You should always be aware that new acquaintances invariably look to such things when forming important first impressions."

"Or, as Lord Mountbatten was fond of saying, if one wishes to run with the hounds, one should take care to avoid looking like a fox," Laszlo added with a chuckle.

"A brilliant man," Clarissa said to Sims, nodding her head as if confirming the veracity of her own statement. "One of the first of the royal family in Britain, if not *the* first, to understand the post-war imperative of realpolitik."

"I suppose he was one of your clients," Sims said with heavy sarcasm.

"Alas," Laszlo shook his head sadly, "no. But not for lack of effort on my part, I assure you. Mortality, I'm afraid, was seldom on his mind."

"Unlike Herr von Goethe," Clarissa reminded him.

"Ah, yes, Johann Wolfgang von Goethe." Laszlo smiled. "Many thought him stiff and formal to a fault, but trust me when I tell you that in the company of a few good friends, well, Herr Doktor Goethe could bend an elbow with the best of them. He was also a man who appreciated the need to ensure that a sudden and unexpected death did not rob him of the opportunity to share his final thought with a soon-to-be grieving world."

"And his final words were . . . ?" Sims hated to have to ask but felt compelled to do so.

Laszlo leaned forward and lowered his voice. *"Mehr licht."*

"Which means?"

Laszlo leaned back in his seat, unable to hide his disappointment in the young reporter's ignorance of German. "Where did you go to school?" he asked.

"Now, Laszlo, don't be rude," Clarissa interjected. "It is quite possible for one to be reasonably well educated and yet not have a working knowledge of more than two or three languages." She looked at Sims. "*Mehr licht* in English is 'more light.'" She paused and sighed. "Such profundity, such . . ." she paused a beat, searching for the right word, "such opacity."

"One could call it *a riddle wrapped in a mystery inside an enigma*," Laszlo volunteered, smiling. Seeing the blank look on Sims's face, the smile faded. "Winston Churchill," he informed the young reporter.

"I suppose *he* was a client," Sims said. "Churchill, I mean."

"I'm afraid not," Clarissa said, shaking her head sadly. "Mr. Churchill was a difficult man to get to know, socially speaking. To paraphrase Dr. Johnson, who I'm pleased to say *was* a client, Mr. Churchill was a most unclubbable man."

"But a fair watercolorist," Laszlo volunteered. He smiled at Sims. "He painted a charming little landscape for Clarissa."

"Of course, unlike Herr Goethe, not everyone who does business with us chooses final words of such philosophical import," Clarissa said.

"Indeed not," Laszlo agreed. "Remember Rachmaninoff?"

"How could I forget Sergei?" Clarissa asked. "A wonderful man. Hearing him play that evening at the palace of old Count Orloff, in St. Petersburg . . ." Her voice trailed off and she looked at Sims. "Do you remember his last words?"

"Somehow they've managed to slip my mind," Sims replied, a sarcastic smile emphasizing his words.

"*My dear hands. Farewell my poor hands.*" Looking back at Laszlo, she sighed again. "Artists like Sergei come along only once every few generations."

"If then," Laszlo agreed, nodding his head.

"You people don't actually expect me to believe all this, do you?"

Sims asked after several seconds of silence had filled the small room.

"Believe what, Mr. Sims?" Clarissa asked, her eyes wide and questioning.

"This," Sims repeated, waving an arm to take in the entire room. "The notion that you two are actually in the business of selling," he laughed shrilly and shook his head, "last breaths."

"Why, Mr. Sims," Laszlo responded, smiling, "what you believe, and I do not mean to be rude, is of absolutely no consequence. You asked about the nature of our business and," he shrugged, "we told you."

"And just where do you get these so-called last breaths?"

Laszlo, saying nothing, turned his head to look pointedly at the cat, still lounging in the front window.

"Oh, right, the *cat* . . ."

"Grace," Clarissa interjected. "Her name is Grace."

"As I said a minute ago," Sims replied angrily, "you people must think I'm stupid." He stood up and took a small digital camera out of his jacket pocket. "Well, you've made a big mistake." He quickly shot a photograph of Laszlo and Clarissa sitting together on the love seat and another of Grace, staring balefully at him from the window ledge. "What you're running here is nothing more than a scam, a con designed to frighten old people out of what I presume are large sums of money." He turned to leave. "See you in the papers," he said over his shoulder as he walked out the door.

The next morning Sims strolled into the offices of the *Chronicle*, a broad smile on his face and Rachmaninoff's Prelude in C-sharp Minor playing on his iPod.

"The boss wants to see you," one of his colleagues told him before he could even sit down at his bullpen desk. "PDQ."

"Good," Sims replied confidently, "because I want to see her."

He walked quickly to the glassed-in corner office of Margaret Hill, the paper's city editor. "Boss," he began speaking as soon as he crossed the threshold into her office, "you won't believe—"

"I trust," she quickly interrupted, "that you're about to tell me that you've completed all three of the assignments I gave you last week."

"Not quite," Sims replied. "But something far more important has come up, something that you won't—"

"Wait a minute," Margaret interrupted again, a look of serious annoyance on her face. "*I* decide what's important around here, not you. I don't know where you got the notion that you're some sort of investigative reporter-at-large, but if you wish to continue being an employee of this newspaper you'll lose it immediately. Is that clear?"

"Yes, but," he quickly took out the photos he had shown Laszlo and Clarissa the day before and laid them on Margaret's desk, "you don't understand. These people . . ."

Margaret didn't even bother to look down at them. "I know all about Mrs. Ralph Johnson, and Roscoe Wilson, and the little shop out on Union Street."

"You do?" The perplexed look on Sims's face was so comical that Margaret would have laughed had she not been so annoyed.

"An hour ago I received an unexpected visit from Tower Percy." Everyone who worked for the *Chronicle* knew Tower Percy, the paper's executive editor, and more, justly feared him as a man with zero tolerance for perceived shortcomings, personal and professional. "He wanted to know if I was aware that my most junior employee was running around taking clandestine pictures of some of the city's most prominent citizens. It seems that he had gotten an angry telephone call earlier this morning from *his* boss, the publisher of this newspaper. Are you beginning to get the picture?"

"Yes, but . . ."

"But nothing. What these people," she pointed at the photos on her desk, "are doing is none of your, none of our, business. They are private citizens engaged in private matters."

"They're being cheated," Sims interjected. "That couple out on Union Street are running a scam. Look at this." He took a sheet of computer printout from his pocket and handed it to Margaret. "This shows that Mrs. Johnson withdrew one hundred thousand dollars, in cash, from one of her bank accounts two days ago."

"Where did you get this?"

"I have a friend who works for the bank," Sims replied, a proud smile on his face. "A good friend. She got into the database and printed it out for me."

"You're a fool," Margaret said, shaking her head in disgust. "Such a fool, in fact, that I should fire you right now. This," she held up the printout, "or, more accurately, the manner in which you obtained it, is a felony. Worse even than that, however, it proves absolutely nothing. The ultrawealthy, people like Mrs. Johnson and Roscoe Wilson," she glanced down at Sims's photos, "are almost impossible to scam. They are surrounded and protected by attorneys, accountants, financial advisers, and security consultants. It is therefore almost impossible for confidence artists to get close enough to them to ply their trade."

"So one of them got on the phone with our publisher and had the story killed, is that it?"

"Haven't you been listening to me?" Margaret snapped. "There *is* no story. If, once in the proverbial blue moon, a billionaire is flimflammed out of a hundred thousand dollars or so, it's like the tree falling in the forest that no one hears. The Mrs. Ralph Johnsons and the Roscoe Wilsons of the world do not go running to the district attorney and admit publicly to having been made a fool of. And we in the newspaper business," she took the computer printout that Sims had given her and pointedly fed it into the paper shredder next to her desk, "however we might hear about it, do not publicize it." She then picked up the photographs he had taken. "You should know that my boss, the executive editor, suggested in no uncertain terms that I give serious consideration to terminating your employment. I told him, however, that no, you were merely young and foolish, and that I thought you might one day make a good reporter. Henceforth," she paused a second, the better to emphasize her next words, "you will confine your activities on behalf of this newspaper to assignments given to you by me." She slowly fed the photographs into her shredder. "And nothing else. Do you understand?"

Sims nodded but did not speak.

"Good," Margaret said. "Oh, and one other thing," she added, looking at his clothes with obvious distaste. "Do yourself a favor and start paying more attention to your wardrobe. You look like some sort of refugee from the Salvation Army."

Back at his desk, Sims ground his teeth in silent fury and cursed Laszlo and Clarissa and the rich old fools they were so obviously scamming. He knew full well that he could do nothing more on the story himself without risking his job, but . . . A sudden smile tugged at the corners of his mouth as he thought about his cousin Andrew O'Reilly, an officer with the San Francisco Police Department.

Laszlo was seated at the Bösendorfer, playing a Chopin étude, when the SFPD cruiser pulled up to the curb in front of the shop. He looked at Clarissa and raised a single eyebrow.

"I'll call him right now," she said, as if reading his mind. She got up from the love seat and walked back to the small office at the rear of the room, stepping inside and closing the door behind her.

Laszlo rose from the piano and went to the front door, opening it just as the patrolman stepped up to the threshold. "May I be of some assistance, officer?" he asked pleasantly, standing aside to allow the policeman inside.

"My name is O'Reilly, Officer O'Reilly, and I'm here in response to numerous complaints about your business." O'Reilly was young, no more than twenty-three or twenty-four, and possessed of fiery red hair and a beardless, freckled face more suitable, many thought, for the priesthood than law enforcement. "Numerous complaints," he reiterated, thrusting his jaw forward pugnaciously.

Laszlo carefully closed the front door. "Won't you have a seat?"

"What's that cat doing in here?" O'Reilly asked, pointing rudely at Grace.

"Why shouldn't she be here?" Laszlo asked in return. "She owns this business."

O'Reilly's face flushed red with sudden anger. His cousin had warned him that Laszlo could be difficult to deal with. "Keep up with the wise-guy attitude and we can continue this conversation down at the Hall of Justice." He paused a second and glared at Laszlo as if daring him to say something. "As far as that cat goes, it's illegal in San Francisco to keep an animal in a place of business."

"I had no idea," Laszlo replied.

"And ignorance of the law is no excuse," O'Reilly added for good measure. He looked to his right as Clarissa entered the room.

"Dear," Laszlo said, turning to look at her, "this kind gentleman has just informed me that numerous complaints have been lodged regarding Grace's presence here in the shop."

"No, I never," O'Reilly quickly interjected. "I said that there's been numerous complaints about your business, not about the cat."

"But I distinctly remember you saying that Grace is breaking the law by being in here," Laszlo replied.

"The *cat's* not breaking the law, you are, and anyway that's not why I'm here." O'Reilly ran a hand over his face, feeling that somehow he had lost control of the interview before it had even begun. For one thing, he didn't think he'd ever before been in a room with a better-dressed couple. In fact, they reminded him of the wealthy opera patrons he had seen when he had been assigned to traffic control in front of the opera house on opening night. "Listen," he began again, looking from Laszlo to Clarissa and back again, "first off, I want to see your business license."

"Business license?" Clarissa asked, her face a study in wide-eyed innocence. "What is that?"

"You know," O'Reilly said, unconsciously rolling his shoulders in what he thought was a manly fashion, "your license from the City and County of San Francisco to conduct business. Your business license."

"Do we have such a license?" Clarissa asked Laszlo.

"Not that I'm aware of," Laszlo responded calmly. He looked from Clarissa to O'Reilly. "How, exactly, does one go about obtaining a business license?"

"See, I thought there was something fishy about this setup right from the get-go," O'Reilly said, throwing his shoulders back to emphasize his pectoral muscles. "I don't know what it is that you two are trying to pull here, but I'm thinking that unless I get some straight answers, the three of us are going to be taking a little ride downtown."

"To the Hall of Justice?" Laszlo asked.

"You got it, wise guy," O'Reilly replied, already basking in the anticipated glow of the commendation he was now certain he would receive for busting these two con artists.

"What is this Hall of Justice?" Clarissa asked.

"I'm not precisely sure," Laszlo replied, "but I rather doubt, its felicitous name notwithstanding, that it's a pleasant place to be if one is suspected of having engaged in criminal activity." He glanced over O'Reilly's shoulder, toward the front window, and smiled. A black limousine had pulled up and a distinguished-looking older gentleman emerged, followed by a young woman carrying a large, litigation-style leather briefcase. Laszlo looked back at O'Reilly. "Isn't that correct?"

Before O'Reilly could answer, the man and woman opened the front door and came into the shop. Tall, white-haired, and exceedingly well dressed, the gentleman turned immediately to O'Reilly and fixed him with a glare. "What's going here?" he demanded.

"Well, um," O'Reilly licked his lips nervously and cut his eyes from the gentleman to his assistant and back again, "it's kind of hard to explain." He pointed at Laszlo and Clarissa. "These two—"

"Do you know who I am?" the older gentleman brusquely interrupted.

Again O'Reilly looked from the man to his assistant and back, slowly shaking his head.

"This is Judge Martindale," Laszlo gently informed the stricken policeman, using Martindale's honorific title. Martindale, in a career spanning almost sixty years, had been, among other things, a district attorney, a superior-court judge, a justice on the California Supreme Court, a state senator, and a mayor of San Francisco. He was currently the senior partner of San Francisco's largest and most influential law firm and personally represented, among others, Roscoe Wilson, the Silicon Valley entrepreneur.

"I can assure you that I have neither the time nor the inclination to indulge in nonsense," Martindale informed the now-terrified young policeman. To his side, his assistant had taken out a cell phone and was dialing a number. "So I won't ask again," he warned. "What, exactly, is going on here?"

"Well, these two," O'Reilly once again pointed at Laszlo and Clarissa, "I mean, they don't have a business license and—"

"Wait a minute," Martindale snapped as his assistant discreetly tapped him on the elbow and then handed him the cell phone. He turned his back and carried on an intense, sotto voce conversation. After what seemed like several minutes, he turned back to O'Reilly and handed him the cell phone. "Your boss wants to talk to you."

"Sergeant McClorg?" O'Reilly squeaked, the sudden tension causing his voice to rise an octave.

"No," Martindale replied with a grim smile, shaking his head. "Alan Beal. *Chief* Alan Beal."

The color drained from O'Reilly's face as he took the cell phone with a trembling hand. He had never before spoken to the chief of police, indeed had never met him. In any event, the conversation was short, if not sweet, O'Reilly's part limited to a handful of *yes, sirs*, accompanied by vigorous noddings of the head as if the chief could see through the telephone connection. He did not even have to say goodbye, inasmuch as the chief abruptly hung up when he was finished giving orders. O'Reilly handed the cell phone back to the young woman and, without a word, turned and left the shop.

"You couldn't leave well enough alone, could you?"

Roger Sims was standing nervously in the office of his boss, city editor Margaret Hill. Seated in one corner of the office was the newspaper's executive editor, Tower Percy, and behind them, next to the door, stood a uniformed security guard.

"I'm not sure what you—" Sims started to say.

"It was a rhetorical question," Margaret interrupted, disappointment evident in her tone of voice. "You were ordered to forgo any further inquiry into the shop on Union Street."

"I did," Sims replied hastily. "You told me to drop it and I did."

"That's not exactly true, is it?" Tower Percy said from his seat in the corner, his expression one of intense displeasure. "In fact, you contacted your cousin on the police force and asked him to drop by the shop and harass the owners in the hope of sweating incriminating information out of them." He stood up and stepped to the side of Margaret's desk. "We know this because in an effort to save his own job your cousin dropped, you might say, a dime on you."

"I might have spoken to him," Sims allowed, "but—"

"Might have, or did?" Margaret interjected.

"Well, technically, I did, but—"

"Technically?" Margaret's anger at Sims's equivocation was immediate, as was her response. "You're fired." She nodded at the uniformed security guard standing at her door. "He'll accompany you to your desk while you get your personal belongings and then escort you from the building."

"Hey, Sims," one of his fellow reporters, unaware that he had just been fired, called out as he walked out of Margaret's office and into the city room, "I've got another screwball story for you." Several other reporters, also unaware that Sims had just been fired, laughed. "A friend of mine, a nurse at the Laguna Honda hospice, told me that one of her patients reported seeing a cat sucking the breath out of one of the other patients."

The color drained from Sims's face. "What's your friend's name?" he demanded.

"Judith Taylor," his colleague replied. "But I . . ." His voice trailed off as he watched Sims turn and run quickly from the office.

"Yes," the nurse, Judith Taylor, smiled and nodded her head affirmatively, "poor Mr. Sullivan was quite certain he had seen a cat on Mr. Martin's bed. He said he woke up in the middle of the night and looked over and saw it on Mr. Martin's bed."

"Was it an orange cat?" Sims asked. He and Judith were sitting on a bench in the hospice's garden at the Laguna Honda Hospital. He showed her the picture he had taken of Grace. "Did it look like this?"

"You misunderstand. You see, Mr. Sullivan, as are many of our patients in their final days and hours, was not entirely lucid, or at least not all the time. There was no cat; it was merely a figment of his imagination."

"But why would he make up such a thing?"

"I didn't say he made it up—I'm sure it was quite real to him."

"But why a cat? And why would he imagine it sucking the breath out of the old man who died?"

Judith shrugged. "Volunteers bring animals, dogs and cats, to the hospice from time to time to visit the patients. Perhaps Mr. Sullivan saw such a cat and it stuck in his mind. As to it sucking the breath from Mr. Martin, haven't you ever heard the old wives' tale about cats sucking the breath from babies? As I said, in their final days and hours, many, if not most, of our patients are confused, their minds constructing reality from bits and pieces of long-forgotten memories."

"Would it be possible for me to see Mr. Sullivan? I'd like to ask him about what he saw, or thinks he saw."

"Unfortunately he died early this morning." She looked at her watch and stood up. "I'm afraid I've got to get back to work."

"One last question," Sims said. "Have you seen this couple here at the hospice?" He showed her the picture of Laszlo and Clarissa.

Judith studied the photo for a second. "What a beautiful dress," she murmured, more to herself than to Sims.

"Have you seen it before?" Sims pressed, suddenly excited.

Judith hesitated for a second and then handed the photo back. "It's possible. A lot of people, relatives of our patients, pass through here every day. I may have seen it, the dress, and her," she nodded at the photo, "but," she shrugged and turned to leave, "I couldn't say for sure."

Sims left the hospice and drove straight down to the little shop on Union Street, hoping to provoke a confrontation of sorts with Laszlo and Clarissa, although to what end he was not exactly sure.

"What's going on here?"

When Sims got to the shop he was stunned to find it empty of everything save the Bösendorfer, which was being manhandled onto a moving board by two exceptionally large and surly piano movers.

"What does it look like?" one of the movers responded sarcastically.

"I can see that you're taking the piano, but where are the tenants?" Sims asked. "There were two tenants here, a man by the name of Laszlo and and a woman named Clarissa. I don't know their last names."

"Hey, buddy, all we do is move pianos." The mover reached into the bib pocket of his overalls and took out a work order. "See this?" he asked, waving it at Sims. "This says that we're supposed to pick up this piano and bring it back to the store, okay? Other than that, I don't know nothing. Now, why don't you step out of the way," he shooed Sims aside none too gently with one massive arm, "and let us get about our business."

Sims watched the movers horse the grand piano out the front door and onto their truck. He looked around the now-empty shop, noticing that even the gold-leaf lettering, YOUR LAST BREATH, INC., had been carefully removed from the front door.

"What are you doing in here?"

Startled out of his reverie, Sims turned around. "Who are

you?" he asked the short, unpleasant-looking man who had challenged him from the doorway.

"My name is Jones and I own this building," the man responded. His manner softened somewhat. "Are you interested in leasing this space?"

"No," Sims replied, "I'm a reporter with the *Chronicle*," *or, more accurately, I used to be,* he thought but of course did not say, "and I'm trying to locate the tenants who just moved out of this space. I wonder if you could provide me with their forwarding address?"

"I think you've made some sort of mistake," Jones replied. "This space has been unoccupied for the past two or three months."

"No," Sims replied, shaking his head for emphasis. "There's been a tenant in here for at least the past couple of weeks, some sort of business run by a man and woman named Laszlo and Clarissa."

"I don't know what you're talking about," Jones said, looking around the small space. "I bought this building four weeks ago and I can assure you that it was vacant then—in fact, that was one of the conditions of closing. I live in Denver, and shortly after the closing I fired the local real estate company that had been managing the three other buildings I own here in the Bay Area. This is the first chance I've had to get out here to hire another one to get this space leased."

"But I tell you that Laszlo and Clarissa just moved out," Sims insisted, his voice becoming shrill with agitation. "In fact, the piano movers were here picking up the piano not five minutes ago."

Jones looked at Sims much as one might look at a man suspected of being mentally deranged. "I think you should leave now," he finally said, speaking slowly and calmly.

"But—"

"Or I will have to call the police," Jones interrupted, pointedly taking his cell phone from its holster at his belt and flipping it open.

. . .

Nobody could say, with any certainty, when the little shop just a block off Rodeo Drive in Beverly Hills first opened for business. The space had been vacant for some time, something about a bankruptcy involving the absentee owners of the building, and then, one day, a passerby noticed the rather understated gold-leaf lettering on the front door: YOUR LAST BREATH, INC. That and the marmalade cat sleeping in the front window.

Roger Sims simply could not imagine a place where cats own businesses and death can (for a price) be put off for the span of a single breath. A place where, ironically, things could be exactly as they seem, and easy explanations seldom tell the whole story. In his zealous determination to get to the bottom of what was going on in the little shop on Union Street, Sims chose the easy explanation, the only one all his experience told him was possible. Unfortunately, as we have seen, experience does not always prepare us for the truly unexpected, and as Sims focused all his attention on Laszlo and Clarissa, he failed to recognize that the heart of the story all along was the marmalade cat known as Grace, even as she was leading him, step by step, into the Twilight Zone.

FAMILY MAN

Laura Lippman

Submitted for your consideration: A man, a boss, who uses the shield of his family whenever he has to do an unpleasant task. What happens to such a man if that family disappears? Who will he be, how will he act, how does he justify himself? More important, what happens if his family comes back and he's already forgotten who he is?

P aul, could you come in here a minute?"

Bob had spoken, as Bob always spoke, in a casual, friendly tone. But this particular request was pitched slightly higher than usual. Paul wasn't the only one who caught the shrillness. Elena's head snapped up from her work, and Jack appeared to lose his train of thought, pausing in midspiel to catch Paul's eye.

Paul walked into Bob's office. There were only a half-dozen offices on this floor, and some of the managers at Bob's level had to settle for cubicles. But Bob had an office. An office with a credenza, which had always fascinated Paul, as it was unlike anything else on the fourth floor, indeed in all of Brighton Technologies, as far as Paul knew. The credenza looked expensive—real wood, highly polished, possibly cherry or stained to mimic cherry—and was ludicrously out of place amid Brighton's futuristic decor, all metal and glass. Rumor had it that Bob had commissioned the piece upon his promotion, perhaps having figured out that this behemoth would make it that much harder to remove him from his coveted rectangle.

The credenza held a few books that Bob wanted people to think were important to him, books that would establish a side to his personality not on display in the office. Poetry by Wallace Stevens and Ezra Pound, *A Brief History of Time*, by Stephen Hawking, a coffee-table book that had been published in conjunction with a PBS documentary about World War II. Paul, who had been an English major, didn't think Bob had actually read any Stevens, much less Pound. Oh, Bob dropped a poetic allusion here or there, but it was always an obvious chestnut, something everyone knew. "Into the Valley of Death rode the five hundred." Or, "Once upon a midnight dreary." And even these familiar lines never seemed to have anything to do with the moment at hand.

The books, however, didn't even take up a shelf. Most of the credenza was filled with plaques and trophies and photos of Bob's family—his wife, Mona, and the twins, Diane and Dennis, known among Bob's staff as Dumb and Dumber. Which wasn't kind, or even accurate, but when you come to believe that a pair of eleven-year-olds you've never met somehow controls your life—

Bob was saying something about the last quarter's results.

"—Down eleven percent in our sector. Me, I told the big bosses that we just have to take this hit, that things will pick up again, and we'll want to have our best people in place when they do—"

No, Paul thought. *No. Dear fucking God, please no. I'm closing next week on my new condo.* "I'm a good worker."

"Well, as I said, it's not my choice. The big bosses—they don't know the people on the ground, not like I do, what they see is numbers, figures on a ledger. Your salary is higher than most of the people on my team—"

"Because you've given me so many merit raises."

"I know." Bob had an accent that his staff was forever trying to place, quite unlike anything heard here in this corner of the Southwest, where they were used to hearing everything. His *O* sounds were wavering bits of air, smoke rings blown by a teenager. He put *R*s in words that didn't have them, removed them from words that usually relied on them. Elena said it was a mid-Atlantic accent, Jack insisted it was Baltimore or Washington, D.C., and Aimee, Bob's assistant, said she had Googled him and found his mother in a Delaware suburb. Bob swore he was from Philadelphia, the Main Line, even.

"You *know* that I'm getting canned because I've done such good work that I've gotten raises that make me highly paid enough to be a target?"

"Yeah. Ironic, huh?"

Paul thought about this and decided that Bob, for once, was correct about something being ironic. Paul was the highest-paid person on staff because he had been here the longest, performed well, and been given steady merit raises. He also was a year away from being fully vested in Brighton's pension plan. That had probably made him a target, too.

"Paul, you know this isn't my idea." Bob looked gutted. But then, he always did when this moment came. The staff sometimes wondered among themselves if Bob were literally spineless, strung like a venetian blind, nothing but a ropy piece of tissue holding the disks in place. His shoulders were narrow and hunched, and while his gut wasn't large, he couldn't have sucked it in on a bet.

"If I could keep this from happening—" Bob shook his head.

"You could. Tell them to take—" Paul started to name names, decided he was better than that. "Someone else. Tell them I'm valuable, that they'll want someone as fast as me when the clients come back. And they will come back, Bob."

"I wish I could fight these guys," Bob said. "But Diane and Dennis—they start middle school next year and there's all these things they need to do, extracurriculars and the like, that cost money. And you know I'm the—"

Sole provider.

"—Only breadwinner—"

Close enough. Paul would have to remember to tell Jack that Bob had changed it up, introduced a little variety into the speech. Then he realized that he was hearing the speech firsthand, that he would be describing it to his colleagues and friends as he packed up his desk.

"My wife, even when she did work, she worked in retail, on the lowest rungs of the ladder, it's not like we can live off that, and I don't have to tell you that my college funds took a hit, we are so far behind the eight ball now that I keep dropping hints about how community college isn't such a bad deal, if you don't know exactly what you want to do with your life." Bob laughed at the absurdity of this, the notion that his children, whom he considered gifted, would actually have to go to community college. "Anyway, if I was in a position to stand up to these guys, I would. But I'm not, and it wouldn't matter. They're going to do what they want. I wish I could save you, but I can't. They'd just fire me, too, and then I wouldn't be here to protect the others."

Protect them from whom? From you? You've just explained that you can't—or won't—protect anyone.

Bob stood up. "Look, if there's anything I can do for you—"

Paul had a fleeting memory of a movie, a guy who said something clever in this situation, like, "You could go fuck yourself," or, "Please drop dead," only better, more elegant and cheerful, delivered with true élan. He probably wouldn't figure it out for hours, and after many beers. The wit of the staircase, as the French called it.

Instead, he found himself saying, "When do I need to be out?"

"End of this week, although you'll get the full two weeks' severance after that. They don't like employees with proprietary information to stay on. Hey, they wanted me to lock you out of the computer and have security guards escort you out of the building today. I stood up for you, buddy."

"Oh." *Yeah, you're a real stand-up guy, Bob. A tower of Jell-O.*

"I'm really sorry about this, Paul. But at least it's just you, no one else is counting on you. Not that that's why you were chosen," Bob added quickly, probably realizing that it would be actionable to fire someone for the simple fact of not having a wife and child. "I mean, you're lucky, you can move on a dime if you have to, pull up stakes. I love my wife and kids, but in dreams begin nightmares."

"In dreams begin responsibilities," Paul corrected, surprised not so much by Bob's almost-apt allusion to Yeats, a poet he had never before referenced, but the Freudian slip. Of course, Bob probably knew the quote from the Delmore Schwartz story, as most people did, and the title was probably all he knew. Still, it was telling. Was Bob miserable? There would be some comfort, small to be sure, if the life that Bob defended as his reason for being a jerk was making him miserable.

"Right, that's what I said."

"No—" Paul stopped himself. He wasn't going to waste another minute speaking with Bob, this poetry poseur, a man who used books like wallpaper, who knew the title of everything and the meaning of nothing. One day he would be a paltry thing, as Yeats himself would have it, a stick. A stick who was still using the excuse of his wife and children and, by then, his grandchildren, to compromise whatever integrity he had, assuming he'd ever had any. No, Paul was going to go tell Elena and Jack what had happened and then go for a three-hour lunch at Carrabas, drink thirty-seven margaritas, give or take, and put the bill on his final expense account. What could they do, fire him?

Late that afternoon, Bob went for a little spin around the office, taking the temperature of the room. Paul had never come back from lunch, but the others were there, working late to make up for the long, probably boozy lunch with their now ex-colleague. Awful to say, but letting someone go was good for productivity, at least short-term. One of the big bosses claimed he used to like to fire someone his first week on a new job, just to set the tone. "Come to a new place, drop one son of a bitch as a warning, and the others fall into line fast." Bob wasn't like that, though. Bob hated firing people. He popped a Prilosec, washed it down with Diet Coke, moved from desk to desk, checking in. People were courteous, but a little clipped. Paul had been popular with his colleagues.

"Someone had to go," Bob told Jack, the staff alpha dog. "That wasn't my call, and it wasn't my choice. Could have been *two* people. I bargained them down to one."

"This department's been decimated," Jack said. "We can't afford to lose anyone, especially someone who works as hard as Paul."

"I know," Bob said. "That's what I told them."

"And Paul was good at what he did," Elena put in. "Meanwhile, there are others who aren't pulling their weight." She glanced across the room, toward Frank's desk, but he wasn't there. Not even a firing could scare Frank into staying late.

"Let's not get into personalities, Elena. That's not professional."

"Oh, but it is professional to hire someone with no experience in the field because his father was the big boss's college roommate? Jesus, Bob, grow a pair. I've got a six-month-old niece with bigger balls than you."

Elena had always prided herself on talking blunt, like a guy.

"Look, Elena, I don't like how things are done around here, either, sometimes. But what can I do, I have—"

"A wife and two kids," Jack said.

"Well, I do. What would you have me do?"

"The right thing, just once," Elena said. "Not the politically feasible thing. The *right* thing. You're so worried about your kids? What about the example you're setting for them, carrying out orders?"

"Not carrying out orders," Jack said musingly. "That's more Klink, don't you think? Our guy, Bob, he's more Schultz than Klink. He sees nussing, he knows nussing."

It wasn't the first time that the German officers of *Hogan's Heroes* had been invoked in Bob's presence.

"Paul always said you were Klink *and* Schultz," Elena said. "Two Nazis, two Nazis in one! You live in fear of the big bosses, but you're also inept, pretending to be out of the loop. Me, I'd peg you as Ugarte in *Casablanca*. 'You detest me, don't you, Rick?'" Elena did a horrible Peter Lorre imitation.

"You got kids, Elena?" Bob asked. He knew the answer.

"No, but—"

"Well, wait until you do to lecture me on being a parent. You are over the line. You know nothing about being a parent, about what it does to you."

"I'm a parent," Jack said. "I'm also somebody's son. And I know I wouldn't want my father to do sleazy things in my name. Or my wife's name. I wouldn't want someone I presumably love to make me a bad person."

"It's how things are. I can't do anything about their decisions, anyway. Would you rather work in Phil's section? He's a ruthless SOB."

"Yes," Elena said. "But he doesn't expect to be forgiven when he summarily executes someone. Doesn't want to be forgiven, in fact. You pull the trigger, then beg everyone to be your buddy."

"They told me that I had to let Paul go. I could have fallen on my sword, but all that would have meant is that I would have been another guy out there, looking for a job in this economy. I gotta do what's right for my family."

Jack's phone rang and Elena was distracted by the flashing light on her BlackBerry. Tomorrow, they would be happy that it wasn't them. Heck, they were probably happy now and feeling guilty about their relief, which was why they were picking on him. Tomorrow, everything would be fine. Better, perhaps, now that the ax had fallen.

And if the big bosses told him to lose another person on his team—well, then Elena would regret that comment about growing a pair.

Bob woke up late, much later than usual. How had he failed to hear the alarm, the fury of the morning preparations? Why had Mona let him sleep? The kids had a god-awful early bus to school, six forty-five or something like that, and Mona didn't mind if he slept through the chaos of getting them out of the house. But she usually put on another pot of coffee about seven thirty, and if the aroma didn't wake him, she would stick her head in the bedroom door, call his name.

He went downstairs. No coffee? Mona must have something at the school today. It looked like there hadn't been time for breakfast; the only thing in the sink was the old-fashioned glass from which he had sipped several slugs of bourbon last night while watching ESPN, revisiting the conversation with Jack and Ellen, and thinking of other things he should have explained. He didn't mind that they didn't get it, but being thought of as a bad guy— that really hurt.

The refrigerator was pretty sparse—orange juice, a few bottles of beer, a pint of half-and-half past its sell date. He sniffed—no, he wouldn't risk it. And they were out of coffee beans, too, down to the Folgers. What was up with Mona? Maybe she had just run out to the grocery store. He was careful never to wonder aloud just what she did with her days, but the fact was, she *didn't* work. Okay, okay, she didn't work *outside the home*—and while he knew there was a lot of chauffeuring, that the kids' appointments forced her day into odd fragments, stranding her at athletic practices and lessons, it still seemed to him that his wife should be able to get to the grocery store in a timely fashion. And to pick up a little. The house wasn't dirty, exactly, but it had a neglected look, more noticeable in the morning light than it had been last evening. There were stacks of newspapers in the family room off the kitchen, several splayed books lying around, something that Mona normally detested. It was one of the many small tensions between them: he read several books at once, mostly histories and spy thrillers, and Mona went behind him, snapping them shut, so he had to find his place again. Well, good for her, for finally letting go of such a petty complaint. Now if she could just surrender the seven thousand others, realize how good she had it.

He wandered over to the easy chair with his cup of Folgers, thinking only to watch CNN or ESPN before he headed out, but when he pressed the remote—Jesus! It was on some pay-per-view porn station. How could that be? Had Dennie been down here late at night, trying to hack past the parental controls? He pressed the button that pulled up the program guide. When had they ordered Cinemax? Shit, they were going to have to talk to Dennie about this, and when he said "they"—well, in this case, he really meant they. This was one problem that couldn't be left to Mona. She and Dennie would both be mortified. He walked over to the phone to call her on her cell, ask what she knew about their eleven-year-old son's dawning interest in pornography. Gosh, he hoped it was Dennie and not Diane.

It was only then that he noticed that the photo that usually hung above the phone, a portrait taken for a Christmas card three years ago, was gone. Aw, Diane had been complaining about it, said she looked like an obese chipmunk. She was going through a phase. Come to notice—that crazy kid had removed all the photos throughout the den and from the side of the fridge. Not just the photos, but the magnets, too. He glanced at the mud room. Had Mona had another spring cleaning fit? They didn't need much heavy gear here, not often, but there were still enough nippy days in February and March that you wouldn't want to put all the cold-weather coats away in January. Yet they were gone, too. The coats, the shoes, the tennis rackets, Dennie's skateboard . . . Bob felt dizzy. He ran upstairs. Mona's closet was empty, or almost, with just a few of his older suits hanging there, things that no longer fit him. Her sink, her side of the bathroom, had also been cleaned out, only a dusty box of Q-tips stashed in the vanity, along with what looked like a very old bottle of Pepto-Bismol. Had she been sneaking things out of the house bit by bit, plotting this move? Why had she left? Things had seemed fine last night, and by "fine," he meant the same as they always were. They had brisket. He told her about Paul, and Mona said the right things, more or less. He knew that men could be a little obtuse, but there was no way she had signaled any discontent, much less unhappiness so profound that she would leave him.

And take the kids. Had she taken the kids? Or just dropped them off at school and continued on her way to wherever? She couldn't take the kids—he would fight her over that, if only for the principle. He ran to Diane's room first. Like the refrigerator, it had been stripped of every personal item; it was just a twin bed and a desk, and much less pink than Bob recalled. All that color, all that girlishness, had been in the details, he guessed. As for Dennie's room—he threw open the door. It was an office. His office, Bob's office, by all appearances, with a computer, a small CD player, a plasma screen, and a shelf of books, histories and thrillers. There was a can of soda and it wasn't on a coaster. That's when Bob knew that Mona had never been in this room.

And that was when he began to wonder if Mona had ever *been*.

Oh, but he was having a bad dream. He instructed himself to wake up, extricate himself. Nothing happened. He tried to think of something that would make it clear that this was not real life. Not pinching—that seemed silly—but something that couldn't be done in a dream. He sipped from the flat soda in the coaster-less can, picked up the phone and dialed Mona's cell.

"The number you have reached is not a working number . . ."

She could have turned it off, no? Heck, *he* would turn it off, if she hadn't, cancel the contract and screw the cost. He wasn't going to pay for her cell, he wasn't going to pay for anything if she left him. Was this a marital-property state? She was probably entitled to half the house's value no matter what, and they had bought the house ten years ago so there was quite a bit of equity built up, even with house prices falling back. *The house.* He would look up the mortgage, the deed, whatever. You couldn't do that in a dream, not his dreams at any rate. Whenever he had to read in dreams, the text was always gibberish, like the dummy type they used when developing manuals. There was a filing cabinet here and he opened it, reassured by the neatness of the folders, his own handwriting. No dream could produce so much paperwork, so much recognizable and comprehensive verbiage. He pulled out the folder marked "House" and located the mortgage.

It was in his name only.

Okay, that made sense, he was the one who had taken out the loan. It was on the deed, the facsimile copy that you held until you paid the house off, where Mona's name would appear. In fact, she had been worried about that. She had seen some show with that financial lady, the one who was always yelling at women about how they handled their money, and Mona had started fretting about life insurance and whether her name was on the deed and he had taken it out and proved to her that she was covered. He found this now.

And it was in his name only.

He looked through the other files. No birth certificates for Dennie and Diane. His passport and a photocopy, but no one else's. His insurance form claimed he carried individual coverage, not family. He wished. That would be a huge savings. All the documents agreed: he was a single forty-three-year-old. Dazed, overwhelmed, he glanced at the clock. Time to go to work. Whatever was going on, he had to be at work.

He walked out to the garage and saw, instead of his white Jeep Cherokee, a silver Audi R8, the very car that Mona had said he couldn't have, as if she were the boss of the money, as if she contributed a single dime. The Audi cost over a hundred thousand dollars, but shouldn't Bob have some fun in this life? Mona had made it pretty clear that he shouldn't.

He got in, and it felt right, as if he had driven it many times. There were eighteen thousand-plus miles on the odometer, about what he would have put on a car in nine months, given the long commute to work. And there was a woman's lipstick in the well between the bucket seats, a bright, fiery shade that Mona would never wear. Okay, even in the midst of this strange, stomach-churning, disorienting panic, Bob had to admit: things were getting interesting.

The first thing that Bob noticed at the office was the box on Paul's desk, and a few other boxes stacked nearby, then Elena and Jack's contemptuous looks. So yesterday had definitely happened. But what about the last twenty years? He had married Mona a year after he graduated from college. She had worked, at first. In a fashion. But it had quickly become clear that he would have to be a capital-B breadwinner, that it made no sense for Mona to work if she was going to make less money than child care cost. He had more than fulfilled his share of the bargain, and then some. He wasn't even a bad dad, as these things go. He did some of the driving on the weekend, seldom missed a game or a performance. Okay, he almost never drove and he missed most of the events, but he was there for the really important games and performances. He never expressed any resentment at being the family's sole provider, and that was some big pressure. He certainly had not wished that his family would disappear. Well, not exactly. He had felt wistful when he watched the single people on his staff go out after work. He had wondered, from time to time, if he would be invited should he be more available. He suspected not, but preferred not to have this fear confirmed. Besides, he was the boss, and it was better not to be too familiar. It was hard enough, making the tough decisions, only to have employees like Elena and Jack glare at him.

And when a certain kind of woman walked by—yes, yes, he thought about the roads not taken. Who didn't? Screw Jimmy Carter, that didn't count as cheating. Nor did the kind of cheating that Bob had done, sporadically, at conventions here or there. Everyone knew that convention sex was not really cheating. It was more like—networking with benefits.

He unlocked his office. The books were the same, although there was now a volume of Yeats between Stevens and Pound. All the plaques and trophies were gone, and the only photograph on the credenza was a picture of two men in tuxedos, vaguely familiar, although Bob couldn't quite place them. Distant cousins at a wedding? The company's founders? The picture had an old quality, as if it were from decades ago. Yet, his family had existed, he was sure of it. He had memories of them. There was the time that Mona had—well, what had she done, exactly? The night of the twins' birth—when was their birthday? How old were they? What color was their hair?

He began to panic, even as his memories receded further, faster. It was like the time when, bleary from work, he had stopped at an ATM machine and punched his number in wrong. Suddenly, he couldn't remember his code for the life of him, and, after a few failed efforts, he pushed the Cancel button rather than risk the machine holding his card. Bob's father had slipped into dementia before his death a few years ago, but he had been almost seventy, for God's sake. Bob was forty-three. The ATM number had come back to him, once he'd stopped trying so hard.

He called his mother, dialing from memory. See? He wasn't crazy, he existed. He had a mother and he knew where to find her. She lived in a retirement community back east, physically closer to her three other children, but Bob had always been her favorite. She was a doting grandmother, too. She would ask after her grandchildren and, Bob was convinced, thereby bring them back to him. The photos would appear on his credenza; the two strange men in tuxedos—waiters, conductors?—would disappear.

"Hi, Mom."

"Bob!" She was always delighted to hear him call, but today there was an element of surprise as well.

"What's up?"

"Nothing. Nothing new, at least since we spoke Sunday."

He did not remember speaking to her on Sunday.

"Well, I'd just thought I'd check in."

"So you feel better?" his mother asked.

"Um, sure."

"I do think it's for the best. Not that I didn't like her—"

"Didn't like her?" So his mother knew? Yet, she had always doted on Mona.

"Oh, Bob, I didn't have the heart to tell you, when she visited us at Christmas, but I don't think she was very . . . sincere."

"Mona?"

"Mona? Who's Mona? I'm talking about Amy, the one you just broke up with."

Even as his mind tried to figure out who Amy was, he had a sudden image. More of an impression, really. Long legs, dark hair, a big, vivid mouth, sort of everything Mona was not, not that he could really see Mona in his mind's eye. She was fading away, more ghostly by the moment. Short? Freckled? Blond? Blue-eyed? One of the above, none of the above? Definitely not dark, not long-legged, not the kind of woman who—wow, where had *that* memory come from? He blushed, thinking about what Amy had done to him in the powder room at his mother's house outside Wilmington, Delaware, his siblings and their spouses and all the little nieces and nephews just a few feet away, in the living room, Bob gasping in shock, then biting down on his own fist so he wouldn't make any more sounds as Amy went at him like a ravenous little animal. Only, who was Amy?

He told his mother that he was feeling much better, although the opposite was true. He left his office to get a cup of coffee. A cup of coffee, a stiff drink, electroconvulsive shock therapy—he clearly needed *something*. He was so dazed that he caromed off the desk outside his office, the desk that belonged to his assistant. Aimee. *Aimee.* Who had dark hair, long legs, and vivid lips that were conspicuously pale this morning, lips that he suddenly knew were usually tinted the shade of the lipstick he had found in his car.

"Morning, Bob," she said, somehow making them the two most terrifying words he had ever heard. Suddenly, their history was *there*, rushing at him like a montage. It was mainly a montage of sex, heated, nasty, secret sex, like the incident in the powder room. Wonderful sex. Why would he break up with her? True, the memories carried a whiff of crazy, but then, the crazy ones were always best. How did he know that? How could he know that? He had been married to—someone—for . . . a while, a long while. He had never cheated on good old what's-her-name. Well, never cheated in a way that really counted, just a convention here or there, a Christmas party at the old company, back when things were a little more freewheeling. Strange, he could remember those instances in great detail, but he couldn't remember that— who was he trying to remember? Something else was nagging him, something that was making him anxious and fearful. He had forgotten something important. A presentation? A staff meeting?

"Have you thought about what we discussed, Bob? About your decision?"

"Of course," he said. He was clueless.

"And—?"

"I haven't reached a decision just yet." Bob, an old hand at drift- ing off in meetings, had an endless supply of stock expressions guaranteed to ease one back into almost any conversation. Keep it vague, use the other person's words, and eventually the topic will be revealed.

"Well, you better," Aimee said. "By the end of the week, Bob. I meant what I said."

He continued on to the coffee station, feeling as if he had two brains. One was emptying, leaking facts and details slowly but steadily, while the other compartment seemed to be filling with a floodwater of information, so much coming at him at once that he couldn't sort things out. Then, in the next instant, he had all these new vivid memories of sex and golf—not sex *with* golf, but sex, with Aimee and many others, followed by separate memories of exceptional golfing experiences. The other arriving details were slower to cohere, but each one seemed to cost him a piece of his old life. His personal life, through age twenty-one, was consistent between the two spheres. It was there, about the time he met ... what's-her-name, that a chasm opened and his mind separated like an egg. He was Bob, but he had never been married, much less been a, what was it called? A father. He had never been a father. His mother was worried about this. She had lectured him just the other day, when he'd said he was breaking up with Aimee/Amy, that he needed to settle down, if only for the sake of his career and health. "Married men live longer," his mother had said. "And while the bosses can't publicly discriminate against you for being single, other people can't help judging a man who isn't settled."

But they can fire your ass, a voice in Bob's brain said, *for having an affair with your assistant, which is specifically prohibited under the company's sexual harassment policy.*

The voice was not his but Aimee's. She had delivered this warning, he realized, after he had informed her this past Monday that he wanted to stop "seeing" her. Which was a polite word for what had been, and what was supposed to remain, a clandestine relationship. Her arrival on his mother's doorstep during his Christmas visit had been the deciding factor in trying to cool things off. She had introduced herself to Bob's family as his girlfriend before he could do anything. She had used the surname Smith and the not exactly fake first name, making a big point of the fact that it was *not* spelled the French way, as if that were a sufficient disguise. He had realized then that he would have to stop seeing her, but it was hard. For one thing, Aimee seemed to have an unerring instinct for when he might introduce the topic and, even in public, would find a way to start doing things that would distract him.

For another, she could cost him everything. While they were together, she had no interest in bringing anyone's attention to their affair. The secrecy had fueled their encounters. The secrecy and Aimee's craziness. But after the incident over the holidays, he knew he had to end things, and he had finally summoned the nerve Monday, after announcing his plan to his mother on Sunday. He had even considered it a kind of trial run for firing Paul, in fact: dispatch Aimee Monday evening, then tell Paul the bad news on Wednesday. After surviving Aimee's histrionics, it had been a bizarre relief, just doing a straightforward dismissal, although Paul had been kind of a prick about it, and the others had sulked, said Bob had no backbone, made those stupid jokes about Klink and Schultz. They couldn't see the big picture. If Bob didn't bend from time to time, the big bosses would break them all. Now it was Thursday and he had until the end of the week—

To give Paul's job to Aimee. Which made no sense, as he had told Aimee repeatedly. He really did have to trim the payroll in their department. And while Amy would start at the lower end of the pay grade, people would gossip if he brought her in immediately after dumping Paul, maybe even speculate. But if he didn't give her Paul's job, she would tell the big bosses about the affair, and he would be fired.

How had he gotten into this situation? He had vague memories of wanting to be a different kind of guy, someone more stable and steady, like his two brothers and his brother-in-law. He was the big earner in the family and his mother's favorite. She didn't even try to hide that fact, and the others didn't seem to resent it, not much. Perhaps they even felt a little sorry for him, his big salary and big house aside.

Bob somehow managed to get through the day, ignoring Aimee's glares. Ignoring, too, the reproachful looks of his staff, the burning sensation in his gut. He stopped at a restaurant for dinner alone, but he couldn't kill more than an hour. At home, he started to watch ESPN, but took a spin around the satellite, bumping into an interesting batch of programs. Oh, right, he had Cinemax now. He snaked his hand into his pants, but it felt a little lonely. He glanced at his cell phone, noticed that Aimee's number was right there under "A." Not much of a code, but convenient.

"You know what?" he said when she answered. "I think I can swing it."

"Oh, *Bob*," she said. Her voice was warm, moist, almost as if she were there, breathing into his ear. Bob didn't really find his ears that exciting, but Aimee seemed to.

"And, you know, you've shown a talent for discretion." *Other than that time you showed up at my mother's house, uninvited.* "I think we could still continue to work together, even if we're, uh, working together."

"Of course we can, if we're careful. You want me to come over?"

"Yeah."

She was there within the hour. At first, it seemed wildly novel, Aimee crouched between his legs while he watched Cinemax over her head. Then it seemed familiar. They had done this a lot. He had instigated the affair, in fact, although he'd just been picking up on Aimee's signals. The looks she had tossed, the shy, sly touches. Sometimes, in fact, he fell asleep in the chair, without reciprocating. Maybe most of the time. Aimee always said she didn't mind if he was too tired to reciprocate. *You work so hard.* It dawned on him now that she had been much more interested in another kind of reciprocity, a more cold-blooded tit for tat. What was that visit to his mother's all about? A warning, a threat. Then again, when he gave her the job, *she* would be in his debt, with just as much to lose as he had. He could survive a little gossip, a few glares. He—he reached out his hand, and, under the guise of stroking her hair, adjusted Aimee's head, which was blocking his view.

He woke to the smell of coffee.

"I can't believe you fell asleep in your chair again," Mona said.

So it *was* a dream. The kind of dream he hadn't had since he was seventeen or so, judging by the way things felt around his crotch, but obviously a dream. A relief, right? He told himself it was a relief. Strange, though, how in the dream he couldn't retain the details of his real life, while in real life, the dream stayed vivid. Aimee, her threats, her exciting but odd behavior. Well, he always had been hot for her, but never dared to act. He had wanted to, though. Not enough to do anything about it, but enough to wish that he could be a single, unencumbered guy.

Mona brought him a cup of coffee, the real thing, and perched on the arm of the chair. "It's a good thing I came downstairs before the kids were up," she said. "Honey, you left the television on."

"Oh, sorry. Did the noise—"

"It wasn't the noise. But—look, you're entitled to a little fun, as long as we have the parental controls. But you can't *leave* it there, hon."

"There?"

"On those sexy channels. I told you when I agreed to let you have a subscription that you had to be careful. Bad enough for me to start my morning with an image of some woman's behind going up and down, but if one of the twins had come downstairs first—" She glanced at her watch. "Gotta run. I've got a tennis lesson before my pedicure."

Nice life, he thought. *You play tennis, I earn the money, you get to decide what cable channels I'm allowed to have.*

She kissed him on the forehead, leaving what he knew would be a pale pink smear. Eventually, he found the energy to rouse himself and walked through the house, retracing his steps from yesterday. The house had reverted to the chaos of family. He hated to admit it, but he kind of missed the office that had briefly inhabited Dennie's room. But they could do an addition, buy those kinds of furnishings. He drove to work in his good old Jeep Cherokee, barely missing the silver Audi, its power and style.

But when he flipped open the glove compartment to grab his parking pass, he saw a tube of lipstick, as dark as the one from the dream.

In the office, Aimee smiled at him—a normal, pleasant smile, nothing more—then trailed him into his office even though they'd long had an understanding that Bob liked a few minutes to decompress. He hung up his coat on the hook, saw with relief that the credenza was filled with family photographs and the rogue copy of Yeats had disappeared. Yet, the photo of the two men in tuxedos remained on the top shelf. He didn't get that. Who were those guys? What were they to him? Why would a book come and go, while a photo stayed?

"When are you going to announce it?" Aimee asked without preamble. "Last night, you said you'd have to wait three months, until we were in the new quarter, and I'm okay with that. Although I was counting on the pay increase sooner, so if you could help me cover some gaps in my expenses—"

"Last night?"

Her smile was sexy. Creepy-sexy, but sexy. "When I was at your house. Aren't you the naughty one, sneaking me in after everyone had gone to bed?"

"After—"

"And I thought I was the one who liked to take risks. Remember that time in the office, right here, when we thought everyone had left for the night and the custodian almost caught us?"

She seemed on the verge of coming around the desk, re-creating the scene to which she had alluded.

"No. I mean—I remember." He did. He remembered a lot. He remembered too much. Yesterday, it had felt as if his life had broken in half, and his life with Mona and the kids, his real life, had vanished. Today, he had both lives, one overlaid on the other, with a lot of subsequent contradictions. He was a happy family man. A happy family man who apparently had been having the kind of affair that could destroy everything, his work and home lives. "Of course I remember. But, sheesh, Aimee. Not now."

This made her beam with happiness. Happy *not* to have to blow him at 9:25 A.M. He saw now what should have been obvious in any one of his lives: Amy's intimate, uh, ministrations were cold-blooded careerism, a way of getting ahead. Once she had the job, she wouldn't have sex with him anymore, but she would have the history of the sex to control him, blackmail him. He would never be free of her, yet it would never be fun again. The whole affair came back to him and it was an *affair* now, a dark and terrifying counterpoint to his domestic life, full of lies and risks and betrayals. When he had skipped one of the twin's sporting events or performances, chances were he was with Aimee.

But she had started it, although he hadn't realized it at the time. She had pursued him. She had come to his mother's house over Christmas and *Mona had been there*. Mona knew Aimee, of course, and she bought the idea that Aimee was visiting family nearby. Aimee even had a "male cousin" in tow, some guy who chatted happily with Mona in the den, while Bob and Aimee went into the powder room, their visits spaced carefully apart—Jesus, how had this happened? He had always been a good guy, living his life for his family, the sole provider, the breadwinner. He would have to give Aimee the job, but how long would it be before he got caught, trapped in his old lies?

And what's with that goddamn photograph of the two men in tuxedos? It was the one thing that seemed true in all his lives over these two days. Was the photo the answer?

He waited until Aimee had left and reached for the photograph. It was on the top shelf, and he had to stand on tiptoe. It appeared to be insubstantial, a computer printout, not even on proper paper, and the frame was cheap. Funny, he didn't remember the credenza's top shelf being so high. He stretched his arms, his finger grazing the frame, but not quite grasping it. He brushed it, meaning only to scoop it toward him, but lost his balance, lurching into the credenza. After what seemed like a moment of consideration, the credenza returned the favor and swayed forward into his outstretched arms, almost as if they were dancing.

When the crash came, there was a split second of confusion, then the employees who were there by nine thirty ran to Bob's office, but even the half dozen or so who crowded in there were not strong enough to lift the heavy credenza from his body, and, by the time the emergency crews arrived, it was too late for him.

Paul, who had been in the middle of packing yet another box, was among those who gathered. He saw the framed photograph—glass broken, frame splintered—lying a few inches from Bob's hand, which happened to be the only part of Bob that was visible. Had Bob even noticed it? It had been a silly gesture, sneaking into Bob's office Wednesday night and placing the photo there, a bit of nose-thumbing at best, not at all the elegant gesture he had imagined it to be in his beer-fueled imagination.

He wondered why Aimee seemed so stricken. She was a tough cookie, obsequious to Bob's face and contemptuous behind Bob's back, specializing in surprisingly graphic speculation about how inept he must be in bed, how pathetic his cries would be at orgasm, how he had probably never pleased any woman, except Mona, and that was with his big *paycheck*. Aimee had a lot of edge, to risk understatement, but she was bawling like a baby now. Elena and Jack looked more like Paul felt, dazed and horrified. Did he look guilty, too, however?

Paul knew that Bob's death would not spare him. The paperwork had been executed; his exit interview with HR was behind him. He wondered if Bob had even figured out the meaning of the photo, if he had noticed it, much less figured it out. Paul had spent a ridiculous amount of time scouring the Web, looking for an image that would not announce itself too boldly, and was giddy when he found exactly what he needed. The two tuxedoed men, out of context, were not easy to place. But add a monocle to one and a German helmet to the other and they would be instantly recognizable as the actors who played Colonel Klink and Sergeant Schultz, the two reliably inept yes-men of *Hogan's Heroes*, the two halves that made up Bob's personality. Paul had considered trying Peter Lorre, in *Casablanca*, but Lorre was too recognizable. Paul had wanted Bob to puzzle over the photo, wonder at its significance. He had wanted to suggest that Bob was cowardly, and that his cowardice, his fear of any risk, had cut him off from having a truly interesting life. He wanted to say to his former boss, *You are the toady* and *the incompetent, you do the nasty stuff and then pretend to know nothing about.* He wanted to say, *How dare you pretend to love poetry, when there is so little poetry in your soul.* Now he wasn't sure if Bob had even noticed the little frame, tucked among all those plaques and photos and trophies and unopened books.

He went back to packing his desk. A volume of Yeats was there, although he didn't remember having that among his effects. Funny, because it was only two days ago that Bob had made that Freudian slip: *in dreams begin nightmares.* Paul tossed the book into one of his boxes. It wasn't his, but he didn't see how it could hurt, how anyone would miss it.

Poetry makes nothing happen, said W. H. Auden, in memorializing the poet William Butler Yeats. But perhaps the problem is that we don't acknowledge poetry's power, or we deny its role in our day-to-day lives. Or we obscure it, distracted by the petty feuds, rivalries, and tiny discontents, at the office and at home. Bob justified himself by saying that he was a family man and he was forced to live by his own words. As he found out, what's easily said is not so easily done . . . especially in the Twilight Zone.

THE GOOD NEIGHBOR

Whitley Strieber

Jake Martin has it all, the pretty wife, the cute kids, the right car, the nice house. But he wants more and he's just been given the chance of a lifetime, and he's taken it. Of course, there will be consequences. But he's prepared to lose the friend he stabbed in the back and even to trade in the pretty wife for the right wife.

There is one consequence, though, that he cannot be prepared for. Somebody else understands him better than he understands himself, and they are going to confront him in a way he cannot expect. An ambitious man is about to have everything he has gained stripped away, and face his own soul bleeding and naked . . . in the Twilight Zone.

J ake pulled the old Beemer into the driveway, giving himself all the time in the world to savor the surprise that Shirley was about to get. She had been eating him alive over their expenses, over the fact that he never should have bought the house on Alta Vista, over their unpaid mortgage, all that crap. But he'd bought the house so he could entertain people like Charlie and Gil. So it was an investment in the future—that is to say, now.

This was no ordinary promotion, up five grand and shake your hand. No, he was into the big time here. This was lucrative stock options, a place on the bonus list—and, of course, a raise that far exceeded five grand. If things went as well for Bradford this year as they had last, he could be looking at tripling his income. Of course, his boss, Mike, had been passed over, but that was life in the jungle, right?

He stopped in the garage, tucked the bottle of champagne he'd bought to celebrate with under his arm, and went into the house. "Shitty day," he yelled happily, "look out below!"

From upstairs, he heard Shirley's warbling voice shrill, "I got the iron on, honey!"

And, boy, he really could not see her hobnobbing with Rita Bradford and Margaret Harrison at the Burning Tree Country Club. She'd already been a damned iffy hostess at their dinner parties, with that shrill cackle of hers. He had to face the fact that he'd been inspired by the boobs, not the brains, here. As you moved up the ladder, wives counted more and more. She had to be able to sustain an opera weekend in New York with Maggie and Rita and the rest of their posse. She had to be able to make them want her on board.

From now on, he and his wife would be considered a sort of team, and if one could not advance, neither would the other. Example: Andy Card was a senior vice president and he'd been on the waiting list at Burning Tree for years. Why? Leona just did not fit in over there. Behind her back, they called her the Easter Egg, and that kind of summed it up. What would they be calling Shirley, with that voice of hers? The Grackle?

Fine. He'd deal with it.

And here she came, hair up in rollers, wearing a dirty smock, feet bare. "What happened, honey, why are you home early?" Fear made her voice crackle even more sharply. She thought he'd been canned.

"You've been smoking," he said. Another unpleasant habit she couldn't break.

"I've been doing the bills, honey. We're gonna have to skip the mortgage again. So, yeah, I've been smoking."

Smoking was weak. Bradford's entire campus was a no-smoking zone. "Charlie Bradford doesn't like it."

She laughed to herself, shook her head. They'd been here before. She viewed his cultivation of Charlie and Gil with ill-disguised contempt.

He let her see the Wine Cellars bag, then reached in and lifted out the champagne. He held it up. "Shirley, I'm no longer in the marketing department."

"Oh . . . oh, God." She looked at the bottle. Then at his face. "You're . . . not?"

"Yeah, they made me move my stuff out this afternoon."

She reacted as if she'd been struck. "We'll get foreclosed."

Yesterday, that was true. Today, they could put the house on the market, leave it till it sold, and move right over to Terrace Lane, where Gil and Charlie lived, as soon as a house was available. With the kind of money he was making now, they could simply carry this dump until it sold.

"I moved my stuff out of the sixteenth floor and into my new office on the twentieth."

He watched her face. She blinked. Thought.

"But that's—oh my God."

He smiled, a big one, ear to ear.

"Go *on*! You got a promotion, *go on*!"

"It's huge."

From the dining room, little Lissa whispered to Pete, "Daddy got a promotion, Daddy got a promotion!"

And the champagne flowed and Shirley thawed the fine Omaha steaks they'd bought last year.

After dinner and bedtimes, he sat with the calculator, actually figuring out what his new take-home was going to be. Which was a lot of fun.

She was quiet for a long time, watching him, reading. She

turned the TV on and surfed, then cut it off. Finally, she asked him, "What about Mike?"

"He's still where he was."

"But then you—what happened? Did you get his promotion? Did you get Mike's promotion?"

"I got *a* promotion."

"He was your friend!"

"He was passed over. It happens."

"You took Mike's promotion. That's why we've been sucking up to the Bradfords and the Harrisons, isn't it? And it's not right, Jake, it's ugly. What about book club and bridge club—I can't show my face!"

"I just moved you from Alta Vista Avenue to Terrace Lane and all you can think about is some ridiculous midlevel-wives' bridge club? You're headed for Burning Tree, girl!"

"We can't afford Burning Tree. And anyway, how are we going to move? We can't sell this house."

"Of course we can sell this house. I know the market's not perfect, but there've been some decent sales lately. The Carters' place went for two sixty and we've got more frontage."

As he spoke, she stared at him. When he stopped, she kept staring.

"What?"

"I don't think the houses in our neighborhood have any value right now."

"What's that supposed to mean?"

"The Carters—you know. Surely you do."

The Carter place had sold to people just like them, of course. This block wasn't being busted. Certainly not. "All I know is that it has to be a normal sale. This isn't Oakwell Ranch or Lily Dale, for God's sake. We're upscale around here and they don't do upscale, they can't!"

"Hon, I'm pretty sure they're moving in Saturday."

He was stunned, quite frankly, to silence. This was just—well, it was impossible. It meant that this house was worthless. And with him behind on his mortgage two months already, the bank was going to know this very soon, and it would call his note.

Promotion or no promotion, that would force him into bankruptcy.

The Bradford Brands Corporation, Bylaws, Article 15, Board of Directors, Paragraph 5, part ii: "No person in a condition of bankruptcy or operating under the bankruptcy protection of any state or entity in any location whatsoever may sit as a member of the Board of Directors of the Bradford Corporation."

All senior vice presidencies carried mandatory board membership. He felt his underarms getting wet; his head starting to throb. But no, she was wrong, she had to be.

He went into the den and turned on his home computer, then waited for what seemed like a thousand years for the thing to boot. At last, he pulled up the multiple-listing service and checked the listing . . . and the world ended.

Oh, they'd made an effort to hide it, but it was clear enough. The buyers had numbers, not names.

The doorbell rang, causing him to almost jump through his skin. Who would it be at this hour? Only one guess—

And, indeed, it was one of his neighbors, Ed Trillian. Or no, there was George Montague back there in the shadows, too.

He opened the door for them. Nobody spoke. As he was taking them into the den, the bell rang again. This time it was Adam Dane and Tom Ford. So that was the street, except, of course, for Carter himself. But he wasn't around anymore. He'd gone under with the collapse of Capital Fiscal. The house was in foreclosure. The block was being busted by the guy's damn bank.

He got the guys into the den, closed the door and locked it. He already knew what he was going to propose, and there was absolutely no way Shirley was going to hear one damn word of it. She'd start shrieking like a banshee, and he did not need that. "Obviously," he said, "we're in trouble."

"I'm under water on my mortgage," Adam said.

"We're in escrow here and in Dallas," Tom added. He'd recently gotten a new job there. "If we lose this sale, then we also can't close down there. We're up on cinder blocks."

Ed Trillian said, "I find them fascinating."

"Yeah, I had an ant farm when I was a kid," Jake said. "They were fascinating, too. You just didn't want the damn things in bed with you." He shook his head. "You know, before this all happened, I thought I hated al Qaeda. I thought I hated the Taliban. Raghead bastards. I have to tell you, though, I had no damn idea what hate was. And I hate these things—good God damn, but I do hate them."

"Okay, we all do, Jake. But we gotta focus on our problem."

Tom could not have been more right. "Absolutely," Jake said. "And God willing, we will hurt them somehow."

"Yeah, maybe, but what we gotta do is sell out," George announced.

Jake saw red. Just saw red. He knew he was advancing on George, he knew he was yelling and George was cringing—and then he felt strong arms gripping him, felt himself being pulled back—and there was George sitting on the floor with blood trickling out of his gaping, astonished mouth, and Jake's right fist hurt like hell.

"Jesus, Jake!"

"Sorry! Sorry! But—George." He shook off Tom and Ed. "Lemme go, I got it. I got it under control." He looked down at George. "Buddy—sorry—you just—man! You shocked me there! SELL OUT? No. What we gotta do is tear out some goddamn throats. That's the question on the table."

Tom said, "The only offers we're gonna get will be from the bastards who just busted this block, and they will be for pennies on the dollar."

"But . . . my mortgage is a hundred and eighty grand," George said. "That's my absolute minimum."

Was the man a moron? Born yesterday? Jake did not suffer fools gladly, but this fool was still rubbing his jaw, so it was time to try to tone himself down. "George," he said in as reasonable a tone as he could manage, "you will be lucky if they offer you fifteen thousand dollars. Ten. If that."

George stared. Silent. He had finally realized that he would be left renting a trailer and paying off a mortgage on a house he no longer owned. Just like the rest of them.

"Maybe it won't be that bad," Ed said. "'Cause I already have my offer. It's for about half the value of the house. Take it by eight tonight or forget it."

Jake felt his stomach kind of congeal, a sensation he'd never experienced before. He knew exactly why Ed had gotten a slightly decent offer.

"I could do that," George said. "I could live with that. With half."

"That would work for me," Tom added. "Just. If I put the savings I have left into the closing up here, I think I could still make it."

Jake saw that he had to play this out carefully. "Okay," he said, "who here does not have a mortgage?"

There was a silence. Finally, Ed said, "Well, I guess I'm about paid off. Next month, in fact."

"Which is why they made you a real offer. Us, they don't need to stroke. We're all under water on our mortgages. They *want* us to walk away from our houses. If we're foreclosed, the banks will sell our places for ten cents on the dollar. That's how block busting works."

George turned a desperate face to Ed Trillian, who looked at the floor. "Just telling you guys is all," Ed said. "But I gotta take it."

"You're destroying us. You know that," Adam Dane said.

"You're my friends—"

"Then tell the bastards no!" Jake shouted.

"Our houses are worthless!" Ed said.

"Not yours," Jake said, forcing calm into his voice. "Yours is gonna bring you a cool hundred grand!"

"Which I have to take! And don't you come at me, Jake. Don't you get physical. And I'm sorry for you guys. I am so genuinely sorry. But I don't make the laws."

Jake realized that he'd played that card. "Look, do us a favor and just get outta here."

"Guys, I had to." He backed toward the door. "It's a hundred grand, don't you see that?"

Nobody said anything. Nobody could, because it was indeed a hundred grand, and they did, indeed, see that.

He slipped out. And now, Jake saw, the way was clear. "Okay, guys, I'm going to propose something. It will be a shock, but before you start yelling, I want you to think. Carefully. What I am going to propose is that we burn them out."

"Burn . . . the Trillians?"

Dear heaven, how did Tom Ford manage to make the money he did? Did the man even have an IQ? "No, Tom, leave him be. He's doing exactly what any one of us would do if we had the chance. I am talking about our new neighbors."

All three men looked at him, and, one by one, he met their eyes with his determination and his defiance and the purity of the hate he felt for the vile creatures who were invading their beautiful world.

Nobody spoke until, finally, Adam said, "You're not gonna get away with a thing like that."

"Look, it's been done. A lot, in fact."

"A lot? Jake, that's more like once," George said. "And eleven guys went to jail, as I recall."

"The neighborhood was saved. If the scum get burned out, they give up. That's the message of the Michigan Eleven."

"I'm not going to jail," George said. "Screw that."

The general assent told Jake he was in trouble with these guys, and that must not be. The filth had to be kept out of the neighborhood. Period. Life-or-death struggle. "First off, we don't have to get caught, and if we do it right, we won't."

They just stared at him. Did not believe a word of it. He thought fast. "Okay, we'll vote. But let's base it on an assumption."

"No assumptions, Jake."

"Hear me out, George. Jesus! Assume that I have a plan that absolutely, convincingly will not get us caught. Would you do it then?" Jake thrust up his own hand. Tom started to raise his, then stopped. George never even started. Adam fidgeted with one of the many coasters Shirley kept on the damn table. "Guys?"

"It's a crime," Adam said.

"Wait a second, now. Let's be clear. There has been a crime committed, no question about that. The crime is that this block has been busted. That's the crime. People protecting their homes, I'm sorry, but I feel no guilt." He looked at Adam. "You know it's true." Slowly, Adam raised his hand. Then Tom. Then, finally, George. *And thank you, God.*

Now for the next step. Burning the empty house wasn't going to be enough, and Jake knew this. "Now we're together. But this has to be handled very, very carefully. First, my best guess is that the cops are going to be keeping an eye on the house."

"Do we know that?" Adam asked.

"We assume it." And here came the crucial twist in logic that was either going to work or it wasn't. And it had to. He needed these guys, he could not do this alone. "Right now, if we do the house like in Michigan, the cops are gonna be watching and we will get caught."

"So how do we solve that?"

"Do it later. After the garbage has moved in. Because once they've arrived, no cop is gonna come near the place. No need."

The silence was that of death, of the tomb, of profound human fear.

Finally, George whispered, "We can't go near it, either. My God."

"But we can, George. Nobody expects it, but to us, our homes and our families are more important even than our fear."

Adam crossed and uncrossed his legs. Tom went over to the little fridge and pulled out a beer. "Okay," he said. George nodded.

"We let them settle in. And here's the beauty of it. Who's to know they didn't start the fire themselves? An accident. Nobody knows what they do in their houses because nobody goes near them. Plus, who's going to investigate, and what would they look for? Nobody knows. No, if we do this while they're inside, we're not going to have a problem."

George drank beer, sucking nervously. Tom turned on the TV and surfed, clicking the remote with an angry, jabbing motion.

"So," Jake continued, "we make a plan, then we wait until they're in, then—poof." He tried to laugh. It did not work. He cleared his throat.

Finally, Adam said, "We can't kill them."

"Of course not," Jake said. "We'll start it in the basement. Give them time to get out. Plenty of time."

"They'll call the fire department," Tom said. "It'll get put out. They'll demand a police investigation."

"They do not make phone calls," Jake said.

"You know this?" George asked.

He didn't, but the whole idea of their using things like emergency services struck him as just damn improbable. "I know it."

Tom surfed awhile longer. George cracked another beer and left with it. Then Adam and Tom took off. Jake went up to bed. Shirley was already asleep. He lay close to the edge on his side, his back turned to her. He thought long thoughts about life as it was now, and the world and what it was coming to, and how a man had to make his success because there was damn well nobody else who was going to do it for him.

When morning came, both of the Trillians' cars were gone and there was a black panel truck in front of the Carter place. Nobody was wasting any time, it seemed. As he backed out of his garage on the way to work, Jake thought that they ought to burn the Trillian place, too. Useless gesture, but satisfying.

Just before noon, he found one of the mailroom guys standing in his doorway with a FedEx envelope. When Jake saw that it was from City Savings and Trust, he stuffed it into his briefcase. It was their demand letter, of course.

On the way home, he stopped at Lowe's and bought some emergency candles. As he drove up the street, he saw that the Carters' pretty lawn was now covered with that black goop they sprayed everywhere, and workers from some government agency were coating the house with it. Black, black, black, inside and out—that was their only color. The junk smelled like—well, a dead neighborhood. Ruined lives. Or, to be more precise, sewage mixed with burned hair.

He moved through Friday like a zombie, doing his work, which consisted of filling out requisition forms for his new desk, office chair, curtains, you name it—the list was long and the budget generous.

That afternoon, he stopped in the middle of Alta Vista and looked carefully and long at what had been the Carter place. What was it now, a hovel? Call the damn thing a slum.

Saturday morning dawned, and Jake woke up to Pete and Lissa's excited shouts from the front yard. One glance out the window and he was into his sandals and downstairs. "Shirley, the kids are out there!"

Shirley came in from the kitchen. "It's no big deal, they don't hurt people."

"There could be radiation, anything!" He went out onto the front porch. "Come on, boobalas," he said gently. "We can watch from inside."

At that moment, the sun went out. Jake looked up to see a vast blackness spreading across the sky like a gigantic lid coming down on the world. The air became still and dense, as if a storm was brewing. This was followed by the first whiff of the legendary stench that accompanied the bastards, and when he caught the fetid, rotten scent, Jake had to choke back his loathing.

Up and down the street, doors slammed as people came out. George and his wife, Tom and his kids, Adam and Tina Dane.

"The thing," Shirley said, "isn't it . . . decrepit?"

"It's filthy," Jake said. "Their junk is all filthy."

You could see open areas with gridwork behind them, places where it had been gouged by something, other places where big, black panels were hanging off.

"Has it been attacked?" Pete asked.

"Nobody knows what happens out there," Jake explained. "It's a total unknown."

Added to the stink from across the street, a smell of hot metal and burning plastic wafted down from what Jake was increasingly coming to think of as an interstellar jalopy. The thing clanked like a busted washing machine.

With a gigantic, echoing creak, a big trapdoor slowly opened onto a dark maw.

"We need to go inside right now," Jake said. Somehow, being exposed to that opening—being seen by *them*—was making him darned uncomfortable. Who knew what they were capable of? Maybe they read minds, who knew? "Get inside," Jake shouted up and down the street. "Everybody! NOW!"

Added to the clanking came the sound of every dog in the neighborhood going berserk, howling, barking, making sounds you don't often hear, the screeches and roars of dog insanity.

Jake got his family into the house, but he had to literally drag the kids, who were absolutely fascinated.

He let them watch from behind the curtains, though. And, for a few minutes, nothing happened. Then there was movement in the blackness. Slowly, objects came down on ropes. Black objects, black ropes.

"It's furniture," Shirley whispered.

You could see that there were chairs coming down, tables, even what looked like some kind of stove made of more black tubing than Jake had ever seen in one place before. The chairs were tall and narrow, with seats indented to fit the sitters' bones. Everything was black.

Then rope ladders, black as night, were dropped, and first one and then another of the great, gangling creatures came slowly, clumsily down.

"My God," Jake said, "look at them."

"They're fascinatingly strange."

"They look like bugs covered with . . . what is that, some kind of . . . tar?"

At night, they flew, feeding, it was believed, on bats and owls and insects. When they took flight, they sounded the way they looked, like gigantic blowflies.

"Look at their faces," Pete said, his voice quavering.

Jake could see the humanity in their lips. "They look like some kind of crossbreed," he said. The eyes were insectoid, but the lips could have been on the face of anyone anywhere, they were that human.

Shirley's hand slipped into his. "That was the bank guy. They wanted us to know we need to get our basics out."

He hadn't even heard the phone ring.

"I'll get packing," she said, tears in her voice.

"Yeah, you do that," he said. He hoped he sounded convincing, but he was worried. He knew no more about the capabilities of the aliens than anybody else did. They were sickening, but they were also powerful, and now he had to face that power.

He watched them drag their belongings into the black, ruined house. They moved like snakes mixed with spiders, alternately writhing and jerking along. They were the ugliest things Jake had ever seen, a grotesque abortion of evolution. God only knew what sort of hideous, misbegotten world they came from.

As the sun went down, Jake went into the garage and checked the gas in his lawnmower can. Three-quarters full. He'd use a little, George would use a little, Adam would use a little, they'd do it together. Very late, after the creatures had done their night flying and come home to roost.

The things probably wouldn't be in any danger, but if they were—if they burned—oh, how beautiful it would be.

Shortly after eleven, Jake heard the drone of the creatures leaving the house, flying off into the night.

He texted the agreed signal: *"Nice evening, let's suck beer."*

They'd met one more time about what they now referred to as "the matter." Jake had laid out the plan and they had arranged this signal. The fear would be incredible, they knew that. They would help one another. The Carters had been gregarious neighbors, so everybody knew the house.

The plan was to hang out here until the creatures returned, then do the deed. Move in fast, get out. Simple as that. Except for one thing: nobody was replying.

Jake repeated the text. He had expected at least one defector, probably George, but not all three, surely not all three.

Then there came a sound—tapping, very soft. He went to the front door. Tom was out there. He opened the door onto a stricken man.

"You're not backing out," he said.

"Jake, they're the most awful things I've ever seen."

"I know it. But we have to do this."

"If we have to get close to them, to touch them—I just can't do it."

"We won't! We won't even see them."

"We'll be alone in there, Jake. With them. God knows what will happen to us, Jake. What we need to do is just get the hell out of here. Live to fight another day."

He let him go. What else could he do? He'd just have to take all the risk himself. But this neighborhood would pay him back— it would pay him back in full. How, he did not yet know, but he would find a way.

Jake sat in the den, doing research, googling for information about them—as if he hadn't done all this before. The problem was, there was so much crap out there, you just could not tell what to believe. What he was most curious about was their ability to read minds.

One o'clock slowly edged into two. How long did the damn things stay out? At this rate, they'd eat every bat in town in a matter of days. *God, why did you have to send us these horrors? Why not beautiful white angels, or just any damn thing that isn't so hideous?*

At last, he heard a buzzing, faint at first—then dying away—then—no—yes! Oh, yes, that was them, they were coming home.

He turned off the TV, then went to the front window and looked out just as the last gangly shadow landed on the roof and disappeared down the chimney.

Okay, now, just give it a few minutes, then you move.

He waited until the minute hand past through two twenty, then headed to the garage. Working quickly, he dropped two emergency candles into his pocket, then picked up the can of gas and went out the door that opened into the side yard.

It was so quiet you could hear the lawns sighing. The smell of the place across the street was appalling . . . and then again, there was the much nicer odor of the gas he was carrying.

Rather than try to creep up on the place, he decided on a swift approach. Quiet as could be.

His plan was to go around the back of the house and use the cellar entrance, but as soon as he stepped into the black muck that covered the lawn, he realized that it was tacky. Every step he took made a sound, so he had to go to the front door instead. He would get rid of the shoes after the deed was done. All the clothes. If the cops found raw gas or something on them, he was done. To minimize the sound, he walked on the edges of his feet.

As he approached the porch, he could see that the front door had actually been removed. In its place was a black curtain that was blowing gently in the night wind. Well, this was a break. So far, so good.

Carefully, he touched the curtain. Felt like ordinary cloth. Burlap, maybe. He drew it back, and almost fell backward off the porch, the stench was so terrible. A dense, acidic, rotted stink that forced him to somehow swallow an almost uncontrollable sound of loathing. Bugs and cigarette smoke and tar and, was that ammonia?

Inside, the floors were bare and dry, not tacky like the lawn. So at least he could be quiet.

He opened the gas can—and cursed himself for not having loosened the damn cap before he even started. In this silence, the scraping sound seemed gigantic.

God, but the air was awful. Was it going to give him cancer or something? Just kill him right here and now? What a life—you finally kill off some jerk, you get the dream promotion—and this happens. Usually, his luck was good. Usually.

He went through to the kitchen and worked his way backward, splashing gas. Once he was at the front door again, he waved the curtain to disperse the fumes so that he could safely light one of the emergency candles.

The match lit the whole room, an amazingly bright flare. The windows were black, of course, so it wouldn't be seen from outside, but what about them, what about upstairs?

He touched the match to the wick of the candle, set it in the middle of the floor, and left fast. The fumes were strong, and they were going to go any second.

He crossed the black lawn and, never mind the noise, stopped to pull off his shoes, then crossed the empty street and ran up to his garage. He put the gas and the spare emergency candles away, stashed the shoes in the trunk of his car, then went straight upstairs.

Shirley stirred. "Where were you?" she murmured.

"Bathroom."

"Oh . . ."

Dropping off his clothes, he went close to her and folded her into his arms. She might not be a trophy wife, but she was warm and she felt good against him. She sighed, kissed him, and opened herself to him. For an instant, he was in touch with the sweet sensuality that had drawn him to her in the first place, and the love he made to her was genuine.

In the middle of their passion, he heard a faint thudding sound, not even a boom, and, a moment later, saw orange shadows begin flickering across the ceiling.

It had damn well worked! It had *worked*! But he had to play this very cool. He kept on with Shirley until he could feel her getting uneasy, then see her eyes growing wide as she looked past him. She said, "What the hell?"

He turned away from her, made himself gasp, then rolled off her. "Oh my God!"

They came up out of the bed together, which could not have been more perfect, because this alibi would stand up even to one of the new lie readers, because Shirley really would believe without question that he'd been here the whole time.

He raised the blinds and was absolutely horrified at what he saw. The entire house was a ball of red, raging flames. That black stuff must be inflammable. He hadn't thought of that. But there could be no question about one thing. Nothing was coming out of there alive.

Except—"Jake, look! LOOK!"

One of the creatures, its angular body sparking with blue flames, came staggering out onto the front porch and collapsed.

Without a word of warning, Shirley took off running. She was already downstairs and out the front door, dragging one of their bedsheets, before he could so much as catch up with her. "Jesus, Shirley, slow down!"

"We have to help!"

The house was a wall of fire, and the creature on the ground lay still, smoke coming up from its body.

Shirley threw the sheet over it.

In the distance, sirens were rising, getting louder fast.

She went down to it.

"Honey, don't touch it!"

"Jake, he's breathing!" She pulled the sheet back, and in the flickering firelight Jake saw that the creature was alive, and their eyes met, and he saw the lips—the delicate, complex line of the lips—part just slightly. And he saw something there that he did not understand and did not expect, which touched his heart with pity so great that he sobbed aloud.

"Oh, Jake," Shirley breathed. "Jake, he's so delicate. Oh, he's so light and delicate."

The firemen came, and, as the situation was being brought under control, an EMS truck appeared. They collected the creature in what looked like a big black pan with no handles. All this time, the creature's eyes never left Jake.

Did it know?

Maybe, but the days passed and there was no reappearance of the aliens, no questions from the cops. The city engineers came with bulldozers and scraped off the ruins, and rolled out artificial turf. A builder bought the lot, and within weeks a new house was going up, a nice, substantial house . . . for people.

Property values stabilized, and Tom closed without a hitch and went off to his new life in Dallas. The Trillians, happily enough, had already taken the hundred grand the block buster had offered them, and a very nice new family bought their house from him.

But this didn't matter to Jake, because he was installed in a lovely home just three doors down from Gil Harrison's place on Terrace Lane.

Mike accepted Jake's promotion with such good grace that Jake decided it was too good. He began keeping a secret Mike file, because he knew damn well that he'd made an enemy, and, in the end, one of them would have to go. Still, they played golf together and took their kids to movies together, just like always. And Jake built his file.

The aliens not only stayed away from Alta Vista, they never came back to this side of town.

Until one night very late, they did. Or rather, one of them did.

The huge buzzing sound woke Jake up immediately. In fact, it caused him to leap right out of the new brass bed he'd insisted they buy. He wanted a king. He wanted grandeur. Where he slept was important.

The sound stopped, and for an instant he allowed himself to hope that the thing had flown on. But then he heard from the roof, *scritch, scritch*.

Then he saw, coming down past a back window, the outline of a thin, segmented body and legs. Hideous. Loathsome. In one of its long, complicated claws was a gasoline can.

"Jesus!" He turned to wake Shirley, but she flopped on the bed like a dead fish. "We gotta get out of here!" He shook her and shook her. Nothing. She could not be waked up. Then he ran into Lissa's room. Her eyes were open but they were strange and dark and she could not be waked up, either. Pete was crying, but when Jake tried to open his door, it seemed to be stuck. He turned to go back and get Lissa, but her door slammed and the join just disappeared. Before his eyes, it became a wall.

He smelled gasoline.

Running downstairs, he cried out, "No! Oh, for God's sake, *no!*"

There it was in the middle of their wide living room, standing there. The gas can was open. The alien stank like a corpse bloating in a steam room, a stench at once sour with rot and nauseating with the sick sweetness of unbathed skin. Its eyes were filmed with mucus, its lips wrinkled and withered. It raised its foul, insectoid face to him and the thin line of its lips parted into what had to be the ugliest smile Jake had ever seen or known possible, a look so malevolent that he thought it literally could have killed a weaker man.

It lifted the gas can and poured. The gas gurgled out, splashing over his four-thousand-dollar couch.

"Please! Please stop!"

It tilted the can back, then stood still, staring at him. The can remained positioned in its claws, which undulated along the red surface like restless snakes. He felt that stare, a million accusing arrows driving deep into his soul. He thought, *I have to kill it.*

Then it spoke, its voice at once like the rasp of a great cicada and the song of an angel, and it said, "You cannot kill me."

Which was true, because Jake could not move a muscle. Jake was alive, he was conscious, but his body had been frozen solid.

It smiled again, and this time, despite his disgust and his white-hot hate, Jake saw the grief. "You killed my whole family. I am old and now I am left alone, and you have deprived my children and my grandchildren of their young lives."

From upstairs came the sounds of Lissa and Pete and Shirley hammering on their doors and screaming and crying.

Every muscle in his body, every cell of him, strove to break the paralysis. He whispered, "Please don't hurt my family." And then, again, he saw the pain in that vile face, and knew that the thick mucus dripping from the eyes was its equivalent of tears. And his heart opened a little, and he rasped out a dry, unwilling whisper, "Forgive me."

Again the voice came, singing like an angel, rasping like a bug. "I can forgive you, but you have marked your soul and my forgiveness cannot erase it." In its tone, it seemed to communicate something like gentle acceptance, but also great sadness. "We came here," it said, "to rescue souls." It sighed. "I am going to show you what you will not allow yourself to see. I am going to show you yourself as you appear to us."

Jake became aware of a trembling deep in his body, and then a sense of something changing along his spine, as if he was being opened. His body seemed to disappear around him like so much dust.

It was death. The damn thing was killing him and he had to break this paralysis, he had to get away, he could not let it burn the house, burn his wife and kids—

"Because you asked for forgiveness, there is still a tiny part of your soul that's healthy, Jake, trapped beneath the greed and the cruelty and the hate that defines you. So I will give you a blessing. I will give you a chance to repair your soul by helping others."

"And you won't hurt my family."

Slowly, it shook its monstrous head. "Love your enemy," it said. Then it pointed toward the kitchen. "Jake, just walk through that door."

"Walk . . . into the kitchen? That's it?"

"Through that door."

Immediately, Jake crossed the living room, went through the dining room, and pushed his way into the . . . kitchen.

Whereupon everything changed. There were strange sounds, booming like a great heart beating hard, sucking noises, deafening roars. And there was heat, and tight confinement and pain, there was red raging pain in every inch of his body.

All around him there was something pulsating, a huge, thick mass of something that he didn't understand, that was something animalistic, an orifice of some kind.

Wild terror made him struggle, but it was useless, he could not move even a finger.

The creature had tricked him. He was being eaten alive, but by what he could not imagine.

Then light came, immeasurably bright. Clanging, huge sounds. Something like a face, but immense, blurry and terrible, with great, dark eyes and long, thin claws that clattered as they quested toward him.

Then he knew: up there in the mists and immensity of these bizarre surroundings was one of the aliens, its head bobbing as it peered at him.

A voice boomed out, big as a liner's enormous foghorn, "He's here! He's out! We have our little boy, we have our child at last!"

He was swept up into fierce, amazing cold, into agonizing dryness that seemed to burn his skin off his body.

Was he burning? Had the creature lit the gasoline? He thought these must be death throes, and all this light was the fire that was consuming him.

Then a shape swept down out of the haze, and he saw that it was an alien face, the eyes gleaming, the lips twisted in one of their hideous smiles.

Then hands grasped him, enclosing him in their wriggling, snakelike fingers. He realized that he was a baby again, and—but no, this was impossible, this couldn't happen.

Then they moved him, his body tiny in their great hands, and he was lifted before a mirror, and he saw in that mirror a tiny black bug of a creature, wet and writhing, its little fingers wriggling like worms, its legs those of a stick-insect running helplessly in the air.

He screamed. He screamed as he had never screamed before. And then he heard a tinkling sound, gentle like a spray of water, and knew that it was laughter, and the rattling, kindly voice of an angel said, "Oh, little one, you are so *loud*."

"I think he's hungry, hon."

"Of course he is, my dear little man."

There came toward him a red button dripping with a white substance, and it was beautiful to him, so much so that his heart began roaring, and his whole body struggled and fought to get closer.

He let himself be pressed against his mother's red, flowing breast, and he felt himself in her claws, and his whole body vibrated with the delight of her touch, a burning, furious pleasure, and then he saw, like a great sun, her teat bouncing toward his mouth, and his lips caressed it and he tasted of his mother's milk.

It has been called the milk of forgetting, mother's milk, for its sweetness fills both the body and the mind, washing us clean of our pasts. We are left empty by its fumes and flavor, ready to try again in the land of life. And we set out once more, seeking in ourselves the compassion and the tenderness—the innocence in experience—that is our one true goal.

Jake became once again an empty baby full of hungers and vibrant with possibilities, a dark little insect shrieking for its mother, its little claws grasping the teat, its narrow lips sucking with all its might, feeling the hot delight of the milk in its throat.

While his father held his tiny foot and his mother caressed his black, bald head, the little creature drank at his mother's teat. As gently as that, Jake fell away into the past, and he gained the great chance to repair the evil he had done by living among the angels and doing their hard work of salvation, and was born again.

Jake Martin had a treasure map, and he was mean enough and hard enough to follow it all the way to the end of the line. But he was given a second chance by somebody he neither understood nor expected, but who had the sort of powers—and the sort of heart—that you find only in the Twilight Zone.

EL MOE

Rod Serling

It is my privilege to include this previously unpublished treatment that gives a glimpse into the mind of Rod Serling. This treatment for "El Moe" is Rod at his classic best, showing incredible attention to detail, fully developed characters, and the trademark twists that his episodes were known for. Although we don't know if this treatment was written as a *Twilight Zone* episode, it is very easy to see how this plot might have played out on the small screen. . . .

The Mexican side of the Texas–Mexico border, circa early 1920s. It's a time of turmoil and tension; Model As and bandoliers and Federales; a running, bleeding, protracted three-way battle between tyrants, bandits, and the patient, long-suffering peon who stands in the middle of both.

A small Mexican town. Siesta time in a hot noon sun. Horses sleep on their feet; men sleep under their sombreros; dogs sleep in the shade of the men; even flies sleep. Off in the distance there is a sound like thunder. A dog pricks up an ear and opens one eye. A horse whinnies. A fly buzzes off and finally the sleeping men awake to the noise. The noise becomes an object. A Cavalry troop of Federales, resplendent in ornate uniforms, led by an iron-jawed, pig-eyed Colonel of Cavalry. This is Ruiz. He leads his men through the village. They steal a few chickens, a couple of pigs. They drink everything in sight in the cantina and break what they can't drink. Most explicit: this is a weekly raid and nobody holds up a hand against them. Nobody dares. The Colonel visits the home of an ancient Mexican. He's badgered and bullied. They ask him what became of the legendary hero known as The Falcon. Where is this champion of the little man who rode across the dusty earth ten years before—a brace of pistols and a cutlass shining in the sun? This black-bearded beauty who used to strike down the Federales—only to disappear after a battle. Almost everyone agrees that he was killed and buried, but a persistent little legend says that he is only biding his time—ready to come back in the defense of the men and the soil. The Colonel and his men leave and the wizened little parchment-thin patriarch retires to a back room of his house, opens up a secret panel to reveal pictures of The Falcon. There he is in paint—big and resplendent—bush-bearded and every inch the hero. The old man gazes sadly upon the portrait. "El Nombre de Dios—El Falcon—if you are still alive, come back and give us salvation. In or out of the grave—come back to us."

His name is Moe Weintraub. He's a peddler of nostrums, pots and pans, liniments, and anything else he can lay his hands on that can be turned over for a dime profit. He speaks fluent Spanish because for a period in an altogether misbegotten life, he had spent some Army time and served on many a foray into Mexican territory hunting down bandits. He's glib, tough as nails, shrewd, and reprehensibly without a single suggestion of honor. He would sell himself if indeed the body were sellable. He's in a little Texas border town, setting up his wagon—spewing out his usual line of bullshit. He doesn't notice two Mexicans staring at him from across the piazza and he's quite unaware of the fact that no sooner has he been seen than the two Mexicans saddle up and ride like hell south. Straight to the village. Straight to the old man. El Fal-

con lives! He has been seen. True, he has no pistols or saber. He has
a spindle-shanked, splay-footed nag attached to a wagon that is
pre-Custer. The luxurious beard is down to a small, straggle-forked
Van Dyke. But what the hell can you expect from a man who's
been dead over a decade?

And this is what happens. A delegation of hard-pressed Mexican
peons, including the old man, recrosses the border and latches onto
El Moe while he's hiding from an irate sheriff and equally irate citizens who have just paid a dollar a slug for what tastes like panther
piss but is far less salutary in its effects—medicinal or otherwise.
They recognize him. They tell him. They know who he is. Please—
shed your disguise. Give up your anonymity. Come back and lead
your people in their fight against tyranny. Weintraub, though ini-
tially denying he is who they think he is, nonetheless ultimately
accompanies them. He does this out of honor, compassion, and
gut-level courage—also because a posse of vigilantes has appeared
and is about to string him up by the cayunes.

Thumbnail chronology of events. El Moe has about as much military knowledge as the Vatican Swiss Guard. He doesn't know tactics from tacos, but he's being fed, wined, dined, worshiped, and
fallen in love with by the old man's granddaughter. Deep in his
tequila, he maps out a campaign against Colonel Ruiz's Cavalry.
He does this by throwing darts against a map while he's in such a
stupor that he can't see the wall. The Mexicans whisper amongst
themselves. The Falcon has indicated a battle to be fought in a narrow mountain defile impossible to defend. Impossible to take
cover. Impossible to win. But it is The Falcon's considered tactical
judgment. So, like sheep they follow this bleary-eyed drunk into
what should be their last battle. What happens is that the place is
so impossible to fight in that Ruiz and his men file in, rifles slung,

altogether unprepared for battle. It's an absolutely impossible place to fight in, but the Mexicans fight there and they win and The Falcon is looked on with awe, as well as the accustomed reverence. His fame travels across the parched lands. Through the tiny villages. Ultimately to filter through the echelons to the General Staff of the Federales. In the next battle, the god topples. The clay feet show. The Falcon turns into Moe Weintraub. And he's captured.

The General lays it out for him. The Falcon *is* dead. But if Weintraub will continue to play the role and come over to their side, leading the Federales, salaried by the Federales—the legend will dissolve. Weintraub is horrified by the suggestion. To betray his men who believed in him? To play Judas to these Christians? To sell his soul for a pottage of silver? It takes him fully five seconds to agree. And off he goes—the display-case General—on his way to wreck a dream.

But someplace it happens. Why—who's to know? Maybe it's the hidden well that is tapped and suddenly produces courage. Or maybe every man can suddenly become a giant. But Weintraub becomes El Moe—that slashing, brave giant of a Mexican Litvak. He finds his own well of courage. He escapes the Federales, goes to his friends, admits his deceptions, and then calls on them to fight the next day.

And what of the strategy? The tactics? El Moe is cross-eyed with tequila and his head is the size of the Andes. Once again out come the darts. And once again an improbable battle is fought in an improbable place. And once again—improbably—the good guys win.

El Moe is dead. They can't find his body. But the last eyewitness saw him fall from his horse, shot 114 times. The second Falcon has been consigned to the earth. But another legend has been born. El Moe. He's a battle cry. He's an avenging ghost. He's a threat to tyranny so long as it exists. El Moe.

There he is—on a train with his new Mexican bride. Moe Weintraub, heading north through Texas—still conning, still cheating, still lying—but adored by his beautiful wife and perversely admired by all the vigilantes who will pursue him—probably for the rest of his life.

ABOUT THE AUTHORS

Kelley Armstrong is the author of the *New York Times* bestselling "Women of the Otherworld" paranormal suspense series, the "Darkest Powers" YA urban fantasy trilogy, and the Nadia Stafford crime series. She grew up in Ontario, Canada, where she still lives with her family. A former computer programmer, she's now escaped her corporate cubicle and hopes never to return.

Alan Brennert was executive story consultant on the 1980s CBS network revival of *The Twilight Zone* and wrote some of its most well-remembered episodes, including "Her Pilgrim Soul" and "A Message from Charity." He has won a Nebula Award for his short story "Ma Qui" and an Emmy Award as a producer for *L.A. Law*. More recently, he is the author of the bestselling novels *Moloka'i* and *Honolulu*.

Deborah Chester is the internationally published author of thirty-eight novels in several genres, primarily science fiction and fantasy. Her most recent books include *The Pearls* and *The Crown*. She's also the John Crain Presidential Professor at the

University of Oklahoma, where she teaches short-story and novel writing. For more information, go to www.deborahchester.com.

Jim DeFelice is the author of several novels, including *Leopards Kill* and the forthcoming *Helios*. Look for him on the Web at www.jimdefelice.com.

With her home office a *Twilight Zone* landscape of mannequins in vintage dress, no wonder award-winning ex-journalist and novelist **Carole Nelson Douglas**'s fifty-four books offer surreal *TZ* touches. They include two Vegas-set series: the Midnight Louie, feline PI, mysteries partially narrated by a "Sam Spade with hair-balls," and the Delilah Street, Paranormal Investigator, noir urban fantasies of werewolf mobsters and silver-screen zombies. Douglas was the first author of a Sherlockian series with a female protagonist, diva-detective Irene Adler, the only woman to outwit Holmes, debuting with the *New York Times* Notable Book of the Year *Good Night, Mr. Holmes*. Visit her website at www.carolenelsondouglas.com.

David Hagberg is a former U.S. Air Force cryptographer who has traveled extensively in Europe, the Arctic, and the Caribbean. He has published nearly seventy novels of suspense, including the bestselling *Soldier of God*, *Allah's Scorpion*, *Dance with the Dragon*, and the *New York Times* bestseller *The Expediter*. He has been nominated three times for the Mystery Writers of America Edgar Allan Poe award and was nominated for the American Book Award. He and his wife make their home in Sarasota, Florida. His website can be found at www.david-hagberg.com.

Earl Hamner was born in 1923 in a small village in Virginia's Blue Ridge Mountains. Much of his writing is rooted in his growing up in a large and loving family during the Great Depression. Today he lives with his wife of fifty-four years in Studio City, California, where he continues to write and care for his collection of over fifty bonsai. He describes himself as "a good-looking old thing who doesn't look a day over eighty-four." For more self-congratulations, go to www.earlhamner.com.

Joe R. Lansdale is the author of thirty novels and over two hundred short works. He has written screenplays, teleplays, and comics. His latest book is the short-story collection *Sanctified and Chicken Fried* from University of Texas Press, and forthcoming in June from Knopf is *Vanilla Ride*, his new Hap Collins and Leonard Pine novel.

Laura Lippman has published fourteen novels and a collection of short stories. She has won virtually every prize given for mystery fiction in the United States, including the Edgar, Anthony, Shamus, Agatha, and Quill Awards. She lives in Baltimore.

Author of four novels (*Cutdown*, *Causes of Action*, *Tropical Heat* and, most recently, *Coyote Moon*), as well as a collection of short stories (*Jackson Street and Other Soldier Stories*), which won the California Book Award for First Fiction, **John Miller** is a full-time writer and artist. His short stories have appeared in, among others, *The William & Mary Review*, *Crosscurrents*, *The Missouri Review*, *North Dakota Quarterly*, and *Ellery Queen's Mystery Magazine*. A native North Carolinian, Miller resides in the Pacific Northwest.

Mike Resnick is the all-time leading award winner, living or dead, for short science fiction (according to *Locus*). He has won five Hugos, plus other major awards in the United States, France, Spain, Japan, Croatia, and Poland, and has been nominated for major awards in England and Italy. He is the author of sixty novels, well over two hundred short stories, and two screenplays, and is the editor of almost fifty anthologies. His work has been translated into twenty-three languages.

Lezli Robyn is an Australian writer who sold her first couple of stories in the closing months of 2008, and in the three months since then has sold to *Asimov's*, *Analog*, and other magazines, as well as science fiction markets as distant as China and Russia, alone or in collaboration with Mike Resnick. She is currently working on her first novel.

Lucia St. Clair Robson's first novel, *Ride the Wind*, appeared on the *New York Times* Best Seller List and won the Western Writers of America's Golden Spur award. It has been continuously in print for twenty-seven years. She has written eight other historical novels, the most recent of which is *Last Train from Cuernavaca*. *Kirkus Reviews* wrote, "Few novelists working today have a better grasp of early American history than Robson."

Robert J. (Bob) Serling is Rod Serling's older brother and a prolific author himself, with twenty-five published nonfiction and fiction works, mostly dealing with the airline and aerospace industries. Among his seven novels was the bestselling *The President's Plane Is Missing*. Before becoming a full-time freelance author, he was aviation editor of United Press International, and now at age ninety is regarded by his peers as the dean of aviation writers. He served as technical adviser on Rod's acclaimed *TZ* episode "Odyssey of Flight 33."

Rod Serling (1924–1975) worked in the television area for twenty-five years, developing, in addition to the landmark *Twilight Zone* series, *Night Gallery* and *The Loner*, and countless drama anthologies, including *Requiem for a Heavyweight* and *Patterns*. During his career he won more Emmy Awards for dramatic writing than anyone in history. He also wrote the screenplay for the very first *Planet of the Apes* film, which embodied everything Serling was interested in as a writer. He continued to write for television while teaching in Ithaca, New York, until his death in 1975, leaving an indelible imprint on television that would inspire countless future writers and artists.

R. L. Stine is one of the bestselling children's authors in history. His book series—Goosebumps, Fear Street, The Nightmare Room, Mostly Ghostly, and Rotten School—have sold more than 350 million copies around the world. Stine says his job is to "terrify kids." But his proudest accomplishment is the millions of kids he has motivated to read. His adult-thriller titles include *Superstitious*, *The Sitter*, and *Eye Candy*. He is currently at work on a new batch of Goosebumps titles. Stine lives in New York City with his wife, Jane.

Whitley Strieber is the author of such books as *The Wolfen*, *The Hunger*, *Communion*, and *Superstorm*, which have all been made into feature films, and many other bestsellers, including *Billy*, *Majestic*, *The Grays*, *2012*, and, most recently, *Critical Mass*. His website, www.unknowncountry.com, is the largest website in the world featuring daily news at the edge of science and reality.

Tad Williams is the *New York Times* bestselling author of some fourteen books for adults, which have been translated into twenty-three languages and sell worldwide. Among his bestsellers are *The Dragonbone Chair*, *The Otherland Cycle*, and *Shadowmarch*. He lives and works with his wife, Deborah Beale, and their family in the San Francisco Bay Area.

William F. Wu, Ph.D., is a six-time nominee for the Hugo, Nebula, and World Fantasy Awards and the author of the six-volume young-adult science fiction series titled Isaac Asimov's Robots in Time. He is the author of thirteen novels, one short-story collection, and sixty short stories as well as one book of literary criticism. Wu's short story "Wong's Lost and Found Emporium," a multiple-award nominee, was adapted into an episode of *The Twilight Zone* from the 1980s and is available on DVD. He lives in Palmdale, California, with his wife, Fulian Wu, and their son, Alan.

Timothy Zahn has been writing science fiction for over a quarter of a century. In that time he has published thirty-six novels, over eighty short stories and novelettes, and four collections of short fiction. Best known for his eight *Star Wars* novels, he is also the author of the Quadrail series (*Night Train to Rigel*, *The Third Lynx*, *Odd Girl Out*, and the upcoming *The Domino Pattern*), the Cobra series (including the upcoming *Cobra Alliance*), and the young-adult Dragonback series. His latest novel is *From the Ashes*, a prequel to the movie *Terminator Salvation*. The Zahn family lives on the Oregon coast.

ABOUT THE EDITOR

Carol Serling has been involved with the writing career of her husband from its very inception, and all through *The Twilight Zone* years she was his first reader and toughest critic. Since her husband's death in 1975, Carol has maintained a self-contained industry working with the literary and cinematic legacy that Rod left behind . . . the latest work being this anthology written in the spirit of the *Zone*.